SPLITTING
THE ATOM

SPLITTING THE ATOM

STEPHEN AMIDON

BLOOMSBURY

First published in Great Britain 1990
Copyright © Stephen Amidon 1990

Bloomsbury Publishing Ltd, 2 Soho Square, London w1v 5de

A CIP catalogue record for this book
is available from the British Library

isbn 0 7475 0568 3

10 9 8 7 6 5 4 3 2 1

Typeset by Hewer Text Composition Services, Edinburgh
Printed in Great Britain by Butler & Tanner Ltd, Frome and London

Things could never be the same again after Eddie and Matthew
Merriweather's twenty-second birthday – Eddie is dead and Matthew has to
come to terms with a new existence without his complex and dangerous twin.
The accident knocks Walter, their father, out of kilter too, as his sudden
self-awareness exposes cracks in the edifice of security in which he has tried to
shelter himself and his family.

Eddie's death leaves an emptiness that is not easy to fill, causing both
Matthew and Walter to undertake separate journeys in their search for
whatever it is they are looking for, while Helen and Beth, Eddie's mother and
girlfriend, can only cope by retreating into the familiarity of their once-
secure surroundings. Matthew ricochets between his rebellious friends and a
love affair with a sad, beautiful refugee. Walter is forced to confront the fact
that his apparently successful career has been built on a giant lie. Out of this
confusion a new understanding gradually emerges. But it's not until Walter
holes up in his father-in-law's house in Greece and finds the courage to put his
thoughts on tape that all can be, at last, laid to rest.

A thoughtful and moving study of father-and-son relationships, *Splitting the
Atom* is Stephen Amidon's first novel, a debut of truly outstanding clarity and
vision.

FOR CARYL

SOARING

'Hey Matt, wake up.'
Eddie stood in the doorway, framed by the hall's lesser darkness.

'Happy birthday,' he said in a hoarse voice.

Matthew raised himself to his elbows, straining against a sheet that was damp and twisted from bad dreams.

'Same to you.'

Eddie walked into the room and sat on the edge of the bed. His hair and lab coat were tussled by sleeplessness. He smelled of sweat and coffee.

'What time is it?' Matthew asked, his thumping heart beginning to slow.

'Early still.'

Matthew sat up now, breaking free from his covers and scuttling back in the bed until his back rested against the headboard. He pressed the inside edges of his eyes for a moment, culling two drops of creamy rheum from them.

'You been working?' he asked.

'Yeah.' Eddie said. 'Just got off.'

'What rotation you on?'

'O.B.'

'How is that?'

Eddie didn't answer. Matthew could see his eyes now in the light from the digital clock – brilliant, yet distant. As if some great energy had recently flared in them and was now slowly fading away.

'I remembered something while I was working last night, Matt,' he said. 'About us. It just . . . came to me. Out of nowhere.'

'What's that?'

'About when we were in the womb.'

Matthew felt a charge of fear pulse through his flesh.

'Eddie . . .'

'About how we used to fight,' Eddie continued, his bright eyes intent. 'Remember? Pressed together like that? Wrestling and shoving, all the

3

time. Not for position or anything. Just . . . fighting. I could see it again last night, so clearly. Us kicking and slapping through the fluid. In slow motion, almost. It was . . . relentless. Don't you remember?'

Matthew shook his head slightly.

'And the only thing that would make us stop would be when dad would talk to us. When he'd put his mouth right up to mom's belly and tell us to settle down in there. He thought it was a joke because he didn't know that we could hear him. We'd just huddle there, not knowing what this voice was but scared to shit by it. It was so . . . close. So close. Remember?'

'No, I don't,' Matthew whispered.

Eddie idly twisted the top sheet around his hand.

'Yeah, well, I do.'

There was a long silence.

'What the fuck made you think of all this, Eddie?' Matthew asked softly.

His eyes widened a little. Matthew could see him tighten his grip on the gnarled sheets.

'A woman came in last night. Young, strong, yuppie-type. First pregnancy. They'd done a scan several months earlier and determined she was going to have twins. Well, everything went fine for the first few hours, but when the contractions started coming hot and heavy we began to monitor some major foetal distress. The attending did a couple procedures to chill things out but it was no good. The panic signals kept coming with each contraction. Stronger and stronger. It soon became clear that a C-section was indicated. They got in there pretty quick, but it was too late – one of them had already died. What we discovered was that they were monozy . . . they were identical . . . and they shared the same amniotic sac. It's a rare condition but not unheard of. And what had happened was that when the contractions started to really rock one of them had grabbed a hold of the other's umbilical cord and squeezed it every time the muscles bore down on him. Gradually, bit by bit, his fear caused him to choke his brother to death. You should have seen them, Matt. Lying there. The dead one all blue, the other as healthy as a fucking horse, gripping that cord like it was the only thing keeping him from falling into the abyss. It took the attending ages to pry that damned hand loose. I couldn't take my eyes off them. You should have seen . . .'

Matthew noticed that Eddie's hand was beginning to twitch from the pressure it applied to the twisted rope of sheets.

'Why didn't you do it, Matt?' he whispered, leaning close. 'You had me. You could've . . .'

'Why didn't you?' Matthew asked, believing for a moment.

Eddie released the sheet and fell to the bed, laughing quietly for a moment. There was a long silence.

'Anyway,' he said. 'That's what I remembered.'

Later that morning, Matthew's father tapped gently on the door to his room, then inched it open. Matthew was still in bed, flipping through a magazine. He took several seconds to look up from it. Walter was wearing the baggy khaki pants and blue windbreaker he jokingly called his flight suit.

'Ready?' he asked.

Matthew closed and folded the magazine.

'I don't think I'm going to go,' he said after a moment.

Walter pushed the door open a little wider, but didn't step into the room.

'I wish you would, Matt,' he said. 'There's plenty of space.'

Not for me, Matthew thought. There was a long pause.

'It's my gift to you, you know,' Walter continued, his voice level with calm persuasion. 'To you both. I think you'd find it . . . thrilling. And yet peaceful, too. It takes your mind . . .'

Walter paused. The crow's feet around his eyes stretched and smoothed as he envisioned the flight.

'It'll be the ride of your life, Matt. Guaranteed.' He ducked his head slightly, trying to catch his son's eye. 'You can make an exception this one time, can't you?'

'I don't think so,' Matthew said, his eyes averted.

'And why's that?' Walter asked, controlling his anger. For an instant, Matthew wondered if Eddie might not be right. Perhaps he could remember Walter's voice speaking to them in the womb. Frightening them. Perhaps that was why he hated it so much now.

'I've got a headache.'

Walter looked around the room for a moment, as if suddenly discovering something distasteful about it. Keys and coins rattled accusations from his large pockets.

'All right,' he said, closing the door as he backed away.

Matthew finally got out of bed in mid-afternoon, in time to watch from his window as the passing glider was pulled gradually to altitude by its chugging tow plane. For an instant, the woven steel line which connected the two crafts caught the afternoon sun and flared with the brilliance of a lit fuse, only to return quickly to near invisibility. Matthew drew a bead on the trailing plane with an outstretched finger, then released an imaginary shot with a jerk of his wrist. The glider continued its ascent unaltered, disappearing behind a rogue cloud. Matthew moved slowly away from the window until the backs of his thighs hit the bed. He hesitated a moment, then tumbled on to the mattress, his arms spread to absorb the shock. A spring snapped beneath the pressure and reverberated through the bed for several seconds.

When it stopped, Matthew could hear the tow plane droning in the opposite direction. The glider was free now. He turned his attention below, where he could hear the sounds of his mother preparing the surprise downstairs. He was supposed to have gone to the airport with his father and Eddie as a way of making himself scarce so that his mother could prepare the food and get all the guests into their hiding places. The surprise party was a family convention which had been in operation since he and Eddie were an age when everything was a surprise. It was an institution, protected as they grew older by the willing suspension of disbelief by everyone involved. Yet now, when nothing seemed to surprise him and everything was to be disbelieved, Matthew couldn't bring himself to make the effort. He knew he should go somewhere else until that party was ready, but instead remained in his room, wondering why he couldn't bring himself just to leave this place altogether. Once and for all. Go to the city. Film school in California or backpacking in Europe. Just go. But something kept him here. Some dark fascination. A strong yet barely visible bond he couldn't break.

He scissored out of bed and left his room, pausing at the top of the stairs to hear what was going on below. Just the sound of Helen in the kitchen. He slid down the steps, the flesh of his palm squeaking against the railing. He hit the ground with a deliberate thud.

'Stay out of the family room,' his mother called.

He walked into the kitchen, ignoring the cellophane-covered salad bowls and the trays of chicken and burgers ready for the barbeque. Helen stood before the whirring microwave oven, staring through its tinted glass door. She was already dressed for the party in a deep purple dress and black silk scarf. Her black hair was molded into a single rigid wave from her forehead to the nape of her neck. Matthew joined her in watching a solitary wishbone vibrate in the oven's invisible heat. A small deposit of liquid bubbled out of its dark cleft.

'It was still damp,' she said absently. 'This way it'll be sure to crack later.'

Matthew nodded grimly at the prospect of another of the day's customs – splitting the wishbone with Eddie. He looked at his reflection in the oven door. His eyes were dull and puffy from the long night. Walter's eyes, he thought. Only without the stoic exhaustion. Eddie's eyes, without the electrifying madness.

'Hey, mom?'

Helen looked up from the oven.

'Which one of us was born first?'

She smiled slightly as she remembered.

'You were, Matthew. By six minutes. I've told you this, haven't I?'

'I guess. I couldn't remember for some reason.'

'Why do you ask?'

'Just wanted to know who won.'

'Won what? The race?'

'No, the fight.'

She stopped smiling.

'What on earth are you talking about?'

Matthew picked at a potato salad on the counter. The oven continued to whirr.

'Eddie told me this morning that we used to fight in the womb.'

Helen smiled slightly and shook her head.

'Well, I don't know about that. But some days there was some awful kicking going on down there.' She hesitated a moment. 'I've never told you this, but it broke one of my ribs once. The kicking. Just a hair-brained fracture or whatever they call it. But still . . .'

'So which one of us do you think was the culprit?' Matthew asked.

'Who do *you* think?'

They both smiled and stared again at the shimmering bone.

'Why didn't you go with them?' Helen asked, taking advantage of the rare moment of good humor.

Matthew shrugged.

'Well, I suppose that's a good reason for ruining the surprise,' she said bitterly.

'What surprise?' Matthew asked, still watching the oven.

'Oh, Matt.'

'You know I'm not into this soaring,' he added quickly.

'Is that all?' she asked.

'No,' Matthew said, watching the timer count down. 'That's not all.'

'Then what is it? He intended it as his gift, you know.'

'What do you want me to say, mom? Are you dying to hear the truth?

7

All right.' He looked at her. 'The truth is that I'm not in on their code, mom. I'm not on the team. I'm the odd man out. That's why. I don't care about all this derring-do or whatever the fuck it is they share. I never have and I might as well avail myself of this landmark occasion to stop pretending I do.'

'Your father doesn't see it that way at all,' Helen said. 'He thinks you're just being hurtful.'

'Yeah, well, he would.'

They were quiet for a minute. The oven switched off with a prolonged high-pitched tone. The bone continued to crackle in the darkness, its marrow cauterizing into a breakable consistency.

'Besides,' he said, nodding towards it. 'We all know whose side it's going to break on, don't we?'

He eventually relented beneath his mother's hurt gaze, however, leaving the house on his old three-speed bicycle. He'd drive around the subdivision a while, maybe go to the mall, then meet Eddie and Walter so that they could return home together for the surprise. As he left his street a car approaching from the opposite direction flashed its lights at him and began to slow. He stopped his bicycle parallel to the driver's side. It was Eddie's girlfriend Beth, on her way to the house. Stacks of paper cups, bags of potato chips and liter-sized bottles of soft drink covered the seat beside her. He could also see the cake, with its boldly scripted '22'.

'Hey, Beth.'

She smiled strangely at him as she slowly raised her hands. Before Matthew could figure out what she was doing, there was a flash of blue-white light and a loud explosion. He fell backwards, tipping the bicycle into the gutter and rolling on to the brief expanse of lawn between the sidewalk and the street. As he came to rest on his back he could see a web of multi-colored streamers descending over him. Beyond them, he could see that the sky was darkening with low, fast storm clouds. The car door slammed.

'Oh Matt, I'm sorry. I didn't think it would be so loud.'

The streamers settled on top of him. Beth began to laugh. Matthew smiled back at her as she dropped on to the damp grass beside him.

'It's a party favor,' she said, gingerly picking the streamers from him. 'I wanted to give you a surprise in spite of your surly self.'

'Yeah, well, do me a favor . . .'

He sat up next to her, brushing the paper into the gutter.

'You'll live,' she said as she helped him extricate himself from the net of colored paper.

'Rumor has it.'

'Hey, I thought you were going to hang out with Eddie and your dad until later,' she said. 'My dad's sort of waiting for you.'

'Yeah, I know,' he said. 'But that's really their thing, the flying. Their . . . rush.' He patted the turf below him. 'I'm ground bound. So I thought I'd kill some time on my own.'

Beth shook her head in gentle reproach.

'You're always, so . . .' she began, but didn't finish.

'Hey, Beth, what's the first thing you remember? Your first memory?'

She thought for a moment.

'I guess it would be when I was a baby, in Houston, and my parents took me to this park or something because JFK and Jackie were going to be there. Something for NASA I think. I remember my mom holding me as we stood beside the big reflecting pool and then there was a big commotion – I guess it must have been the Kennedys arriving – and we were jostled real hard and all of a sudden mom dropped me into the pool. I landed on my back and just sort of sank. And what I can remember is looking up at all the people staring down at me as I floated to the bottom – it was only like a couple of feet deep – and how the way their faces wavered in the disturbed water made it look like they were laughing. So after dad pulled me out I started to laugh because I thought that was what I was supposed to do since everyone else was. Laughing. Dad says that they took me over to meet JFK after that – all soaking – and that Jackie said what a brave girl I was for not crying. But I don't remember that. Just the sinking and laughing.' She looked at Matthew. 'So what's yours?'

'I don't know,' Matthew said. 'I mean, I'm not sure.'

There was a long silence.

'Have you seen Eddie?' he asked eventually.

'He stopped by for a few minutes this morning,' she said. 'Why?'

'Did he say anything about last night?'

She shook her head.

'Why?' she asked.

'Nothing, really.' He began to tear small clumps of grass from the ground. 'It's just that sometimes he . . . sometimes he scares me.' He smiled with slight embarrassment, but his face became somber after a moment.

'How do you mean?' Beth asked.

'He seems a bit . . . out of control, recently. Don't you think?'

She laughed softly.

'Well, yeah, sure. But that's his way. You know that.' She tapped Matthew's leg a few times. 'It's why we love him, right? He's the supernova and we're the cold moons. Your words, Matty.'

'No, I don't mean the crazy shit he does,' Matthew said, tossing the torn grass into the air. 'I mean what he's thinking. The things he seems to see. To remember.'

Beth watched the wind blow the grass across the street. Her eyes glazed a bit.

'He has these dreams sometimes . . .' She looked at him. 'Is that what you mean?'

'I guess. I don't know.'

'Then I don't know, either. But I'll tell you one thing, Matt. I don't think you're any more scared of him than he is of you. Or maybe you're both scared of something else. Something you share. That place you both go, sometimes.'

Matthew let it drop. He took advantage of their proximity to look her over. She wore one of her father's NASA sweatshirts and a pair of Eddie's knee-length swimming trunks, making each look as if it had been designed for her. She still hadn't gained much weight, although he could tell that her tiny waist was beginning to disappear and her breasts had swollen somewhat. A few veins had risen to the surface of her long legs. Yet he still wouldn't have known she was pregnant if she and Eddie hadn't confided in him. The main change was that she was more beautiful – her pale skin animated by some deep-sourced light, her brown eyes larger, clearer. Even her blonde hair seemed to be richer. And there was a hush to her voice.

'How you feeling?' Matthew asked.

'Don't ask,' Beth said, performing a mock retch. 'Every morning.'

'Ah well. It'll pass.'

'This I've noticed.'

They both looked at Matthew's bicycle, teetering on the curb, its front wheel spinning slowly in the gathering breeze.

'So when are you guys going to go public?' Matthew asked.

She unfurled a dud streamer.

'Moments after we set a date for the wedding.'

'So you're really going ahead with that?'

She looked at him.

'What does that mean?' she asked sharply.

'Nothing. Just . . . it's a funny thing to do.'

She began tearing small bits from the end of the streamer.

'Maybe to you, Matthew,' she said angrily. 'But then everything is to you, isn't it? Funny, I mean.'

He looked down at the grass, then up at the sky.

'Looks like rain,' he said.

'Maybe you should go over there and make sure they know about that,' she said coldly. 'My dad'll be there still.'

He stood and righted his bicycle.

'See you at the party,' he said.

Beth said nothing as she watched him ride away.

He was caught in a hailstorm a few blocks later. The stones were as large as marbles, forcing Matthew to turn his bicycle into the parking lot of the large stone Presbyterian church which his family had attended regularly until a few years previously. He carried his bicycle up the steps leading to the main door and took refuge in the arched portico. From inside the church, he could hear the sounds of the organ. Someone was tuning it, playing the opening bars of the Doxology over and over, pausing occasionally to make adjustments. The hail continued to fall with a strange violence, as if to assert its right to intrude on the warm spring afternoon. The stones that splintered on the concrete sounded like slaps, while those that hit the ground thudded, like body blows.

Matthew looked across the parking lot to the field where they had begun to lay the foundation to the new church. He thought back to all the games he had played there, all the Sunday afternoons he and Eddie had spent racing around its expanse. Softball in the summer and football in the autumn and snowball fights in the winter. The twilit games of kick-the-can or hide-and-seek to celebrate the lengthening days of spring. The carnival contests on holidays. Almost always calmly supervised by their father, still wearing his tie from church. Teaching them with a patience that would drive Matthew to tears of rage.

The abrupt storm made Matthew remember one event in particular – the balloon launch. It had been held during the spring, when he and Eddie were ten. One of Walter's big events. The idea was for each student in the church school to launch a helium balloon with his name attached. Whoever discovered the balloon when it landed was instructed to send word to the church of where the balloon had touched down. Walter would then be able to calculate how much the sponsors, who pledged pennies for each mile a balloon would travel, would owe. The money raised was to support the starving or the ill, or someone.

An hour before the event, Eddie had taken Matthew and a few other boys to the tool shed at the back of the church where Walter had stored the canister containing the helium. After figuring out how to open the sealed valve, he challenged each boy to inhale a lungful, then shout out an obscenity. They were soon falling about in laughter at the sound of their artificially high-pitched voices. When Eddie's turn came, he took several dramatic moments to figure out what to say. Finally, after gulping down a blast from the canister, he pulled himself up to the window and yelled 'God is a jerk' as loudly as his gassed throat would allow. The others were silenced by his daring, except Matthew, who immediately took his second lungful and shouted the same phrase, his voice loud and high. Eddie countered with a louder, more defiant call, 'God is a jerk.' They could hear it echoing outside, through the church's stone structure. The other boys grew frightened and left. The twins didn't notice, however, continuing their competition for several more rounds, their temples pounding from the helium as each dared to shriek the phrase slightly louder than the last. Finally, the door opened. Their father looked at them for several seconds without saying anything, his eyes lingering on Eddie.

'Come on,' he said eventually. 'You'll make yourselves sick with that stuff.'

Now, as the hail beat down, Matthew remembered with grim satisfaction his feeling of triumph as he followed his father from the shed.

The launch proved a disaster. A small, hard squall blew up at the last moment to replace the favorable breeze which had prevailed all day. It caught the balloons just after Walter called for the kids to release them, pushing them back to earth, where they scuttled along the grasstops until becoming involved in a row of rose bushes or slamming into the church's irregular stone walls. Before long they had all exploded, their bright plastic husks littering the well-kept lawn.

Matthew's reverie was broken when someone emerged from the church. It was the choir leader, a fat, enthusiastic man with many chins and fingers so short that Matthew had often wondered how he could play the hymns on the organ. He was wearing a black sportscoat over a T-shirt which bore the slogan 'Think Globally'. Matthew and Eddie had served a short stint in his choir as boys, but had soon escaped service by singing too loudly, a practice which was anathema among the suburban Presbyterians. Yet now, upon seeing Matthew, the choir director opened his mouth in a dumb-show of joyful surprise and extended his hand. Matthew's took it limply. There was a moment of silence as each realized they didn't remember the other's name.

'So how are you?' the choir director asked.

'Good.'

'Haven't seen much of you recently. But we've been hearing great things about you.'

'That's my brother you're thinking of,' Matthew said. 'I'm the one who writes for *Profiles*.'

'Oh,' he said, blinking. 'Yes. I've read some of those things.'

The man paused for a moment, then continued, undaunted.

'So how's your dad? Haven't seen too much of him, either.'

'He's okay, I guess. His plant closed down.'

'Yes, we heard,' he said, sniffing. 'I'm sure that's quite a blow, although some people think that's a good thing. The plant closure, I mean. Does he have anything else lined up?'

Matthew shook his head.

'Not really. But I'm sure he'll find something,' Matthew said. 'Although there's still no telling if it'll be, uh, a good thing.'

The man recoiled slightly, his pudgy face furrowing in confusion and suspected insult.

'Well, gotta run,' he said, tapping a sheath of music papers decisively against his thigh. 'Give Walter my best, will you?'

Matthew nodded once. The man walked sideways down the icy steps like a giant crab, then rushed in a stiff-legged run to the parking lot, holding his papers above his head.

Moments later, the hailstorm stopped abruptly. An emerging sun illuminated the bits of ice that lay scattered on the concrete, causing them to flare brilliantly as they melted. Matthew crunched as many of them as he could beneath his bicycle's wheels as he headed off to meet his father and brother.

The airport was quiet. The prefab hangars and pilots' shack seemed to be deserted. Matthew wondered for a moment if he had missed them, yet his father's car was still in the parking lot, drenched from the brief storm. Matthew pedalled slowly up the muddy driveway, carefully swerving around the many ruts. He dropped his bicycle by the door of the shack and entered, expecting to meet Beth's father, Dean, who piloted his father's tow plane.

There was no one in the room, however. Just an insistent, disembodied voice. It took Matthew a moment to realize that it was coming from the off-the-hook phone on the desk. He walked across the room and picked up the receiver.

'Please hang up the phone,' came the tinny voice. 'Please hang up the phone.'

Matthew replaced the receiver and looked at the desk. Creamed coffee in a conical plastic cup. A scanner whose red lights flared in panicky succession. Binoculars. A picture of Beth and Eddie at the medical school graduation. Matthew looked around the shack again. He wondered where everyone was.

He walked to the window overlooking the runway. That, too, was deserted. A half-mile beyond, past some parked planes and across an empty field, Matthew could see a strange light moving erratically above the approach pond, like a sparkler in the hand of a child. He watched it dance for a moment, fascinated. Then, after his eyes became accustomed to the brilliant light, he saw something else – the belly of his father's glider lying perfectly still on the pond's surface.

He ran quickly to the door, but stopped before passing through it. He put his ear up to its cool wood, listening for some sound of danger, some warning of what was to come. Silence. For an instant he was struck by a childish thought – if there were no noise, then nothing could be wrong. He quickly came to his senses and jerked the door open, racing around the side of the shack and heading out across the field. He could hear the Dopplered wail of sirens now, coming at him from contradictory horizons.

He ran steadily across the uncut grass, unable to bring himself to sprint. As he drew closer to the pond he could see Dean's surplus jeep, as well as the four-wheelers of the volunteer firemen who had just arrived. The glider lay almost exactly in the middle of the pond. There was a narrow gash in its bottom, as if it had been gutted. It seemed to shudder for a moment, but then became perfectly still. Matthew could now see that the light he had watched from the shack came from a high tension wire which danced a few feet above the pond, spitting out clusters of sparks which died quickly in the stagnant water. It was watched warily by the rescue workers who had begun to wade to the upsidedown plane. One man ignored the wire, however, as he walked away from the plane, churning his knees like a fullback to move quickly through the silty pond. Matthew stopped abruptly when he saw that it was Dean, carrying Eddie in his arms. He noticed that his brother's hands were clenched in half-fists, that his elbow-locked arms bounced with the rhythms of Dean's stride.

Upon reaching the shore, Dean placed Eddie gently in the thick weeds and began to give him mouth-to-mouth. Matthew walked at an angle to them to get a better view, still lingering several yards away. He could see his brother's open eyes now, a thrilled light brightening them. Two men in white jackets jogged past. One gently pulled Dean away, the other went to work on Eddie. Dean looked up at Matthew, his eyes confused. Foamy spittle ringed his mouth. Veins throbbed through his muscular neck.

Matthew looked past him to see Walter being helped ashore by two firemen. His soaked blue windbreaker clung to his body like skin about to shed. Viscid water dripped from his flattened hair. His open mouth bled and he limped somewhat, but he seemed otherwise unhurt. He stared at the slimy water in front of him until he reached the shore, when he looked up. His glance darted quickly over Eddie, meeting Matthew's. He made a small gesture of recognition with his right hand, but then both averted their eyes.

Matthew's attention was again caught by the dancing wire, which continued to pour sparks into the water. The way it moved fascinated him. Erratic. Like a living thing. Then he heard his father's voice, speaking his name with a strange matter-of-factness. As if he wanted to explain something. It sounded close. Too close. Matthew backed slowly away from it, his eyes still fixed on the light. He stumbled on a tuft of weed after just a few steps, falling backwards into the brush. Twigs and thick stems cracked beneath him like brittle bones, and a canopy of disturbed insects immediately enveloped him. Some were fireflies, which flared angrily at being awakened before dusk. More emergency vehicles pulled up, their red and blue sirens pulsing. Matthew closed his eyes against all the light.

SPRING FORWARD, FALL BACK

E ddie called them monsters. Matthew believed him. He called them electric beasts, savage machines who used the long black whips they held in their massive steel claws to destroy everything in their path. They were an invading army, he said, marching out in long lines from their secret fortresses to burn down the city with the sparkling fire that ran through their veins. There would be no survivors. Look Matty, he'd say, pointing at the blurred horizon into which the line of giant metal skeletons disappeared. They might be still now, but soon they will attack and kill us all. Look Matty, he'd say. They're monsters. You can't stop them. You can't.

Then Matthew would begin to cry. But Eddie would persist, cruelly whispering into his brother's reddening ear. Look at them. Do you think they can be stopped? Look at the shadows they cast. Nothing can stop them, Matty. Nothing at all.

'Edward!' Walter would call from the stationwagon's front seat, staring at them through the rear-view mirror's grim mediation. He'd tilt the mirror towards Eddie, commanding silence, a muttered apology. Then toward Matthew, who would receive a single, soothing nod. And then one last look at Eddie. Matthew could see that his father's eyes were different this time – wide, searching, a little scared. Finally he'd set the mirror aright and return his eyes to whatever highway, whatever journey was at hand.

Now, as he drove with his father through gray morning chill, the powerline pylons that crossed the quiet land seemed to Matthew as benign as the barren trees that surrounded them. Wireless, dull with weather, graffiti-scarred, their once menacing arms half-raised in exhausted surrender. Nothing like monsters. If there was movement it was haggard retreat, as if they'd been beaten by an unexpected defence. Some were even imprisoned in small pens of chainlink fence. Not much of an army, Matthew thought. They could only claim one victim.

Stop it, he told himself. Just stop.

19

He looked at his father behind the wheel, his head held perfectly still by the plastic neckbrace. Walter's eyes were busy, though, scanning the fog-shrouded road ahead through the computer delayed sweeps of the wipers. Nothing soothing in those eyes now, Matthew thought. Just that same look of bewilderment and quiet alarm that crossed them when he'd look for the second time at Eddie.

'How much longer?'

Walter pressed a button on the console that said 'Elpsd'.

'About twenty minutes.'

They had passed well out of the suburbs and were into farm country. Although it was not yet fully dawn, the fields were busy with activity. There had been an early frost that night, forcing the farmers to take extraordinary measures to protect their unripe crops. Smudge pots smoldered in nearly every field, sending billows of black smoke through squat, gnarled trees. Massive sheets of white nylon or dark gray plastic covered the ground crops. When the smudge smoke would blow in these fields the tarps looked like parachutes floating through storm clouds. In some fields there were groups of men in slickers spraying water on vine-encrusted trellises that were illuminated by banks of fluorescent lights. The air shimmered above them as the moisture evaporated into encroaching darkness.

Walter and Matthew had been travelling for over an hour, speaking only a few curt phrases, arguing over who was to drive and which radio station they would play. Walter had kept the keys; the radio stayed silent. Matthew dozed off soon after they started, sleeping dreamlessly until Walter awakened him with a gentle touch on the forearm so he could watch the odometer click over to 50,000.

They soon passed out of the farm region, into lowland marshes. The gamy odor of the swamps – a brew of brittle grass, fetid water and long-dead meat – seeped through the car's ventilation system. The road became a series of gentle undulations that caused the car to rock rhythmically. They made a long curve and the familiar outline of the power station appeared through the haze of a just-risen sun.

'The monster factory.'

'What?' asked Walter, turning slightly in the confines of his brace.

'Nothing.'

Nothing's the word, Walter thought as he looked at the station's familiar mass, noticing that one of the twin coolant towers had already begun to come down. The roof of the turbine hall was also almost gone. They don't waste any time, he thought.

It was to have been called Olympic One, but now was simply called the unit. The mistake. UPU's Folly. Walter thought of the various states he had seen the plant through: the broken earth of the opening ceremony, the laying of the foundation, the ascending mass of five years' construction. Then had come the delays – protests, court battles, charges that the plant's effluent would have heated the adjacent bay, uncoupling the long thin foodchain and ruining the native fishing industry. News reports, hearings, a commission. All licenses had been revoked, construction suspended within months of completion. After several months of controversy, the station was abandoned altogether by the parent utility, UPU. A film studio was rumored to be on the verge of purchasing the basic structure. What they didn't want was up for auction to urban contractors. The core was to be sold by Walter.

But there were no domestic buyers. The industry was in a slump. So Walter had begun to court overseas buyers, travelling extensively, lunching at embassies, setting his alarm for four a.m. to phone distant executives in their offices. It was a slow, exhausting process for him, with each initial eagerness dampened by bureaucracy and delay.

Today he was to meet officials from an East African nation that had recently unearthed a profound vein of radiant minerals. He had asked Matthew to come along to make a videotape of the reactor for him to use in sales presentations. His son had agreed reluctantly.

Walter brought the car to a stop a half mile from the station's gate. A small flock of gulls hovered over the road ahead. They seemed to be taking turns landing and taking off, stopping only to pick up what looked to be bits of pavement, which they then carried about twenty feet in the air and dropped on to the road.

'Have you seen this?' Walter asked.

Matthew shook his head as his father inched the car forward.

'They bring shells from the bay here and drop them on the road so they'll crack open,' he said, almost upon them now. 'It's better than boulders. They don't lose them to the waves. It's an easy target.'

He hit the sedan's basso horn and flashed the highbeams. The birds scattered. As he accelerated they could hear the shells crunching beneath the car's hard rubber.

'We'll do it for them,' Walter said softly.

A reversing truck crossed their path as they entered the yard, a shrill klaxon bleating beneath its hood.

'What's that noise?' Matthew asked.

'It's automatic,' Walter explained. 'When it's in reverse. Because of the blind spots.'

Matthew looked above the truck's dustcloud at the power station. The buildings were dull with disuse and fatigue. They have the feel of ruins, he thought. The first building was the squat generator hall. Men in sky-blue hard-hats stood on top of it on the last remaining section of roof, warming their hands over a fifty-five gallon drum that emitted sparks and smoke. Beyond that was the containment building, a factory-like structure. To either side of it were the tall coolant towers, dull white inverted cones. The left one was enveloped by scaffolding and large cranes that had removed the concrete from its top half, exposing a skeleton of iron bars and wiring. The other was intact. There were dozens of other shacks and bunkers situated irregularly around the lot, through which a sourceless blue mist swirled. There were no windows in any of the buildings.

Matthew thought for a minute how he would go about filming this beast. Lots of wide pans, slow zooms, slower fades. Cheap stuff. Gimmicks. Although he knew how to use a videocam, he knew that this was just more make-work from his father. Like the summer jobs painting hydrants and clearing weeds at the plant, or the month doing light draughtsmanship for the toad-faced UPU engineers. Just another thing to keep the fuck-up busy, Matthew thought. If Walter had wanted to make a solid sales video he could get one of the slick, hungry city firms for not much more than the five hundred he'd allocated for Matthew. Ah well, he thought. The ties that bind me up.

Walter pulled the sedan to the back of the turbine hall and parked in an alley between it and the containment building. A forklift idled nearby, its driver dozing over the wheel, a smoking pipe dangling from his mouth. Matthew turned to get the cane from the back seat.

'Might as well leave it,' Walter said.

'Are you sure?'

'Yes. I don't want to get into the habit of it.'

Matthew shrugged and slid from the car. Walter maneuvered himself out with difficulty. They met at the trunk. Matthew removed his pistolgrip camera, the light meter and the portable strobe. He held up the meter and turned a sundial circle.

'Bad light,' he said.

'Well, do what you can,' Walter replied as he limped into the turbine hall.

*

The Africans arrived in an unwashed white stepvan with diplomatic plates. Someone had written 'Wash Me' in its dust. There were three officials – tall, thin men in tapered suits. They were similar in appearance, with moustaches, sharp cheekbones and narrow hips. Except that one of them was an albino, his red eyes and white flesh making him look like a negative exposure of the other two. He appeared to be the leader. They were accompanied by an elegantly dressed woman who served as their interpreter.

Matthew watched his father greet them at the entrance to the turbine hall with curt bows and an unwavering smile. With the interpreter taking a discreet position at his side he made an introductory speech. The Africans were all manners and gentle irony as they listened. Matthew, standing several yards off, raised the camera to his shoulder and looked at his father through the gridded viewfinder. He's wearing his game face, Matthew thought. Walter spoke in measured, uniform paragraphs, his hands spread open before him, as if he were assessing the volume, judging the mass, of the words he spoke. As he paused to let the interpreter pass the language on, Matthew noticed that his father's eyes crept momentarily away, focusing on some vague, distant horizon.

Matthew thought of the times his father had spoken to him and Eddie this way. During time outs in church league basketball games, when the score was close. The times he'd called the family together to explain that they were moving again. Before letting them into the garage to see a new car, or the lounge to see a new television or stereo. Once, upon returning from a vacation to the shore, Walter had called them together before letting them enter the house. He stood above them on the front porch, surrounded by insects that clicked futilely against the yellow night bulb. Their cat, Boomer, a twenty-pound monster who kept them awake with screeching copulations in the backyard shrubs, was dead. Someone had poisoned him, Walter explained. It must have happened far away, he said, because no one around here would do that. Yet Boomer had managed to struggle all the way home, dying on the back porch, one paw resting gently against the glass door. He had come back to those he loved, Walter explained with quiet pathos, to make his final farewells. The boys, who cared little for the cat, were soon in tears. Matthew remembered weeping again that night as he lay in bed, not with sorrow but with rage at his father for making him feel that way. Something in him had been revolted by the emotions, terrified at the power his father had to raise them in him.

Matthew turned his view from Walter to the interpreter. She looked to be in her late twenties, with long legs and a long neck, gently curving hips and breasts. She had large eyes that moved with slow deliberation, as if marking everything in their field of vision. Her mouth was full, pouted by irony or sensuality or both. Her lucent brown skin looked softer to Matthew than other skin he had touched. He felt a surge of desire as he watched her eyes shift with languid concentration from Walter to the albino, as he watched her breasts sway slightly beneath the bold pattern of her blouse. Then she caught him looking at her. Matthew lowered the camera. She was smiling at him, wagging her finger playfully.

Walter led his party into the building and Matthew set off to film. He thought he'd start with a shot of natural power, then segue into a long-shot of the plant. The sun was still masked by haze, so he left the complex and trudged down the narrow path to the bay in order to film the waves. The first stretch he came to wouldn't do – there were no rocks to provide contrast, no breakers. He headed down shore to where he knew there was a rocky cove.

The beach's sand gave way to a scrub field littered with garbage and piles of shells. Matthew made his way slowly through the field, careful not to cut himself on the broken glass or jagged hunks of metal that lay hidden in the weeds. He then passed through a series of artificial dunes formed around the frames of abandoned cars. He came to the cove, an unshielded, rock-strewn inlet about two hundred yards across its mouth. Matthew stopped abruptly.

A whale had been washed ashore. It lay in the hard sand, jostled slightly by an ebbing tide. He approached it slowly. The tide had rolled it on to its side, leaving one surprised eye open to the sky. Sporadic gurgles came from its spout, and the barnacles on its underbelly were still damp. It must have washed up overnight, Matthew thought. Purple fluid bubbled from its mouth and a short puncture near its dorsal fin. An infinity of sand crabs hustled about in the shade. The wind shifted and a great rancid smell caused Matthew to back away.

He waited for the wind to fade, then stepped up to within an arm's distance, avoiding the growing puddle of gore. He reached out and stroked the hard, smooth patch beneath the eye, then knocked on it like a shy guest. There was no response. He gently pressed his finger into the animal's eye. The membrane gave a little, layering under the pressure. Some of the ubiquitous purple fluid seeped through the duct, staining his finger. He wiped it off on the whale, making several small 'X' designs.

'You the law?'

Matthew turned to see two men approaching him from the dunes. They were both wearing baseball caps, overalls and rubber boots. The taller of the two, a skinny man with long sideburns and an intent, slightly moronic stare, was carrying a chainsaw. The other, a fat, bouncy man with a beard and mirror sunglasses, carried a crowbar and a plastic trash bag.

'No,' Matthew said.

'Good.' It was the fat one who was talking. 'Don't get no ideas, cause we spotted this sucker first.'

'I don't have any ideas,' Matthew said.

'Good.' He made a few tentative jabs at the whale's mouth with the steel toe of his boot.

'What are you going to do?'

The fat one stared at Matthew through his sunglasses.

'Gonna git sumdem teeth,' the tall one said.

'Hundred bucks a throw,' the fat one added coldly. 'We sell 'em to tourists. You gotta problem with us making a livin'?'

Matthew shook his head and began to walk away. When he reached the dune he heard the chainsaw kick on, its high-pitched whine plunging periodically. He squatted in a cluster of weed and filmed the men as they cut into the whale, until the fat one looked in his direction. Matthew turned off his camera and walked quickly away.

He returned to a deserted edge of the complex to make some slow panoramas of the buildings. The sky had cleared, marked now only by high clouds and seams of jet vapor. He put a filter over his lens and took a slow zoom of the sun.

As he finished, the man in the forklift drove up to him. Matthew lowered his camera.

'Hey,' he said, tapping out his pipe against the yellow roll bar. The billows of his chin shook slightly with the action.

'Hello,' Matthew said.

'You work for that film studio?' the man asked.

Matthew shook his head.

'Oh. Cause my daughter wants to be in that film they're gonna make here.'

Matthew shrugged.

'She'll do anything,' the man continued, working the pipe's bowl with his small finger. 'Make coffee. She'll take her shirt off if you pay her something.'

'Sorry,' Matthew said. 'I can't help you.'

'Yeah,' the man said, sticking the pipe in his breast pocket. 'She'll figure something out. Wanna ride?'

Matthew stepped on to a steel prong and let the man drive him to the containment building.

'Watch your head.'

The interpreter passed on Walter's warning to the trailing officials, who laughed. One of them said something.

'He says he'd need a mirror to do that,' the interpreter said.

Walter smiled sourly. She rolled her eyes in agreement.

They were moving through the lower levels of the containment building, towards the core. The way was narrow, so Walter found himself talking over his shoulder or giving stooped lectures beneath naked bulbs and elbow joints. The pain in his back was throbbing. He wished he'd brought the cane. His only consolation was that now that he was shorter he bumped his head less often.

The Africans were giving nothing away. They were impressed at the right times, inquisitive during the gaps, indulgent if Walter lost his place. They seemed to have done their homework – the albino had Soviet and French technical training. Yet there was an impassive expanse between them which Walter couldn't cross. A great, ironic gulf that made him feel at times as if these were inquisitors from some powerful bureau, gathering evidence against him for a verdict on unspecified charges. He didn't like this selling, he decided. He lacked the instincts.

They passed through a long corridor lined with burned-out lights. Walter took the penlight from his breast pocket and illuminated the way. The low ceiling and darkness triggered a swell of memory that he vainly resisted. He heard again his voice speaking his son's name, felt the damp mud of the walls, smelled the dank odors of rot and mud. 'Eddie?' he could hear his voice echo.

There was a sharp click and an oath he didn't understand. He turned around to the laughter of his guests. The albino had walked into a jutting pipe, causing his hard-hat to fall from his head. He rubbed furiously at his forehead and glared at the other two men, who grew solemn.

'We're almost there,' Walter said.

Matthew had to pass through several red-bulb rooms filled with stacks of unattached insulation and spools of multicolored wire to reach the reactor hall. He used his strobe to light the way. In the room before the spiral staircase something caught his eye – a single drop of blood dangling from the end of a piece of copper pipe. He stared at it a moment, then ran his finger over it, creating a long smear. He heard voices ahead and quickly climbed the helix stairs to the reactor hall.

It was a hangar-like structure whose walls were lined by intricate webs of piping. On the ceiling were the tracks of a giant mobile crane whose large hook hung above Matthew like an out of order *deus ex machina*. The floor was thick concrete that absorbed his footfalls without echo.

In the center of the hall was a domed structure, the inner containment building that covered the reactor. It was the size of a small house, with two-foot thick walls of concrete and lead. After making several long zooms of it, Matthew entered the hut through a heavy iron door held open by a wrench. Inside, there was a square walkway around a pit about twenty yards across. He looked into the hole, at the gray cube punctured by long, cylindrical holes. Thin beams of light shone through them from some source below, through the graphite dust suspended in the hut's air, on to the lead roof. It looked like a planetarium display. Matthew felt a brief wave of fear, then laughed at himself. He checked his light meter and decided to use the strobe. He made several pans across the surface, then knelt to make a penetrating zoom through one of the holes into the reactor's core.

There was a rustling behind him.

'So there's a little bird in the egg.'

Matthew turned. It was the interpreter. She was alone.

'Hello,' he said, switching off his camera.

'I'm taking five,' she said, stepping up beside him. She went on to her toes and peered over the guardrail.

'Where are the others?' Matthew asked.

She pointed into the pit with a theatrical, downward looping gesture. He nodded, taking in lavender vapors from her skin. As she leaned forward her blouse flapped open, exposing a breast. The nipple was small, walnut dark.

'What are those holes for?' she asked, nodding toward the reactor.

'For the rods. You put them in to absorb the reaction. Control it.'

'So,' she said, nodding.

There was an uneasy silence.

'I'm Matthew.'

'And I'm Eleni Desta,' she said with mock formality, extending her hand. It was soft, warm. 'You are the director of this movie we are acting in, I see.'

'I'm only helping out my father.'

'So he is your father. I thought.'

'Do we look so much alike?'

'Look alike? Oh yes, I suppose. I can see that. But that is not how I could tell. It is the way you look at him that is the proof.' She narrowed her eyes. 'Hard. No forgiveness. A son's look. Not a worker's.'

Matthew looked at her for a moment, then into the pit. She laughed gently, as if to concede that she had gone too far.

'What happened to him?' she asked. 'His injuries?'

'He was in an accident. A plane crash.'

'People don't usually survive those.'

'No,' Matthew said.

He wanted to change the subject.

'Do you work at the embassy?'

'Oh no,' she said, laughing at some absurdity to the notion. 'Just sometimes I come along when they need to speak. No, I'm a singer. Or I should say I'm learning to sing.'

'Are you at a university?'

'No. I am at a restaurant.'

They watched each other laugh for a moment.

'And you? Are you at a university? Or maybe a restaurant.'

'I finished college last year. Currently I'm trying to forget everything I learned.'

Her smile collapsed.

'You can do that,' she said, nodding. 'It can be done.'

They were silent for a moment. Matthew was confused by her sudden seriousness. She looked at her watch.

'I should go back,' she said.

'Okay.' He pointed to her wrist. 'Do you know about tonight?'

'Yes.'

'Okay.'

'Well, I will see you again I hope.'

'Yes.'

Walter watched the van's exhaust fumes dissipate in the late-afternoon wind. The Africans had left abruptly, with formal thanks and arch glances among themselves. Somebody would write a report, somebody would read it. I don't need this, Walter thought, I really don't.

The pain in his back agreed with rippling pulses that ran from his neck to his knees. He leaned against the hood of his sedan, letting the metal's coolness numb his flesh. As he stretched he could see that they were preparing to bring down another section of concrete from the left tower. The wrecking crane was in position, its large ball cocked menacingly. There were some shouts, then a long blast of what sounded like a foghorn. The ball was released, swinging through a heavy arc, connecting with the top section of the tower. There was a brief hesitation as cracks went out through the concrete, then a great tumbling. The stone hit the ground with a series of thuds. Walter watched the dust rise around the ruins for a moment, then looked back up at the shortened tower. Only a few ribs of bent steel remained.

A plane appeared above them. It had long, thin wings and a narrow fuselage whose fibers reflected the light of the lowering sun. Dixon Firefly, Walter thought. Or perhaps a modified Condor. He watched as it proceeded in a slow, noiseless path toward the bay. A short dash of vapor hovered behind it, marking a brief release of ballast.

Suddenly, it banked and began to soar upwards. Ah, he's found one, Walter thought. His heart sped sympathetically. The plane continued its upward gyre for about thirty seconds, completing almost two full circles before levelling off in a southerly tack with several hundred feet more altitude. Not a big one, Walter thought. But still, a lift.

The control room was located at the top of the turbine hall. It was a square room with a high ceiling and dozens of disconnected clocks. The walls were covered by complex designs mapping the plant's piping and electrical systems, as well as a wall-sized map of the bay region's power grid. They reminded Matthew of primitive cave drawings. Long consoles with meters, dials and screens hugged the walls below them. In the center of the room was a large conference table surrounded by bolted chairs. It was covered with blueprints and softdrink cans.

There was a man at the far end, staring intently at a computer screen. Matthew recognized him – André Brand, the chief engineer. He was a short, thin man, about sixty. His face and limbs were a network of angles, like the pipes that ran through the plant. He had a goatee and long, stringy hair pulled behind large ears. He wore a plaid shirt, safari pants and weathered deck shoes. Matthew walked noisily across the room, yet Brand didn't look up until Matthew stood over him.

'Hello, Dr Brand.'

He squinted at Matthew, frowning slightly.

'Walter's son,' he said with grim factuality.

Matthew nodded.

'Sit, sit.'

He entered the information on the screen into the computer's memory with a sharp punch of his index finger.

'What are you working on?' Matthew asked as he pulled up a folding chair.

'Oh, just farting around with a database a friend sent me. It lists the fundamental characteristics of the world's major geophysical anomalies. You know, water spouts, locust clouds, the Bermuda Triangle.'

He finished working on the computer and removed the disk. He nodded to Matthew's camera.

'What's all this?' he asked.

'Making a video.'

'For sales?'

Matthew nodded and Brand shook his head in disgust.

'Yeah, I saw that bunch who came in here this morning. And Walter's talking about going to Mexico next month. Jesus. Let's give matches to the children.'

He picked up a large coffee mug from the console and took a frowning sip.

'Would you like a cup of putative coffee?'

When Matthew hesitated he produced a half-empty bottle of bourbon from the floor beside his chair. Matthew nodded and grabbed a paper cup from an inverted stack on the table.

'Heavy water,' Brand said as he poured.

Matthew took a long drink.

'Your dad . . .' Brand said. He shook his head. 'It's a good thing he's so tough.'

Matthew shrugged non-commitally. Brand looked at his eyes.

'You think not?'

'I wouldn't know,' Matthew said.

'Ah, okay.' He looked at the blank screen. 'You have your own ideas about all this, this toughness thing. You can tell me all about it, eh? Fair enough. I can understand that. But listen. I've worked with a lot of men, my friend. Seen them in lots of situations. Boot camp, cocktail parties, watching their kids fuck up little league games. Burying wives or just leaving them. All kinds of men in all kinds of places. Most of them are miserable shits, some luck out, a few even get smart. But very few are self-possessed. Very few can hold on in the shitstorm. Just . . . hold on. He can.'

'And that's good?'

'Okay, right. If you're . . .' He raised his eyebrows.

'Twenty-two.'

'Then it isn't. I can understand that. But there's a question of perspective at work here that you have to keep in mind. It's sort of like, like we're walking on a Möbius strip. You're chugging along and suddenly, for no apparent reason, you find yourself inside out, upside down, in reverse. And you can't for God's sake remember getting off the straight and narrow. You haven't done a thing. But there you are . . .'

He swirled the liquid in his mug.

'So what looks like toughness when you're twenty-two might turn out to be weak and stupid when you're our age. And vice versa.' He finished off his drink, the liquor wilting his mouth's sternness. 'So, yeah, I think he is tough. I think so.'

They were staying at the nearby Best Western where Walter had spent his weeknights while overseeing the plant's construction. Matthew had often wondered why they lived so far from his father's work, until he had seen a map on Walter's desk showing the primary evacuation zone in case of an accident at the plant. The city of Advance lay just outside the red circle.

After watching the national news from their twin beds, they headed out in search of a restaurant. They drove into the town of Eastern, a fishing and tourist village that had prospered briefly during Olympic's construction, only to ebb back into tatty quietude after building was halted. The only evidence of the momentary boom were the partially-built apartment blocks and office complexes that resolutely absorbed salt air along the road leading into town.

They passed several diners with signs advertising 'Meat, 2 Veg, Cof, $2.98', as well as a handful of modular fast-food restaurants. Walter slowed before a barn-like steakhouse with a giant iron cow grazing in the middle of the parking lot, but Matthew shook his head. They were running out of town.

'Wait, dad. Turn around. I saw something.'

Walter executed a graceful turn through a gap in the median and pulled across the scanty traffic into the parking lot of an outdoor shopping mall. There were drugstores, baby clothing outlets, insurance shops, a lit-up grocery store. Some kids sat on the hoods of cars docked around a fluttering streetlight.

'In the corner. There.'

Walter pulled to the lot's corner, where a dozen or so cars were assembled in two uneven rows. As the radio antenna lowered automatically into the hood they looked at the restaurant.

It was called The Arbor of the Moon's Enchantment. There were two flickering signs in the window: 'Japanese Cuisine' and 'Budweiser'. It looked like all the other storefronts, except the windows had been covered with colored paper and the dark wood door bore a gravened Japanese character. A string of paper lanterns hung from the roof of the walkway.

'All right?'

'Yes.'

They were greeted by a shrivelled Japanese hostess who asked them if they wanted sushi or hibachi. They chose the cooked food and were wordlessly led into a spacious room of about ten large, low tables that were surrounded by legless benches and topped by domed exhaust hoods. Several strings of paper lanterns criss-crossed the steamy, noisy room. The walls were covered by a skin of thin bamboo. Posters of volcanic mountains, bent-legged birds and flawless gardens hung at regular intervals.

They were led to the only empty table, in a poorly-lit corner. They sat at an angle from each other, facing the other diners. The closest table to them was occupied by a group of slightly drunken teenage couples. The girls wore shiny gowns of peach or sky blue or lavender, and had pale, drooping flowers strapped to their wrists. One of them, a fragile-looking redhead, stared intently at Matthew and Walter. Her large eyes showed great distress, yet she sat quietly, allowing her muscular date to grip her shoulder. The boys wore ill-fitting tuxedos with matching pastel cummerbunds and clip-on bow ties. They seemed to be passing something beneath the table. All bore expressions of leering expectancy, as if waiting for a practical joke to run its course.

'Prom night,' Matthew said.

'No,' Walter said. 'Wrong season for that. This would be Homecoming.'

A plump young white woman in a faded kimono and running shoes approached them with parchment menus. As she handed them out, Matthew noticed that one of her false fingernails had come unglued and swung from her fingertip like a shutter in a storm. She took their drink orders. Walter chose the warm sake, Matthew a bottled beer.

'Your cook will be Hiro,' she said.

Walter took a gulp of water and stared at the teens. He chewed the crushed ice from his glass slowly, seeming to remember something. Matthew followed his gaze. The teens had grown silent, their attention commanded by a cook who had begun to work at their table. He was a thin young Japanese man in an immaculate white smock and high cylindrical hat. He cooked on the large griddle at the table's center, performing skilful, mischievous stunts accompanied by clownish grunts and deadpan asides. He twirled the pepper shaker like a baton; he sheathed and unsheathed his knife with mock fury; he tossed shrimptails into the air and caught them in his pocket or hat. Once, a piece of food got away from him and landed in the spray-stiff hair of one of the girls. The teens laughed and applauded his performance, their astonished eyes dancing in the rising steam. Even the redhead seemed to be enjoying the performance.

'Did I ever tell you the story of my prom?'

'They're not prom goers, dad,' Matthew said sarcastically. 'They're Home . . .'

'That was the night my father died,' Walter continued, ignoring him.

The waitress returned with their drinks, placing them on small napkins with paintings of wildfowl on them. She flourished her pad, staring blankly at a point somewhere between Matthew and Walter. They ordered shrimp. She collected the menus and moved off, her kimono rustling.

'Go ahead,' Matthew said softly.

Walter chewed on crushed ice as his eyes returned to the memory.

'Do you have themes at your proms now?' he asked. 'You know, for decorations and what not. To enable you to create a little world. Well, we did back in Grand Rapids. I remember, ours was Atlantis. Undersea paradise was the idea. Boy, looking at those kids really brings a picture of it to my mind. Aqua-blue bunting, cardboard mermaids and glowing watercolor fishes, a papier-mâché re-creation of Davy Jones's Locker with chestfulls of treasure, skulls and crossbones. And this mannequin dressed up as, um, what's that guy's name with the big fork?'

'Poseidon.'

'Yes, yes. Anyway, since I was mechanically inclined, the committee asked me to help them with the prom's centerpiece. They gave me free rein. So what I decided to do was make a fountain. We put that dummy in the middle of one of those, uh, kiddie wading pools, then rigged a pneumatic fountain using some weights and an old sprinkler. You see, you can . . .'

Walter paused, smiling self-deprecatingly.

'Well, never mind the details. So anyway, we had a fountain in and around Poseidon, with colored lights angling up from the pool's bottom, creating these rippling effects on the cafeteria walls. I'll tell you, Matt, it was beautiful. Everybody thought so. Everybody. As the evening wore on, people, you know, got wilder. Some of the more sophisticated types even had some liquor. We all started dancing in and out of the water. Just skipping through it. Finally, some guys got the brilliant idea of taking the crown and beard and fork from the mannequin and giving them to me to wear. You know, cause I'd built this contraption. And of course I was promptly pushed into the water.'

He paused, his smile fading as he chewed more ice.

'Then I saw my cousin Carl, who was a state trooper, standing there, staring at me in the water. I thought for a second I was in trouble or something. But then I saw that his face was more sad than stern. I draped a tablecloth over my shoulders and followed him into the parking lot. There were some kids out there drinking and they got real nervous when they saw Carl but he didn't even notice them. Then he told me that my father had killed himself. In the garage. He'd just locked it up and run one of those engines he used to tinker with until . . .'

He tried to swallow more ice from his cup, but it was stuck to the bottom. He swished the cup through small circles, dislodging the chips. Something else seemed to come to his mind.

'You know, Matthew, there's something you should know . . .'

He was interrupted by the arrival of their cook, pushing a cart laden with raw food and utensils. He was different from the cook at the other table – shorter, older, more dour with his square jaw and muscular crew cut.

'Gentlemah . . .'

He flicked some drops of water on to the griddle to test its heat. They sizzled into steam which disappeared up the hooded vent.

'I am Hiro.'

34

Matthew and Walter nodded at the cook, who went to work with efficient, unceremonious movements. He splashed sesame oil on the griddle, then threw chopped onions and sprouts into the steaming liquid. He poked at them for a moment with a spatula and dumped a mound of starchy rice on the griddle's edge.

'Where you from?' he asked sullenly, making it clear that small talk was obligatory.

'Advance,' they said together.

'I know it,' Hiro nodded.

He took a bowl of shrimps from his tray and dumped them on to the table. Their still-active sympathetic nervous systems reacted to the heat, causing them to contract embryonically. Hiro pulled a large knife from its holster and, after sharpening it briefly on a whetstone, began cutting off the shrimps' heads and tails. He did not flourish the knife acrobatically, make noises or flip bits of food into the air. Instead, he cut with a savage, three stroke rhythm – head, tail, then a cleansing slap of the blade against the table's metal. As he worked, they noticed several discolored scars on his hands.

'Where are you from?' Walter asked.

'Hokkaido. You know?'

Walter spread his hands.

'Islah. In the nor. Many cranes. Many snow.'

He laced the meal with spice and soy.

'Do you ever want to go back?' Walter asked softly.

Hiro stopped in mid-gesture. He looked at Walter, then at the steam as it was sucked into the rumbling hood. He frowned and slowly shook his head.

'I know,' Walter said. 'I know.'

The game had gone into extra innings, yet the home team's starter was still on the mound. Walter thought back to the pitcher's rookie season with Detroit, the same year that the boys were born. He had been a brash, pencil-necked fastballer who refused on principle to throw curves with two strikes. Now, however, he was a paunchy veteran with long sock stirrups and gray-flecked sideburns, and he threw nothing but knuckleballs. He had been traded around both leagues, yet now had returned to the Tigers to end his career. He worked slowly, deliberately, taking long breathers between batters, standing behind the mound, rubbing down the ball or collecting sweat from the brim of his cap. And always, just before charging up the mound to face the next batter, he'd stare up at a point on the roof of the stadium, his eyes unfocused, tired, almost sad. My kind of player, Walter thought.

Matthew came out of the bathroom, rubbing his long wet hair with a towel. He stared at the screen for a moment.

'Look at this guy,' he said with scorn.

'He's great,' Walter said. 'Tenth inning. One earned run. Four hits, all on the ground. He's great.'

'I don't know,' Matthew said, flopping into his bed.

You will, Walter thought.

'They'll get to him,' Matthew continued. 'It's just a matter of time.'

'Well, sure. But look how long he's held out.'

'What, throwing junk.'

'A knuckler isn't junk, Matt.'

'Then what is it?'

'It's a way of staying in the game.'

'My theory is if you can't throw heat you shouldn't be on the mound.'

'Some theory,' Walter said, tugging at his brace with a crooked finger.

They watched in silence. The next batter was a long-limbed rookie who hit the first pitch for a towering home run on to the stadium's roof. As he trotted around the bases the camera cut back to the pitcher, who stood on the back slope of the mound, examining his fingernails. Soon the manager joined him. He spoke for a few seconds, then asked for the ball. The veteran walked from the field, superstitiously stepping on the first base line with his left foot.

'Ha,' Matthew said.

Walter shrugged and raised himself laboriously from the bed. You'll see, he thought as he limped to the bathroom.

When he came out Matthew was sitting on the edge of his bed, looking at the carpet. The aggression was gone. He seemed troubled. Walter lowered himself carefully on to his throne of pillows.

'Dad.'

Walter turned slightly within the confines of his brace.

'What is it you were going to say?' Matthew asked. 'At the restaurant. Before the cook came.'

Walter looked up at the ceiling. Tell him, he thought.

'Nothing.'

Matthew's eyes constricted with momentary anger, but then he shrugged and turned away. He picked up his watch from the night stand and stared at its face.

'Which way is it, anyway?' he asked. 'I can never remember.'

'Back. Spring forward, fall back.'

Ice machines gave clattering birth to new cubes as Matthew walked the hotel halls. They were deserted except for salesmen who'd checked in late and groups of high schoolers who raced from room to room, supressing pubic laughs as they hurried past him. Most had changed into new clothes – jeans and denim skirts, emblazoned T-shirts, running shoes. From behind closed doors he could hear muffled voices and television music.

Walter had dozed off just after the game, yet Matthew had been unable to sleep. He spent five minutes under the sunlamp in the bathroom, yet that failed to tire him. He dressed and left the room but found the bar closed. So he wandered the halls, hoping to burn off the deep anger and frustration that always welled in him when he spent time with his father.

Someone hissed at him from a slightly ajar door. It was a boy dressed in a rented tux. There was some great stain on the ruffled shirt. His face was puffy yet his eyes were lucid, as if he'd just been awakened from a long sleep.

'Hey man, you gotta help us.'

Matthew paused. You've got the wrong guy, he thought.

'What's the matter?' he asked, approaching the room.

'It's Donna, man. She's flipped. We can't monitor her no more.'

The boy pulled the door open and let Matthew into the room, which stank of rummy vomit. Empty bottles and bits of clothing lay on most of the surfaces. One of the inner drapes had been pulled from the window, lying in a soiled heap in a corner. Someone had written 'zoned' on the mirror with a bar of soap.

There were five kids in the room. There were two other boys leaning against the far wall, inexpertly smoking filterless cigarettes. They had thick necks, Mohawk haircuts and wore Atholton Wrestling T-shirts. They were trying to look casual, yet their eyes were scared, and they nervously stroked their brushes of hair with open palms.

A red-haired girl sat cross-legged on the bed, her head bowed so that her face was hidden. She was naked except for a bra, which had a small pink cloth flower over the front clasp. Matthew noticed that her hands were bound by a cord that had been ripped from the drapes. Every

37

ten seconds or so she took a deep breath, which she released with a slow moan. Another girl, still in her dance dress, sat beside her, trying to comfort her by gently rubbing a lock of her red hair between her fingers. Nobody said anything.

'Well, the obvious question is why is she tied up?' Matthew asked.

'I told you, man. She's freaked,' the boy in the tuxedo explained.

'So?'

There was a confused silence.

'So? So she might hurt herself, is what.'

'She doesn't look so dangerous.'

'Look at her face,' one of the thick-necked boys said.

Matthew stepped up to the bed and raised the girl's head by placing a finger beneath her chin. It was the girl who'd stared at them in the restaurant. There were four long gashes on either side of her face, running from her cheekbone to her chin. He looked at her hands. Her fingernails, which were decorated with small tattoos of stars or glitter, were stained with blood and spools of flesh. She was smiling, staring down some great distance. Her eyes were large and green and brilliant. Hello Eddie, Matthew thought.

'What's she had?'

'One rum and coke,' said a wrestler.

Matthew looked up.

'I swear to God,' said the boy in the tux.

'What should we do?' the other girl asked.

'Give me a wet towel,' Matthew said, looking into her eyes. One of the wrestlers moved quickly. Matthew used it to gently daub her wounds. As he worked the girl looked at him. Her smile faded, the brilliance of her eyes diminished.

'My face,' she said.

'Yes,' Matthew said. 'I know. But it's all right now.'

He threw the towel on the rug and untied her hands. It took several seconds – the cord had been bound into a dozen crude knots. When her hands were free the girl closed her eyes and rubbed her wrists. Matthew turned to the others.

'She'll be all right. It's over. Help her get dressed.'

They nodded obediently.

That night he dreamed he was a bird in the midst of a feeding frenzy. Dozens of fellow birds fed on a swarm of green insects that had flown into their midst. All around him were the sounds of flapping wings, the shrieks of terror and satiation. He was disgusted by the spectacle and tried to fly away yet kept bumping into an invisible wall, some sort of acrylic dome. Then, one of the insects flew into his mouth. He tried to dislodge it, yet he had no hands, just stubby wings that couldn't reach his face. The bug scuttled about furiously in his mouth, chirping loudly. It had a hundred thrashing limbs. Matthew tried to bite it to stop the noise, yet it only grew louder.

He awoke to the steady, two-pulse sound of his father's alarm wristwatch. He reached across the divide between the beds to his father's dangling arm and switched it off. Walter's skin felt damp with cool sweat. Matthew gently touched his wrist, feeling the racing, erratic pulse. He raised himself to an elbow and looked at his father in the soft light. He lay on his back, his wide-open mouth puffing irregularly. His eyes fluttered rapidly, as if disturbed by wind. He's dreaming of him too, Matthew thought.

He gently removed the watch from Walter's wrist and set it back an hour, to the new time.

CAREERING

M atthew moved quietly through the empty house, trying not to disturb anything, careful not to leave a trace. He had been here over an hour, taking note of all the valuables, making sure that he closed the drawers and closets tightly, that he returned the vases and appliances to their proper islands in the shallow sea of dust. As he moved from room to room, the only sounds he could hear were the rumble of the heating system and the clicks of various digital clocks. Once the phone rang, but an answering machine took the call.

All that was left to do now were the kitchen and basement. He had already taped eight and a half minutes' worth of possessions – panning over the baby grand and china cabinet, zooming into fur-stuffed closets and drawers of polished silver, casting strobes on to wood-colored consoles of electronic equipment. He had filmed the garage's tools and machinery, as well as the attic's holiday ornaments and outgrown toys. The remaining things would have to be squeezed into ninety seconds. No house got more than ten minutes of tape.

This was his job. He worked through several insurance agencies, making videos of households to file with their larger homeowners' policies. The agencies were willing to pay for the videos in order to discourage fraud and overpayment. He could have made good money if he worked hard, but he was content to just get by.

This was his second job since graduating from college. After moving back home he'd worked as a calendar editor and film critic for *Profiles*, a weekly suburban tabloid. The paper was a mass circulation advertiser that was distributed free in supermarkets, shops and the foyers of restaurants. It contained personality profiles, consumer reports and arts reviews. No hard news or features. It was owned by a mass media corporation and run by boozy middle-aged reporters who'd outlived their usefulness on the corporation's urban dailies.

Matthew found the calendar work to be a grind but enjoyed the film reviewing, especially the paragraph-length blurbs for the movie listings section. He had started off trying to cultivate the discursive, modest tone of his college professors, but soon saw he was only boring. So he developed a style that was all acid wit and fierce irony, often writing sections of the review before even seeing the movie. Angry letters began to appear from readers, and Matthew was given a small raise. Then the manager of the eight-cinema complex at the mall asked for a meeting with the publisher. Business was off a little. Couldn't their paper be a bit more positive? More supportive? Help him sell some popcorn? He took out a color ad on the back page to cement this new, mutually beneficial relationship. Matthew was relegated to just the calendar section, replaced as film critic by a retired high-school English teacher. He quit the magazine altogether.

During his tenure at the magazine and in the months after, he'd also worked sporadically on several film treatments, none of which was finished. The first was about a medical student from a comfortable suburban home who spends a summer working with migrant laborers in a rural health clinic. He discovers that a local agri-business is exposing them to poison and decides to intervene, convincing several illegal immigrants to testify. Matthew wanted the student's decision to have ambiguous moral repercussions but couldn't decide what those would be. Then there was the story of the man who had been a champion miler in high school and college, yet wasn't quite world class material. He ended up as a pacemaker in international meets, leading the other runners through three laps and dropping out. The opening shot was to be of his face the moment he stepped off the track and let the others pass – a look of exhaustion, envy, sorrow. He gets involved with drug smuggling, but Matthew couldn't think of how or to what end. Then there was the story of the suicide pact between two lovers from wealthy suburban families. The movie opened on the day of their attempt, which was botched – only the boy died. The girl went on to do something, but Matthew wasn't sure what. That one was to have lots of music. Anthems. Matthew abandoned them all at approximately the same point, around the sixth page, where the momentum of the initial idea was slowed by the friction of accumulating irony, then stopped dead against the wall of hard work needed to carry it through.

He'd also sent off an application to a West Coast film school. An essay, some screenwriting fragments, a short film on the choreography of teens in and around the mall on Friday night. He'd even been interviewed by a laconic graduate of the school who worked as an editor for a local television station. That morning, before setting off to make the insurance film of the house, he'd received the rejection. It was not a standard letter, but a lengthy, personal note from the school's assistant dean. He wrote of Matthew's 'undeniable' skill and wished they had room for him and other 'similarly sharp-eyed applicants'. But given the volume of applications, they had to choose students who also possessed 'more humanistic' skills. Matthew's abilities seemed 'too tentative, cold, undeveloped'. They focussed on 'insignificant detail', showing a 'fascination with the prose of the world that serves as a barrier to emotional resonance'. His work was, in short, 'almost French'. He wished Matthew well and suggested he investigate 'something along more commercial lines'. Matthew had folded the letter several times before throwing it away.

He was just about done with the kitchen. As he rooted through the last cabinets he was startled by a prolonged, shrill tone, followed by a loud whirring noise. It took him a moment before he realized that the microwave oven had come on. Set on timer. Everything in these houses is set on timers, he thought. He stepped up to the tinted glass and watched as a massive frozen roast began to thaw, sending slow streams of bloody water through the glass pan.

When he finished filming, Matthew took a beer from the refrigerator and settled into a large reclining chair in the lounge. It was mid-afternoon – he didn't have to be out until dusk. The room was the usual collection of trophies, photo portraits of children, great books with uncracked spines, fake antique barometers and compasses. They are so still, these houses, he thought.

Matthew thought of his family's homes. There had been five since their birth, growing telescopically with Walter's career advancements. First there was the creaky, drafty apartment in Ann Arbor where they'd spent their infancies. His memories of there were simple sensations, isolated incidents. The sound of tricycle wheels across polished wood floors. The smell of milk warming in the stove's gas heat. The time the mailman threw their softball so high it disappeared from sight. The cigarette smoke from the students Walter tutored, swirling slowly through the drafts. The sound of the marching band rehearsing in the field across the street, waking them from their afternoon naps.

Then, when he and Eddie were four, there was the two-bedroom yellow house outside Cincinnati. The memories there were more continuous, more complete. Walter's nightly return from work – loose tied, prickle faced, smelling of exhaust fumes, of sweat and car vinyl. He remembered travelling to nursery school in the red bus with the fat woman driver who drank beer from bottles wrapped in paper bags. The times he and Eddie were jeered for sharing a rug during naptime at kindergarten. Walter taking them to Riverfront Stadium to see Bench and Rose and Perez and Morgan on Saturday afternoons. Matthew remembered the way his father would rail against the artificial turf every time a grounder skipped through the infield. Afterwards they'd go for a dinner of Four Star chili, then sit on the stationwagon's tailgate as they ate soft ice cream and watched teenagers rumble past.

Most of all, he remembered the long afternoons playing in the small, fenced-in yard strewn with cones from the single looming pine. He and Eddie would mount tremendous battles with armies of molded plastic soldiers, setting them up all over the yard. They always fought to bitter, entrenched draws, after which the inarguably dead were consigned to technicolor pyres that billowed thick black smoke through the neighbors' gardens. Tumuli of hard, formless plastic eventually littered the sandbox. Then Walter and Helen had gone to an energy exhibition in London, and Eddie's gift upon their return had been a squad of the Queen's Own Lifeguard model soldiers. From then on he was invincible, his troops' tassled peak caps, silver breastplates and Wilkinson swords far superior to Matthew's dull green GIs.

And there was the fragile corpse of the praying mantis, held in Eddie's cupped hands, its shattered antennae moving a little in his brother's breath. Look, Matty. Look.

Then, when they were nine, it was the large North Jersey ranch house with its neatly sodded lawn that Walter would cut with the tractor mower they weren't allowed to ride. In the back yard there was a large, above-ground circular pool that gave off clouds of steam on cold mornings. Matthew and Eddie practically lived in the water during the humid Jersey Augusts, emerging only at lunchtime to sprint into the kitchen, where they would shiver through lunch, then fidget away the obligatory half hour before returning to the pool. Walter would join them after returning from work and they'd take turns diving from his shoulders or swimming beneath his legs. Then, all three would move in clockwise unison along the pool's rim, creating a whirlpool with their mass. The current would eventually begin to move faster than the boys' small limbs could carry them. Walter would then move into the pool's center and watch as the twins were carried by the current through rapid, bobbing circles, plucking them out only when they called to him in fear or exhaustion. Matthew always called first, Eddie only after one or two dousings. Once he did not call out at all, dragged deep underneath the surface when he caught a lungful of chlorinated water. Walter had to go under to get him. Matthew remembered his brother's eyes as he greedily took in air upon surfacing – thrilled, burning with a frantic light. Walter held him tight, saying comforting words, but soon found that Eddie's gasps were laughter. They never made the whirlpool again.

A few years later, when the prototype fast breeder whose construction he was overseeing became operational, Walter received a large bonus and they moved to a bigger house in the same town. Matthew remembered their quiet awe as they walked through the gratuitous rooms and played with the intercom system. The backyard was an immense lawn dotted with dowel-propped fruit and berry trees that instantly became boundaries for their ballgames. One of the trees bore a perpetual harvest of small, dull-red berries that the lore of the neighborhood children held to be poisonous. If you touched or stepped on one, Matthew and Eddie were told, you had to rub it off right away with leaves or grass. There was even a vague story about two girls, Japanese exchange students, who had eaten the berries and died, their bodies shipped back home in small black coffins.

After hearing its story, Eddie had spent the entire morning staring at the tree. Finally, around lunchtime, he organized about a dozen of the block's kids around it. Without a word he plucked a handful of berries from the tree and placed them in his mouth, chewing them with parted lips. The kids had yelled, one or two cried. Eddie concluded by swallowing with a loud gulp, bowing, then emitting a reedy belch. He opened his mouth to show the bright dye that harmlessly coated his tongue and teeth.

It was at the second Jersey house that Matthew began to spend time alone, away from Eddie and his new, rough friends. He would often wander into the woods behind the house with a book about Doc Savage or John Carter of Mars, hiding in the small, litter-strewn clearing that had once been used by vagrants. He would lie in the ivy, reading and imagining himself in various heroic situations. He soon created a small library of fantasies that he would re-run, intact, in his imagination. Other times, he would walk around the circle of rain-embedded stones that had been the vagrants' campfire, imagining that he was ascending some great spiral staircase into the sky. Moving always counterclockwise, he imagined himself topping the trees and peering down on the roofs of the subdivision and weaving cars of the interstate; then breaking through the clouds and seeing where the rain was made; moving through the thinning atmosphere where the last thing you could hear is the barking of a dog; into space clotted with small stars and syrupy black air; then beyond space, to where there were new colors. He would strain to see one, hyperventilating or pressing his eyelids, yet he could never manage. His mother's call or the crash of his brother approaching through the foliage would break the reverie, and he'd climb patiently down the spiral before returning home.

And finally, when he was fourteen, they moved to the mock Colonial in Advance, the planned city in Maryland. It was a little larger than the second Jersey house, but the thrill of size was gone. It had a large basement which also served as a garage, a ground floor of aluminum siding and a second floor of treated wood shingles. In the back was a large elevated deck with an in-built gas barbecue. The lawn was tiered with railroad ties and would flood sometimes in the spring rains.

Matthew finished his beer, absently crushing it into an hour-glass shape. Time to go. As he stood, he noticed a line of video cassettes on top of the television. He walked over and read them. The usual collection of movies, family events, mini-series. A wedding. Matthew selected one called 'Hallow' and inserted it in the machine.

There was a storm of checkered static, out of which slowly emerged a vision of a party. He heard the shrieks of children and pressed the mute button. The three sisters whose photos filled the house's walls and shelves stood in line for the camera. They were dressed as a witch, a ghost, and a comic-book character. There was a series of wavering shots of them posing, eating, rummaging about the close-cropped yard in search of hidden candy. Then there was another interval of static, followed by a long section of the girls playing a game Matthew remembered. Each girl would reach blindly into one of several boxes, having to guess its contents. You were told beforehand that inside was part of a human body – eyes, fingers, veins, a heart. In fact, the boxes contained peeled grapes, sausages, cooked spaghetti, a plastic bag filled with pudding. The first two girls squealed with delighted disgust as they dipped in their hands. But the third girl, the one in the ghost costume, recoiled in terror after exploring the first box. Tears seeped from her mask and she refused to go on, wriggling her hands frantically before her. She looked just beyond the camera, shaking her head each time the camera dipped. A hand emerged from the right edge of the picture, beckoning her to play. Finally, she ran off, and the storm of static broke again.

Matthew rewound the tape. I know that game, he thought. When the tape reached the beginning he simultaneously pressed the 'play' and 'record' buttons. He waited until the tape ran through, removed it from the machine and returned it to its case. Then, he quietly left the house.

He drove slowly through Advance's sapling-lined streets. There was little traffic – school buses, Volvos with baby seats in the back, service vans. Rakes of water moved across some of the lawns, as if clearing the air around the houses of something unseen. A group of skinny runners from the local high school loped by his car as he waited at a stop sign, causing him to think back to his own track career. He had wanted to be a distance runner, but soon earned a reputation for not finishing races. He went out too quickly. The coach eventually told him he either had to quit the team or become a rabbit, pacing the better runners through the early stages of a race. Matthew soon became expert at it, leading two of the team's runners to school records. One day, however, he had just kept on going, finishing the race ahead of the runners he was supposed to have paced. He quit soon after.

On one of the quieter streets, Matthew slowed to watch some workmen in bulky protective suits as they attached a hose from a tanker truck to the base of an aluminum-armored house. The yard they worked in was cordoned off by long ropes that held pennants bearing warning skulls. Matthew soon figured out that they were pumping extra insulation into the walls. A small amount leaked as they worked, coating the perfect shrubbery that lined the house's foundation. It was pink, light, like frosting or cotton candy.

Advance was a city that had been born on a developer's map twenty years earlier. It had been one of the earliest settlements in that part of the country, an outpost for settlers pushing inland from the bay. The developers had kept the old name as a sign of the city's newness, its bold originality. It was built on spent, nutrient-drained farmland that was cheaply bought and easily dozed. Cow ponds were transformed into recreational lakes for paddle boats and swimming; pastures were molded into concentric subdivisions; barns into dinner theatres or recreation centers. Fences and stone walls were used to align cul-de-sacs, golfdominiums, bicycle paths.

The city was divided into a half dozen townships. Each had its own community center, which consisted of a small shopping mall, civic offices, schools, recreation facilities. The residential streets swirled around these centers in complex configurations. The civic architecture was called environmental – single-storey office buildings, all-wood playgrounds, windowless schools with open-plan classrooms. The residential architecture was an uneasy blend of aluminum and wood. There were also several large apartment complexes of stucco or painted brick. The streets were lined with baby elms and fledgling oaks that provided no shade. Everything sprung up as planned on the ten-meter relief map at the developer's tinted-window headquarters, between the city's central shopping mall and largest lake.

The only element of whimsy were the names of the streets. There were cul-de-sacs called Pandora's Box, The Conundrum, Zeno's Way, and streets called Descartes Path, Gatsby Green, Jacob's Ladder. While working at the weekly magazine, Matthew had discovered that the developer had given his brilliant, dissolute son the job of naming the roads. The boy, a philosophy major in his seventh undergraduate year, had committed suicide soon after submitting his work. His despairing father had stood resolutely by the names despite pressure from his board.

Twenty years later, construction was ongoing, expansion seemed perpetual. Orange-ribboned stakes marked sections of undeveloped pasture. Dislodged tree trunks smoldered for days in lots being prepared for building. A second garbage dump was about to be opened. Muddy tracks of earthmovers lined residential streets, and long-haired young men with tattoos and hard-hats occasionally called out from the sites to carriage-pushing housewives.

Matthew turned off the residential streets in order to take a shortcut through the golf course. It was situated near the town's center, lined by transplanted cypress trees and retirement condos. He had to drive slowly in order to avoid hitting the weaving carts operated by bandy-legged old golfers in brightly checked pants and face-shadowing visors.

He stopped near the fourteenth tee, once again caught up by memory. The hole was a dogleg to the right, a long par four that bent around a small lake of murky water. The tee's elevation above the water tempted many golfers to try to drive over the hazard, rather than laying up and playing around it. Many balls ended up in the water. The hole was rarely birdied.

Eddie had gone in first, wearing only his track shorts. He walked slowly, probing the bottom with his feet. His back muscles shimmered in the moonlight as his body reacted to the water's chill. At chest-deep he stopped, cocking his head as he leaned slightly to one side and reached deeper into the water. He then ducked quickly beneath the surface. Seconds later he emerged, holding the dimpled ball above his head.

'Come on in,' he said, tossing the ball to shore, near their bag. 'Water's great.'

Matthew waded in, trembling with the sharp shock of cold. The bottom was mud covered by a slick skin of slime that kept his feet from sinking in. Strands of spongy weed floated around his ankles and knees as he moved deeper. Ahead, Eddie went under again with a muffled splash.

Matthew felt the hard form of a ball beneath his feet. He tried several times to lift it with curled toes, but the water's pressure pried it loose before it reached his hand. He hesitated a moment, then went under and collected the prize from the mud, his eyes and mouth firmly shut against the foul water.

They retrieved several dozen balls from the hazard this way. Practice ranges bought them at five dollars a dozen, so on a good night they could make twenty or thirty dollars. Technically, they were trespassing, but there was no watchman and the police didn't care. The only sounds were the cars passing on the road above, the dogs barking in the nearby condos. Somewhere, a burglar alarm sounded for a few minutes, then switched off. As they moved about the lake Matthew had a strong feeling of isolation, as if he and Eddie were at sea, slipping past some hostile shore.

Then, something like a cold hose whipped Matthew's leg. He stumbled violently backwards in the waist-deep water.

'What the hell was that?' he whispered to Eddie.

'What?'

'It was like an icicle. But it moved.'

'Snake.'

'Don't say that.'

'Seriously. They dig your warm skin.'

Matthew stared at his brother's smiling face.

'Don't worry, Matty. They can't open their mouths under water. But I can . . .'

He disappeared beneath the surface, the hazard swallowing his laughter. Matthew braced himself for his brother's assault. A street cleaning truck passed on the street above, its flashing orange light playing across the water rippled by Eddie's dive. Matthew looked around the lake for his brother's slickened hair, listened for that first sighing breath. Nothing.

'Eddie?'

He began to wade toward the point where Eddie dived, moving his arms in front of him like a man making his way through an opposing crowd.

'Hey, Eddie.'

Frustrated by the bottom's slipperiness, he began to swim. When he reached the vanishing point he was surprised to find the water to be over his head. A picture of infinite depths flashed in his mind as he trod water.

'Eddie.'

But it was absurd to speak. He went under and discovered it was ten feet to the bottom. The strands of weed were longer here, sharper. The mud, free from the encasing slime, sucked greedily at his probing hands. He opened his eyes for an instant and saw a dark yet radiant color that was new to him. He tried to look around but the stinging was too much. His chest began to tighten and he darted to the surface, his ears popping violently.

He again scanned the lake, but there were only his own disturbances, rippling away from him. He took a deep breath and prepared to dive again, but was stopped by a strange noise. Laughter. Why is someone laughing at this? Then there was a splash near him, followed by another, and another. He looked to the shore.

Eddie was sprawled on the cropped grass of the fairway, his shoulders caped by a brilliant towel. Golf balls surrounded him, glistening white in the moonlight. He tossed one into the pond, not far from Matthew.

'Lose something?' he asked.

As his brother laughed another cold hose slid against Matthew's leg – languid, gentle, almost loving.

Around him were the echoed sounds of closing. Heavy doors thudded together; security grills rattled shut; chalkboard signs scraped across the walkway. The central fountain's hiss diminished into the faint sound of dripping water. Even the invisible speakers grew silent, their muzak cut off in mid swell.

Matthew walked slowly, taking an indirect route to the shop. He liked the mall when empty of shoppers. It had the same quelling power as the cathedral in the city. Only without the obligations of religion or art. But those things don't matter, he thought. It's that quality of sound and light that people want. That sense of nothingness, of insignificance in the face of their own creations.

He could see his mother behind the shop's glass night doors. The neon sign still burned – Helen's Gifts. She stood behind the counter, holding an unfurled register tape that followed the contour of her leg to the floor. Occasionally, she would enter numbers into a small adding machine. Surrounding her were shelves of porcelain and terracotta figurines, china serving dishes in the shape of fish or vegetables, *cloisonné* vases containing silk and paper flowers.

She'd started the business two years earlier with Walter's bonus money. She had done it originally to alleviate the boredom, to get out of the empty house, yet had soon made back her husband's investment and was now turning a profit. Her strategy was to take roughly half the items for sale on consignment, thereby minimizing the amount of money she had to give to wholesalers. It's ironic, Matthew thought as he approached. Her immigrant father had spent all those years working behind a counter because he had no choice. And now here was his daughter, doing it because she wanted to.

He rapped on the glass. She looked quickly and held up a finger as she completed a final tally.

'Just finishing,' she said as they pulled open the doors. Matthew kissed her soft cheek. 'Thanks for coming to pick me up.'

'How's business?' Matthew asked.

'Steady,' she said, reclosing the door. 'Steadily bad. People aren't interested in gifts these days, it seems.'

Matthew sat on a stool behind the counter. He watched in silence as she continued her closing procedure, punching an elaborate code into the register.

'What's news?' she asked over her shoulder.

Matthew put his feet against the counter and tilted back the stool.

'Nothing. The film school people rejected me.'

She turned to him.

'Oh,' she said, scrutinizing his face, trying to gauge his feelings. 'I'm sorry.'

He shrugged.

'What are you going to do?' Helen asked softly as she looked back to the register.

'Don't know. Keep on keeping on.'

'You should do something, you know.'

He looked at a row of shiny porcelain figurines of child dancers.

'You sound like dad.'

She looked up sharply.

'It's not inconceivable that your father should say things that are right and true.'

'I think I'm going to go into the city,' Matthew said quickly. 'You know, move there. I know this guy who has a place.'

'So does that mean you're going to get a job or go to school or become a gangster or what?'

'I just want to be on the scene.'

She looked at him for a moment, then returned to her work. Matthew got up from the stool and strolled around the shop, examining the merchandise, until she finished.

'Your father called. He'll be coming home tonight,' she said, locking off the register.

Matthew shrugged.

'Well, try to control your excitement,' she said.

'What am I supposed to say?' he asked. 'Okay. Great. Saint Walter will be returning from among the heathens . . .'

'What's that supposed to mean?'

'Nothing,' Matthew said. 'Never mind.'

'Tell me, Matthew.'

He returned to his stool, taking a magnetic paperclip holder from the desk.

'All right.'

He pried a paperclip from the magnet and dropped it back on. It hit with too much force, though, and fell to the carpet.

'I'm just tired of him. I'm tired of his suffering. It's like he's this genius at pain and because I'm not, because I'm so fucking numb about it all, then I'm cold and inhuman and a rotten person. Every time I look into his face I feel as if he knows all these great and profound things about what's happened and I don't know anything. It's like, I don't know, he's a master martyr and wants me to be his apprentice. So I just get pissed off because I don't want to be that. I don't want to suffer like him. I don't want to be in on his dark secrets or whatever. I don't want to learn anything from him. So don't be surprised when I won't let him teach me.'

'Well, I just don't understand that.'

'I just don't need him, mom. It's that simple. I mean I love him and if I look back to ten years ago there are good things there, but now I think he's a failure. An across-the-board failure. I don't want to be told things by him. I don't want his wisdom, cause look where it got him.'

She stared at him but didn't say anything.

'So that's the reason,' Matthew said softly, picking the paperclip from the floor.

Helen took the keys from the register's lock.

'We should go,' she said.

Matthew was sitting in the dark family room, flipping through the channels with the remote control and nursing a long-neck beer, when his father returned. He pretended to be dozing when he heard Walter shoulder open the front door, hoping he would just go upstairs. But Walter dumped his bags near the foot of the stairs and went into the kitchen. A few moments later he entered the room and said his son's name.

Matthew pretended to awake. Walter stood in the doorway, holding a tall glass of milk and several slices of unadorned white bread. He had been in Mexico City for nearly a week, making sales presentations to the energy ministry. His suit was rumpled with travel, his tie loosened to the second button of his shirt. His eyes were bloodshot, the lids puffy with jetlag. Matthew noticed he no longer wore the neckbrace.

'Hey dad.' He pressed the mute button. 'How'd it go?'

Walter lowered himself heavily into a leather reclining chair. He stared distractedly at the television.

'You know, I suppose I can get used to the notion of bribing people to make a deal. I just can't get used to the idea of bribing them to *consider* making a deal.'

'They ask for bribes? Really?'

'Well, not literally. What happens is you hire them as a consultant for something insignificant, give them a fat retainer. Then they'll sit down with you and talk turkey.' He took a sip of milk. 'Consultants. We've entered the age of the consultant, Matthew. The ultimate nonentity. Nobody knows who they are, nobody knows why they are, nobody even knows what they do. You can't see or touch or hear them. All we know is how much they cost. That they have to be paid.'

He finished the milk.

'How was the flight?' Matthew asked.

'Fine, except for take off. Jesus. Mexico City. You don't take off from there, you just go level and the ground falls away. We taxied for about eight miles, it seemed. Low throttle. I thought perhaps we were just going to drive up to Houston. Then we bump up to about one hundred feet. And hold. And hold. We're towered over by those volcanos. Below there's a shanty town. So close

you can see what's for dinner, you can see the naked kids' bottoms.'

He paused as he rubbed the bridge of his nose.

'And then, well, the ground just fell away. We're high in the sky
without even ascending.'

They watched the silent television.

'Anyway,' Walter said, standing up slowly. 'I almost forgot.'

He left the room for a moment, then returned with a carrier bag.

'Brought you something.'

Matthew sat forward on the couch as his father rummaged through
the luggage. He thought of the gifts Walter bought them when they were
young. Headdresses from Saudi Arabia. Berets from Paris. Robes from
Japan.

'Ah. Here.'

He handed Matthew a small object wrapped in a newspaper that bore
advertisements for masked Mexican wrestlers. Matthew smiled slightly
as he unwrapped the gift. It was a small, crudely carved clay statue of
a grotesque Indian deity with bulging eyes, jutting tongue and claw-like
hands. An indeterminate blob of clay protruded from between its legs.
Matthew held it up in television light, nodding admiringly.

'Your mother sent me on a wild goose chase for her shop, looking
for statues. Everything was either Catholic icons or crude stuff like this.
Personally I think it's ugly but I figured you . . .'

'I like it,' Matthew said quietly. 'I do.'

Walter nodded for a moment, then reached into his bag again, this
time pulling out a scroll. He handed it to Matthew.

'This is strange,' he said to Matthew as he unrolled the parchment.
It was an illustration of a cockfight, drawn in childish, two-dimensional
figures. 'A man I was meeting with told me about these. They're done by
Indians in the southern part of the country, which I guess is still pretty
savage. They're not very professional, the drawings, I don't think. But
the paper is interesting. What do you think it is?'

'Papyrus?'

'Skin. Human skin.'

'What?' Matthew asked, looking more closely at the drawing.

'No kidding. What they do is, the artist will peel off the top layer
of the skin from his arm or his leg. Again and again, over a period
of weeks, pressing the bits together and treating it with some kind of
sappy substance. Then when there's enough it's stretched and dried.
You can see that it's skin if you examine it closely.'

He leaned forward and ran his finger over the uneven surface. Matthew held up the statuette next to the drawing.

'Which one is mine?' he asked, his voice suddenly bitter.

Walter moved away from him slightly.

'What?'

'You bought two. Which one is for me?'

'Both. I don't understand,' Walter said.

'You know what I mean,' Matthew said. 'You know exactly.'

'Matt . . .'

'So which one is it?'

'Both, I said.'

'It can't be both, Dad.'

He held them up.

'I can't take both. You know how it is. So tell me.'

'Matt, it was just habit.'

'Tell me.'

Walter stood and, shaking his head, walked slowly from the room, his shoulders stooped with jetlag.

The only people on the streets were joggers whose reflecting crosses bobbed in the car's headlights. The yellow streetlights gave them a sickly pallor, making them look like patients wandering the grounds of a hospital. Matthew realized this was the last night he would spend in this town. He decided to visit the Ashes.

He parked in the street and walked around the side of the large house. As he stepped over the drainage spout something at the edge of the bushes which separated the yards caught his attention. An animal, crouched, perfectly still. Matthew let his eyes grow accustomed to the irregular light. It was a possum. He took a step towards it.

'Hey,' he said, putting out his hand like a dice player. He'd once seen Eddie entrance one so that it let him scratch its belly. 'Hey.'

The animal took a half step backwards and made a hissing noise that sounded like a machine releasing a small portion of some great pressure within it. Matthew could see several thick strands of cottony foam criss-crossing its mouth. A car passed and he could see its eyes for an instant – the one blind white, the other darting wildly back and forth.

Matthew leapt to his feet, stumbling backwards. The animal fled, careering maniacally across the yard and disappearing into a drainage ditch, from where Matthew could hear it hiss again.

*

57

He drummed gently on the sliding glass door until they noticed him, turning unsurprised from the television. Beth flashed him a wan smile, while the two boys with her looked at each other to see who would let him in. Finally, the taller of the two shuffled over and removed the two-by-four that barred the door. He wore a T-shirt that bore the phrase 'T-shirt' in large letters across the front.

Matthew nodded to him and stepped into the room, which smelled of new carpets. He bent over the couch and kissed Beth's averted, passive face. She looked tired, numb, as if the anesthetic were still in effect. Her eyes were almost lost in the shadows of her cheekbones; her widow's peak seemed like a gash on her forehead. Out of the corner of his eye Matthew saw the second boy, who was wearing a lilac polo shirt, smooth his moustache and smile grimly at the first.

'What's on?' Matthew asked.

'*Guys and Dolls*,' said the first boy.

'It's great,' said the other, clutching an oversized pillow to his abdomen.

Great, Matthew thought. He climbed over the couch and sat on the floor beside Beth. He noticed that there were several half-moon scars on her left ankle. Eddie's jagged, uncut toenails. Matthew remembered his own similar scars from years ago.

Beth leaned forward and picked up the remote control from the coffee table. She squinted at the screen, gently tapping the selector against her thigh.

'Is the color right?' she asked.

Nobody answered. She pressed the green switch a few times, then returned it to its original level. Matthew looked again at the half-moon scars on her ankles.

There had been showers that morning. Twice the skies cleared, only to cloud back over quickly with low, dark clouds that moved as fast as a squadron of helicopters. The car radio spoke of flooding on secondary roads as they drove in silence.

The building was in a medical park. It was brick and had no windows. There was a heavy metal door attended by a security guard who picked at his teeth with a coffee stirrer.

The room was empty when they arrived but soon crowded to overflowing. There was a young black woman on her own, another with an elderly man who stroked her neck. There was a group of three

Spanish-speaking women who appeared to be friends. There was a young girl and her young boyfriend and their mothers.

Beth had first been taken into a conference room by a very tall woman with curly hair who gently touched her back as they walked. She emerged about five minutes later. Matthew asked what they had talked about. Beth said she couldn't remember.

They called her about half an hour later. When she was gone Matthew watched a nurse feed the goldfish in a large tank. One of the teens' mothers kept on glancing at him. He tied and retied his shoes until he broke a lace.

A nurse came out after only about ten minutes and beckoned for Matthew to come into the inner room. It was filled with reclining chairs and sinks. Beth sat in one of the chairs, staring at the ceiling. A nurse was taking her blood pressure.

They left when she was stable, about a half hour later. The rain had stopped for the day, it seemed. Matthew drove slowly, avoiding potholes or sharp turns. They had to stop at a drugstore to fill an antibiotic prescription. He left the car running, left Beth looking at the puddles, a gnarled paper tissue oozing from her fist.

She was in the same position when he returned. He put the pills on the seat between them and drove slowly through the parking lot.

'Drive through that,' she said, nodding towards a large puddle.

Matthew drove through it slowly, only making waves.

'Now that one,' she said. 'Faster.'

Matthew hit the second puddle at about twenty miles per hour. There was a small splash.

'Come on, Matthew.'

He looped around the lot and drove quickly through the first puddle. It made a sound like rending cloth.

'Go faster, faster.'

He pressed the accelerator and bolted through the second puddle, then turned sharply and headed toward the first. He hit it at fifty. There was a tremendous splash that soaked the side windows. All the dashboard lights flashed and the car stalled. Matthew let it coast to the edge of the lot, then tried fruitlessly to turn it over.

'Something's flooded,' he said.

She began to shake and he thought she was laughing. But she was crying. He took her cold hand in his.

When the movie ended the two boys said they were going dancing at a club called 'Panache'. Beth said she was tired and Matthew just stared at them. They left with petulant shrugs.

'So how are you?' he asked her.

'Come upstairs. I want to show you something.'

She disappeared into the bathroom when they entered the room. He sat on the edge of her canopied bed. The room was almost unchanged from the first time he and Eddie had seen it, eight years earlier. There were the cream colored lampshades, the Degas prints of stretching dancers, the clusters of dried flowers. There was the shelf of dolls from several nations: Flamenco dancers, mädchen in lederhosen, the geisha with the chipped face. There were the photos of Beth's youth – posing in a tutu; seated at the wheel of a convertible in the driveway of their Houston home; trying on her father's helmet as he smiled broadly. And the framed photo of Eddie in his lab coat, leaning casually against the trunk of a cherry tree in full bloom. You will be the best man, he had told Matthew that day.

She emerged from the bathroom, clutching a large white towel in front of her.

'Look.'

She lowered the towel, showing him her breasts. They seemed too large against her small ribs and narrow shoulders. The moist aureoles seemed to have been stretched. Bluish veins showed near her armpits. Matthew remained seated at the edge of the bed.

'Does it hurt?' he asked.

She shook her head.

'Not really pain. Just a sort of tenderness. A pressure. It would be good if . . .'

She stepped closer to him.

'Matthew.'

He silenced her with a gesture, then closed his eyes. He felt her hands on either side of his head. He parted his lips, careful to cover his teeth. The liquid was warm, sweet.

Matthew walked through the dark den, opened a sliding glass door and stepped into the pool area. Dying coals glowed in the grill. He caught a whiff of charred fat as he walked past. At the other side of the pool Dean peered intently into a telescope, tilted upwards at a severe angle. In his left hand he held his Apollo mug. At his feet was a bottle of schnapps and a dirty plate.

He was a former astronaut who had never broken the envelope, who had been held in reserve status through his entire tenure at NASA. After retiring he had moved from Houston to run the gliderport just outside Advance. He also gave lectures at elementary schools and ran seminars at the Air and Space Museum in the city. But his main passion were the long nights he spent by his pool, grilling hamburgers, watching the sky, keeping records of what he saw to post on the computer bulletin board of the stargazing organization to which he belonged. Matthew and Eddie had spent several of those long nights with him, sitting in backward-angled deck chairs as Dean taught them the constellations and showed them how ancient mariners had used astrolocation to navigate. Darting bats would interrupt the lectures as they skimmed the pool's surface for insects. One night he'd left a message for them to come after midnight, having received a news flash over the modem that a star was in trouble. They'd arrived just in time to see the wavering light of a prehistoric extinction.

Matthew walked quietly around the pool. He stared at Dean's crewcut and muscular neck.

'Colonel Ashe,' he said with mock formality.

'Matt,' Ashe said, unsurprised, still looking into the telescope.

'What's on the grid tonight?' Matthew asked.

'Big noise, big noise. Soviet bird's in trouble. Failed to reach its proper orbit. It's wobbling all over the place. Should re-enter over North America tonight.'

'Damn. Is there anybody on it?'

'Oh no. She's unmanned. Comsat. Just a bit of space junk. But it should make a nice burn.' Matthew dropped into a chair.

'These sodium lights,' Ashe said. 'I'll tell you. They're the greatest thing since tight pussy.'

'Why's that?'

He moved the scope through a wide stretch of sky.

'Visibility, Matt. With your basic white fluorescent light, ground level stargazing is a royal pain in the ass. Too much surface light. They make this sort of, uh, tent of glare that just fuzzes the hell out of everything. Real shitstorm of light. Your basic low-intensity sodium yellow, however, produces practically no glare whatsoever. It's the only thing the hippies who designed this place got right.' He moved the lens. 'No refraction.' He moved it again. 'No noise.'

He checked his watch, then returned the telescope to its resting position. He took the chair beside Matt's, pouring out a cup of schnapps.

A slight breeze kicked up, disturbing the wind chimes and stationary kites that hung about the yard.

'We've built so much and lit so much on the ground that we can't even get a good look at the goddamned sky. Now what kind of sense does that make?'

'No sense, Colonel.'

'Damned straight. So, how you be? You seen Beth?'

Matthew nodded.

'She's looking good,' he said.

'Still too damned thin,' Ashe said, shaking his head. 'Spends too much time on that couch. I tell her to get a job or go back to school or something.' He took a sip. 'But she just prefers parking on that damned couch.'

They listened to a brief animal skirmish in a hedge several yards away. Matthew recognized the pressurized hiss.

'So what have you been up to?'

'Nothing,' Matthew said. 'I think I'm going to go into the city for a while. I've a friend there who has a place.'

'What you gonna do there?'

'I'm still trying to decide.'

Ashe laughed quietly.

'You sound like your dad, Matt.'

'What do you mean?'

'On the edge. On the prowl. Always on the move. Always trying to decide.'

Matthew frowned into the pool.

'I used to be a bit of a wanderer. I know the feeling,' Ashe said, leaning back in his chair and looking up at the sky. 'I remember when I was in training. Out in Arizona. This was before Beth was born. When I'd get three days Louise and I would hop into the T-bird, batten down the roof and . . .' He stretched out his flat hand toward some horizon. 'Dallas. Juárez. L.A. Truth or Consequences. Santa Fe. You know Santa Fe? That's a hell of a place. Best kept secret in the country next to who killed JFK.' He took a sip. 'Used to stay at a hotel there called La Fonda. Great old flop, that. Art deco lobby, big windows in the rooms, shoeshines whistling as you walked to breakfast. And the air up there. Thin, clear, clean. Upper atmosphere stuff. We'd always overstay, have to race home.'

He paused for a moment, his eyes remembering.

'There's this road in New Mexico. Damn if I can't see it now. Man, would we drive that sucker. Start in Santa Fe when the bars closed. Roof down, Louise's hair all wild. Seven thousand feet, mountains all around. Slight downgrade for about a hundred miles – you hit seventy without even trying. Then, after we came down a ways and dawn had broke, we'd be in these rolling hills, covered with pine trees. Sometimes you'd see the ranchers staring at the horizon as their horses drank from a pond. Down a ways further we'd hit the semi-arid desert. Sage, some tall grass, spindly ass trees. Coyotes on the side of the road with their shit-eating grins. Then – we're in Arizona now – you hit the painted desert. Mesa, craggy rocks, quartz formations that bend the sunlight every which way. Red, yellow, salmon pink, purple. Then it's the petrified forest. You can't see too many of those old trunks, but they're there. Know how that works?'

Matthew shook his head.

'Well, the water those trees drank way back then was so full of minerals that eventually the tree's cells would get all clogged and turn to stone. The hardness just seeped in. Amazing. Anyway, after that it's desert until you hit Route 40, then its just a short way to the meteor crater where we trained. Biggest in the world. Must be, hell, two hundred yards in diameter. Used to run our ass ragged on that boy.'

He took a sip.

'And that's where the road ends. That's it.'

Matthew couldn't think of anything to say.

'There!' Ashe called, leaping to his feet and pointing skywards.

Matthew followed his gesture in time to see a scar of light crease the sky, then fade.

'That was it. The Soviet bird. Burning up.' He turned to Matthew. 'Make a wish.'

Matthew looked at the dark sky. But he could think of nothing, nothing at all.

BUILDING PYRAMIDS

W alter stood perfectly still before the long marble altar of urinals, presenting an offering of three thousand nautical miles' worth of urine on to a smoking chlorine wafer. He stared at the wall in front of him, still dazed by the pressurized cabin and night-long turbulence. Ghosts of scrubbed out graffiti appeared on the tile. 'Don't look here, the joke's in your hand.' 'Charybdis sucks.' 'Why? When? Where?' As he finished the urinals exploded raucously with automatic flush. The great piss god is pleased, Walter thought. But only for now, the hungry bastard. He knows I'm on the installment plan. He stepped back from the spray, jostling his penis into its cotton nest.

The man continued to speak in the stall behind him, his voice insistent, monotonous. Walter had suspected a desperate liaison or perhaps insanity when he first heard him, but the voice was solitary, sober, rational. He bent slightly to look beneath the door and saw shoes of polished leather, partially draped by dark silk pants. As the urinals gurgled into silence, Walter realized that the man was speaking into a dictaphone.

'Tell him I do not want partial payment, Les. I do not want an amenable settlement. I want it all. Every tack, every paperclip, every scrap of paper. He gets nothing. Nada. I want him to be strung up by the short hairs and left to dry. Do you understand, Les? I want it all.'

You can have it, Walter thought. As he walked into the terminal something bright and quick approached his head. He ducked and a mechanized bird soared past him, a metal feather rustling his hair. The brilliant toy smacked against a wall and fell to its back, moving its wings frantically on the carpet. Walter squatted over it and stopped the turning key on its underbelly.

'Sorry, man.'

A young black man wearing three baseball caps and a smock stood above him, his face vaguely apologetic.

'It ain't 'posed to do that. It flies in circles.'

'That's all right.'

Walter stood slowly and the two men examined the tin bird.

'The wings seem to have stabilized somehow,' Walter explained. 'You'll have to reposition this left one at a lower angle so it'll pull it into a circling pattern. You see, the drag ratio now is not sufficient . . .'

'Yeah, I see what you mean, man. So you wanna buy it? I'll let you have it at cost.'

'No thanks,' Walter said, handing back the bird, releasing the key.

'You wanna Falcon's hat?' the man asked above the racket of the bird's renewed flapping.

'Please move away from the door. The doors will not close until they are clear. Please move away . . .'

Tourists smiled incredulously at the disembodied voice, while the business travellers cast impatient glances at Walter. He knew his buckling left knee was the culprit, puncturing the laser plane of the inter-terminal subway's doors. But the spasms of pain in his back prevented him from moving. All he could do was to wait for it to pass. He had learned not to fight it, this companion pain that had staked a claim to the tract of flesh and muscle running from his right hip to just below his left ear, like a stubborn tribe inhabiting both slopes of his spine's valley. It flared up in savage uprisings when intruded upon by heat, stress, jetlag, too much coffee or too little scotch. The doctors said it would be there in one form or another for the rest of his life, the product of several inoperable slivers of bone in the tissue surrounding his spine. He'd quickly learned not to try to domesticate this tribe, to let them have their rampages. Perhaps they would settle eventually on their own. Evolve, civilize. So he remained still, despite the remonstrations of the simulated voice.

'Um, excuse me, sir. I believe she, it, means you.'

Walter turned his head as far as his neck would permit. A small woman with a webbed hat was looking up at him sympathetically. The pain noticed the interloper and beat a retreat.

'Yes. Thank you.'

He moved back slowly, allowing the doors to shut and the train to slide soundlessly into the dark, dead air of the tunnel.

Walter inserted his silver VIP card into the vertical slot, causing the heavy wood door to click open. Soft light and laughter greeted him, followed by wafts of chemical pine and roasted peanuts. He stepped into the sanctum, the door closing softly behind him.

About twenty people in business suits sprawled on low chairs that were positioned at acute, conversational angles to one another. A few wore cowboy hats. There were three speaking groups, plus several loners reading plastic-bound reports or watching a game show on television. A bartender in a bow tie and red vest worked a crossword behind a napkin-strewn counter. Walter checked the departure time on the screen above the door as he made his way towards a group of unoccupied chairs overlooking the tarmac and runways.

He sat heavily and set his alarm watch, hoping to sleep through the layover. It had been just over twenty-four hours since he had left Taipei. Anchorage, Seattle, and now, Atlanta. He looked across the lounge, wondering if he should hazard a drink before dozing off. The bartenders in these places always wear bow ties and red vests, he thought. God, I hope the Chinese make a decent offer. Half closing his eyes, he looked at the steady migration of planes that rattled the tinted glass before him with thrusts of revving engines. He soon closed his eyes completely and let his body sink into the soft cushions. The tight pain in his back was slowly unravelling.

'Walter?'

No, pissgod, he thought. I gave at the office. Go away. You can't judge me now. Not yet.

'Walter?'

He opened his eyes to discover an unjudging, ungodly face hovering over him. An insect's face, really. Its watchful, predatory eyes flickered behind thick mucal bubbles. Antennae of hair protruded from its nostrils and earholes. Its mouth was formed into a broad smile that seemed to mask a flicking, predatory tongue. The skin was viscous, the lips drawn white. No, not a god's face at all, Walter thought. The face of something you spray, then find when you move the refrigerator.

'For goodness sake, it *is* you.'

Walter's pain tightened, forcing him upright in the chair. He knew this face.

'Hello, Thomas,' he said, unsure whether he were speaking a first or last name. 'I didn't recognize you at first. You're . . .'

'Thinner, richer and on top of my game,' Thomas hissed, perching weightlessly in the chair next to Walter's. Walter couldn't think of a response.

'Jesus, how long's it been?' Thomas asked, his magnified eyes blinking. 'Ten years?'

'Must be, must be.' His smile broadened somehow. 'Double over-time.'

'That's right,' Walter said. 'So what are you up to these days?'

Thomas produced a business card from an inner pocket with a fluid, practised gesture, holding it out between pincer fingers. Walter took it, reading 'Kelvin Thomas' then 'Manager, Third Tier'. In the upper right corner was a figure of a pyramid, with a picture of Thomas's floating, smiling head in the middle.

'I'm with Puritan Enterprises.'

Walter nodded noncommittally, staring at the small bloodstains on the man's shirt collar from a host of shaving nicks.

'Heard of us?'

'Not really. Just stories.'

'Direct sales, Walter. Nationwide. We market all sorts of things, straight to the consumer. Cut out the middle man. Cotton balls. Bee pollen. Hand lotion. Miniature Bibles. Air fresheners.'

'But weren't you with the Bureau of Weights and Measures?' Walter asked.

'No more. Got off that treadmill years ago. No room for advancement there, Walter. Too many chiefs, not enough braves. You know. Whereas now, I have four hundred people under me, buried in the bedrock. It was a bit rough when I first started out, going door to door, organizing sales parties. You know. But after you reach twenty thou in sales they let you start recruiting, co-ordinating. Then you get your mitts on distribution. That's where the real money is. All you do is pick good people and let them do all the work. Then they start recruiting and you're bumped up another level. Then the recruits recruit and, bingo, you're up one more notch. I haven't touched a product in four years, recruited a salesperson in two and a half. All I do now is answer the phone, attend management seminars and deposit checks. I figure in a year I'll be one level from the top. Second tier, Walter. Do you know what that means?'

Walter shook his head.

'Pure money. Passive income. Don't have to lift a finger. Just collect eight percent of eight percent of eight percent . . .' His voice trailed off, reverberating into some rarified zone of income and leisure.

'So how are *you*, Walter? Hard times in the industry I hear.'

'I guess our time has just about come. You know Olympic's been locked down.'

'So I hear, so I hear.'

'Well, I'm sorting out the debris of that, and then . . .' Walter's voice trailed off into a different rarified zone. Thomas's eyes began to flicker.

'Would you mind some friendly advice?' he asked.

'Only if it doesn't involve selling air fresheners.'

The momentary spasm of offense on Thomas's face was quickly controlled.

'No, well, of course not. But I do know someone who can help place you. You know. Help you find a new situation. First rate headhunter. Specializes in big ticket engineering jobs, I believe. Power. Construction. Weapons. Name's David Passer. I met him at a motivational weekend in Santa Barbara a month or so back. He works out of his ranch in Arizona. Outside Phoenix, I believe. You can get his number from Dun and Brad.'

'Passer?'

'David Passer.'

'Thanks, Kelvin. I'll keep that in mind.'

They watched a group of men in jumpsuits and headphones direct a widebody to an accordion offloading tendril. Walter had known Thomas when they were opposing coaches in the interdenominational youth basketball league. Thomas's board-crashing Baptist squad had been the only real rivals to Walter's fast-breaking Presbyterian team. They split their two regular season games and met in the league championship. It was played at a university auditorium before a small, noisy crowd whose cheers echoed through the rafters and empty upper bleachers. During slow intervals all you could hear were the squeak of rubber soles, shouted instructions from the bench, the slap of the ball.

The Baptists maintained a slim lead through most of the game, with Thomas's abnormally tall son controlling the boards. Only Eddie's aggressive defense and Matthew's foul shooting had kept them close.

'Double overtime,' Walter said softly.

'That shot Eddie made,' Thomas said, his face softening into human contours now.

Two points down, four seconds left in regulation. Eddie had stolen a pass at midcourt, wheeled, thrown the ball overhand toward the basket. Swish. Nothing but net.

'Just the way we practised it,' Walter said with an ironic smile.

The first overtime had been slow, both teams treading cautiously through unexplored territory. Baskets were traded up until the buzzer. Second overtime. Sensing his team's fatigue, Walter decided to take the air out of the ball, play for the last shot. But Thomas's boy controlled the tip, and the Baptists also began to play for one final shot. Walter signalled for Matthew to foul Thomas. It was Matthew's fifth and final. Thomas missed the front end of the one and one and Eddie came down with the rebound. Dribbling expertly behind the back, between the legs, he worked the clock down to thirty seconds. Walter signalled for a time out to set up a play but Eddie ignored him, dribbling wildly into a corner, launching a desperate jump shot with over ten seconds on the clock. Air ball. The Baptists scored easily on a fast break. Game.

'How are your boys?' Thomas asked, as if he'd just run through the same memory.

Walter paused.

'Eddie died three months ago when I crashed our glider.'

Thomas jerked back in his chair and removed his glasses. He looked at the tarmac for a moment, then back at Walter.

'My God. Walter.'

'Matt's fine, considering. A bit confused, a bit lost. As we all are.'

'Walter . . .'

Walter's alarm watch sounded. The two men shook hands silently and Walter walked off to make his connection.

Walter tried to keep his head still as he looked for skulls in the diminishing ice of his drink. He thought he'd seen one a moment ago, but now he couldn't be sure. Months earlier, a man he'd met on a plane had described how he made a living by travelling to colleges and clubs, giving a slide lecture that showed how advertisers used subliminal images of sex and death to sell products. Walter conceded the sex but was dubious about death. So the man showed him a liquor ad from the inflight magazine in which he claimed the highball's ice cubes were purposefully formed to resemble human skulls. Walter turned the magazine several ways but still hadn't seen it. How could death be a selling point anyway, he asked? What was alluring about that? *That's* why it's subliminal, the man replied. *That's* how it worked. Now, as the scotch burrowed into the sighing ice in his glass, Walter thought he could see the man's point.

'Stop moving your head.'

Walter let Helen reposition his head, then continue cutting his hair. The tribe of pain was strangely reticent as he sat in the stiff chair in the middle of the kitchen. He shivered a little, the ragged towel around his shirtless torso providing little protection against the house's evening chill. The loose locks of hair itched on his shoulders.

He watched Helen's reflection in the oven's stainless steel. She moved with the deliberate, careful motions he'd first seen at the funeral and which had since become her way. Her style, Walter thought. That's what grief settles down to after the initial shock. A style, a manner, a new kind of movement. The raincoated governor overflying the tornado's swath has a style: grim assurance, manly sympathy. The victims he comforts have another style: numb optimism, stunned relief. The limp-haired young woman doctor in the famine zone has her style: efficient pity, busy detachment. Helen's style was this new deliberation, this careful slowness that seemed to let nothing pass unexamined, that allowed for no mistakes of omission. And what's mine? He wondered.

'There's more gray,' she said, lifting a section of hair with the comb and letting it fall slowly back to his head.

'Ah well.'

He thought of when he first met her. She was a freshman at Michigan, he was a junior. She was quiet and shy, yet resolutely determined to move beyond her parents' immigrant past, to leave 'the neighborhood' for college, for a teaching job, for a detached house in a community that smelled of something other than sweat and food. He remembered her at the fraternity mixers – the unpicked wallflower who willed herself to the dancefloor, the girl who doggedly pursued lines of questioning in class despite being from a family where women kept quiet.

When they'd started dating Walter had been fascinated by her Greek heritage, prodding her with questions about language and custom. She had been reluctant at first, failing to see what was so exotic about it. Yet she gradually opened up and eventually invited him to her Orthodox church and Sunday dinner at her family's squat brownstone in Little Greece. Walter had found her mother a mystery and her sisters, a gum-smacking trainee beautician and a pregnant wife of a loutish bartender, repulsive. But he'd been enchanted by the church's sweet incense, the aromatic food and, above all, Helen's father.

Constantine was not a tall man, nor was he very muscular. Yet there was something in the intensity of his eyes, the hardness of his jaw and the spread of his hands that gave the sense of great power. He was gentle and humorous, though, making fun of his spotty English while employing a complex grammar of nods, winks and gestures to communicate with Walter. There was an ancient story about the tasting of wine that he had told Walter that afternoon, yet Walter had since forgotten it. He had asked Helen if she knew it, but it was a story for the men.

He had come to Detroit as a boy of fourteen, just after World War One. His father had been killed by renegade Turks, leaving Constantine the head of a family of four sisters and an infirm mother. He'd left them behind in the village as he travelled to America to make them money, working double shifts installing running boards at General Motors. He lived in a dormitory with other Greeks and Italians and Poles, his only social life being church, occasional dinner with distant relatives, and the once-a-month dances at the National Guard Armory. He had every other paycheck remanded to a Greek bank to provide for his family and go toward his sisters' dowries. It took ten years to make enough to marry them all off.

He returned to the village as a hero. A meeting with Helen's mother was arranged, and they were married within the month. He brought her back to Detroit at the first possible moment, secretly admitting he could no longer abide his old home. She was a beautiful, stubborn sixteen-year-old who bore three daughters and died homesick forty years later, having learned only a few words of English.

Constantine had not gone back to GM upon their return, instead opening a diner at 13 Mile and Utica that catered to hard-hats and motorcycle cops. He worked hard enough to buy a good house and send his one bright child to college. He died of a heart attack not long after she had graduated and married. The funeral had been attended by most of the Greek community and an escort of motorcycle cops for whom he'd fixed eggs and hash browns for years.

As Helen trimmed his sideburns, Walter remembered their wedding. His fraternity buddies rolling their eyes at the ornate church and strange language. The three large rings passed over their heads by the stern-eyed, full-bearded priest who'd surprised them by cracking crude jokes during the intervals of music. The sour wine in the beaded chalice, the smell of incense on the gilded tabernacle. The rubbery dry lips of the black-clad old women who kissed his cheek with a strange fury. The worry beads and coins pressed quietly into his palm for luck. And above all else, Helen's breathtaking beauty in the century-old lace and pearl veil brought over from Greece. Afterwards, Constantine had plucked Walter from the line of handkerchief-joined dancers and given him two hundred dollar bills as his *plika*, apologizing that he couldn't give more. He'd then shown Walter a sepia photograph of a slightly rundown stucco house, explaining it was a piece of property he owned in his home village of Nostopathios in Greece.

'Now hit's hyours,' he'd said solemnly, his voice cracking with emotion, his wavering hand causing the photo to flutter slightly. 'Hyou feex, hit's a new home.'

Walter was struck by the primitive beauty of the surrounding valley, the strong simplicity of the house's structure. Yet before he could thank Constantine he was pulled back into the dizzying dance.

'So you think they'll agree?' Helen asked, clipping a combful of Walter's hair. 'You think they'll buy?'

Walter watched the spray of hair float to the linoleum.

'Well, yes. I get the feeling they want it, even though they're driving such a hard bargain.'

'Do you think it will be good for them?'

'They can handle it. They're cautious people. Not at all reckless.'

'And then?'

'Well, then it's a question of arranging transport . . .'

'I'm talking about *you*, Walter,' Helen interrupted. 'Remember him? The guy getting the haircut?'

Walter looked out the window above the sink.

'I don't know. UPU's offer to stay on as a troubleshooter doesn't really do much for me. I was thinking about getting out of the business altogether. Getting into home improvement, maybe.'

Helen stopped clipping.

'What?'

'I had this idea on the plane coming home. Just retire from the industry altogether. Start my own business. Home improvements.'

'What kind of home improvements?'

'You name it. Converting basements and garages into rec rooms. Installing sound systems and track lighting. Wooden decks, wet bars. You know, the whole nine yards.'

Helen maintained a dubious silence as she continued cutting, squaring the back of his hair.

'It would be good to work with tools again,' Walter continued. 'To have blueprints in my hands. To be useful. See a job through.'

'Would you?'

'What?'

'See it through?'

'What do you mean?'

'I mean that I really can't see how you could square that sort of life with what you are now. I don't think you could settle down like that just now. I don't think you could be satisfied with that sort of stillness. With all that peace.'

She's right, he thought. She's right.

'It's just . . . It's just that now I'm only slipping. I'm trying to move forward but my efforts just cause me to slip back. It's like when you're a kid and you try to run up an icy slope and your momentum runs out before you reach the top. And your efforts to get new momentum just make you fall back. So I figure if I can just stay still, hold on to everything with both hands, dig in, then I won't slip any more.'

'And what's so bad about slipping? What's so hot about this particular slope?' she asked, coming around in front of him. She looked at his head clinically. 'It's not entirely straight. Just a bit more.'

She clipped at his bangs.

'Have you heard from Matthew?' Walter asked.

'No.'

'Not at all?'

'Well, not in several weeks. He's living with some friends from school in the city. They don't have a phone.'

'Did he say what he was doing?'

'Something artistic. Temping. I don't know.'

'I don't get it,' Walter said.

'That's what I said to him. Do you want to know what he said?'

Walter nodded as much as the cold scissors would allow.

'He said he doesn't want to make your mistakes.'

'Fair enough.' Walter then laughed. 'Lord, neither do I!'

'There,' Helen said, stepping away and examining him, removing the towel. She took a mirror from the counter and held it in front of his face. Walter nodded grimly.

Walter jolted awake, his heart racing. He lay still for a moment, trying to decide if the noise had been in the house or in a dream. All he could hear were the usual electric hums and his wife's slow breathing. Outside, a dog barked at some great distance. The last thing you hear, he thought.

He felt the pressure of Helen's sleeping body against his. He examined it without moving, concentrating on each point of pressure. It had changed so much since the first nights they spent together in the bear-menaced Smoky Mountain honeymoon cottage. Some areas had grown softer, others harder. Her breasts and hips had softened, as had her face. Yet her hands had become firmer, tougher, more knowing. And her hair, so soft then, had become stiff with years of discipline, fatigue, control.

He slid away from her and slowly raised himself to a seated position. The clock read four-twelve. He felt the pain protest the awakening, threaten revenge. It took him several minutes to urge it into wakeful, grudging compliance. One day it will just say no, he thought. He stood and shuffled out of the room. The house was cold and dark, silent except for the brush of his feet on the carpet and the rattle of their aging refrigerator.

Walter eased himself down the steps, peering over the tomb-cool railing for signs of forced entry. Everything seemed quiet. He hesitated at the bottom of the steps, listening for intruders. He heard nothing. The front door was bolted, the kitchen seemed still.

My pyramid, he thought. Built with a mortgage that will outlive me, become my legacy. Cool, dark, solid. That above all – solid. Walter thought of the bedrock of that solidity: the payments, the insurance, the furniture. Brick after brick. A vagrant memory flashed through his mind of a matinée he'd seen as a boy, about thieves who'd broken into a mummy's tomb, unleasing some deadly curse.

'Matthew?' he asked quietly. 'Matt?'

He made a slow circuit of the ground floor. Everything was bolted, no alarms had been tripped. Good, he thought, making his way back to the stairway. I don't need to be a hero. Then he remembered the basement, the small windows tucked in against the ceiling.

As the suspended banks of fluorescent lights flickered on, Walter thought he detected movement, something scuttling into shadow. He hesitated, looking for a second movement. Nothing. Just a trick on his eyes. There was nobody down here. He walked slowly down the creaking stairs anyway.

It was a square room with cinderblock walls and a ceiling of puffy pink insulation held in place by knotted two-by-fours. The floor was concrete that had cracked in several places with pressure from the water table, letting through small amounts of moss and mud. A dehumidifier had to be run continually in the spring, condensing several buckets of water which they poured down the stone sink with hook faucets.

He paused and looked down at his large workbench. Meters, plugs, sockets, screws and nails lay scattered on the table top, covered by dust. Rows of cluttered pigeonholes lined the back of the bench. Some were empty. An eclectic array of tools hung from pegs on the wall. Oozing batteries and spools of wire were crammed beneath the bench.

Walter thought of all the things he had built with these tools. Bookshelves and furniture for the boys during the first years of their lives. The miniature dragsters he had helped them with for their soapbox derby, teaching them the trick of using dry graphite lubricant rather than the oily ones that would drain during the early rounds of the competition. Eddie's red bullet had nudged Matt's uncarved blue slab in the finals. And then there was the glider, built over those long evenings with Eddie at Dean's hangar. Walter thought of the sound of that work, the feel of it. The regular scrape of the plane. The howls of the drill. The stains that blueprints left. The sander's shriek as it spat out showers of sparks.

There was a noise in the far corner, behind the stack of mover's boxes that held Christmas decorations and outgrown clothes. Walter hesitated, contemplating retreat. But he moved quickly to the basement floor, grabbing a lug wrench from above the bench. He walked quietly to a position where he could see behind the boxes.

A boy crouched in the shadow, looking through a crack. He hadn't seen that Walter had moved up beside him. He looked to be in his mid teens, wearing filthy painter's overalls and no shoes. He was holding something tight against his chest. His hair looked as if someone had been gripping him by it. As Walter examined his face he saw the seismic divide of a cleft skull, the mongoloid slope of the brow.

It was Dan Llewelyn's boy, from down the street. The coin thief. He was severely retarded, yet had a genius for breaking and entering. Once he'd gained entry to a house he would seek out the shiniest objects, usually coins, arranging them on the floor in strange patterns or taking them home to his beleaguered parents, who dutifully returned them the following day. The neighbors had been tolerant at first, but slowly a muted suburban uproar had risen. The boy had been committed. He's probably escaped, Walter thought. Or maybe his folks got him out.

He saw Walter.

'Hello,' Walter said, placing the wrench on a cardboard box.

The boy smiled up at him serenely.

'What you got there?'

The boy looked at the objects against his chest, as if deciding what to do with them. He finally held them out to Walter, who recognized the model mounted soldiers he'd brought one of the boys from London.

He could see that the boy had arranged the remainder of the soldiers in a star formation behind him.

'How did you get in here?' Walter asked.

The boy continued holding out the horsemen.

'How did you get in?'

But Llewelyn's boy wasn't talking, simply smiling through puffy, twisted lips.

'Okay,' Walter said. 'Go ahead and play.'

He walked away from the smiling boy, who quickly returned to his game. Walter could hear him making quiet noises to accompany the movement of the horsemen. He'd call Llewelyn after the sun came up.

Helen stood at the top of the basement stairs, clutching her robe to her neck.

'Who were you talking to?' she asked.

'Somebody's boy. Let's let him play for a while.'

BLACK WATER AND ANSWERS

M atthew lay perfectly still on the top bunk's sagging mattress, watching Ben add to the mural that now covered nearly half of the room's clinically white wall, as well as the door to the bathroom. He used the broad felt-tipped markers he carried with him everywhere, working slowly, passing the marker a few inches above the wall before drawing a line. He then examined each stroke for several seconds with a cocked head before adding to it or moving on. Matthew noticed that Ben never redid his work, never altered a line once it was drawn.

The mural depicted a great, panicked exodus over a ravaged country-side, away from some great catastrophe or impending menace. There were people from many races, creatures from several species – trios of troubadours carrying electric guitars and chainsaws; teams of marauding midgets armed with clown-headed cudgels; leering satyrs who entered foam-mouthed bitches from the rear; mouthless children with winged feet; palace guards on mini bikes; thousand-legged insects wearing sunglasses and fake moustaches; pteradactyls with rifles and crossed gunbelts; fat men on toilet-seat rickshaws reading pornographic maga-zines; sack-carrying hags who kicked out at the rodents that tried to suck their pendant breasts. The land they passed over was barren, rutted, litter strewn, dotted with burned-out wrecks of autos and clean skeletons. Matthew rolled on to his back after staring at the mural for a few minutes, waves of feverish darkness lapping at the edges of his vision.

Max came back into the room, carrying food in his arms, pockets and half-zipped leather jacket. He dumped the food on the bed, then shed his jacket and jeans, stripping down to the light green hospital gown they were supposed to wear. He gestured to the bounty on the white sheets.

'Check this out. They're going to have a banquet or something down-stairs. I could have got more but, alack, I heard somebody coming.'

Matthew leaned over the edge of the bunk and looked at the food.

There were several whole lobsters belly-up on the pillow, a cellophane covered bowl of three bean salad, cold cuts of roast beef and turkey breast, flaking croissants, florets of raw vegetables. There were also two bottles of champagne and several imported beers, coated with bits of clinging crushed ice that melted on the bed.

Ben reached over and took some bread and beer, while Max began violently to tear the limbs from a lobster. Matthew remained on his bunk, trying to suppress the powerful nausea that had been renewed by the food's rich odors. He watched Max's face, studying the erratic movements of its scars and distortions as he chewed. He still found it hard not to look at Max's deforming burn scars – shiny, waxen whirlpools of flesh that swirled around the basin of his eye, rushed down the stream of his temple, tumbled over the waterfall of his jaw. The scar on his cheek was the worst, a deep fold of flesh in which bristles of unshaveable hair grew on a small, still-fertile patch. The left side of his face was intact, showing that he had once been handsome. Dense, severe eyebrows that hedged a prominent forehead; dark, deeply set eyes; cheeks that sloped concavely into full lips and a strong jaw. Max caught Matthew staring at him and grinned broadly, showing bits of orange shell staining his teeth. Matthew looked at the sprinkler on the high ceiling. There was an archipelago of red stains not far from it. Don't even ask, Matthew told himself, closing his eyes. He tried to swallow the resilient puddle of bile at the back of his throat, yet it bounced back elastically.

It was the experiment's first day. They had arrived at the Institute in the early morning, given their histories, given blood. A nurse had checked their temperatures, blood pressures and heart rates. A doctor had dilated their pupils, palpated their chests and necks, prodded their kidneys with his athletic fingers. Finally, dressed in the green paper gowns, they'd been led to a room full of sinks and trays and examination tables, where their necks had been numbed by surface anesthetics and the pellets introduced into an artery.

The researcher, a quiet man with large hands and a close gray beard, had explained to them that he was interested in seeing whether the drug contained in the pellet would enter the section of the kidney it was designed to treat. To check this, he added a mildly radioactive label to the pellet. This would allow him to trace its progress through the body. After entering the kidney and, hopefully, going to the proper place, the label would then be painlessly passed through the urinary tract. If there were any difficulties with its passing, which was highly unlikely, they could easily pluck it from the body with a catheter. Either way, the experiment would be over when the label was out of their system – no more than twenty-four hours.

'What's its half-life?' Matthew asked.

'Something like six months. But that's not a factor here,' the researcher explained impatiently. He had also said there might be nausea and low-level fever involved, but that it was nothing to worry about.

Matthew felt something cold and hard on his chest. He opened his eyes to see a lobster directly above him, its antennae shimmering.

'Methinks sometimes young Merriweather has no more wit than a Christian or an ordinary man has: but he is a great eater of lobster and I believe that does harm to his wit,' Max said, turning the lobster with each syllable. Matthew waved him away.

'Not hungry?' Max asked.

'I feel like shit.'

'What – stomach, fever?'

'Yeah.'

'No sweat, man. S.O.P. This is nothing. Very manageable. You should have been with us last year when we guineaed for this nouveau chemo thing that had us mewling and puking every half hour. There were some very distressed personages in that gig I'm here to say. One fellow even threw a petit mal. I copped some of those moves for my next role. Mad Tom. You know it?'

He bent into a performance posture, but Matthew closed his eyes.

'Anyway,' Max said, straightening. 'It'll pass. Is this the first time you've ever done anything like this?'

'Yeah.' Matthew said. Then he remembered. 'Well, I did do something similar when I was a kid.'

'A kid? Really? What?'

'Well . . .' Matthew sat up laboriously in the bunk. He noticed that Ben had stopped in mid-figure and turned to listen.

'You see?' Max said to Ben. 'I tell you this man is a born storyteller. He even rises from the dead to tell his tales.'

'It was when we were about nine,' Matthew said. 'Our family had just moved to New Jersey and didn't know anyone. So my parents were making a big effort to meet people. Socialize, get involved. They joined all these groups – bridge club, gourmet club, travelogue club. Your basic middle-class gig. I remember the nights they were the hosts. Eddie and I used to watch from our room at the top of the steps. They used those Sterno flames to cook fondue with – you could see those steady blue flames wavering in the dining room. Neil Diamond on the stereo in the lounge. And all the men wearing white shoes and plaid sportscoats.'

'Hey man, the Sixties were tough for everybody,' Max said, clearing the food from his bed and flopping on to it.

'Anyway, one of the things my folks got into was the local product testing center, some kind of a marketing research outfit for kids' shit. Right near the mall. I don't know what they could have been thinking of. Some sort of strange fit of participatory capitalism, I think. Anyway, every once in a while we'd get a call and my mom would trundle me and Eddie into the car and take us down there to interact with the latest creations.

'It was a small, you know, bland building. Just one big central room, flanked by offices and storage closets. What happened was that on Saturday morning or after school they'd get a bunch of us kids together and try out stuff on us to see what we thought of it before they decided whether or not to put it on the market. I guess they have these places all over or something. So we'd just sit around and eat cereal or try out some new action doll or play board games. Whatever. These women with clipboards would supervise us from a discreet distance, adding helpful pointers when somebody would try to eat a truck or see if Barbie had nipples.'

'She doesn't,' Max said.

'Then, when we started to get bored, the women with clipboards would move in and ask us questions. Could you figure out how to put it together? What about the yellow ones, why didn't you eat those? Too sweet? We were a pretty tough bunch of critics, though I'm pretty sure we were instrumental in giving the nod to Lucky Charms.'

'Damn,' Max said.

'I guess we went about a dozen times altogether. Pretty routine stuff, except for this one day. The last time we did it, actually. We were doing toys that day. There was a helicopter with remote controls, building blocks without sharp edges, maybe some trucks. One of the things we were shown were these strange balls, these eight balls with a little window on the bottom. They were 'bout as big as a softball and had this inky liquid inside and all these bits of paper with answers on them. What you would do is ask a question, then shake it up and turn it over. One of the bits of paper, which were black with white letters on them I think, would then float up and appear in the window. And that would be your answer. You know, 'yes' or 'soon' or 'maybe' or 'never' or whatever.'

'I remember those things,' Max said. 'An early ancestor of the Ouija Board.'

'So we were all sitting around, about a dozen of us, asking stupid questions and getting *non sequitur* answers. It was pretty much fun, really, only my brother wasn't into it at all. After about two minutes he said, "This is dumb," and threw the fucking thing to the parquet floor. Really hard. It cracked, but didn't break. So he picked it up and did it again. This time it splits open like an egg. There's black water and answers everywhere. We couldn't believe it. We're just sitting there. Even the ladies with the clipboards were mesmerized. So Eddie starts collecting the bits of paper from the floor and sticking them to our foreheads, dubbing us with these new names. "You're yes," "You're happiness," "You're never" – all the way round the room.'

'Which were you?' Max asked.

'I think I was "maybe".'

Max smiled his twisted smile.

'This brother of yours . . .'

Matthew nodded in agreement, then looked at Ben, who had returned to his mural. He was putting the finishing touches on a large ruptured egg that disgorged dozens of words with spindly legs and sharp-taloned claws. They chased children into the hills.

Matthew had gone to live with Ben and Max after leaving Advance. He knew Ben from college – they had been the only two students in a course on Italian cinema. Since his father worked as a maintenance man in the college's cafeteria, Ben was able to attend at reduced tuition. He had graduated with honors in English and taken a part-time job designing and repairing diorama mannequins at a church museum on the Beltway. Max was an actor who was employed as a stock fool at a Shakespeare theater and had done some bit work in horror movies.

The apartment was a group of unconverted basement storage rooms in a large brick warehouse near the subway switching yard. The warehouse was contracted to the federal government, who used it to store World War Two documents. Ben and Matthew had rented the basement from a holding company to use as studio space and lived there despite the fact that it wasn't zoned residential. No one ever checked.

There was only one entrance, a metal door at the bottom of a short well of concrete steps. There were four large rooms, each with concrete floors, cinderblock walls and ceilings that snowed cracked masonry when freight trains passed. A small amount of natural light was provided by dirty windows high on the wall.

They used the first room as the kitchen. Water came from a solitary spigot at the end of a bent copper pipe. Below it was a dented fifty-five-gallon drum that echoed with continual drips. A tattered card table stood in the center of the room, surrounded by large, wooden spools that served as chairs. Scattered about the floor were several hotplates, a microwave oven, a small refrigerator and a coffee pot, all connected to a jumbled web of extension wires. There were also several cracked plastic coolers crammed with cans of generic food and packets of rancid government cheese.

There was a decrepit water boiler in Max's room, about eight feet long and four feet wide. He had sawn off the top half of it, leaving a large metal tub which he lined with styrofoam. This was his bed. On the many pipes emanating from it he'd hung clothes, stacked books and plants. Long planks of plywood propped up by cinderblocks lined the walls, forming workbenches that were covered with masks, fishing tackle boxes full of make-up, bits of costume, model theatrical sets, photographic negatives. A small mound of spent carbon dioxide canisters rested beneath one of the benches. There was a television and VCR on a stand at the edge of the bed. The room was lit by red and yellow light bulbs on unshaded lamps. Thick, unmatched rug remnants covered the floor.

Ben's room was more austere. There was a small bed of woven mats and fringed blankets in the center of the floor. There was no other furniture, just stacks of drawings and long scrolls of manila paper that had been covered with his work. A single theatrical spotlight in an upper corner of the room provided the light, along with rows of candles that had formed a multicolored glacier of wax around his bed.

The room left to Matthew was lined with five-foot-high filing cabinets stuffed with yellowing casualty lists from the European Theater and requisition orders for Atlantic convoys. He had emptied a few of them, using them to store his clothes, books and video equipment. He bought a hammock from a camping store and slung it between two cabinets. A single fifty-watt bulb provided the room's only illumination. He considered hanging some posters or buying plants but never got around to it.

The apartment's remaining room was a tiny bathroom that consisted of a disconnected, moss-filled sink and a small toilet with a chain flush. Max told Matt to use it as seldomly as possible because it backed up. There were plenty of empty lots and buildings around.

Matthew couldn't sleep the first night at the apartment. He would jerk awake each time he'd begin to drop off, compelled by a violent shock he couldn't define. He'd lie in his swaying hammock, trying in vain to remember his dream, then listening to the apartment to find out whether or not something there had awakened him. But all he heard were the metallic shrieks of trains at the nearby switching yard and the muffled garble of television noise from Max's room.

Near dawn, he dressed and wandered into the next lot, perching on an abandoned refrigerator and watching the empty subway trains embark. There was a live section of track opposite him, where the trains would shoot up showers of sparks that died quickly in the dead weeds that surrounded the yard. After a while the dread that had been tormenting Matthew all night came upon him with full force. The feeling that he had something difficult and perhaps painful to do, that something had been left undone and it was up to him to take care of it. A childish feeling, but still intense. He watched the sparks until the dawn chill became too great, then headed back into the bunker apartment, still not knowing what it was he should do.

A nurse entered their room. She was a young woman with a sharp, pretty face and very large hips. She silently handed out specimen bottles and took their blood pressure when they came out of the bathroom. While she worked she looked occasionally at the mural, emitting short, angry sighs and shaking her head. She finished her work quickly and made for the door, but turned before leaving the room.

'That's going to come out of your pay,' she said, pointing to the mural. 'Room damage.'

There was a long silence.

'It's in the rules,' she added feebly.

'Go piss up a rope,' Max said from his bed. The nurse left the room, the specimen bottles tinkling with her disgust.

Ben ignored her. He was used to trouble about the mural. It had caused him to be beaten up several times, maced by a real estate agent, arrested twice and profiled in the Style supplement of a major newspaper. He had begun work on it a year earlier, painting it throughout the city, on every available surface – sidewalks, subway station posters, bits of wind-tossed garbage, the sides of delivery vans caught in traffic, the collars of dogs awaiting their masters outside shops, coats draped on the backs of chairs in outdoor cafés. Despite the disparity of surface, the mural was a continuous work, depicting the chaotic exodus with unity and precision.

He had recently been arrested for vandalizing a 'Starving Artist' sale at a Holiday Inn near the Beltway. He had broken in late one night and painted his mural on the displayed watercolors, altering each painting rather than drawing over it, leaving each watercolor's basic structure unchanged. His grotesques tramped on the hedges and cut down the trees of autumnal landscapes; they occupied quiet riverside houses for orgies and sprayed graffiti on quaint watermills; they urinated on still-life bouquets of flowers and stuffed themselves with bowls of fruit; they kidnapped puppies and slaughtered kittens.

At his trial Ben had pleaded guilty to one charge of wilful destruction, singling out a landscape on which he'd made an error that smudged out some of the background. He plead *nolo contendere* to the rest of the charges and was ordered to make restorations. Yet he had no money. So the judge sentenced him to one hundred hours of community service. A splenetic court officer had him scraping and sanding graffiti off subway trains for the first week, but had relented in the face of Ben's silence, having him instead give drawing lessons to autistic children who were wards of the city.

Matthew had stopped by at the school where Ben was working during one of his meandering journeys through town. He found him in a room with ten children, seated around a low table with small chairs. The walls were covered with dirty blackboards, a long chart with the alphabet in capital and small letters, cartoon portraits of astronauts, presidents and inventors.

Matthew looked in, unnoticed. Ben and the children worked with equal absorption, filling page after page with broad-stroked drawings. Ben would look up occasionally from his own work to help one of the children. Some of them waited patiently as he wordlessly added a line or a figure, others violently snatched back their paper or tried to shove away his hand, making menacing, preverbal grunts. Yet he gently persisted until he'd made his point.

Matthew stepped into the room. Only Ben looked up.

'Hello Matthew,' he said in a quiet voice. 'It's good you've come. There's something you have to see.'

Matthew followed him to a shelf near a cracked window at the back of the room. Ben fumbled through a stack of crinkled paper, finally finding a sheath bound by a large clip.

'Look at these.'

Matthew examined the crude drawings. There were about a dozen of them, all of a single scene – a man in a top hat hanging from a leafless tree. A large bicycle leaned against the trunk. There were several long-toothed black birds circling in the sky. Flowers grew from the man's eyes, his mouth and ears.

'Look at the quality of this kid's line,' Ben said. 'Here. And here. This. And this.'

After the nurse had gone Max turned on the television. He flipped manically through the channels, spending no more than a few seconds on each one. He had once told Matthew that he didn't care about stories, that a story took his mind off the momentary images and gestures he really cared about. He sometimes dragged Matthew and Ben to suburban cinema complexes, where they could wander from film to film for one admission fee.

He stopped for a moment on a station that played an old movie Matthew recognized. It had been one of Eddie's favorites. Matthew remembered being terrified the time they had watched it as boys. About a year ago, Eddie had awoken Matthew and told him it was the late movie. They had watched it in silence.

The movie had just reached its climactic scene. An old king and his soldiers had trapped the young hero and his two lieutenants in the ruins of a cliff-top temple. The soldiers drew their swords, yet the king stopped them. Muttering vague imprecations, he sowed a handful of gleaming teeth he had cut from a monster in the ground before them. There was a tremor of the earth, and two lines of armed skeletons sprouted from the scattered teeth. They stood at disciplined attention, grinning fleshlessly at the young men.

On the old man's orders the skeletons attacked with a ferocious cry and clatter of bones, tenaciously driving the young men through the ruins. The skeletons moved with remarkable agility, leaping, tumbling, brandishing their weapons with living poise, with human skill. The young men fought hard, yet their slashes and parries couldn't find flesh. The skeletons had soon killed two of the young men, grinning over their slaughtered bodies. Realizing he could not defeat the already dead, the young hero plunged over the cliff into the tranquil waters of the sea and swam strongly to a waiting ship. The camera panned back until the ship could be seen as an image in a reflecting pool, into which two gods peered with satisfaction.

'Look at that,' Max said, turning off the sound. 'Utter perfection.

God, I love that stuff. Animation, boys. The perfect art. Cartoons, fx, frame-by-frame puppetry. The only remaining visionary art. The only art form capable of expressing our culture's soul, the only one that can give form to our myths. You know why?'

Matthew and Ben stared at him.

'Because it's the only art that does not accept limitations,' Max continued. 'Nothing is impossible in animation. No problems with the palate, no actors trying to give their own interpretations, no readers with paltry imaginations. The creator controls everything. The only limitations are the limitations of your technology. That's why it's the ultimate American art. Give me old Disney or Harryhausen over Melville or Whistler or Arthur Miller any day of the week.'

The local news came on. They watched in silence as various crimes, meetings, traffic situations were reported. There were some commercials, followed by a report of a news conference about a new international theater festival. A pale young man dressed in a kimono and bow tie spoke into a microphone on a long dais, surrounded by middle-aged men in suits and wire-frame glasses. Matthew saw some of the men were colleagues of his father's from the utility company. Above them was the sign 'UPU presents the First Annual Festival of International Theater'. The pale young man unscrolled a poster that read 'Get FIT!' to general applause and flashing bulbs. Max leapt from the bed and pointed at the screen, a vagrant vein rippling through his brow like a loose hose.

'You fucker!' he yelled at the pale young man. 'You super-serviceable asshole!'

He looked frantically around the room, finally finding a spare specimen bottle. He threw it into the television screen, which shattered with a storm of smoke and sparks. There were some popping noises from behind it, casting menacing shadows on the wall. Ben reached over and pulled the plug from the socket.

'I don't like that guy,' Max said.

Matthew watched the protruding vein flutter above Max's eye.

'I really don't.'

Max was an actor who had spent the last three years in rep at the theater group attached to the national Shakespeare library. He had quickly developed a reputation as a masterful clown, performing the roles of Launce, Costard and the gravedigger in *Hamlet* to critical acclaim. Yet his real triumphs were in the roles of Shakespeare's grotesques, playing

92

Shylock with a cringing ferocity, Bottom with a crude and maskless sexuality, Malvolio as a furiously repressed homosexual, Tom O'Bedlam with spitting insanity. Critics and audiences hardly knew how to react to his shameless ugliness, his aggressive use of his deforming scars. He would sometimes stroll from the stage and directly address individuals in the audience, twisting Shakespeare's language into direct assaults upon them. His greatest role was as Caliban, playing the savage as a slobbering would-be rapist who can only understand the language of violence and domination. His next performance was to be the lead in *Richard III*, yet he quit before rehearsals started, claiming that Shakespeare had become 'impossible' for him to perform.

He had not been on stage since, supporting himself by working as a bicycle messenger in the city's business district and by doing occasional voice-overs for local advertisers. He spoke occasionally about doing his own show, but had no concrete plans. He was forever searching for ideas for it, seeing the world around him in terms of this ideal performance. The configuration of a crowd on a subway platform, the sound a man made when they saw him pulled from a mangled truck, the face of a woman speaking angrily in a frosted phone booth – he added them all to his grammar of gestures. Even his wild speech and aggressive rudeness seemed designed to provoke reactions that he could one day use in performance.

Only once had he almost been enticed back to the stage. Two months earlier he had been approached by the Boy Wonder director of the new theater festival to perform in the festival's central show, a big-budget adaptation of *Prometheus Bound*. Max was offered the role of Mercury. Broke and bored, he accepted reluctantly.

The festival had been organized with the boundless energy and growing reputation of the Boy Wonder, who had directed prize-winning productions of *Fidelio* and *All My Sons* while still a student at Juilliard. Since then he had been guest director at various theaters and festivals, winning further plaudits and enthusiastic press. He had even been offered a job in movies, yet made a much-publicized refusal, saying his true vocation was the theater. He had then proposed the idea of a yearly international theater festival. Everyone was enthusiastic, and corporate sponsors lined up, with United Public Utilities contributing the basic grant.

There would be five shows, shown in repertory over a two-month period. A Russian director who had recently been swapped for some diplomats would lead an all-émigré cast in a stage adaptation of *Dead*

Souls. A group from Colombia would do their impressionistic fantasy piece about the search for a lost city, a production whose use of nudity and graphic violence 'had shocked audiences in Europe'. Then there would be a production of *The Playboy of the Western World* by an Irish group formed exclusively of unemployed youths. The fourth production was by a Japanese butoh dance troupe, a group of five men with shaved heads and white-painted bodies who performed slow, embryonic dances to rhythmic music. Their most notorious piece involved having themselves lowered from the top of tall buildings in a slow mime of birth.

The final production, a new interpretation of Aeschylus's *Prometheus Bound,* was to be directed by the Boy Wonder himself. He had announced his intention of using a variety of minimalist acting techniques, as well as large video screens and laser-enhanced lighting, to present the Greek classic.

Max lasted for six rehearsals. He had clashed several times with the Boy Wonder over blocking and interpretation, finally accusing him in front of the entire cast of not having the balls to approach the text without an array of technique and technology. The director, sitting in the sound booth at the top of the theater, had fired Max over the p.a. Max had tried to scale the back wall in order to get at him, but had been restrained by a snatch squad of bearded teckies.

So Max had returned to his retirement, still speaking vaguely about doing a show. He would wander the city, provoking it for an idea, for a story. Matthew and Ben followed, close planets to his hot sun of anarchic energy. They never stayed in one place for long, striding through gallery openings and shopping malls, gulping draft beer in strip bars, shifting through late shows at movie houses or music clubs. Sometimes Matthew brought the videocam, casting its inquisitive strobe on Max as he howled at drunks or pounded on restaurant windows or insulted jammed traffic.

Matthew was good at this wandering. Since leaving Advance he had done little else. When Max and Ben would work at their day jobs he would go out alone. Sometimes he took his camera, but usually he went empty-handed. He soon developed a routine, staying in the apartment until just after the noon news, then taking the subway into the city's museum district. He would buy a sandwich from a vendor van, then wander through a museum or sculpture garden. Sometimes he would see people like himself, not in school, without the look of employment.

They would eye each other from hostile distances, as if some great secret were on the verge of being divulged should they come in contact. On a good day he would find a beautiful, solitary woman, perhaps a tourist from Europe or South America, and follow her at a discreet distance.

At mid-afternoon he would visit the café between the two wings of the National Gallery, watching the tourists pass on the mechanized walkways, drinking coffee or beer at a corner table until lightheaded. Then he would ride the subways through the rush hour, changing cars and lines randomly, letting the flow of the commuters carry him, emerging occasionally to have a drink in happy hour bars. He was constantly handed leaflets, which he collected in the filing cabinets at his apartment. Sometimes he would witness crimes – fights, petty thefts, violent genital gropes – during the surge of a crowd. He would see Ben's mural occasionally, on the platform posters or on the walls beside the escalators. When the crowds thinned he headed back to the apartment for a canned dinner and whatever Max and Ben had planned.

He also went to the zoo. It was not too crowded on weekdays and the houses had an animal warmth. He liked to watch the mating of swans, with their ferocious bites, their entwined necks and flapping wings. Once, in the monkey house, he had seen a group of uniformed children attacked. They had been laughing at a cage full of chimpanzees when, without warning, the chimps struck back, pelting the children with pebbles, feces, scraps of food. Some seemed to be pointing out particular children as targets with their long fingers. A few raised pink bottoms to the bars and peed ferociously. The children fled in panic, though not before several were soiled and one boy was cut above the eye with a wedge of concrete. Keepers had to enter the cage with lassoes and syringes and restore order.

Meanwhile Matthew went for job interviews, even though the dividends from the UPU shares his parents had given him upon graduation provided enough money to get by. He took a test at a government employment center, having to type out 'Every Good Boy Does Fine' and 'Excellence Is Its Own Reward' as many times as possible in a minute. He'd then gone into a room where a man with a red beard and averted eyes asked him where he saw himself in five years. Matthew said he didn't know, maybe in California or Japan. The man had then asked why he wanted a job with the government. Matthew said really he didn't. The man had written something on a form, then thanked Matthew and told him to stay in touch. Matthew had also submitted some of his tapes to a place called ArtSpace, where videos were displayed on dozens of screens above installations and wall hangings. A man named St Ivie had screened them in his office while Matthew sat in the lobby, staring at a 'Get FIT' poster. The man had sent the tapes back out with a secretary who thanked him and asked him to try again.

Some days he would stay home and get drunk in the afternoons, downing beer after beer as he flipped through the TV stations or listened to records. Eventually he would doze off. Max or Ben would wake him in the evening and it would be like a new day.

One day, he had run into Dean Ashe in the lobby of the Air and Space Museum. He was wearing a plaid sportscoat with a nametag across the breast pocket. His broad smile released minty vapors.

'So the rumors about you being hijacked to Beirut aren't true after all,' he said as he gripped Matthew's hand.

'Hello, Colonel,' Matthew said.

They stood for a moment in awkward silence beneath the suspended aircraft.

'So Matt, how the hell have you been?'

'Busy.'

'That's good, that's good.'

They looked up at Lindbergh's *Spirit of St Louis*, swaying slightly in the conditioned air.

'And you?' Matthew asked.

'Conferences and more conferences. Shooting the shit with the desk jocks. You know.'

'Sounds all right.'

'Beats working.' He looked at his polished shoes for a minute. 'Your folks sorta been wondering about you.'

'I'm okay.'

'Yeah? Well, I'll pass that on. Anything else?'

'How are they?' Matthew asked.

'Pretty well, it seems. I mean considering. Drove your dad to Dulles a few days ago. He's off to Taiwan again. Looks like they're gonna make the deal.'

Matthew looked up at the aircraft.

'I don't know.' Ashe said. 'Tell truth, he seems tired. Pasty skin, sagging shoulders. Must be all that travelling. Sorta seems like he doesn't know if he's coming or going.'

'Come on, Dean. He loves it.'

'You really think that?' Ashe asked slowly.

'I don't know.'

Ashe nodded up at the planes.

'It's hard to imagine they ever flew, the way they got 'em strung up in here.'

Matthew remained silent.

'Well, anyway. I'll tell your folks I saw you and you're still a hippy.'

'Thanks,' Matthew said as he walked away.

'Although you could call your mom, you know.'

'Christ, Dean, I'm twenty-two.'

'Shit boy,' Ashe called after him. 'I'm twice that and I still call my old momma. And she's *mean*.'

Matthew laughed in spite of himself.

He had arranged to meet Helen in the underground café between the two wings of the gallery. He rode the mechanical walkway, staring distractedly at the faces of the people propelled in the opposite direction. It was not until Eleni had passed him that he remembered her. Those wide eyes, the graceful sweep of her cheekbones, the radiant dark skin. He turned and saw that she had turned too. She was smiling that beautiful smile and wagging her finger playfully at him.

'So . . .' he heard her say.

He contemplated leaping over the divide on to her track but saw two beefy museum guards standing directly behind him. They stared at him, thick arms crossed over thicker chests.

'Don't even think about it,' the first said.

The second one turned to the first.

'You know what they say,' he said.

'What's that?' asked the second.

'Once you go black there's no going back.'

They laughed and Matthew turned around. There was a hundred yards to go on his ride, which seemed to have slowed. By the time he reached the end and doubled back she had disappeared into the throng of students and tourists. He went back to the tunnel to meet his mother.

Helen stood by a stack of trays. She was dressed in a dark blue suit. He realized she must have come from work. She stared at the artificial waterfall that ran over the outside of a large window at the opposite side of the tunnel. Her eyes looked tired, and she seemed to let the sight of water soothe them.

'Mom?'

She turned to him and, for an instant, her eyes remained blank, impassive, like they'd been at the funeral. Matthew felt a wave of fear through his back and guts. Then she smiled warmly and embraced him.

'Thank you for calling,' she said.

They moved uneasily through the cafeteria line, choosing cellophane-wrapped salads from beds of chipped ice. They had to wait for a new pot of coffee to brew. The woman at the register took Helen's money without a word.

They found a table near the water-drenched window. There was a small pamphlet on it advertising perfumes. The table was spotted with flattened crumbs and ovals of dried liquid. Helen picked up the pamphlet, scratched the raised section and smelled it. She frowned slightly and dropped it back on the table.

'So how's the scene?' she asked.

Matthew laughed quietly to himself as he pulled the cellophane skin from his food.

'All right.'

'Are you, um, on it?'

'Sort of next to it.'

'Is that better than being, let's say, under it?'

'Traditionally.'

'Matthew,' she asked as she serrated the pamphlet's edges, 'what are we talking about?'

He shrugged and plucked a sheet of limp lettuce from his salad, dangling it between them.

'I don't know, mom. But I get the feeling it'll end up being about how disappointed dad is in me.'

'Well, that statement's sort of a self-fulfilling prophecy, isn't it?'

'I know what I'm doing.'

'Who on earth says you don't? Hey.'

He shrugged.

'No one.'

Helen caught herself shredding the pamphlet and gathered the bits into a small pile.

'So?' she asked.

The words made Matthew think of Eleni for a moment. He was surprised how badly he'd wanted to see her. He looked at his mother's expectant eyes.

'So,' he said.

'Matthew, I'm not capable of chattering with you just now. So I would like it if you would tell me how you're doing and perhaps even what you're doing, although that's not so important to me.'

He nodded for a moment.

'I've been doing a lot of thinking, mom. I'm with these guys now who are very challenging. I'm starting to realize how little I know and how much of what I am is crap. I'm, it's like, getting rid of a lot of excess baggage.' He dropped the lettuce back into the bowl. 'I suppose the only part of it all that you would understand is that I'm not being a martyr.'

'What are you saying?' she asked with sudden fury. 'Why do you keep saying that? What's wrong with you? Where do you get these expectations from? Good Lord, sometimes I think you two boys are just . . . vacuums. Just one way mirrors or . . . whatever. Even Edward, dead.'

She collected her thoughts.

'A child starts out wanting you to be God,' she said matter-of-factly. 'Well, you can't be that, so it expects you to be a hero. And when you fail at that, well . . .' She shook her head and looked back at the waterfall. 'Of course he's a martyr. What else have you, has anyone, left for him to be?'

Matthew rubbed his thumb over a spot on the table, raising several thin spools of grease.

'You know something,' Helen said, calm now. 'You won't want to hear this, but you're always saying hard things under the banner of truth, so I'll tell you. You're just like him. You remind me so very much of him, when he was young, when I first knew him. So probing, so demanding, so restless. Up all day and night slaying imaginary dragons. So intent on being decent and truthful. So hard on everyone, especially yourselves.'

She leaned towards him.

'It's a very attractive quality, Matthew. It's probably a good one. But it has cost him so very dearly. It has forced him to lose a lot.'

'Then why doesn't he change?'

'Because it's his character. You don't change your character.'

Their eyes met over the uneaten food.

'It's both your characters.'

Not long after Max broke the television, a doctor in a tuxedo came into the room. He was a tall man with gray temples who smelled of distant cologne. He had a penlight in his left hand which he clicked on and off, casting small circles of light on the tile floor.

'Good evening,' he said briskly, taking in Ben's growing mural, the shattered television. 'Is everything all right in here?'

'Fine,' Max said politely, 'except I think there's something wrong with the TV.'

The doctor frowned and nodded.

'I've just read the latest scans. All's well. Things are proceeding along the proper channels. I thought I'd give you a bit of a check up.'

He raised an eyebrow, looking for a volunteer.

'Okay,' Matthew said, lowering himself from his bunk.

The doctor gestured for him to sit on the edge of the lower bunk and pulled up a stool opposite him. Matthew noticed how his pants rode up, showing small patches of tanned skin covered by white down.

'How do you feel?'

'A bit feverish.'

'Don't worry. That's expected. Any nausea?'

'Some.'

'Dizziness?'

'Some.'

'All right. I'm going to check some things. Would you take off your shirt please?'

Matthew complied. The doctor gently vised Matthew's wrist between his thumb and finger, measuring the pulse against his watch. He then gently palpated Matthew's armpits, his neck, his solar plexus. He concluded each probe with a gentle caress. He removed a tongue depresser from the inner pocket of his jacket and moved aside the mass of Matthew's tongue, peering into him with the penlight. Finally, he opened Matthew's eyelids and looked closely into his eyes, their faces almost touching. He pulled away, nodding once.

'Everything's fine,' he said. Only then did he look at Matthew's entire face. He sat up in surprise.

'What?' Matthew asked.

'Were you related to Edward Merriweather?'

'He was my brother.'

'Twins?'

'Yes.'

The doctor looked absently at Ben's mural, again clicking his penlight on and off.

'He was a brilliant student. Quite a dynamic and supple mind. A great loss that.'

Matthew didn't say anything. The doctor stood and gestured towards the wall and the television.

'This is all very interesting, but I'm afraid it will have to come out of your fee,' he said before walking from the room.

Matthew turned to Max to see his reaction, yet Max ignored the doctor's remark, staring at Matthew with an intense, dark scrutiny. Matthew turned away, remembering all the times recently that he'd suffered under that look.

Max had not liked Matthew. He had ignored him for the first few days Matthew lived at the bunker apartment, making it clear he was deferring to Ben when he allowed Matthew to join their nightly romps. The few times Matthew would speak or make suggestions, Max would listen with a half smile, then snort and shake his head. When Matthew would ask him a question he would pretend not to know the answer or make a sarcastic remark.

One night, about two weeks after Matthew had moved in, they had their confrontation. They had been to a play but left at intermission, coming home to watch television in Max's room. Ben had gone to bed after a few cartoons. Matthew and Max sat in silence, drinking lukewarm generic beer, watching old comedy shows on UHF. Matthew felt uneasy but felt a strange desire to be with Max.

'Matt,' Max said suddenly after finishing the dregs of a beer. 'Can I ask you something?'

Matthew looked at him.

'What are you?'

Matthew said nothing.

'Let me rephrase. I'm an actor. Ben's a painter. You are a . . .'

He made an exhortatory gesture.

'Max – ' Matthew said uneasily.

'No, just listen for a second. I have this nagging suspicion about you.'

'What's that?'

'Well, I have this little theory about you. Would you like to hear it? I think you're an insect. Of the wannabee variety. Yeah, I think that's it. You wanna be creative, committed, recognized. Somebody solid, a force to be reckoned with. Am I right? You want to be a success. Get shit written about you in the Sunday supplements, get advances and royalties so you can get a nice flop, go to parties at embassies and townhouses and lofts. Right? Correct me if I'm wrong here. Yet between this goal and reality the insect has come across one small obstacle, a bit of netting, a roach motel.'

'Which is?'

'You don't have the guts to say what you have to. You're afraid to bleed from the appropriate wounds. I mean, you've got taste and maybe talent and you're clever enough to know whose rules to follow. You'll probably even make it, now that I think about it. Climb your way to the top of the turd, like all good insects. But the fact remains you haven't got any balls.'

'That's not true.'

'Prove it, bug,' Max said, popping open another beer. 'You fucking suburban kids with your irony and your ambition. Man, you're everywhere. A plague of you is upon our nation. At the theater, in the clubs, in the galleries. You're smart bugs, too. Almost as smart as your fucking parents. And you're going about your business the same way they did their corporate suburban gigs. Cocktail parties, meetings, agents. All that positive energy. All that canniness. All those contacts and deals. Watching, getting smart, keeping up. Only you're gonna be boho, right? You're ironic. You know.' He took a long sip. 'Asshole.'

'You're an obnoxious shit,' Matthew said angrily.

'Yeah, so what?' Max reached forward with his toe to change the channel. Matthew stared hard at the shifting bone and muscle of his face. He felt like lashing out, but kept still.

'The funny thing is,' Max continued. 'I get the feeling you've got something sort of pure and nasty in you. Something ugly, something brilliant.' He looked Matthew in the eye. 'Yeah, I believe so. The problem is you're too fucking clever and ironic to stare it down. You dance around it, you don't want to bite it or put your dick in it. Because it's hot. Because it hurts.'

He finished his beer and lay back on the haphazard rugs.

'It's too bad you're such a fucking wimp, Merriweather. It really is. Because when we walk around and I see you about and see what you almost know I think maybe you can do something. I think maybe we could even do something together. But then, man, I don't know.'

He looked sharply at Matthew.

'I just don't know. Because I don't know what you are. What the fuck are you?'

Matthew hadn't answered.

After that, Max had been less hard on him. He assumed Matthew would come along with him and Ben, he gave him advice on movies or exhibitions or sites that were worth seeing. He was especially eager to hear stories about Matthew's childhood, about Eddie and Walter. Yet it wasn't until the incident at Pompeii Pizza that the barrier of condescension and contempt came completely down.

They had stopped in for slices of pizza and long-neck beers a few days after Max had been fired from the FIT show. There had been a small grease fire earlier and the dining room still smelled of smoke. It was busy with students and people who had just come out of the cinema. Max led Ben and Matthew sullenly through the line to their usual table in the back corner. They ate in silence, then lingered over their beers, watching a man on the sidewalk try to sell shrivelled roses to passing couples.

A group of four loudly laughing men entered the restaurant. They were all wearing FIT T-shirts and carrying leather folders. They were led to the line by a fat man with slicked back hair and red sneakers. Max stared hard at them.

'You know these guys?' Matthew asked.

'That fat mother-fucker is the assistant director of *Prometheus*. The others are actors.'

'Let's go,' Matthew said.

'No, hold on,' Max said. 'I want to talk to this douche bag.'

They had made their way through the line and approached the only empty table, adjacent to Matthew's. It wasn't until after they were seated that the fat man saw Max, who raised his beer in mock salute. Everybody stopped talking.

'Well, if it isn't the rebel without applause,' the fat man said. The actors snickered. Max said nothing. 'How is the wonderful world of unemployment?'

Max continued his silent smile.

'You know, Max, a certain director has been in touch with a certain union to see that a certain member is going to be suspended.'

Max took out his wallet and removed his Equity card from a plastic sheath. He took the lighter from his shirt pocket and lit the thin card, holding it in his hand until the fire extinguished. The actors at the other table gasped.

'You're crazy,' the fat man said. 'You're finished in the business. You really are. We're going . . .'

Max threw his beer bottle at him. It sailed past Matthew's head and hit the fat man in the chest. He emitted a nasal cough, spat a small spray. One of the actors tried to stand, yet Ben was quickly on his

103

feet, knocking him back into his chair and holding him there with one hand. The actor sitting on the far side of the fat man stood, looked at his watch and walked quickly from the restaurant. The other actor remained quiet, staring warily at Ben.

Max was trying to make his way around the table to get at the fat man, yet was restrained by hard-gutted kitchen staff who'd appeared with the sound of the bottle rattling across the tile floor. They were speaking calming words in a foreign tongue.

'Could you guys let me go for, let's say, thirty seconds?' Max said, his voice controlled. 'So I could rip this fat faggot's dick off and shove it down his throat? No? Twenty then. Fifteen.'

'You're an asshole, Cvenovich,' the fat man said, his falsetto voice slowed by mock calm. 'One day it'll get you in trouble.'

Matthew moved for the first time in the incident, springing across the short divide between the two tables. He grabbed the fat man by the throat, standing him up. He tried for a moment to pry Matthew's hands away, yet then had to use his hands to keep himself from falling over backwards. Matthew bore down on him. He could hear shouts and scuffles around him, yet remained undisturbed. He moved his face over the fat man's, looking closely into his eyes. The fat man looked around in panic, blinking furiously. A drop of spittle appeared at the side of his mouth. Sputtering gurgles sounded from deep within the flesh beneath Matthew's fingers. Veins burrowed across his forehead like the spoor of some subterranean animal. Matthew could feel their pulses race in unison as he pressed his thumbs harder into the soft flesh around the windpipe.

Then the man's eyes unfocussed. He looked above Matthew's head, as if he were tracking the flight of a just-launched rocket. His eyelashes were fluttering. Matthew could see dandruff in them.

Ben's large hand gathered Matthew's collar at the back of the neck and pulled him away. Matthew released the fat neck, noticing the perfect impressions of his fingers in the pink flesh. Two of the staff moved close yet didn't touch him. The fat man slumped in his chair, coughing. Matthew noticed that Max now stood in front of him. He was gesturing away the staff, looking from Matthew's eyes to the street. He put a hand on Matthew's chest.

'Matt. Hey. Are you in there? Okay, easy. You with me? Good. Listen up. Here's the plan. We're gonna walk out of here now. You follow me, and Ben'll be walking behind you. Just be easy. Matt?'

*

After the doctor left Max lay on his bed, staring at the ceiling. Matthew and Ben watched him, waiting. After about ten minutes he sat up quickly.

'You just about done?' he asked Ben, who nodded. 'Okay then, that's it. They're gonna fuck with our fee. Let's go. End of experiment.'

The halls were deserted. Their rapid footfalls echoed back at them like the sounds of pursuit.

'Where is everybody?' Matthew asked.

Max stopped before a blank door, pressing his ear to it. He gently turned the knob and it clicked open. They stepped in, entering a large room lit by bluish light. It smelled of sweat and rubber. There was a regular mechanical wheeze emanating from a large, tentacled machine. Bunk beds lined the side and back walls, each containing two men in pale green hospital gowns. Their mouths and noses were covered by clear masks that were hooked up to the machine's tentacles. They were all conscious, yet seemed disoriented. One shook his head slowly against his pillow; another moved his hand above him, as if clearing away webs. A third was trying to sit up but could only manage brief launches that dropped him heavily back to the mattress. They were all short, with shiny black hair, brown skin and broad faces. Most had wide moustaches. Max and Matthew and Ben backed out of the room, closing the door gently behind them.

'This one,' Max said, stopping before a door at the end of the hall. It too was unlocked. This room was brightly lit by fluorescent light. Soft disco music played on an unseen stereo. Two tall black men stood with their backs to the door, a jar-littered table between them. Their gowns flapped open. In front of them were music stands holding pornographic magazines. The man on the left stroked himself with his right hand. The man on the right, with his left. In their free hands they held large test tubes, taken from a long rack on the table between them.

'That's the sixth,' said the man on the right. 'Now what's the seventh?'

'Taj Mahal,' said the one on the left.

'No, man, you already said that.'

'Damn . . .'

They descended a floor. These halls were dirtier, cluttered with tied-off garbage bags. There was a strong smell of ammonia in the air.

'Where is everybody?'

Max tried several doors, finally finding one open. The room was full

105

of cages. Max turned on the lights, which flickered on slowly. There was a wheeled cart next to the door, filled with dead rhesus monkeys. Their necks were broken. Ben poked one on the forehead, causing its head to flop against its back.

'Check it out,' Max said, approaching a stack of cages. Each contained a German Shepherd puppy. Steel clamps bound their feet to the cage floor, while a snug metal ring around their midsection further immobilized them. Each wore a helmet that had an elaborate mask at the front which pried their eyelids permanently open. Two nipple droppers attached to a water bottle at the top of the cage kept their eyes lubricated. Electrodal wires emerged from their ears and necks, running to a monitor at the bottom of the cage, which contained a clock that showed elapsed time. On some of the monitors it was less than ten hours, on others more than fifty. One of the dogs, whose clock had stopped just short of seventy-four, was dead.

'Looks like they're seeing how long they can keep their eyes open,' Max said.

Ben stepped up to the nearest cage, whose dog had been immobilized for nearly twenty hours.

'I think I'm gonna take this one,' he said, opening the cage and releasing the binding rings. It took him several painstaking minutes to remove the wires and eyelid clamps. The dog remained impassive as he worked.

'Blink,' he said when he finished. The dog obliged. Ben lifted it to the floor, where it sat quietly blinking.

'Maybe we should rig up a leash,' Matthew said.

'It's okay,' Ben said.

There was a banquet on the ground floor. They could hear it from the stairs, the sound of metal on china, the hum of human voices, the shuffle of chairs. They could smell roasted flesh, tobacco smoke, sweat activated perfumes. Max gestured for quiet as he led them across a coat-cluttered lobby to the entrance. Ben was carrying the dog, who slept quietly. The sign outside the door read 'National Gnotobiology Foundation Annual Banquet'. On a flower-shrouded easel next to it was a photograph of a man with a high forehead, tired eyes and a crooked nose. It said 'In Memoriam, Dr Leonard Drinkwater'.

They slipped unnoticed into the large room, standing in shadows against the back wall. The room was filled with several dozen round tables with numbered bouquets in the middle. Most of the guests were in their sixties or seventies. The men wore baggy tuxedos, the women crinkled gowns. Beige-jacketed waiters moved quietly among the tables, collecting dirty plates, filling coffee cups. Some of the men lit cigars, others tipped back their chairs to talk to guests at adjoining tables. A few of the women were speaking too, although most stared absently at the tablecloth.

Max nodded to the buffet table. Infra-red light bulbs illuminated the remaining food-tureens of steaming vegetables, silver trays of fish and chicken, glass bowls of salad, straw baskets of pill-shaped rolls. An empty tray stood at one end, soiled with brown lettuce and lobster antennae. At the other end of the table a boy in a white tunic and tall chef's hat aimlessly cut slivers of flesh from a slab of roast beef.

Max walked nonchalantly up to the buffet, holding out a dish to the boy, who eagerly filled it with several slices of the fat-trimmed beef. Max returned and gave it to Ben, who fed it to the now awake dog.

There was a shriek of amplified noise. A man had stepped up to the rostrum at the front of the room and was adjusting the microphone. He took a stack of creased index cards from his jacket pocket. It was the doctor who had examined them.

A waiter carrying a stainless steel pitcher walked by them.

'Excuse me, son,' Max said, stopping him with a hand on the elbow. 'Do you have a match?'

The waiter handed Max a disposable lighter, then hurried off to refill glasses. The doctor tapped the microphone with his finger.

'Is this on? Can you hear me?'

'No,' somebody from the crowd called.

There was general laughter. The speaker smiled indulgently.

'That must be Terry Fritz,' he said. There was more knowing laughter. 'Now, I'd like to start by welcoming you all and congratulating everyone on a splendid year. I think you'll all agree that the past twelve months have seen tremendous strides forward in the creation and maintenance of workable germ-free environments.'

There was muted applause.

'Now, before we get down to the awards, let me take a few minutes to remember our recently departed and much missed colleague, Lennie Drinkwater.' He paused and there were murmurs of accord. 'Now, how is it we can best remember the dead? Well, one way is by their achievements. And Lennie's were legion, as I need hardly tell you. But there's more to a man's life than what he did. There's the legacy of what he was, the quality of his character, that lives on in all those who . . .'

'Alas poor Lennie!' Max called out. 'I knew him well.'

Heads turned, chairs scraped, people whispered. The speaker shielded his eyes against the spotlight, trying to see.

'As I was saying . . .' he continued.

'The evil that men do lives after them, the good is oft interred with their bones. So let it be with Lennie.'

'Who is that?' the doctor asked.

'For indeed, there was a goodness in the worm that bit him,' Max continued.

'Would somebody escort that man out?' the speaker said sternly.

There were scrapes as several of the guests arose. Some of the waiters moved towards them, too. The dog growled defensively as Matthew and Ben edged toward the door. Max moved in the opposite direction, leaping on to the buffet. He flicked on the lighter and held it to the sprinkler valve on the ceiling.

'Come on,' he said impatiently as the doctors and waiters closed in. 'Come on.'

There was a loud click somewhere, a tremor through the ceiling. Everybody stopped and looked up in time to see the monsoon erupt. Women were toppled, cigars ripped from mouths, glasses and dishes knocked to the floor, bouquets shredded. Max leapt down from the buffet and strode past the doctors and waiters, who were cringing beneath the torrent.

They lay perfectly still in the gentle curve of the satellite dish, covered by a web of thin wires. They rested like spokes, with their feet at the dish's center, their heads near the rim. The dog slept between them, its legs and ears twitching through a dreamy chase. Sporadic vibrations shook the cool metal below, which Ben had partially covered with a few figures staring open-mouthed at the sky.

Security guards had blocked the front exit as they attempted their escape, while soaking guests clogged the way to the back. So Max had led them up a flight of service steps to the roof, where they'd climbed into the dish. Fire engines had come and gone, banquet guests had departed with angry slams of sedan doors. At one point they'd heard footsteps and the squelched static of a walkie-talkie just below them, but the guard had not thought to look in the dish. Now, nearing dawn, all was quiet.

'I've got an idea,' Max said. Ben and Matthew waited. 'Let's do a show.'

108

'What show?' Matthew asked.

He raised himself to an elbow.

'Their show,' he said, nodding toward the city.

'I don't get it.'

'Yeah, yeah,' he said, growing excited. 'Their show. What we do is, we rent a place right near the theater and we put on our own little festival. To run at the same time as theirs. Or maybe we could do it in the street right outside the theater. Or maybe in the lobby.'

Ben smiled, his eyes closed.

'Gosh,' Max continued, 'I bet we could just ruin their day.'

'Which play do we do?'

'You tell me, Matt.'

Matthew shrugged. A traffic helicopter raced over them on its first flight of the rush hour.

'Write me one,' Max said. 'I'm serious.'

'About what?'

'About that place you go sometimes. When you talk about your croaked brother or your fuck-up dad. Where you were that night you choked fat shit at Pompeii.' He thought for a moment. 'I can't do it. I can't organize my thoughts enough to go there. I don't have the key, you know? I try to pound down the door and get into that place twenty-four hours a day but it's no good. I can't get in. But you, man, you fucking live there. I can see it in your eyes sometimes, even though you're basically a faggot. Write me that place. I'll do the rest. We'll have a festival. We'll give them their fucking fit.'

Matthew thought for a moment.

'Yeah, but what would the story be?'

'Make it about Prometheus,' Ben said, his eyes still closed.

Max sat upright.

'Yeah,' he said, his eyes widening. 'Yes, yes, yes.'

'I don't know,' Matthew said.

Max stood unsteadily in the dish, which groaned under his weight and shifted slightly. Another helicopter passed over them. He looked down at Matthew.

'Be not afeard,' he called out over the hovering copter's beating sound. 'The isle is full of noises, sounds and sweet airs, that give delight and hurt not.' He spread his arms and spun once in the dish. 'Sometimes a thousand twangling instruments will hum about mine ears; and sometimes voices, that, if I then had waked after a long sleep, will make me sleep again.' He squatted next to Matthew, their faces close. He was whispering now. 'And then, in dreaming, the clouds methought would open, and show riches ready to drop upon me, that when I waked I cried to dream again.'

The helicopter passed again, its flashing red light casting the day's first shadows across the valleys of Max's face.

'All right,' Matthew said. 'I'll see if I can put something together.'

BEAST RULES, OK

The massive stone church cast a late afternoon shadow which covered the small graveyard and crept halfway up the windowless wall of the abrupt new building beside it. Workmen in white jumpsuits and baseball caps moved on the scaffolding that enveloped the church, preparing panels of stainless steel glass for removal. A long orange van had been backed to the church's vestibule, its loading ramp running over the broad steps. Several aged pews leaned on end against the side of the truck. At the back of the church an old man scraped paint and rust from the cemetery gate.

Walter parked in the lot of the church, near the scarred elm that had served both as the sixth station of the Good Friday processional and the left field foul line on softball Saturdays. He sat in the car for a while as the engine settled, watching the workmen. He thought of his days as lay deacon at the church, in charge of the Sunday school. The slide presentations. The award Bibles. The boys in suits they outgrew soon after purchase. The girls smelling of soap and strawberry gum. The disastrous balloon launch. The unanswerable questions about God's face, the color of heaven. Walter shook off the spell of memory and slid slowly from the car, fetching the bucket, the brush and the jug of turpentine from the trunk.

He avoided the graveyard as he headed toward the new building, looping around the far edge of the lot so that he passed a flatbed trailer that contained several steel dumpsters. One was marked 'paper', another 'green glass', the third 'clear'. A tall man with a beard stood before the trailer, standing at the back of a pick-up truck. A young girl was perched on his shoulder, throwing bottles he handed her from bags on the pick-up's bed into the appropriate dumpsters. The young girl's eyes were brilliant with delight at the violence of the shattering bottles. Walter watched her for a moment, remembering.

The early classes had ended and the children were assembling outside the hall of worship for the main service. They were edgy with nervous energy; summer had just begun. As he tried to keep them still Walter noticed Matthew standing alone at the back, looking worried. He approached his son and asked where Eddie was. After a moment's hesitation, Matthew led him to the boiler-room door. Walter felt a brief moment of panic when he saw it open.

He knew that beneath the century-old church was a complex maze of basement rooms that housed the church's heating, storage and sewage facilities. Walter also knew that deep within it was an emptied catacomb that had once been part of the graveyard. It had been discovered about twenty years previously, the feverish brainchild of an eccentric turn-of-the-century minister who had later converted to Catholicism. Health authorities and officials from the national council had been called in after it was discovered and had decided that the catacombs were unhygienic and irregular. The occupant corpses had been unceremoniously transferred to conventional graves near the homes of traceable ancestors. The only access to the vacant catacombs that had not been sealed was through the boiler room, whose heavy metal door was kept tightly locked.

Walter sent the children into church and dug up a flashlight from a closet. He entered the labyrinth. The first room contained the rusty boiler with its humid pipes. It was lit by a single yellow bulb. The next rooms were similarly lit and used for storage, containing rotting pews, styrofoam angels that were punctured by insect tunnels, choir uniforms of faded purple and gold. After these were rooms that were empty of everything except thick water pipes that didn't reach the floor and stationary puddles of ancient crud. Some of these rooms had no lights, though some daylight came through weed-shrouded grills leading to the parking lot.

At the end of one of these rooms was a short passage, about four feet high. The floor was old planks. Walter hesitated for a moment, then duck-walked through it, fetid clay staining the flapping extremities of his suit. He emerged into a long, rectangular room with what appeared to be shelves or doorless cupboards on the walls. The floor was old brick, the ceiling sagging beams. He let the flashlight play around the room for a moment, making tentative stabs of illumination into the cavities.

'Eddie,' he said quietly.

'Eddie,' another voice said.

He shone the light to the corner where the voice had come from. It wavered in a compact strobe of his fear. On the floor, he could see the clump of Eddie's discarded suit. Steam seemed to rise from it. He walked across the room.

Eddie sat naked at the back of the cavity. His knees were drawn up
to his chest. Wet clay streaked his face, his exposed ribs, his legs. He
was smiling.

'What are you doing here, Edward?' Walter asked gently.

'Listening.'

Walter looked into his son's lightened eyes.

'To what?'

'The kids.'

'Come out and put your clothes on,' Walter said firmly.

Eddie slithered from the wall and quickly put his suit back on. He
looked at his father.

'Don't you hear them?'

Walter shook his head.

The sliding glass doors had motifs of crosses and stars to make sure
that no one walked into them. They sprung open automatically before
Walter's approach and he entered a carpeted lobby filled with large
plants and small couches. There were several bulletin boards bearing
mimeographed announcements and posters in the bold, naive styles of
children. On the far wall was a large sign in bulging letters: 'Advance
Interdenominational Fellowship Center'. A young woman sat at the
reception desk, chewing a pencil as she eyed Walter.

'Reverend Dixon?' Walter asked, switching his bucket from one hand
to the other.

'One hundred and eleven,' the woman said, nodding toward a hallway,
the pencil still in her mouth.

Walter found the office at the end of a long corridor. He noticed that
the nameplate had been pried from the door, leaving a bright, empty
rectangle. He looked in. Books and pictures were stacked on every
available surface except the empty shelves. A man in his sixties, his
gray hair crewcut, his mouth semicircled by a thick moustache, stood
behind the desk, loading books into a cardboard box. He wore black
clerical trousers and a Baltimore Colts T-shirt. Before loading a book
he would read the spine, then open it and leaf through several pages,
stopping to read random passages.

Walter rapped quietly on the door. Dixon looked up and smiled.

'For crying out loud.'

They shook hands warmly. Dixon noticed the bucket.

'Walter, listen, that's not necessary. Leon will take care of that.'

'It's all right. I'll do it. I want to.'

Dixon shrugged and gestured for Walter to place it near the door.

'These vandals,' he said. 'They aren't the first corrupt generation, our young. But I do believe they're the first whose corruption was inevitable.'

He sat on the edge of his desk.

'So, Walter, how the hell are you?'

Walter folded his arms and smiled at Dixon, shaking his head.

'What?' Dixon asked innocently.

'You know,' Walter said, still smiling.

'Come on, Merriweather, don't make me,' he said, grimacing.

'Let's see it, Dave.'

'Oh shit. All right. Come on.'

Dixon shook his head with mock reluctance and led Walter across the hallway to a door that bore a sign reading 'The David L. Dixon Memorial Meditation Room'. Dixon tapped the sign.

'Do you believe this shit?'

Walter pushed gently past him into the large room. He depressed a switch and tracklights flickered on.

It was decorated in the same manner as the lobby, with modular furniture in primary colors, magazine racks and drooping plants in earthen pots. A coffee maker and small refrigerator hummed in a corner. Above them was a photograph of a man in a shirt buttoned at the collar. He had a scraggly beard and large, ironic eyes that were rimmed with dark gulleys. The sign beneath it urged members to write to the government that imprisoned him.

'Oh no,' Walter said, catching sight of an oil painting hanging from the far wall.

'Oh yes,' Dixon said.

Walter walked across the thick carpet to scrutinize the portrait of Dixon. It was painted in caked oil that made him look twenty years younger and twenty pounds heavier. It captured his face's severity while omitting its humor and kindness.

'My legacy,' Dixon said sadly. 'I mean, look at this crap.'

'Who did it?' Walter asked, squinting at the signature.

'Some yid they commissioned. I mean, what did he use as a model? A chub? Halibut? Judas Priest . . .'

Walter shook his head, smiling ruefully.

'Now I need a beer,' Dixon said, opening the refrigerator and unhitching two cans from their plastic harness. Walter followed him back to his office.

Dixon cleared the debris from his chair, revealing an oft-taped crack in the vinyl. He sat heavily and popped his beer as Walter unfolded a metal chair opposite him.

'So how are things in the atom smashing biz,' Dixon asked, sucking foam from the can's opening.

Walter gave the top of his can several cautionary taps before opening it.

'I'm travelling a lot,' he said. 'Trying to unload the unit. It's a bit of a runaround.'

'Where you been?' Dixon asked, elevating a heavy eyebrow.

'Oh God, don't ask. Mexico City. Seoul. Sao Paulo. Taiwan. Mostly there, to Taipei. They seem most interested in the technology.'

'Nice to see all those places, though.'

'Are you kidding? It's airport to hotel to board room to hotel to airport. I hear nothing but English and eat nothing but French.'

'So what happens when you wrap it up?'

Walter shrugged.

'I don't know, Dave. UPU would resituate me but I just don't know. That might be a bit too much. I think I might need something else just now. Something new. I have this feeling of, what . . .'

Dixon sat forward slightly, his chair groaning with concern.

'Go ahead, Walter,' he said gently.

'Dread. I suppose I'd have to call it. A deep dread I can't shake if I'm doing the same old thing.'

'Dread of what?'

'Of, what do I call it?' He looked at his palms. 'The familiar. The usual. It's as if I've come to fear all the places where my histories and my capabilities are.'

'That's understandable,' Dixon said.

'Is it?' Walter asked distantly, still examining his hands. They sat in silence for a moment.

'Well, anyway,' Walter said. 'I've an appointment to see a headhunter in Phoenix next month. I'll see what he has to say.'

He looked up, forcing a smile.

'So how about you, reverend? What are your plans?'

'Judas, we're worse off than you guys. You think *your* services are no longer needed. What do you think I can do? Missionary work in the South Bronx? Inspirational manuals for MBAs? Yeah, that's it. The one-minute minister.'

They laughed.

'Actually, I've had an offer from some other cashiered clerics that I think I'm going to take them up on. They're buying a bee farm up in Alberta. No shit, Walter. A bee farm. I've seen it, spent a few weeks there last year. Half a dozen cottages, thirty acres. Cost me five grand and I have to chip in on the work. Nothing heavy – repairs, wood chipping, honey dipping. I'll be able to catch up on my reading. Write acerbic letters to the editor. Do some cross country skiing. You ever done that?'

Walter shook his head.

'I discovered it about twenty years ago. Me and some old college buddies have gone every few years since. Lake Tremblant, outside Montreal. We called it fear and tremblant. What you do is you go out at night. Damn, it's beautiful. Big moon, no wind. New wax under your feet. Skin bursting with that very V.O. on your hip. We just head out across that frozen lake. Sometimes you can hear the ice groan beneath you. It's a real grind at first, but after about half an hour you hit your stride, catch your second wind. That's when it happens. That's when it gets good.'

He sipped at his beer.

'I remember one night in particular. Very cold, very clear. The only clouds were our breath. Full moon, too. After about half an hour of chugging along I looked up at the big radiant fella and thought to myself – so why aren't you moving, Dave? Why are you standing still? Then I looked around and knew I was moving, going at a fairly good clip. I looked up again and I wasn't. But I was. You see? For those hypnotic moments I was both moving and not moving. It didn't matter. All the energy I pumped into my legs came back to me, right back to me.'

They drank their beers silently, thinking about second wind, until a man appeared in the doorway. He was young and muscular, dressed in a minister's uniform. Body hair billowed from beneath his stiff collar. He had deep-set black eyes.

'Ah, my heir apparently,' Dixon said. 'Walter, I'd like for you to meet the most recently reverend Jackson Gaines. Just graduated from Princeton and days away from being Interdom's new Presbyterian pulpit pounder.'

Walter stood and suffered the man's athletic grip. Raquetball, he thought. His face looked familiar.

'Walter used to be a lay deacon at the defunct First United. He was in charge of education. Currently he's lapsed, choosing instead to . . .'

'I know Mr Merriweather,' Gaines said in a strangely high voice that allowed Walter to recognize him.

'Ah, yes. Yes, we've met.'

Dixon looked confused. Walter turned to him.

'I met Reverend Gaines a few years ago while he was in the process of pouring blood on the hood of my new Olds.'

'Not necessarily orthodox behaviour,' Dixon said, still confused.

'It was at a protest outside of Olympic,' Gaines explained in a condescending whine. 'We'd been barred from picketing by a judge sympathetic to UPU, so we decided to form a human chain. When that was broken by the security forces we cast symbolic blood on to the cars of the management.'

'Which left a symbolic stain on my finish,' Walter said.

'Hey, are you guys going to duke it out or are you going to knock it off?' Dixon said.

Walter laughed. Gaines made a brief show of restraining himself from further comment.

'Have you seen the custodian?' he asked Dixon.

'Leon went off to get some solvents to clean up the symbolic protest outside.'

'Yes, of course. If you see him could you tell him I need some help setting up the teleprompter? I want to rehearse my Sunday talk.'

'Jackson solos this week for the first time,' Dixon said.

'What's the theme?' Walter asked.

'Job.'

'And what is it you say about the old moaner?' Walter asked.

Gaines eyes flickered at Dixon, their confidence fading a little.

'Well,' he said haltingly. 'Several things. I suppose the gist of the sermon is that Job was only able to truly become a man through suffering and renewed commitment.' He began to gain momentum. 'Before Satan's wager, Job was not unlike the basic member of America's suburban middle class. Of our congregation. Money, family, respect. Pious as far as his lifestyle would allow. Confident that his supposedly good works would be repaid. But his piety was cheap, his rewards not truly earned. It was only when the Lord challenged him, made him question and suffer, that he became truly a believer. Then I tie that point into social commitment, showing how belief only becomes meaningful when it costs something. When you have to give something up for it.'

Walter nodded.

'Sounds reasonable to me.' He paused for a moment, smiling self-deprecatingly. 'I once taught Job to a bunch of fourteen-year-old boys. Goodness, what a mess I made of that.'

'How's that?' Gaines asked.

'Well, they weren't impressed by it very much. They thought the story was, uh, gross. You know – ashes, sores. But my son Matthew had a good question.'

'Which was?'

'Well, he didn't see why Job was given a new family in the end. I mean, if it had only been a joke, a bet, why wasn't his old family brought back to life? Whatever happened to them?'

'That's good,' Dixon said, laughing softly. 'Yes, that's very good. Good old doubting Matt. My favorite cynic.'

'He asked me why Job didn't get back on that pile of shit until God squared this family thing with him.'

'And what did you tell him?' Gaines asked.

Walter shrugged.

'I told you I made a mess of it.'

Some of the tombstones had been toppled, most were scarred with red spray-paint that spelled out a single phrase, repeated in crude, bold strokes over the names and dates and remembrances. **Beast Rules, OK**. Walter shifted the bucket from one hand to the other as he walked to Eddie's grave. The stone hadn't been tipped, only sprayed, the single phrase at a diagonal across the name and dates. Walter squatted before the stone, the pain protesting this awkward position. He re-read the new inscription.

'Okay,' he agreed.

He splashed some turpentine into the bucket. The fumes brought protective tears to his eyes. He let the fumes dissipate for a moment, then dipped the brush's wiry bristles into the liquid and began to remove the paint from the marble. It came off easily, yet left a shadow on the bright stone. Walter scrubbed furiously, scraping some skin from the heel of his hand and causing his back to spasm violently. It was no use. The stone was stained.

He sat on the damp ground and rested his back. He watched for a while as the removers lowered an awkwardly shaped organ pipe from an upper window of the old church. He then ran his hand over the foliage around him. The sod had not yet fully taken root, yet the recent weeds and sprouts of veronica were firmly in. As he looked at the ground he discovered another plant, near the base of the scarred stone. It was light green, resinous in texture, with small spliced leaves. Walter tussled it curiously for a moment, trying to figure out what it was. Finally, he picked a small bunch of lower leaves, scrutinizing them in the pale sunlight. He smelled them but only detected dirt and chlorophyll. He rubbed a leaf into pulp between his thumb and fingers. There was still no distinctive odor. He placed the remaining leaves in his mouth. They were so bitter that he almost gagged. Yet after the initial swell of distaste there was something soothing, something rich in the pulp. He closed his eyes and swallowed.

Walter coasted to a stop before the small security shed. The guard dozed inside, his small head held aloft by the thick muscle of his neck. Walter stilled the engine, slid slowly from the car and approached the corrugated shack.

He stared through the streaked window, his breath creating amoebas of mist on the glass. Surrounding the guard were stacks of guns and porno magazines, a portable police scanner whose lights rippled in steady waves, an oozing plaid thermos, balls of soiled tin foil, two cans of insect spray. What a job, Walter thought. He looked at the lumps of muscle beneath the cheap uniform, the sloping brow. He wondered where this kid would have been generations earlier, after three years as pulling guard at the local high, after the early marriage and mortgage on the house with a small back yard. Pouring molten steel in Bethlehem, maybe. Or cutting a path for Route 40 in the granite and limestone above Asheville. Bumping bananas and bad transistors off a steamer in Baltimore. But now, Walter thought, now he gets to stay awake in this dog house, poised to chase away his boss's kids.

Walter drummed the cool glass. The guard's puffy eyelids drew open like loading dock doors, then slammed shut, their drawchain released. Walter drummed again. The guard awakened this time, touching the gun on his hip. He recognized Walter and stood quickly, frowning apologetically as he opened the door. A strong odor of sweat and insecticide rushed out.

'Hello, Mr Merriweather.'

'Hello, Duane,' Walter said, taking in the nametag. 'How is everything tonight?'

'Um, it's okay. Some kids on bikes came by earlier but I ran them off.' He looked at his watch. 'My two-ten rounds are coming up.'

'Good.'

'Oh yeah. Dr Brand is in there,' Duane said, his face folding back into a crude conspiratorial smile.

'Yes, yes, I'm meeting him,' Walter said, making to move off.

'Mr Merriweather?'

'Yes?' He said, stopping.

'Um, well, there's a problem, sir.'

He hesitated, fumbling nervously with the strap of his holster. The scanner spluttered in the shed behind him, then quieted.

'Go ahead, Duane,' Walter said.

'That tower there, sir.' He nodded toward the remaining cooling tower, then shook his head and furrowed the rubbery flesh of his brow. 'It's just that I ain't gonna be going in there no more, Mr Merriweather. Not at no five dollar per. You can call my superviser, Mr Farousseh, if you wanna, but . . .'

'That bad?'

'Are you serious? They're breedin' or sumpin'. I mean, if they were just a couple I could pop 'em. But I don't know, there's like a zillion of 'em in there. Maybe two.' He shook his head, his eyes downcast in thick determination. 'It's just that I'm not gonna go in there no more. You can call Mr Farousseh . . .'

Walter held up a quieting hand, then tapped Duane's broad shoulder with it.

'Don't worry. That's fine. We'll let them be the guards.'

They stood silently in the cold night.

'They really gonna make movies in there?' Duane asked.

'That's the plan.'

'Big league,' he said, looking at the tower in admiration. 'You think they need extras? Stunt men?'

'Could. I'll keep my ears open.'

'Thanks,' Duane said. He looked at Walter. 'You like movies?'

Walter nodded.

'Who's your favorite star?'

Walter thought for a moment.

'I'd have to say Tracy.'

'Tracy? I don't know her. Who's she?'

'No, no. Spencer Tracy. He was a man.'

Duane looked sceptical.

'Was he tough?'

Walter nodded slowly.

*

He found Brand hunched over a console in the control room, his face colored blue by the light from a half-dozen computer screens. He looked intently from screen to screen. Occasionally, he'd touch a keyboard with the tentative stab of a first-time typist, then squint at the corresponding terminal. He was wearing a light brown robe and grainy sandals. His hair was long enough now to be pulled back into a stubby ponytail.

'Hello, André,' Walter said.

Brand wheeled in his chair, his face grimacing in recognition.

'Walter. I'm glad you came.'

'No problem, André.'

He took a position behind Brand's chair.

'I didn't know the simulator was still connected,' Walter said, leaning over the chair.

'Yeah. I'm just running something,' Brand said distantly. He punched several more keys. Walter watched the numbers and the charts transfigure.

'Pull a rod or you're going to have a little backwash in three,' he said. 'You'll need a mop.'

'It's not up to me to pull a rod, Walter,' Brand said grimly. 'This isn't my deal here.'

'I don't understand.'

'You will,' Brand said, punching in data with small, definitive gestures. Walter moved to a chair several yards away. Brand scrutinized him with impassive eyes.

'You're moving better, Walter. How are you? How are the travels? What's it been, a month?'

'I'm fine, André. Tired.' He sat slowly. 'The Mexican situation turned out to be the fiasco we all knew it would be. Somebody back-doored us in Seoul. But the Nationalist Chinese look very, very possible.'

A troubled look shifted through the crags of Brand's face.

'So how are you, André?'

'I'm retired is how I am,' he said curtly. 'As of Monday.'

Walter stiffened in his chair, causing it to swivel slightly.

'Retired?'

'That's right. I had a nasty confab with CEO Mock last week. All sorts of epithets and unretractables were hurled. The upshot of the whole affair was that I got a year's salary and a bum's rush to the elevator.'

'Did anything specific bring this on?'

'Everything specific brought it on, my friend.'

Walter waited for an explanation but none came.

'So what are you going to do?' Walter asked. 'Teach?'

'No way. Like I said, I'm retired. I've taken a cottage down bay. I'm gonna do some writing, design some software. Work out some ideas, basically.'

Their eyes met for a brief instant, then spun off in separate orbits. Walter thought about how much Brand had changed from the dour, efficient number-cruncher he had met ten years earlier. So sober then, so diligent. Unwilling to go beyond the patterns numbers made. Yet recently he had become sloppy, vague, fascinated by cheap mysteries, worthless anomalies, cosmic pseudoriddles. Walter had seen the books in his office: *Psychic Advances Behind the Iron Curtain, The Stones of Easter Island, Worlds in Collision.* His file cabinets had become jammed with xeroxed articles about black holes and watery triangles, prehistoric desert lines and inescapable sarcophagi. Mental candy for a toothless dotage, Walter thought.

'What sort of ideas?'

Brand's oyster eyes dilated slightly.

'Ah. Well, it's something that's been on my mind for a long time. Maybe since Trinity. I'm going to work it into a book.' He cupped his hand, fingers facing outward, and ran it in front of his face. 'The history of the myth of the atom in America.'

'Sounds like I'll need some coffee for this one,' Walter said, stretching to his feet. He inserted a conical cup in a plastic holder and poured out some thick coffee from the unbreakable glass pot.

'You see,' Brand persisted, 'it occured to me that the reason we're in such bad shape, why we've failed so utterly here, is because the atom is not reality but only an explanation of it. It's a myth. You see, after Trinity, after Hiroshima, the atom became like what a god must have been to the savages. The way it was and the way it was going to be. No ifs, ands or buts. Only the average schmuck on the street couldn't see it, couldn't touch it. He couldn't approach it. So they had to have priests, crazy mediums with their sweatshirts and Teutonic accents and strange hair, to worship this god. And it was a pretty good god for a while. It could slay the feared barbarians. It could bring light, it could bring heat. It could run the dryer. It could motor us around the world if we were so inclined. Project our tiny voices far into the cold, cold void. And all this god asked from us in return was that we believed in it. Make the odd sacrifice to it. What a great thing, huh? A god who showed up with the flick of a switch.'

'So what happened?'

'What happens to all minor gods? They die when the price of belief becomes too high. This little sprite with his balls spinning round his cluster head screwed up in reverse. He became too big, too tough. He went from a friendly to a bad-ass. He became a specter of danger, menace, death. He was measured in throw weight and six-digit body counts, he brought mushroom clouds and terminal sunburns and unfortunate lumps in the tissues and glands. To hell with this god, the people said. He's too expensive. We don't like this god any more.'

'So who replaces him up above?'

'Whoever's turn it is, really. White powder god. Virus god. Bran god. Something. I don't give a damn, really.'

Walter watched Brand's face as the security guard walked by the room, stopping to turn the time key on the wall in the rounds recorder slung over his shoulder. He thought again about Brand's life. The heavy-legged wife who'd died. The daughter who had become a liability lawyer and never called. The mornings he'd find Brand on the computer, his body gamy, his chin all stubble, his eyes red with sleeplessness.

'Why did you want to see me, André?'

Brand's features sharpened to their customary sourness.

'I've come upon something that I think you should know about.' He leaned over the console. 'That you definitely should know about.'

Brand pulled at his bottom lip for a moment, searching for the right words or perhaps gathering courage.

'I was at UPU a few weeks ago, making the rounds, and I ran into Henry Braithwaite. From legal. It was after lunch so he was of course shit-faced drunk. Anyway, he hijacked me into his office and I had to listen to his drivel for about an hour. His wife has left him or they were going to remove his prostate or something. In order to change the subject I asked him what he was working on. He blurted out "Oh, the Chapter Eleven for Olympic".'

Walter sat up in his chair, the pain tightening hard in his back.

'Come again?'

'My sentiments exactly. He realized he'd put his foot in it and tried to deflect but I would have none of that. After some hemming and hawing he explained himself, making me promise it would never leave his cheesy office.'

'So should you be telling me this?' Walter asked reflexively.

'Don't be noble till I'm finished, Walter,' Brand said. He paused for a moment. 'The bottom line is that UPU has no intention of selling this reactor. They *want* to take a bath with it. There's no movie company. There are no contractors from the city. There are no Chinese. It's all a big house of cards. Blue smoke and mirrors. None of those deals will be okayed by the board. Every one will fall through.'

'I don't understand.'

'It's simple, really. This,' he gestured around him, 'was never meant to be.'

'André, please, hold the philosophy for a while,' Walter said impatiently.

'No philosophy, Walter. Facts. UPU never intended for us to go on-line. This whole enterprise is a giant fraud dreamed up during the oil embargo. UPU was in bad, bad shape back then, worse than anyone imagined. Massive debt to the ragheads, poor spending, union trouble, safety cock-ups, fraud, mismanagement. They needed cash, lots of it, post haste. But with the sheiks on one side, Ralph Nader on the other, there was no way they were going to get any rate increases past the legislature or the commission. So what to do? Build this behemoth. A perfect source of short-term revenue. Bonds were floated, loans secured. They were even able to win a small rate increase with their stories of the atom god and his beneficence. The solution to all their short-term problems. Yet there was a problem – what to do with the behemoth when he became a big boy. I mean, there was no way they could afford to operate it. You know the costs it would take to fire this thing up. Salaries, juice, material, PR. There was no money left. It had all disappeared into the cracks. So the one little nicety, the one fact upon which UPU's whole scheme was predicated, was that we would never go on-line. Never ever. All the good after bad, all that fraud and funny money would have to come out then. Olympic would have to be closed out in such a manner that would never allow UPU to recoup their losses. I mean, they couldn't just walk away from it. The utility commission would have massacred them. So they needed a crisis. Something beyond their control. A mitigating circumstance.'

'Little fishes.'

'Not originally, my friend. Originally it was you and I.'

Their eyes met.

'That's right. It was all worked out. Blueprints were going to be altered, weld points compromised, stress lines weakened. Then, just after start-up, there was going to be an accident. Not a big one, mind you. Just a small cloud. Just a small puddle. Enough to trip some wires, kill some chickens, scare the citizenry. The place would have to be sealed up forever. A sarcophagus in which UPU's little scheme would be forever buried. And in the ensuing investigation the chief engineer would be hung out to dry.'

'How do you know this?'

'It's all in here,' he said, tapping the computer. 'I've figured it all out. It took a few weeks, but it's all in here. They were going to slip it by me. Because they knew I was a loser. They knew I'd let my guard down. That's why they hired me.' He took a deep breath. 'So anyway, after the barbecue, it would have been me. Look at these mistakes, they would have said. Look at these fudged tests, these illegible blueprints. UPU would be red-faced and apologetic, but personnel miscalculations aren't sufficient ground for the commission to make the whole utility suffer by denying them enough of a rate increase to recoup one hundred percent of the loss. Nader would get his pound of flesh, and UPU would get their bread.'

'My God.'

'But then along comes this environmental survey. A blessing for them, really. Far less messy, far more sympathetic. But it does leave one small dilemma. A perfectly sound and useable structure. The commission would tell them no rate increase. Sell it, boys. To the market. What are there, six Republicans on the commission now? But that would have meant significant losses of – ?'

'Fifty cents on the dollar.'

'So they need to execute one more con. The famous "We tried to sell it but there were no serious buyers" routine.'

'I don't think I want to hear the rest of this.'

'And since every fraud needs a front,' Brand went on relentlessly, 'and since they already had an aces one at the helm, they decided to put you on the mill. Send you all over the globe trying to peddle this thing. Borneo, Antarctica, Bora Bora. It doesn't matter. The more far flung the better. They would have sabotaged and nitpicked any deal you made. Then, when the commission's hearing rolls around, who is the star witness? Good old Merriweather. Mr Integrity. Young Abe Lincoln. Solid citizen. Suffers through family tragedy yet never leaves his post. And you get up before the commission and tell them all about your travels. Did you make slides by the way? Those long trips. Those frustrating meetings with corrupt officials you refused to bribe. Insultingly low offers. The Chinese looked good but there were unforeseen complications at the last minute. The commission nods its collective head. UPU was right, it can't be sold. They're satisfied that all has been done in good faith. They figure if Walt can't do it, nobody can. The gavel comes down. Rate increase allowed to cover one hundred percent of the losses. Shelter is given, momma bankruptcy cuddles UPU to her warm and milky breast. They get their money back without having to go to the expense and effort of running this sonofabitch. And a lot of board members with slick construction contracts and portable toilet companies and automatic yearly bonuses have done very well by it all, thank you.'

Brand stopped, the elation of speech passing from his face.

'It's true, my dear friend.'

'I know,' Walter said. 'I know.'

He could sense their presence the instant he entered the tower. An added density of darkness, a mass of positive black. He could hear them after a moment – the rustle of short flights, the click of talons on concrete, the copulative flurries. And something else, something he did not receive through his senses. A presonic shudder that resonated in his body's cavities, his nasal passages, his lungs and scrotum. Sounding the pain in his back as if it were the bass string of a master's instrument. It came in waves, in pulses, an indecipherable code relayed through his tissues and nerves from a distant station far outside his body. So this is it, Walter thought. The divine whisper. He stepped forward and felt the wind of wings on his face.

Eddie had killed it. Snapped its thin neck, gently, so you could barely see the damage. Held it in his cupped hands. Walter had gently prodded it with his finger, then explained to Eddie that you shouldn't kill this insect. It was harmless. Useful. But Eddie refused to understand. It's all right, dad. Walter remembered flushing it, watching its limbs spread in the bluewater whirlpool.

A single red light began to pulse at the top of the tower, followed hard by loud shrieks from a klaxon. The sound and light moved chaotically through the tower, forcing the bats into confused flight. They bounced off the walls, collided with each other, their echolocation disabled by the careering sound. Walter crouched, shielding his head from the creatures that flew by him. He felt a pincer pressure on his shoulder and brushed something leathery away. The windbreaker's skin remained unbroken.

The klaxon stopped abruptly, though the light persisted. The bats were able to organize their flights and race through the open roof. Brand's simulation had run its course, reaching its fantasy accident.

Walter stood perfectly still in the rain of fecal spores and bits of fur, letting his heart and breathing calm.

Yet a more profound panic soon took over, a scattering within him, a spinning off of what was solid, what was earned and possessed. He looked at the warning light on the thick walls and felt some great structure within him that had slowly been cracking had finally crumbled into dust and jagged bits. It was just survival now, he knew. Preservation. Holding on. That was all the redemption there would be.

The hum in his body was gone. He laughed a little, realizing it had been nothing holy after all. Just the probing radar of those blind creatures.

PROMETHEUS DOWNBOUND

'Hey, Matthew, do you know anything about electricity?' Max called down from above.

'A little.'

'Okay, good. You're in charge of lights. Come up here.'

Matthew walked the length of the Friends Meeting Hall they had rented for their performance. It was a modest brick building in a fashionable residential and boutique district, just a few blocks from the theater where FIT was being held. The rent was high, but it was the only thing available in that part of town. Max knew the Hall's cultural affairs director, Christine Bevaqua, who had been an audio librarian at the Shakespeare library when he was in rep there. She was a nervous, bird-like woman who listened with attentive nods and continually 'looked in' on them to see if they wanted tea.

The hall was about a hundred feet long, forty wide. It was made of dark wood and off-white plaster and smelled of old polish. At one end were three double doors, above which were two small block windows looking out from a projection room. At the other end was a stage, three steps above the floor. It was backed by a dirty maroon curtain that hid a brick wall and stacks of old hymnals. Folding chairs lined the hall's side walls, resting below windows covered by frayed beige curtains. Domed lamps hung from the ceiling, their light muted by layers of dead insects in the glass basins.

This was their first full rehearsal here, three weeks before their play opened. Max had scheduled performances on Thursday through Sunday for two consecutive weekends, with an option to carry on if it proved a success. Mrs Bevaqua had agreed to sell advance tickets for them.

Matthew had written the script over a four-day period in which he did little else. He rarely left his room, and when he tried to eat or sleep or head out into the city to clear his head, he found himself rushing back to his room for a reworking or an addition. Max read the script several times after Matthew gave it to him, then left the apartment without

133

a word. He returned an hour later, carrying a quart bottle of vodka, looking happy.

'Yes,' he said to Matthew, dancing around the room. 'Fucking yes. That's it. I mean, it's awful and it's just what I want. Everything that's wrong about it is right. You have no idea how perfect this is for what we have to do, you poor naive earnest motherfucker.' Matthew had asked him what he'd meant but Max had only told him that he would see.

Matthew left the main hall and climbed the cluttered stairs to the small projection room. Max stood above the electrical board he had stolen from the storage room of an old theater. It was an archaic, rusting machine, a quilt of over-rides, broken knobs, hot-wired connections. Several long cracks in its structure had been crudely soldered together.

'I'll need you to run about thirty lights plus the sound system from this,' Max said.

'I don't know, Max,' Matthew said, looking at the board.

'You'll do it,' Max said, striding from the room.

Maybe, Matthew thought. He turned the heavy board over and began to sort out the multicolored pasta of wire beneath.

Max clapped his hands in a slow rhythm, then listened as the sound echoed through the hall. He walked to a different point and repeated the procedure, stamping his bare feet on the floor for a different quality of sound. He considered what he heard for a moment, then turned to Matthew and Ben, who were sitting near the back of the hall. He pointed to Blink, sleeping between them, his legs and ears twitching.

'Could we get him to speak?'

Ben placed his sketch pad on his lap and frowned as he inspected the sleeping dog.

'Come on, Ben,' Max said. 'That's the perfect sound.'

Ben nodded grimly and gently touched the dog's flank. He looked up, startled, then began to wag his tail.

'Hey,' Ben said softly.

Blink responded with a sharp bark. Max nodded, then dashed to the stage.

'Again.'

'Hey.'

The dog barked. Max moved.

'Hey.'

The dog barked.

'Perfect,' Max said, clapping his hands once loudly. 'I'll be able to hear the audience as clearly as it hears me.'

'Does that matter?' Matthew asked.

He ignored the question, looking up.

'But these lights. They're no fucking good. I want a supernova in here. We're going to need about ten more instruments. Strobes. Gels. I want this place to explode with light.'

'Hey, Max,' Matthew said.

'What?'

'Money's what,' Matthew said. 'I just paid Bevaqua the rent. We have like eighty bucks left.'

Max's face formed into a twisted smile.

'Yeah, Matthew, I was meaning to talk to you about that . . .'

The building was made of dark glass. Matthew stood on the opposite side of the street, watching reflected clouds. A jet's image slithered over the panes. The people coming out of the building's doors were shocked by the cold, drawing their clothes to their necks and breaking into annoyed trots. Those who were passing watched themselves in the glass, often making small, incongruous gestures, as if to ensure it was really them.

Matthew crossed the street, shrouded in the frosted exhaust of taxis and limousines. He reached out his hand to push open the door, but it snapped open before he could touch it, drawing him into a large, silent lobby. A black man with ritual facial scars and a baggy rayon uniform gave him a clipboard to sign, then showed him to the elevators.

Matthew found an empty car and punched the appropriate floor. The elevator ascended with great speed. He felt a sharp scrotal motility that forced him to cup his testicles in his hand for a moment.

The car stopped several floors short of his destination. Two tall young men with slicked-back hair and tailored blue suits got on. They looked at the grid of buttons without touching it, then cast cursory glances at Matthew. They seemed unimpressed by his long hair and surplus clothes. One of the men pounded a rolled-up sheaf of papers into his hand. The doors closed.

'What a wimp,' said the first one.

'Definitely,' said the second.

'We should cut him off.'

'At the knees.'

'You know what it is with him, don't you?' asked the first.

'Sure,' said the second, jangling coins in his pocket. 'He's afraid to go for it.'

'They all are in that firm,' said the first, banging the sheaf against the brass wall now. 'It's a faggot firm.'

The elevator stopped at an intermediate floor. The doors opened and closed without anyone getting on or off.

'Sometimes,' the first man said, pointing his sheaf in front of him, 'I daydream about walking in there with an Uzi and opening up on the whole firm.'

'Yeah,' the second man said, rattling his keys quickly. 'In slow motion.'

'But first I'd pork that Monica.'

'Definitely.'

'Up her ass. Chocolate tunnel of love. Then I'd blow her away, too.'

'Bitch.'

'For sure.'

They reached the top floor. The two young men went off to the left, towards a law firm. Matthew headed towards the brokerage firm to the right. He passed through a large glass door to a reception area where two women sat at a long desk. They wore headphones and put through call after call as they stared, eyes unfocused, at the wall in front of them. Matthew looked at the wall. It was made of mirrored tiles. Two workmen crawled from opposite sides of the desk, tearing the carpet from the floor. They used small, hooked knives. Matthew waited patiently for about a minute as everyone worked on, ignoring him.

'I'm here to see Mr Bruce,' he announced finally.

One of the women pointed towards a door. After he walked off the men tore away the section of carpet he'd been standing on, making a violent rending noise.

Matthew entered a large, open room of computer consoles and phone banks. Several dozen men and women talked excitedly into receivers or to one another. Everyone seemed to be watching a plane that passed, except a group of old people in overcoats sitting in a far corner of the room. They were staring at an electronic board on which letters and numbers scrolled by quickly. Some held scraps of paper, others sandwiches or cups of coffee. One of them drooled unwittingly on to his wool scarf.

'I'm looking for Mr Bruce,' Matthew said to the closest person, a blonde woman wearing a bow tie. She nodded toward a man opposite her. He was broad-shouldered, with sandy hair, brown eyes and thick lips. He wore a large school ring on his right hand, a thick gold wedding band on his left. A pair of sunglasses rested on his head. Matthew pulled up a chair and waited for him to finish speaking on the phone.

'Yes?' he asked.

'I'm Matthew Merriweather. I called earlier. About the UPU stock.'

The man nodded once as he typed rapidly on his keyboard. He picked up a pencil as he stared at the figures.

'Don't sell,' he said, tapping the keyboard lightly with the pencil.

'I have to.'

'Isn't there something else you can liquidate?'

'Breakfast.'

Bruce gave a brief smile.

'The reason I think you shouldn't sell is because UPU stock is down just now,' he said with slow condescension. 'Way down.'

'How come?'

'Well, the word was that they were on the rebound after the Olympic fiasco. On the verge of being able to cover their losses by raising rates, thereby protecting the shareholders. Things were looking good share-wise. Only now, some asshole who was in charge of selling the plant or something has written a letter to the NRC which makes it seem that UPU has been less than honest about the whole nuclear thing. So the rate increase is on indefinite hold while the commission investigates. And UPU stocks are about as valuable as real estate in Haiti. So my considered advice is you should wait until they sort out this whistle-blowing schmuck and clean up the mess he's caused. Why are you smiling?'

'Sell anyway,' Matthew said. 'I need the money to invest in something else.'

The broker shook his head, then touched some keys.

'You're gonna take a bath.'

'That's okay, I could use one.'

'No, no, no . . .'

Max jumped from the stage, flattening a half-empty beer can into a disc, sending small torrents of suds into the floor's cracks. He stared at them for a moment, taking measured breaths.

'You guys are going to have to get these fucking cues down. They have to be absolutely microscopically perfect. Or else we're . . .'

He kicked the can, which soared through a low arc before chipping the wall. Max looked up at Matthew in the projection room.

'Come down here a second.'

Matthew switched off the rumbling board and walked slowly down the cluttered stairs. They had been working on sound and light cues for over two hours. He walked into the hall, wandering through the posters Ben was painting. Blink sat at the foot of the stage, eating a BLT sandwich from a cardboard plate.

'Sit,' Max said, handing him a beer. 'Ben?'

They sat on the floor in front of the stage.

'Matthew, those light cues are too slow.'

'Well, Max, there's a reason for that. I'm running fifty units on a board that was made for sixteen. I've got copper pennies and uninsulated wire and, Jesus, who knows what else . . .'

'You have to make it work.'

'Right. You say that. But it's fucking scary up there with all this smoke and stuff.'

'So?'

They stared at each other. Max got up and jumped on the stage.

'Listen,' he said. 'I understand. You're thinking that maybe if we're ballpark on these light and sound cues, a little loose, then it's no big deal. Because we got a decent script and I'm going to go fucking berserk up here.' He shook his head. 'No way. Forget it. It has to be flat fucking perfect.'

Matthew looked away, shaking his head slightly.

'And I'll tell you why,' Max said resolutely, his voice controlled. 'Because the idea here is not to impress people or get reviewed or get fulfilled. The idea is to rock the world of every person who is stupid enough to walk through that door. Rip out vital organs. Change personalities. Soil underwear.' He pointed to the empty auditorium. '*They're* the enemy. You don't ingratiate an enemy, you don't cut him a break. You defeat him. In this case, you defeat his imagination. All right?'

Matthew and Ben watched him patiently. Blink continued on the sandwich.

'And the only way we're going to do that is to be perfect. Letter fucking perfect. We have to establish authority over them, convince them we're artistically perfect. We have to be transparent. No seams, no personalities, no human passion. Pure art. Then we nuke 'em. Pre-empt their imaginations, block all avenues of intellectual escape. They won't be able to say "they're punks" or "they're sloppy" or "they're pretentious shits". They won't have time for such thoughts. They'll just think these guys are perfect and I'm sweating piss here, so I must be some kind of bourgeois pseudo shit.' He paused. 'I'm right about this, you guys. I've been there a few times. Just for a few moments, but I've still been there. As Shylock or Caliban or Mad Tom. I've shown these people their fucking lousy souls and I've felt this ripple of dread go through the theater. Only I've never sustained . . .'

He pressed his palms into his temples, shutting his eyes furiously, as if against some blinding light. Blink stood up and walked over to him, wagging his tail as he stared up at his face. The dog then sidled over to Ben, who began to scratch his belly, forcing his hind legs into frantic reflex.

'It's just that this is a great fucking text, Matt,' Max said softly. 'I mean, it's artless and unstructured as a scream. Every word is like something being torn. So if we get it into good form, then . . .'

Mrs Bevaqua had materialized at the hall's entrance. She was wearing a knit frock and sandals. Her wiry, gray-streaked hair was pulled into a bun at the back of her head. She held a large earthen tea mug.

'What?' Max asked sharply.

'I wanted to speak with you guys about the voltage of your lights.'

'What about it?'

'Well, don't you think it might be excessive?'

'No,' Max said rudely. Matthew stared at him, yet remained quiet.

'Well, I spoke with the janitor – '

'The janitor!' Max leapt from the stage. 'I don't care what that besotted pustule thinks. He couldn't even screw in a light bulb! The janitor. Jesus, do you believe this dame? I say it's fine. All right?'

The woman hesitated.

'Blink,' Max said. The dog stood and growled.

'All right,' Mrs Bevaqua said, dematerializing.

'Hippy moron,' Max said. 'Okay, enough balloon juice. Let's do it again.'

Matthew climbed back up the stairs. In the booth, he looked at the large, rusting board. The metal around several of the knobs was charred with recent heat. He switched it on and listened to the usual concerto of hisses, cracks and rattles. He had to remember the next time they got drunk to ask Max how he'd burned his face.

'Hey, Max,' he called down through the window. 'I'm not too sure.'

139

Max looked up at the platform, smiling.

'Me neither.'

He laughed hysterically for a moment, then rubbed furiously at the bridge of his nose.

'Line,' he commanded.

The glass discs began to pulse, a wind crossed the tunnel. Commuters stepped to the platform's edge, shoving creased newspapers into their armpits and changing briefcases from one hand to the other. The train came into view and glided quietly to a stop. The people began to shuffle on or off, as solemn as prisoners exchanged during an unending war. Matthew, weighed down by parcels, waited until the warning klaxon sounded, then stepped on to the subway. He found a solitary seat at the front of the car, obscured by a panel of tinted glass. When the train jerked into motion he looked around. He couldn't see them.

He relaxed in his seat and examined the programs he'd picked up from the printers. Ben's cover was a crude, chiaroscuro drawing that ran from front to back. It showed a man in a business suit chained to a rock, a grotesque bird tearing at the flesh of his side. On the rock below him a wing-footed skinhead spraypainted 'Prometheus Downbound' and 'Throw a FIT'. On the inside of the program were two densely-typed pages of Max's manifesto, punctuated by numerous exclamation marks and bold-faced words. There was no mention of their names.

Matthew repacked the parcel and again looked around the car for the two men who had been following him since he left the printers. One, a tall, muscular white man with tinted glasses, had twice tugged Matthew's sleeve while the second, a short-limbed black man, had muttered, 'Yo'. Matthew had stopped the first time, but they didn't speak to him, only smiled expectantly. The second time Matthew had jerked away from them and descended into the subway.

He didn't see them. The car had thinned out now, most of the commuters having switched to a suburban line. The remaining occupants were mostly black women with head-shrouding scarves, stuffed plastic bags and wild children, or long-haired men in army jackets and tennis shoes who bobbed their heads to the sounds of earphones.

A bland voice from the intercom announced Matthew's stop. He walked to the door and stood, legs wide, as the train pulled into the station. He felt his weight shift back and forth like a small tide. There was momentary hesitation after the car stopped, then the doors parted with a sigh.

They caught up with him a half-block from the station exit. There were no words, just strong hands maneuvering him into an alley. They stood him up against a crumbling wall. Matthew clutched the parcels to his chest. The black man moved close.

'I thaid yo. Didn't you hear me?'

Matthew nodded.

'Well then you're one wily motherfucker.'

Matthew said nothing.

'Now, I believe you have thomthing for us.'

'I don't understand,' Matthew said, his mouth sticky with dry mucus.

'I don't underthtand,' the black man said in a mocking voice.

'I don't.'

'Don't say that, Doctor Kildare. Just, don't say that.'

So Matthew said nothing, looking at the tall white man. He wore a leather weightlifter's belt over sweatpants and a T-shirt that said 'Who Dares Wins'. He seemed impervious to the cold. His tinted glasses darkened as the sun came out from behind a cloud.

'Now, as I said, I believe you have something for us?'

There was a reedy whistling noise from the entrance to the alley. A young boy dressed in a toy Indian headdress stared at them, blowing rhythmically into a hotdog-shaped whistle.

'Go,' the black man ordered. The boy walked away, still tooting.

'Money?' Matthew asked. 'Do you want money?'

'No, man, *you* want money. We want a package of goodieth.'

'I don't know you,' Matthew said. 'I don't have anything for you.'

The black man shook his head and smiled, gazing at the wall beside Matthew's head.

'You see,' he said, his face hazing over in soliloquy. 'You see, thum people, man. They always be fuckin' wit chou. Thum people just always, just always be that way. And you doctor thkool motherfuckers are the worst. It's like we do a deal and we do our thing but then it's like you don't even wanna know about it. It's like it never even happened. I mean, you're telling me you don't even like know me or nothing. I can't believe you even thaid that given our predictamint we have now. I can't even believe that. Yo Dennis, do you believe that?'

Dennis punched Matthew in the face, causing his head to bounce off the wall.

'Hey,' Matthew said.

'Hey,' the black man mocked, taking the parcels from Matthew and tearing them open.

Dennis spun Matthew around, steadied him, then punched him in the back of the head. Matthew felt a shift in his nose as it hit the wall. He tasted warm blood and realized he was sitting on the ground, a piece of brick irritating the bottom of his thigh. For no reason, he counted backwards from ten. He then began to collect the parcels, which had been torn and dropped on the ground. Dennis and the black man had gone, yet there was a shuffling wheeze behind him. Matthew turned slowly, careful to keep his head tilted back. The little boy with the headdress stood just a few feet away. He stared blankly at Matthew, the hotdog whistle sounding between his lips.

He walked unsteadily to the apartment, bunging up his nostrils with his thumb and forefinger. He swallowed a lot of blood. It was nauseating at first, but the warm liquid gradually calmed him. He managed to keep the programs from being soiled.

Ben was in his room, printing posters. He had set up a small, hand-rolled press on which he printed black and white posters using the same design as the program cover. At the bottom the time and place of the performance were written in letters that sprouted roots, arms, penises, weapons. Hundreds of the posters were hung to dry over a web of ropes running throughout the room. Ben's hands, arms, neck and ripped T-shirt were smudged black with ink. Blink lay at his feet, also stained.

'I gah the stuh,' Matthew said, his nose still closed.

Ben looked up.

'What happened?' he asked.

'I gah my az kid,' Matthew said.

'Really?'

'Some guys thaw I was my brolla.'

Ben gently removed Matthew's hand from his nose and examined it.

'It's not broken,' he said. 'Wait here.'

Ben returned to his machine and removed the lithograph plate. He moved quickly to the kitchen. Matthew heard running water, the sound of scrubbing. Blink came and sat before him, placing a paw on Matthew's thigh, wanting to play. Ben returned and affixed the dripping clean lithograph to the roller.

'Come here,' he said, directing Matthew to the printer. 'Now, could you bleed on this plate for a minute?'

'Wuh?'

'Just let the blood run on it. Just for a minute.'

Matthew leaned over the press. The blood trickled freely into the plate's many grooves.

'You can use this,' Ben said, handing him a wad of cotton. Matthew daubed his nose, then coated the plate. Ben fed a piece of paper through the machine.

'Good,' he said, holding the fresh poster up for Matthew to see. 'Good.'

Max squinted up at the booth as the sound and light died out.

'Perfect. Fucking perfect.'

Matthew looked down at him from the shadows, his heart racing with the power of Max's performance. The words are no longer mine, he thought. They're his now.

Max leapt from the stage and began slipping into his clothes. Ben looked up from his drawing, smiling.

'It's tight. Those cues are on, on, on. Those pinheads at the festival are dead in the water. Oh yes. We're tight.'

He shielded his eyes and looked up at the booth.

'Come on down, Merriweather. Let's get some food and beverage.'

Matthew closed down the rattling board, careful not to touch metal, having burned himself several times during rehearsals. He raced down the steps.

'Yeah,' Max was saying. 'It will be a very interesting show.'

Pompeii Pizza was closed. Max leaned forward, hands in pockets, feet stamping at the cold as he read aloud the Public Health notice taped to the door. Inside, they could see men in masks and hooded caps spraying beneath the booths and ovens.

'I know a place where we can go,' Max said, plunging on.

It was the coldest night of the year. Steam came from everywhere – mouths, exhausts, fresh turds, sidewalk grills. The few people they saw had their faces wrapped with scarves or held gloved hands to their mouths. The sky was close, yet it hadn't snowed.

They passed through the business and government district, abandoned except for furtive cabs and the tattered people who tried to warm themselves in the clouds of Federal steam that came from the large periscope vents. It seemed to Matthew that their arms and legs beckoned him into the swirling heat.

'The thing about theater,' Max said, stepping up between Matthew

143

and Ben, 'is that it's impossible. I mean the idea that there is this thing where there are people on a stage doing something and people in the audience checking it out is absurd. Maybe a few hundred years ago, but not now. People are too emotionally dead. Numb. Their fucking imaginations have been caved in by movies and television and all that shit. No, it's impossible.'

'So what is it we're doing?' Matthew asked.

'Something different. We're going to present the people who have the misfortune to see our show with a different scenario altogether. That's why there are no actors, no credits. Actors are unnecessary. We're going to be so good and so tight and so anonymous that they're going to find themselves smack dab in the middle of some very unholy shit. They're going to pay for being at this show.'

'I don't see where that happens in the script,' Matthew said.

'Yeah, well, Merriweather, you incredible asshole, the script might suffer a mutation or two as the situation warrants.'

'Such as?'

'Such as you'll see.'

'Hey Max, who wrote the fucking thing?'

Max stopped so abruptly that he slid a few feet on the icy pavement. Matthew also stopped and faced him. Ben stood a few feet off, discreetly between them.

'Why, you did, Matt,' Max said with false sweetness.

'Yeah, well, that's right,' Matthew said, averting his eyes.

There was a long silence.

'Say it,' Max said coldly.

'All right,' Matthew said, looking at him now. 'I know you asked me to write it and Ben gave me the idea, but there are some things in there which are mine. There are some things there I have to say. Which are important. Real, maybe.'

'Yes, I thought I whiffed the stink of self-expression there,' Max said. 'But I've just about cleaned all that up.'

'Leaving what?' Matthew asked.

'You'll see,' Max said.

He turned to walk away, but Matthew grabbed his arm and jerked him back face-to-face.

'Leaving what?' Matthew repeated.

Max slapped Matthew's arm away and Ben moved closer. Max then pulled up his hands and smiled.

'Matthew, there's something you don't understand. You're just the builder here. All you've done is given me a frame on which I'll hang my madness. I've stolen whatever you put into that script that's precious. So don't fuck with this, or you'll be the enemy like everyone else.'

'Let's go,' Ben said. 'It's cold.'

They approached a brightly lit intersection, crowded with service vehicles and scurrying workmen. A portable generator chugged in the middle of the road, feeding a jackhammer that periodically erupted. As they drew closer they could see the problem; a water main had burst, spewing gushes of water that froze upon reaching the night air. Both gutters were clogged with foot-thick glaciers. The hammer operator had opened a segment of the street, and several men in orange helmets descended into the hole. Water had splashed on them all, causing glistening drops of ice to form on their clothes, on their hair and faces.

The restaurant was called The Nile. It was at the end of a small, unlit street dominated by the backs of windowless government buildings.

They stepped through a foyer of cane furniture and pictures. There were several watercolor portraits of a sharp-eyed black man with a twisted moustache, as well as a photograph of a barefooted runner racing along cobblestone streets. They passed through a door of beads into a dimly lit dining room, with several low circular tables in the middle and smaller booths along the walls. It was about half full with languid diners, sprawled on pillows or hunched over their booths. At the far end was a small stage where a slight, bald man sat cross-legged, emptying saliva from a long wooden flute.

'There,' Max said, striding toward an empty booth near the back of the restaurant. The wall above the booth was decorated with pictures of saints done in a colorful, Byzantine style. Ben began to scribble reproductions of some of them on the paper table covering, ripping away finished sketches and shoving them in his pockets.

They ordered the standard meal and were brought it quickly, as if they'd been expected. It consisted of a large tray of shredded meat and boiled vegetables, bowls of yogurt and clusters of fresh salad. They ate by ripping hand-sized chunks from a large sheet of rubbery bread and scooping the food with it. It was spicy, so they cooled themselves by eating the yogurt and drinking from a large, labelless bottle of sweet wine. Max explained that when they finished the waitress would measure what they'd drunk and charge them by the inch.

As they ate a woman joined the slight man on stage. It was Eleni.

She wore jeans, a loose white shirt and a bright scarf of several colors. She said something to the old man, who nodded okay and lay the flute on his lap. She looked up at the ceiling and tapped her right index finger rhythmically into her left palm. After four beats she began to sing, unaccompanied.

The tune began as a single vowel, a tremulous 'ah' that she held for fifteen seconds or so. She then began to flutter between octaves, like a bird or insect amid dry buds, changing sometimes after just one or two beats, other times after eight or twelve. Occasionally she would leap abruptly over several octaves, or maintain several beats of songful silence. Yet she never strayed far from that touchstone vowel, that tremulous 'ah' which sounded sometimes like laughter, other times tears. The song ended.

'There,' Max said, pointing at her with a piece of bread. 'That.'

The flautist interrupted the scattered applause with a mad dash of joyous sound. She joined him when the tune was established, singing words now, telling a story in her native tongue.

They played for about a half hour. Max and Ben left during the set to hang posters, figuring no cops would be out on so cold a night. Matthew stayed behind to hear the music, drinking several more inches of wine. The waitress cleared the table and brought him a small carafe of strong coffee and a skull-like censer that burned a stick of incense. It reminded Matthew of the baptisms of distant cousins at the Greek church in Detroit. When the music finished he made his way through the pillows and sprawled diners and incense smoke. She saw him approaching.

'So,' she said, smiling broadly. She stood and kissed him on the cheek. Her skin was damp from the performance. She smelled of spice.

'Hello,' he said, confused by the kiss.

'How is the beast?'

He thought for a moment, then remembered.

'Oh,' Matthew said. 'He's out.'

'Out and about,' she agreed.

They were silent for a moment.

'You sing beautifully,' he said.

She rolled her eyes.

'No, really.'

'Have you eaten?' she asked.

Matthew nodded.

'Do you like the wat?'

'Yes.'

146

'Spicy,' she said, widening her eyes. 'Hot.'

He nodded.

'Eleni,' a stern voice called from the kitchen. 'Bichu.'

'Bichu; what does that mean?' Matthew asked.

'Oh, it's another name some people give to me.'

'What does it mean?'

She stepped from the stage.

'You come back to visit me sometime and you'll know. And you can eat again. I'm always here.'

Matthew nodded as she disappeared through the swinging doors.

The festival was scheduled to open on the weekend before their performance. 'Get FIT' posters were appearing in all the authorized places. Some billboards had gone up, too. Ben pasted over some of the posters and scrawled 'Throw a' over 'Get' on others. He even managed to draw his mural across a billboard that overlooked the access ramp to a commuter highway. But it was impossible to get at them all, and those he did deface were soon replaced by fresh advertising.

After the elation of the first good run-throughs, rehearsal had once again become a maddening grind. Max insisted on unwavering perfection and was continually frustrated by the limits of the light system, of the script, of his own skills. He was constantly badgering Matthew to provide more power, more light. Matthew wanted to rent a more sophisticated board yet Max refused, adamantly, inexplicably.

On the night before FIT was to begin Max had walked from the stage ten minutes into the rehearsal, leaving the theater without explanation. Matthew had closed down the groaning board and followed him, leaving Ben to set up the work on posters.

He found him at Pompeii Pizza, staring at a cup of cooling coffee. Matthew sat across from him.

'What?' Matthew asked.

Max looked at him for a moment, then peered out the window.

'Something's missing.'

'Such as?' Matthew asked.

'I don't know. It's starting to be like a play, like a show. It's starting to be like something that people will come to, see, react to, leave.' He looked up. 'It's starting to be the same old shit. I don't want that. I don't want those pricks to leave the same. I want a part of them to stay.'

'Maybe that's impossible,' Matthew said.

147

'Probably,' Max said. 'I'm starting to think that might be true. Maybe something extra-theatrical is going to have to happen.'

'Such as?' Matthew asked.

Max ignored the question.

'And I guess I'm also pissed off about this FIT thing tomorrow night,' he said. 'I don't think we've been able to mount a sufficient challenge to it.'

'Well,' Matthew said, smiling. 'You'll think of something.'

The massive theater center was a confusion of light. There were hooded lanterns resting in the terraced shrubbery, blue spotlights submerged in the fountains, headlights from the creeping limousines. There were floodlights angled against the tall columns at the front of the building, the wavering flashlights of ushers, dappled reflections from the ice-jammed river behind the theater. Above it all, three skyward beams of light cast radiant ovals on the low ceiling of winter cloud.

Max stopped Matthew while they were across the street from the theater. People were arriving steadily, scurrying up the broad white steps.

'I hate it so fucking much,' Max said hoarsely.

'Yeah,' Matthew said, leading him across the street.

They showed their tickets and entered the large lobby, incongruous in their jeans and leather jackets. It was very warm. Most of the men wore broken-in tuxedos, the women chiffon evening dresses that showed tanned backbones, upper arms, chests. Waiters in white jackets moved about with trays of stemmed glasses and bits of fruit and meat on toothpicks. There were also entertainers: clowns, jugglers, illusionists.

Matthew and Max bought bottles of beer from the wet bar, then took up a position near the tall windows overlooking the river. They said little, just swigging and staring hard. Max pointed out the director of the NEA, Matthew recognized a member of Congress. People close by cast surreptitious glances at them, double-taking Max's scarred face.

A performer in whiteface and a French Navy shirt passed, juggling three rubber balls decorated with stars. Max watched him for a moment, sighing sarcastically. He then reached down and unlaced his high-top sneakers.

'Check this out,' he said, removing his shoes.

He walked up behind the juggler and snatched the three balls from the air, one after the other. Before the performer could protest, Max was juggling them, along with his shoes, their red laces flapping in the air. He tossed them with practised expertise, bouncing balls off his forehead or his instep, tossing a shoe between his legs or behind his back. Nearby spectators watched with tentative admiration. Max finished by tossing his missiles higher and higher, close to the massive chandelier in the center of the lobby. The final ball touched a branch, causing a small crystal drop to fall to the carpet beside a young woman with long black hair. She picked it up without being noticed by her elderly escort and dropped it into her drink.

Max let the shoes fall to the carpet and caught the balls in his right hand. He held them out the boy in whiteface, who took them sheepishly. There was applause from a few nearby guests as he put his shoes back on.

'Learn your craft, douche bag,' Max whispered to the white-faced boy.

There was a commotion at the other end of the lobby. Flashbulbs, laughter, the rustle of expensive fabric.

'Come on,' Max said to Matthew as he shouldered his way through the crowd.

The Boy Wonder was making his entrance. He was wearing the usual kimono jacket over black tie and a ruffled shirt. He seemed pale and small as he nodded his way through the surrounding crowd. Two men in tuxedos walked beside him, also nodding and taking proffered hands. One of them was Sandy Mock, the chairman of UPU. He had come to a cocktail party at the Merriweathers' house once at which Matthew and Eddie had tended bar. He had worn white shoes and drunk rye. Near the end of the party he had tripped over a step, falling backwards into a plant. Matthew remembered the strain on the guests' faces as they tried not to notice.

'I gotta talk to this clown,' Max whispered, trying to beat a path towards the Boy Wonder. Matthew tried to follow but was cut off by the crowd. He found himself standing in front of Mock, whose small gray eyes registered surprise and distaste.

'Hello, Mr Mock,' Matthew said.

'Hello, Edward, is it?'

'Matthew.'

'Yes, of course.'

'So, this is a big night for you,' Matthew said, putting himself in the only avenue of escape. Mock smiled indulgently.

'For all of us,' he said.

'It's a shame my dad couldn't make it.'

Mock frowned and looked away.

'You remember him,' Matthew said. 'Blue eyes. Walks with a bit of a limp.'

'He could have been here, son,' Mock said grimly. 'If he knew how to play ball he could have been a lot of places.'

Mock tried to pass, but Matthew grabbed his arm. He leaned close to his rubbery ear, smelling Brut and starch.

'First of all,' Matthew whispered. 'I'm not your goddamned son. And secondly, my father is a fine ballplayer, you flab-ass motherfucker. He taught me everything I know.'

Mock looked at him.

'Yes, I can see that. Now let go of my arm.'

Matthew let him pass. He found Max, who had just finished talking to a shaken-looking Boy Wonder.

'What'd you say?' Matthew asked as they edged towards the balcony stairs.

Max tweaked the nose of the bronzed bust of the building's namesake.

'I invited him to come see our show.'

They had the worst seats in the house. Last row, left corner. Nearly one third of the stage was obstructed for them by an overhanging bank of lights. Matthew felt several seconds of strong vertigo as he stared at the curtain and the stalls, but soon became accustomed to the height.

Dimming lights quieted the crowd. There was about a minute of recorded music, an eight note crescendo of strings, played over and over. The curtain slowly parted. At center stage was the summit of a mountain, about thirty feet high. On an abutment near its top stood a man dressed in loincloths. He was bolted to the rock by thick chains. To the left of the mountain top a hot air balloon rested on stage, nearly fifty feet high. It was decorated with a brilliant blue unicorn. Inside its basket stood two characters in classical military garb, a third in the uniform of a Marine Colonel. They performed a repetitive mime of bolting the man on the mountain to the rock. To the right of the mountain was a thirty-foot-high video screen which displayed random images and words. At the front of the stage, surrounded by the fluff of an imaginary cloud, was a long bowling lane, running crossways. Two tall men in white robes and full, godly beards stood at one end, rolling black balls towards a group of midgets who stood in tenpin position. They would topple when the ball reached them, resetting themselves after several seconds. The Boy Wonder walked the stage, a walkie-talkie in hand. He stopped occasionally to reposition actors or encourage them to move in a different way.

'Jesus,' Max whispered disgustedly.

The play began. Actors spoke their lines in loud, mid-Atlantic accents. They repeated each line, and there was a long pause between them. They moved occasionally in jerky, repetitive motions, like athletes warming up for a competition. The large screen also repeated some of the lines, often in several languages or phonetic configurations. Sometimes swells of the crescendo loop would come through the banks of speakers, drowning out the actors.

Matthew began to look around the theater. The audience were soon fidgeting and shuffling. One man in the stalls leaned forward until his head was almost in his lap. Matthew thought he was sick but then realized he was slipping on earphones to a small tape player. Matthew closed his eyes, but was soon startled by a voice above him.

'Your words declare you mad, and mad indeed!'

He looked up. It was Max, standing on the arms of his chair. His head almost scraped the roof.

'No one could bear you in success!'

There were murmurs and hushing sounds from the stalls. The people around them leaned instinctively away. The actor on the cliff had lost the thread of his dialogue and was gesturing for a cue from one of the men in the balloon. The Boy Wonder looked up, holding his walkie-talkie to his ear.

'But you have not yet learned a wise discretion!' Max continued in a hoarse cry that rattled around the theater.

The Boy Wonder was speaking into the walkie-talkie now. Matthew heard rapid footsteps and could see ushers pointing up from the aisles below. Some were aiming flashlights at them.

'You are far too strong and confident in your weak cleverness,' Max screamed. 'For obstinacy standing alone is the weakest of all things in one whose mind is not possessed by wisdom. Think what a storm, what a triple wave of ruin will rise against you, if you will not hear me, and no escape for you!'

The ushers reached them. Max shoved the first one away, faked out the two others as he leapt over the back of his chair and bolted through a fire exit. Matthew could hear his swift feet rattling on the fire escape. The ushers didn't pursue. They looked at Matthew, who shrugged and smiled.

*

Matthew was the first to arrive for dress rehearsal. They were to open the following evening. Twenty-four tickets had been sold in advance. Max wanted to have the final run-through starting at noon so they would have all night and the next day to make changes or iron out any slow points. Matthew went upstairs and readied the booth, turning on the board to give it sufficient time to warm up. Noon passed and no one arrived. He went back into the main hall to wait.

He looked at the simple set. A desk, a chair, the phones. A large sheet of paper covered the back wall for Ben's mural, to be painted while the show was in progress. He would do a portrait of the audience as they watched the play, an evolving mirror behind the stage.

Matthew sat on the steps, relaxing before the final burst of energy. It had been a good month. Hard, focused, without the usual division of time and boredom. He knew the play would be poorly attended, yet he didn't care. To have worked like this was what mattered. To have done something. He looked up at the quilt of wires running through the ceiling. Even this mess. Especially this mess.

In the past few days, however, Matthew had become worried by Max. He had been distracted, subdued, running through the show with only a fraction of the power of those first rehearsals. He was preoccupied with the sound and light system, worried it would be too weak for his purposes. He seemed to have something planned that he wouldn't share with Matthew and Ben.

Matthew heard a noise and looked up. Mrs Bevaqua had stolen into the hall, armed with her earthen mug.

'Hello,' she said meekly.

Matthew smiled and walked up to her. She smelled of woodsmoke and ink.

'All ready for tomorrow?' she asked.

'As ready as one can be for this sort of thing.'

She nodded for a moment.

'Is . . . *he* here?' she asked.

'No, but he should be soon.'

She looked nervously over her shoulder.

'The reason I ask is because of this.'

She handed Matthew a piece of pink paper.

'This is from the fire inspector. He has to come here and look at everything before you can give a play or performance or whatever. I've told Mr Cvenovich about this several times and he assured me it was taken care of, that you knew all about this. He even said the men had already been here to look it over. Yet now I get this delivered and what's more – '

'We'll handle it,' Matthew said gently.

She looked sceptical, but walked away without further discussion. Matthew read the slip over several times, nervously folding and refolding its edges.

Max arrived fifteen minutes later, breathing heavily, his eyes troubled. Matthew held up the pink paper.

'Max, listen – '

'Is he here?' Max asked, ignoring him. 'He's not here, is he. Have you seen him at all? Damn.'

'Who?'

'Ben. He's gone. Split. I was supposed to meet him at six a.m. at DuPont Circle for some heavy duty postering but he didn't show. I've been back to the flat but he wasn't there.'

Ben had set off after the previous night's rehearsals with a bucket of paste, a brush, a ladder and five hundred posters.

'What do we do?'

'Find him.'

They walked to the door.

'Let me see that paper,' Max said. He took it from Matthew and read it over. A small smile wrinkled his face.

'Good,' he said, balling the paper and tossing it into the gutter. It bounced twice and fell between the grates of a sewer covering. 'Good.'

It took them nearly an hour to locate Ben's trail, at the bottom of a north-bound avenue. The first poster was tacked to an ice-shrouded tree. The next, about fifty yards away, was posted to the cage door of a parking garage. The third was upside down on a phone booth. The fourth was on the hood of a clamped Mercedes.

'Uh oh,' Matthew said.

'He's heading north,' Max said.

They followed Ben's path. The posters were affixed at fifty yard intervals, to whatever surface happened to be available. Matthew and Max followed the trail through the business district, past expensive condos and clothes shops, into the embassy district. They stopped in front of an embassy where a demonstration was just getting started. About two dozen young men with buttoned-up collars and three days' worth of stubble stood chanting, hemmed in by a line of motorcycle police in orange vests and white helmets. Some of the protestors were carrying placards with angry slogans and the picture of a turbaned old man, yet most were empty handed. Max nudged Matthew, gesturing to the place on the sidewalk where two men tried to tear Ben's poster from the faces of several dozen unused banners and placards.

They crossed a frozen bridge, whose guardian buffalo statues had been plastered with their posters. The trail led them to the zoo, where the posters littered trees, paths, cages. In the primate house, a bearded monkey patiently fed the remnants of one to her offspring. They moved out of the zoo and into the tree-lined streets of a suburban neighborhood, where the posters vied for attention with advertisements for garage sales and notices asking for help in finding lost pets. Then they entered a stretch of churches and religious centers of all denominations. They came upon a Buddhist temple, where two monks in orange robes and down jackets examined one of Ben's posters on their corrugated gate. Max approached them.

'Did you see the guy who did this?' he asked.

The monks blinked serenely.

'Yes,' said the first.

'And no,' said the second.

Max turned to Matthew.

'These guys,' he said, gesturing to the monks with his thumb.

'Which is it?' Matthew asked.

'Both.'

'And neither.'

'Like, threats of physical violence and so forth wouldn't induce you guys to be more specific, right?' Max asked.

They continued to blink serenely.

'No, I didn't think so.' He turned to Matthew. 'Let's go.'

The first one stopped them with a gesture while the second reached into a small cloth purse.

'Take these,' he said, handing them two lengths of saffron string. 'It will help bring luck to your journey.'

About a half a mile north of the temple they found Blink sitting and shivering in a field by the access ramp to the Beltway. They saw a poster partially affixed to a large green electrical transformer, several more torn and trampled on the ground beneath it. There were many footprints in an erratic pattern on the ground surrounding the transformer. There was nothing else around except for a small shed at the beginning of the access ramp in which a woman sat with hundreds of plastic-wrapped bouquets of roses that she waited to sell to people caught in rush hour traffic. Traffic moved freely by her now, so she sat locked in the shed, staring at Matthew and Max. They approached her, kicking aside small garbage. Blink stayed by the generator. She eyed them blandly, a fat woman with small eyes and dirty brown hair who took rapid sips from a small bottle of liquor. When they reached the shed she opened a small window.

'Hello boys. Want some roses?'

'How much?' Max asked.

'Two bucks.'

Max nodded to Matthew, who paid her and took the frozen stems. He noticed a handpainted sign on the wall behind her. 'If Life Were Simple, We'd All Die in Graveyards'.

'That's a hell of a burn you got on your face, crispy,' she said.

'Yeah, I know,' Max said.

'You want some schnapps to warm your bones?' she asked. 'Cold as a witch's tit out there.'

'In a brass bra,' Max said, taking the bottle. The woman wheezed her appreciation. He took a pull then passed it back to Matthew. 'Actually, I was hoping if you could tell me if you saw the dude who was with that shepherd there?'

'Paper hanger? Big tall drink of water? Sure did.'

'Could you tell us where he went?'

'Down,' she said, holding her wrists together. 'Cold busted.'

'Oh shit,' Matthew said.

'What happened?'

'Fucking Park Police is what happened. And how. They jumped his bones when he was putting that picture there up. Tried to take his posters away. He just stood there, like he was a statue, holding those posters like you'd hold a baby. They couldn't budge that boy. Ho no. So they started to get hinky, play a little rough. Went upside his head. Bip. That's when your friend laid one of them out. Cold cocked that screw, right up the ass. So the other three go after him with their flashlights. Still took 'em about two minutes to get the cuffs on. The dog tried to intervene but he got one across the chops too. This all happened a couple hours ago. I tried to get the dog in here to warm him up but he don't want to budge.'

Max looked at the frozen ground.

'Okay. Thanks.'

'Hey crispy,' she called after them. 'How'd you get them burns anyways?'

'Playing with matches,' Max said.

'Ain't supposed to do that,' she said, slamming the window against the cold.

They sat at Pompeii Pizza, playing with their saffron strings. Two cups of coffee filled the air between them with cataracts of sour vapor. The restaurant had emptied of its dinner crowd, leaving Max and Matthew alone with the drunks, who played backgammon or talked to themselves.

They had been to the police station, but were informed that Ben wouldn't be arraigned until the following morning. The bail was high, since he would be charged with assaulting an officer as well as trespassing and illegal posting. They asked if they could see him but the sergeant had said not until after he was charged.

They had left Blink behind at the intersection. He wouldn't heed their commands and snapped at them when they tried to use force. Finally the rose woman waddled out of her booth and said if they gave her twenty dollars for food she'd look after him until Ben got out. She could use the protection, she said.

Matthew looked at a passing salt truck.

'What are we going to do about Ben?' he asked.

Max looked up sharply.

'Nothing.'

'Come on, Max. This is serious.'

Max drummed the table.

'What do you propose we do?'

'I don't know,' Matthew said. 'Go back to the station. Go to the arraignment.'

'Why?'

'Just to be there. Let him know about Blink.'

'Listen, Matthew, forget it. There's nothing we can do now. He's gone. He hit a cop. He's had it.' He swirled the coffee in his cup for a moment. 'The thing about Ben is he was either gonna get fucked or he was gonna get famous. Unfortunately it turned out to be the former. And besides, we got a show to do.'

'You're a hard man, Max.'

'Fuckin' right. And so are you.'

Matthew shook his head.

'So what do we do? Go rehearse?'

'Not right yet,' Max said. 'There's something we gotta see first.'

There was different light on the festival theater tonight – three large searchlights shining directly on the front of the building. The lights inside the theater were out, as were the small lights in the surrounding shrubbery and fountains. There was also no light from the street, which had been closed off. Even the reflections from the icy river seemed less brilliant.

The crowd spilled out from the front courtyard into the street. There were several hundred of them, bundled and wrapped against the chill. They seemed less elegant than the crowd on the opening night, younger. A few even warmed themselves around informal bonfires started in Keep Our City Tidy cans. Policemen on robed horses patrolled the perimeters.

Max and Matthew took a position at the back of the crowd. They hadn't spoken since leaving Pompeii Pizza. Matthew felt cold and exhausted. He hoped the performance would be brief. Max showed him his watch.

'I bet these guys start on time,' he said grimly.

Two minutes later the dancers appeared on the roof of the theater. Short, muscular Japanese men dressed in white loincloths. Their heads were shaved and their bodies coated with white chalk. They stood at attention for a moment on the edge of the roof as the crowd quieted. A few people gasped when they noticed them.

There was a short interval of distant music – a low drum, a flute. Then the men crouched and slowly began to crawl over the edge of the roof. Their backs arched as they raised their heads like worms at the end of a table. In perfect unison, they moved into tight foetal crouches and began their slow descent, anchored to the roof only by a thick cord around the right ankle.

They moved slowly, never swaying. Every few feet there was some small gesture of release from their crouch, turning the neck, slightly straightening the leg, spreading the fingers. They moved in perfect unison. Matthew noticed there were no clouds of breath coming from them. The crowd watched in enraptured silence. A videocam hummed somewhere.

When the dancers were about a quarter of the way down, the rope holding the man furthest to the right jerked a little, lowering him a few feet below the others. He coiled back into his foetal crouch, swaying a little. There was a frightened rustling in the crowd. Then the rope snapped. The man dropped quickly, soundlessly to the ground. There was a thud, a loud sigh.

The crowd was silent for a moment. The people began to gasp. Some stood on their toes to see better, others walked quickly away. Doors slammed as men in suits and uniforms poured from within the theater lobby. A policeman on a horse trotted across the street.

'Look,' Max said, pointing up at the remaining three dancers, who were being slowly raised back to the roof. They held on to the ropes above them with one hand, looking over their shoulder at the scene below.

Without thinking, Matthew began to move towards the front of the theater. The crowd moved against him. Some people were crying, others shaking their heads. He soon broke clear and made his way quickly across the terraces. The performer was surrounded by a small crowd of police, photographers and men in suits. Two paramedics knelt over him. One pushed his palms rhythmically into the chalky skin on his chest. Matthew moved to a position where he could see.

The dancer's hands were still balled, like an infant. He lay on his back, his knees drawn up in the air. Everything looked normal, except for the bad angle of his head, staring into the pavement. There was a mass of bone under his right ear, like a cue ball. No blood.

The paramedic stopped massaging his chest. His colleague gently lifted the man's torso from the pavement and moved his head back to a normal position. Matthew saw his face, contracted into the shriek he had not allowed himself to utter. The second paramedic pried open his hands. His fingernails were long, perhaps three inches. They had been painted garish red.

Matthew was aware of Max standing next to him, staring at the corpse. Sirens approached, a helicopter hovered above.

'Let's go,' Matthew said quietly.

The meeting hall was dark, except for the red Exit signs and the wedge of light from the lobby. About twenty people had entered by the time a small woman holding an earthen mug reluctantly shut the door. Some of the audience sat uneasily on a haphazard array of folding chairs, the rest stood near the walls. There were several couples in bluejeans and sweaters; a few black-clad young men with irritated hairstyles; a pasty journalist with a notepad-stuffed denim sportscoat; a group of college girls who looked like they wanted to leave. A pale man who wore a bright kimono over a white jumpsuit stood at the back of the hall. He was accompanied by a fat man with red sneakers and a hawk-eyed woman who wore a leopard-skin blouse.

On stage, a phone was ringing. It had begun to ring before the doors were opened and continued until they were closed. A small spotlight then came up on the answering machine on the desk. After several more rings there was a shriek, followed by a recorded voice.

'Hello. This is Prometheus. I'm tied up at the moment, but if you'd care to leave a message, just wait for the signal . . .'

'Dad, it's me . . .'

There was a click, followed by a dial tone. It sounded for several seconds, then gradually gave way to a live human voice in the exact same key, making the same dead-toned wail. A spotlight came up on its source – a man with his head buried in his hands. He sat behind a desk littered with a dozen phones.

After about thirty seconds he stopped abruptly and walked to the front of the desk. He wore a blue suit and red tie. His face was badly scarred with burn tissue. There was a mechanical groan from the lights above as they brightened.

'Anybody gotta light?' he asked.

There was a long silence. Finally, one of the sallow, black-clad young men in the audience tossed him a box of matches. The man on stage struck one alight and held it close to his face, staring at the flame.

'I just lost my job. Senior veep at U.S. Fire. Just like that, after twenty-seven years with the firm. Started out as apprentice stoker, clawed my way up the ladder. Paid all the right dues; boring meetings, long trips, knives in appropriate backs. I've got the scars to show for it, too. See? And yet now I've been canned. Accused of divulging our secret formula . . .'

The match burned down to his fingertips and sizzled out.

'The funny thing is, it's true. I did it. I gave it away.'

He closed his eyes and inhaled the thick smoke.

'What happened is this. I was approached last year by an anonymous source representing a certain special interest group on whom hard times had fallen. They were cold, hungry, without shelter. Living in crates, living on government cheese. You know the type. This person showed slides, he told stories. If they could only get their frostbitten hands on a bit of the secret formula, he said, they'd be able to pull themselves up by their bootstraps. He also said there would be a nifty retainer in it for me, but I just shrugged that off. I've got money. It wasn't even my conscience that made me do it in the end, although I did pity those poor schmucks. No, there was something else involved. A certain . . . giddiness. A certain defiance. I could break the fire monopoly! I became drunk with the idea of a world in flames. After all those years of slaving for the company, a chance to feel . . . what? Manly. Alive. Free? Free. If that's so, then the joke's on me. Listen.'

He turned to the desk and rewound the answering machine. There was a confusion of shrill, backward voices. When it reached the beginning he pressed 'play'.

'Prometheus? Listen you fool. This is the chairman. We've caught you cold, asshole. Dead to rights. You can't rip off the organization. You can't steal the secret formula. What made you think you could outwit us? It was just a matter of time until we caught you red-handed. As soon as we noticed some embers missing we had you followed, dirtbag. We had everybody followed. We began to notice some discrepancies in your behaviour. Small mistakes, moodiness, woolgathering. Then we saw you make the drop in the dumpster, the briefcase with two smouldering coals. Your buddy got away, but we have you. You're fired, pal. Eighty-sixed. No pension, no nothing. Clean out your desk and hit the pavement.'

There was the click of a phone hanging up, followed by the loud dial tone. The man on stage again began his plaintive moan. The lights increased into a blinding brilliance and there were louder moans in the ceiling. Some of the people in the audience looked up, shielding their eyes. The man stopped his wail.

'You don't know what it's like, do you? To work and sweat and strain, only to find in the end that all you've done is forge your own chains. To come to a point where everything you've done and created is only an image of your slavery . . .'

He bent forward, toward the audience.

'Come a little closer and I'll tell you a secret . . .'

A few of the nearest people leaned forward. The man quickly put the match to his lips and spat a long sheet of flame just over their heads. A few ducked, everyone moved back. The black-clad boy patted the top of his head, then looked at his hand, sniffed it. A few people were muttering indignantly. Someone at the back of the hall left in a hurry.

The phone rang and the lights dimmed. The man stared at it for several seconds, then answered it.

'Hello . . . Oh, hello honey, I was just thinking about you . . . What? Who told you? . . . Oh, . . . Yes, yes . . . Yes . . . I don't know . . . I said I don't know . . . Yes, that's true . . . No, I mean yes . . . There's no answer to that question . . . Nor to that . . . I don't know . . . all right . . . No, I know, I know . . . All right . . .'

He went to hang up the phone but noticed that the cord had entangled his wrist. He tried for a moment to extricate himself but was unable. The phone began to beep a warning signal, the lights began to pulse brighter. There was a popping noise somewhere in the ceiling. A recorded voice came on.

'Please hang up the phone. Please hang up the phone. Please hang up the phone.'

He smashed the phone on the desk until the beeping and the warning stopped. Splinters of plastic showered some of the people in the front of the audience, and everybody moved back a few more steps. The man on stage still couldn't free his hand. The lights dimmed.

'This is unfortunate,' he said, examining the binding cord. 'The incendiary devices will be going off soon, according to plan. In the basement boiler room. No one will notice them at first. Just a slight increase in temperature. A little smoke. By the time the alarm is sounded it will be too late. The top three hundred floors will be trapped. No ladder can reach them. The flames will beat away the helicopters. We'll all be trapped. Damn.'

Another phone rang. The man stared at it. At the back of the theater a door opened and the small woman with her earthen mug led in two large men. The first had thick sideburns and wore a creased white trenchcoat. The second wore a trim blue uniform and carried a walkie-talkie. The woman whispered to them but they ignored her, looking at the ceiling.

The man on stage answered the phone with his free hand.

'Hello? Who? No, no . . . There's no one here by that name. You have a wrong number.'

He tried to hang up the phone, yet found his left wrist now entwined. The phone's warning began to sound, the lights began to flash. The man in the trenchcoat pointed to several areas of the ceiling, twisting his hand in explanation as he whispered to the uniformed man, who nodded and began to weave his way towards the stage.

'But perhaps it's better this way. Yes. I can go up in the flames with all of you. A martyr. What better freedom? What better . . .'

'By order of the fire marshal . . .' the uniformed man said.

'There will be a fire,' the man on stage said.

The uniformed man looked confused for a moment.

'By order of the fire marshal you shall cease . . .'

161

'You can't stop it,' the man on stage said softly. 'With all your men and equipment. It's too late. You can't contain it. The spark is loose. The conflagration inevitable. My dream of a world in flames shall . . .'

'Listen, young man.'

'Why inevitable?' the man in the kimono asked from the back of the theater.

'You know why, Mr Chairman. You've tried to keep it secret for too long. But it's out now. I've broken the monopoly on fire. It will no longer be a weapon of the privileged and the priests. What I've done will allow every drooling rapist to light a path to your daughter's door, every two-bit arsonist to torch your factories, all the counterfeiters to ply their trade by the midnight oil. It's too late. It has already begun. Here. Tonight. This place will be the first to burn.'

'It most certainly will not,' the small woman said.

'And you?' the man in the kimono asked.

'I will be the martyr. The one who brought you fire.'

'Okay, friend,' the uniformed man said. 'Show's over. Let's . . .'

'Lights!' the man on stage yelled.

The uniformed man turned around.

'No, don't . . .'

All the lights flashed on. The audience shielded their eyes. The man in the kimono nodded his head in appreciation as the man on stage spread his bound limbs.

There was an explosive sound in the ceiling and the lights went out. Sparks showered the audience as one end of a large cable that dissected the ceiling came loose and swung through them. It hit the back wall and swung towards the stage. Its erratic light showed the man on stage extricating himself from his bonds. His radiant, wild eyes were fixed on the dancing cord. He stepped to the edge of the stage, waiting for it to swing back to him.

'Don't do that . . .' the uniformed man said.

Max leapt.

The streets were covered with ice from an earlier freezing rain. Salt-spreading trucks passed Matthew as he walked, their flashing yellow lights tossing his shadow around the walls and trees. They moved away with the sound of rattling chains.

He had been walking for over two hours, stopping only to pick icicles from gutter spouts or street signs, holding them tight in his right hand until they melted. When he had flipped the main switch there was a great surge in the board, throwing him from his feet and badly burning his hand. He had run with the pain after leaving the theater, his hand pressed tightly to his chest. Gradually the sharp throbbing had receded until now, a dozen icicles later, it was only a dull ache.

He was cold and tired, yet did not know where to go. His first impulse had been to flee to the apartment, but he thought Mrs Bevaqua might have that address. He'd considered hitching up to Advance, but Beth would be at her father's and he didn't want to see her. He didn't even consider going home. So he wandered.

The final scene at the theater flashed through his mind again. The man in the uniform taming the dancing cable with a wooden chair. The young man patting out the spark that glowed in Mrs Bevaqua's hair. Max, seated dejectedly on the floor, nursing a twisted ankle as the man in the trenchcoat stood over him writing on a drooping pad. The cord had surged away from him at the last moment. And the Boy Wonder, standing near the door that Matthew crept through unnoticed, whispering to the fat man in red sneakers, 'He almost did it, he almost did.'

Matthew soon found himself in the restaurant district. It was quiet due to the storm. No idling cabs, no clots of indecisive couples, no corridors of heated air and laughter. Most of the restaurants were locked down, their cage doors or levered shutters glistening with ice. The all-night bagel shop was empty except for two K-9 policemen and a pink-vested waitress doing her nails.

The door to the Nile gave before Matthew's push. The dining room was empty except for a thin, dreadlocked waiter who was winding a cord around a vacuum cleaner. He looked up at Matthew, smiling, shaking his head.

'Closed,' he said with a fatalistic spread of his fingers.

'I'm looking for Eleni.'

He turned to the kitchen.

'Bichu!'

She emerged a moment later, her arms crossed in front of her. When she saw Matthew she smiled and wagged her finger, but then a serious expression came to her face.

'Are you all right?'

'Yes,' Matthew said. 'Well, sort of.'

'Are you sure? You're very pale.'

Matthew held out his hand.

'I managed to burn myself. Maybe that's why.'

She examined the bubbled, blood-crusted flesh without flinching.

She turned and spoke in dialect to the waiter, who went into the kitchen.

'And how did you do this?' she asked as they sat at the table.

'Doing childish things.' He looked at the burn. 'It happened when someone stole something from me.'

'That happens,' she said, shaking her head gently. The waiter returned with a stack of steaming towels. They smelled of lemon.

'Are you hungry?' she asked, daubing the edges of his wound with a towel.

Matthew nodded and she again spoke to the waiter, who returned to the kitchen.

'So are you through with your childish things?' she asked.

'I hope . . .'

She took a new towel.

'It will sting,' she said. 'But it's what the burn wants.'

She wrapped his hand. He closed his eyes against the pain. After a few seconds it began to soothe. The waiter returned with a wooden tray with the meal. Pasty meat, raw vegetables and mounds of yogurt, all arranged on a sheet of bread. A can of Crucial Brew beer rested to one side. Matthew reached for the food with his unburnt hand, but she stopped him.

'You don't eat with the wrong hand,' she said, gathering meat in a patch of torn bread.

Matthew let her place the food in his mouth.

'Well, how is it?' she asked.

Matthew swallowed and fanned his mouth.

'Hot,' he said.

'And the hand?'

'Cool.'

She nodded.

'So.'

THE HEADHUNTER

The sign said 'Walter Merrywhether'. It was held at a slight downward angle by a short, muscular black man who wore a driver's cap tilted back on his head. He stroked his thin goatee as he blandly watched the off-loading passengers, smiling at any woman who caught his eye. Walter made his way towards him, weaving through stewardesses tugging wheeled suitcases, children with their arms outstretched, fat men who draped garment bags over their shoulders like togas.

'That's me,' he said, nodding toward the sign.

The driver looked Walter up and down.

'You got bags?'

'Just this,' Walter said, tapping the shoulder bag beneath his arm. 'I'm travelling light these days.'

'Heard that,' the driver said, cracking the cardboard sign and depositing it in a sand-filled ashtray. He silently led Walter down the carpeted concourse, beneath a large sign that read 'Welcome to Sky Harbor'. Walter looked around. Men in cowboy hats laughed loudly as they emerged from the bathrooms, hitching up their pants. Mexican women sold flowers from air-conditioned carts. Police chewed toothpicks, ignoring whoever spoke to them. Children squealed as they raced around deserted insurance booths. An airport is an airport is an airport, Walter thought.

The stretch limo was parked in the taxi lane, a front wheel lodged on the curb like an elbow on a bar. As the driver fumbled with the keys, Walter looked at himself in the tinted glass. He was pale and tired from the all night mail-run. I have to stop all this travelling, he thought. He shielded his eyes and looked up at the cloudless sky. Although it was still early morning, the sun shone brilliantly, whiting out the atmosphere like a flashbulb. The driver finally opened the door, revealing two opposing seats with a small table in between. There was a phone, an ice bucket and a small television. Walter hesitated.

'Could I possibly sit up front? With you?'

The driver smiled, his eyes meeting Walter's for the first time.
'Definitely,' he said. 'My name's Lewis.'

There was no beltway, so they had to drive through speed-limited city streets to reach the headhunter's ranch in the hills to the northeast of the city. Lewis explained that the city authorities wanted to build a traffic loop, but the Indians who owned a tract of infertile land to the city's east would not grant permission. The case was in the courts.

'They'll just take it from 'em eventually,' Lewis said. 'They'll just doze that shit and there ain't a damn thing those red boys can do.'

'At least they're going out kicking,' Walter said. 'That's something.'

'Heard that,' Lewis said.

They drove for several miles through the poor neighborhoods in the southern part of the city, passing down street after street of low, washed-out houses whose grassless yards were cluttered with broken toys, booze bottles and skinny dogs looking for shade. The only businesses were auto repair garages, liquor stores, barred convenience shops and bail bondsmen with dual language signs. Puny cacti and limp palm were the only foliage. On almost every corner someone stood waiting for something – a bus, a woman, a child to catch up with them. They all shielded their faces with dirty visors, folded newspapers, cheap sunglasses. They seemed to resent the sun's brightness. Everything moved slowly here, except the tinted limos and brilliant foreign cars that raced to the north.

Lewis crossed beneath an elevated highway, entering the more affluent part of town. The houses were larger here, surrounded by low white walls, lines of shade trees and perfect lawns that glistened under perpetual sprinklers.

'I didn't know there was so much grass down here,' Walter said as they passed a crowded golf course.

Lewis smiled and stroked the long, occasional hairs of his beard.

'There ain't. These fucking snowbirds bring it with 'em from up north or back east or wherever it is they come from. Gotta water it twenty-four, seven, three sixty-five, man. Cut it twice a week, replant it every summer and winter. And you wanna know the funny thing?'

'What's that?'

'Well, most of these old cats come down here to breathe the air, right? No humidity and such? Well, with all these lawns and golf courses and fir trees they sitiated here, now they got pollen. You believe that? Pollen in the damn desert.'

Walter laughed and shook his head. He noticed that on every major intersection there were neat, open-plan shopping malls filled with drug stores, photo finishing labs, maternity clothing outlets, places that sold something called Indian Fry Bread. And insurance agencies, at least one, sometimes two or three per mall. Just after passing a large industrial park of low, windowless buildings they eased to a stop at the back of a traffic jam. Lewis tried to look out of his window to see what the problem was but the view was obscured by a refrigerator truck that slowly leaked some vaporous liquid. He put on the emergency brake and got out of the car to take a look.

Walter settled into the plush seat, closing his eyes and letting the cool air swirl around him. The feeling that had nagged him since leaving Dulles returned, a strange mixture of expectancy and dread. The sense that something important awaited him at the end of this trip, something decisive. He had felt it while waiting to make the connection in Houston, as his ears popped over the lunar landscape of southeastern Arizona, as he adjusted the time on the severance watch UPU had given him anyway, when he saw his butchered name on Lewis's sign. Ah well, he told himself. You'll see soon enough.

He heard a loud hissing above him, rapid bursts of something under great pressure being released. He rolled down his window and looked up. A squadron of hot air balloons passed just a couple hundred feet over the road. He could see the occupants of the lowest one, three fat men in golf hats. Two of them looked up the road with binoculars, while the third looked down at Walter. He smiled and raised a beer can in greeting. Walter smiled back. The man mouthed some words, but Walter couldn't make out what they were.

Lewis slid back into the car, shaking his head.

'Accident. I can see the flashing lights.'

'I'm not surprised, the way these nuts drive.'

'Seriously,' Lewis said.

Traffic began a glacial movement. A young man selling sun visors walked past them on the dotted line.

'Are you from here originally?' Walter asked.

Lewis cast an ironic glance across the front seat.

'This ain't exactly a major black capital.'

Walter laughed.

'So how did you end up here?' Walter asked.

'Come down with Mr Passer from Chicago.'

'How did you get to know him?'

'I was sweeping at the Exchange. Got to talking to him one day and he axed me to run a few messages for him. Let me use his car. Then I started to run all kinds of shit for him, including big time people and some unmentionable bidness too. Then he sent me to chauffeurs' school for two weeks in Santa Barbara. Learned all kinds of things out there. How to make a corner at sixty without spilling bubbly from a glass in the back. How to spin away from kidnappers. How to run a dude down without killing him. And so, here I am.'

'Sounds exciting.'

'Shit,' Lewis said.

They reached the scene of the accident. At first all Walter could see was the ambulance parked in the right lane, the fire engine parked across the median and the fast lane. But as they inched by on the shoulder, Walter could see what had happened. A flatbed truck had run up on to the median, as if it had been cut off. The cab had jackknifed to a sudden stop, its wheels raising large divots of waterlogged sod. The trailer's cargo, a twenty-foot metal statue of a grinning head wearing a cowboy hat, had toppled off the back, landing on the convertible Mercedes that followed the truck. The brim of the statue's hat had sliced through the windshield, pinning the car's two occupants. The elegantly dressed woman in the passenger seat was still alive, shaking her head slowly as an ambulance attendant held her free hand and shielded her eyes from the sparks caused by the fireman's circular saw. The tanned man in the driver's seat was dead, his chest crushed by the brim. His hands were held up before him, pressing into the statue's winking eye. His own eyes were still open.

'Damn,' Lewis said, accelerating into the open road.

They were soon north of the city, driving quickly along an undulating road bordered by bullet-ridden saguaro and signs offering land for development. Three-wheel ATVs crossed their path occasionally, leaving brush strokes of hovering sand behind as they disappeared into the scrub of the open range.

They entered a small town called Carefree at the edge of a range of jagged mountains. The town center was a series of boutiques, restaurants and expensive condos. Women in tennis costumes and helmet-like blonde coiffure, their skin leathery with the sun, walked quickly across elevated wooden sidewalks. Squad cars from private security firms criss-crossed the streets. Walter looked up at the large houses that lined the mountain slopes or rested atop the peaks. Most were in the Spanish style, yet there were also large log cabins, suburban split-levels with aluminum siding, all-glass structures with sharp spires. There was even a large house designed to resemble a medieval castle. Walter noticed that the natural colors were gentler up here, never primary, but rather subtle blends of green and white and brown. The sun was softer here too, less insistent, less punishing.

'Nice place.'

'Shit, man,' Lewis said, shaking his head.

'Is this where Passer lives?'

Lewis nodded to the largest of the nearby mountains. Its slopes were barren of houses.

'He's on the north face of that big boy.'

Its surface was smooth, its slope radical. There was little vegetation, just a few large boulders. It looked like the back of a strong man who had no intention of turning around. They swung off the main road.

There were two signs at the entrance of the road leading to the north face of the mountain. One said 'Passer Peak', the other 'Absolutely No Trespassing'. Walter ran the word over in his mind, thinking how some churches substituted it for 'debts' in the Lord's Prayer. He couldn't see how they were synonymous, really, and wondered for a moment which was closer to the original meaning.

A few hundred yards further ahead the road was crossed by an eight-foot-high chainlink fence that was marked every ten yards by red signs with lightning bolts on them. Lewis stopped the car in front of the gate, next to a short metal post that looked like a periscope. He rolled down his window and unlocked a small door on the face of the post, then punched an elaborate code into a keyboard. There was a subterranean hum, followed by a slow inward swinging of the gate. Walter laughed.

'Seriously,' Lewis said.

The road ascended more sharply after the gate, curving around the mountain's eastern slope. At several points it was bounded on the left by patches of wire mesh that held back fallen rock. The ground grew more colorful as they rose, giving off a dazzling mineral sparkle.

Passer's house came into view as they came around the northeast edge of the mountain. It was a small, white building that seemed to be a natural outcropping of the mountain, a symmetrical ledge, a stroke of erosive genius. In profile, Walter could see that it diminished along the slope from a three-storey façade into a vanishing point at the back, where roof met mountain. The walls were smooth and white, punctuated by a few large, opaque windows. There seemed to be some sort of garden on the roof.

'It's smaller than I thought,' Walter said.

'Man, that's just the tip of the iceberg. Most of it's *in*.'

They pulled into a roundabout at the front of the house, circling an immaculate marble fountain. A menagerie of mermaids, cherubim, unicorns and griffins spouted chlorine-blue water into an elevated bowl, which overflowed into a wading pool where artificial lilies floated. Walter examined it as he stretched out of the car.

'Could use some good old-fashioned bird shit,' he suggested.

'Ain't no birds up here,' Lewis said. ''Cept one kind.'

Walter entered the house alone. Lewis had punched the code into another keyboard, causing the heavy mahogany front door to click open. He said somebody would be with Walter in a minute, then drove off quickly in the limo. Walter stood in the wide, three-storey hall and looked around. The walls were decorated with large sheets of woven cloth depicting dancing figures. Hung as they were, the figures appeared to be tumbling to the ground from a great height. The floor was decorated with ceramic tiles that pictured a bird arising from triangular flames. In the center of the hall was a marble staircase that led to a landing decorated with low tables and clay vases. The house reminded Walter of the monuments he'd taken the boys to when they were young. He closed his eyes and detected the rumble of a distant air conditioner, the smell of marble and polish.

He heard cushioned feet on the stairs and opened his eyes. A tall man in pastel-blue tennis clothes bounded over the last two steps.

'David Passer. May I call you Walter?'

'Hello, yes,' Walter said, extending his hand. Passer let it hang between them for a moment before gripping it. His hand was soft and strong.

'I'm sorry I wasn't here to greet you on your arrival, but my modem was on line to something I didn't want to let slip away.'

Walter nodded indulgently as he scrutinized Passer. He was in his early forties, yet cultivated a younger look. He had black hair clipped into close curls, pipe-cleaner eyebrows and thick, sun-chapped lips lubricated with a coating of petroleum jelly. His eyes were motionless, gray. His tennis shirt was stretched by acquired chest and shoulder muscle, his thick forearms were covered with beds of sun-bleached hair. Yet his wrists and ankles showed his true endomorphic frame, the

172

wristbands rattling when he moved, his socks drooping limply around his shoes.

'Let's go up to the roof, shall we? It's good up there.'

'Fine,' Walter said.

Passer led Walter past the stairs to a small ante-room filled with crated boxes bound by metal bands. They bore Brazilian addresses. There was another keyboard beside a red door, another elaborate code to be punched in. Machinery rattled behind the door for a moment, which eventually slid open to reveal a small elevator car.

Passer pressed the button marked 'R' and the car jerked upwards at a surprising rate. Walter's back protested at yet another ascent and he had to reach for the brass rail to steady himself. Passer noticed the gesture with a brief glance as he cracked his knuckles.

'How was the flight?' he asked.

'Bump all the way,' Walter said. 'Except of course for the three-hour layover in Houston. That was relatively smooth.'

Passer grimaced sympathetically.

'The day that I stopped flying commercially was a happy one indeed,' he said, sounding a deep joint near his left thumb. Touché, Walter thought. The elevator stopped abruptly and the door opened.

The roof was divided into two sections by a long wooden trough full of flowering shrubbery, squat cacti and fruit trees. The eastern half, tiered slightly above the other, was a canopied office consisting of a large desk, a conference table and several chairs. The western half was a swimming pool surrounded by lounge chairs. In a corner of the pool was a statue of a dolphin being ridden by a child carrying a flute. Walter thought for an instant of the paradise he had created on the night of his father's death.

'Let's sit in the shade, if you don't mind,' Passer said. 'I've been sunning too much lately.'

'Sure,' Walter said, following him to the office.

Passer motioned for Walter to sit in a black director's chair. He then took a seat at an oblique angle to Walter in a chair that was slightly higher. So we're going to play this game, Walter thought.

'Would you like a drink?'

'Sure.'

'Beer? The beer down here is outstanding.'

'A beer would work.'

Passer picked up a portable phone receiver from the table beside the chair and dialled three numbers.

'Maria. *Dos cervezas*.'

He replaced the receiver.

'I thought we might speak informally for a while before getting down to specifics. Sound each other out a bit before we pinpoint actual positions that you might fill. Oh, that reminds me.'

He sprang to his feet and walked over to the desk, turning on the power of a computer. He waited for it to warm up, then typed in several commands. He returned to his seat.

'So why don't you tell me a little bit about yourself, Walter,' Passer said.

Walter looked at his hands, which he slowly opened and closed.

'I . . .'

There was a mechanical shuffle on the desk. The computer had begun to print out.

'Your file,' Passer said.

Walter watched the paper being fed through the machine.

'Walter?'

'I'm an engineer . . .'

'Yes?'

'I want to, I don't know, build or work with . . .'

Something in a nearby lemon tree caught his attention. It hovered beside an overripe fruit, its transluscent wings a blur. Its needle beak poked at the fruit's swollen skin, looking for entry. The small crown of feather on its head caught the afternoon sun and glowed brilliantly. It moved to a new fruit with a darting, insect-like motion. Passer followed Walter's gaze.

'Hummingbird.' He cracked his knuckles. 'Haven't you seen one before?'

'No,' Walter said, straining from his seat to get a better look.

'Walter?'

The elevator door opened and the bird flew off to a potted tree on the other side of the pool. A thin young Mexican woman in a dun-colored uniform emerged, carrying a tray with two beers and small dishes full of limes, jalapeno peppers, chips and guacamole. She took a folding table from a stack on the wall and silently set up the food between Walter and Passer. She left quickly.

Passer crushed a lime over his glass of beer, then smeared the rind on the glass's rim. Walter simply drank his. They sat in silence for a moment, Passer looking expectantly at Walter.

'So how does one become a headhunter?' Walter finally asked.

Passer picked a wrinkled pepper from the tray.

'Well, basically, you don't. I mean, I do this because I'm in a position to. I've developed a lot of connections over the years and found myself brokering jobs naturally. So, I decided to go ahead and do it professionally.'

'How did you get into that position? Make all those connections?'

Passer dangled the pepper between them. Walter thought of embryos.

'I got rich,' Passer said quietly. He bit the pepper, forming his mouth into a cool cave after swallowing it. Small beads of perspiration began to form at his hairline, upper lip.

'I've never been rich,' Walter said. 'I don't know how it's done, really. How did you do it?'

Passer reached for another pepper.

'Selling. Selling all sorts of things. Solar panels at first, when I was in school at Champaign. Then Radon venting systems. Surge suppressors. Once I'd socked away a little nestegg I got a position on the commodities exchange in Chicago. You know, livestock options. Boy, that was a grind.' He swallowed the pepper and a few of the beads of sweat broke loose, running part of the way down his face. 'But you know what I learned?'

'You can sell anything?' Walter tried.

Passer shook his head.

'No, that's a myth. There are some things you can't sell. What I learned is that you can only *make* so much money. I mean, as long as money is tied into the amount of work you do, well, that's an awesome limitation on your wealth, don't you think?'

'I've always found that,' Walter said, smiling.

Passer nodded grimly.

'That's when I discovered channelling.'

'Which is?' Walter asked.

Passer looked up at the peak.

'Well, the more I worked in sales, the more I began to suspect that there exists this vast sea of money. There had to be, really. I'd hear rumors about it, catch its scent once in a while. Only it's like the Pacific was five hundred years ago. People know it's there but only a few know where, know how to get to it. So your first job is to find it. That's the hard part. And I did. Then, once you do, you go crazy, because you see that it's unguarded and very, very big. So you immediately start fetching it with a bucket, with your hands. Then, a little later, you get a wheelbarrow. Then a dumptruck. But, you know, there's always a problem, always a hitch. Your arms get tired or night falls or you get a flat. There's always a problem. So then . . . well, you're an engineer, Walter. What do you do?'

'You dig a ditch.'

'That's it. Let gravity and the moon do the work for you. Let nature run its glorious course. That's what I've done. I've all these channels running to me, out here in the desert. Some are just little streams, some are like the Erie Canal. But they always flow, filling up this huge aquafer under my mountain.'

'Good old gravity,' Walter said.

Passer munched another pepper and took a long drink from his beer. Deep gulping noises came from behind his Adam's apple as he swallowed, like the sound of the last of a tub of water rushing into a drain.

'Now, Walter, back to you.' He stood and walked to the desk, ripping the printout sheet from its scroll. 'I've an outline of things here that might be up your alley.'

'Shoot,' Walter said, feeling the first breeze of the evening on his face.

Passer scanned the list.

'As you know, the industry is in a bit of a slump, so there's that limitation placed on us right off the bat. However, there are some decent things going. For instance, the DOE . . .'

Walter smiled ironically and held up his right hand.

'David, if you say the word Hanford I'm going to jump off this roof.'

Passer's pipe-cleaner eyebrows raised and lowered.

'Well, I'm glad you stopped me,' he said. He read on. 'So I guess this waste storage center in South Carolina probably wouldn't do much for you either?'

Walter shook his head slowly. Passer read on, passing over several items with brief, dismissive flurries of his brow.

'Do you speak Afrikaans?' he asked with a grim laugh.

Walter pointed at the sheet.

'David, could you put that away or tear it up or commit it to flames? I don't think I can face that.'

The paper disappeared behind the chair. Passer waited.

'That's a beautiful creature,' Walter said, nodding towards the hummingbird as it flittered through the nearby shrubbery.

'You see them sometimes,' Passer said, still waiting.

'It's funny,' Walter said slowly. 'I came out here not really knowing what I wanted to do. What I was capable of, even. But now, in this air and this sun, I'm thinking, well . . .'

Passer waited.

'I want to build something, something . . .' Walter said.

Passer waited for him to finish his sentence. But Walter remained silent, still looking at the bird.

'I understand,' Passer said slowly. 'Listen, Walter, I have an idea. An offer for you.'

'What's that?' Walter turned his attention back to Passer.

Passer smiled demurely and placed his glass on the ground.

'Come with me,' he said. 'I'll show you.'

They took the elevator down past the floor Walter had come in on. Passer said nothing as they descended, the demure smile wavering across his face. Walter could see two more levels through the elevator's small window before they landed on the bottom floor with a gentle jolt. Passer led Walter into a large room with dark panelled walls and a green pile carpet. There was a wet bar at the far end, backed by a tinted mirror. Man-high stereo speakers rested in each corner. There were chairs, small couches, glass coffee tables. In the center of the room was a large pool table, balls arranged in break formation. Old movie posters lined the walls – W.C. Fields, Erroll Flynn, Bogart. Passer walked quickly through the room, absent-mindedly rolling the cue ball as he passed the table.

They entered a smaller room, with a concrete floor and cinderblock walls. There were several drawing boards covered with blueprints and a metal desk with a phone on it. In the middle of the room was a model of a desert valley, covered with a small village. Two hoses ran out of the bottom of the model to a large sink in a corner of the room. Passer stepped up beside it.

'This is a project I've been thinking of for quite some time,' he explained. 'But I've had a little trouble getting it off the ground.'

'What is it?'

'Well, this is a model of the valley down below this house here. I own it. And I'm going to develop it.'

'What, for housing?'

'Retirement villas. They're a hot item out here, Walter. Growing field, what with people living longer. You heard of Sun City? An entire community for the old, just down the road. Security, medical, recreational – the whole deal. No drag-racing kids, no wetbacks, no B & E, no loud music, no garbage. Well, that's what I want to do out here.' He waved his open hand over the model. 'Develop an entire spread of villas, connect them with paths for the golf carts, stick in a medical and shopping center here, and fence the whole damn thing in.'

Walter stared down at the model. The houses reminded him of the figures on the Monopoly games he used to play with Helen and the boys.

'I don't understand. Do you want me to put up the houses or something? I'm not particularly qual — '

'No, no. Not the houses. Are you kidding? I'm up to my ass in contractors. No, what I need is somebody for this,' he said, pointing to a pond near the medical center. There was a small nozzle in the middle of it.

'What is that, a fountain?'

'That's right, Walter. I'm going to put the highest man-made fountain in the world right in the middle of it. As a selling point. Call the whole thing Fountain Valley. After the Fountain of Youth. That was supposed to be in Florida, which is my main competition.'

'How high?'

'Three hundred feet,' Passer said, walking over to the sink. He opened a faucet, then returned to the model and unscrewed another beneath it. A jet of water came out of the nozzle, rising over a foot high. It looks like a drinking fountain gone mad, Walter thought. The water splashed noisily into the pond, splattering the model hospital and nearby houses with drops of water. Passer closed the faucet below the model. The water slowly drained from the pond.

'Where do you get the water from?'

'Tap a conduit into one of the main waterways.'

'Can you do that?' Walter asked.

'Walter, this is Arizona. If you develop, you can do anything.'

Walter stared at the model.

'I had another guy working on it,' Passer said. 'Headhunted him from the TVA. But I had to let him go. He couldn't handle the power and size. Thought it was wasteful. Can you imagine that? Astonishing. Anyway, I know you're not particularly experienced in waterworks, but from what I understand the technology here is pretty straightforward stuff, right?'

'Well, yes,' Walter said slowly, looking at the draining pond, the dripping nozzle.

'So what do you think? The design is basically there. What I need is somebody to get it built. Somebody like you, who can handle this sort of size and power. That's the thing. When you said that up on the roof about wanting to build something, well, I naturally thought of this. So – what do you think? The pay will be very good, the working conditions – well, you've seen the area.'

Walter stared at the model, thinking how the end of the sentence about wanting to build something was that he wanted to build something simple.

'It's funny,' he said softly. 'I've already built a fountain. First thing I ever built.'

'Really?' Passer raised an eyebrow. 'Well, then . . .'

Walter stopped him with a gesture of his hand.

'I'm not sure I'm your man, David,' he said. 'In fact, all of a sudden, I'm not too sure that I'm anybody's man.'

'I don't understand.'

Walter spread his hands to indicate he couldn't say more.

'I'll tell you what,' Passer said after a moment of silence. 'Don't answer me now. Your plane isn't till tomorrow, right? Why don't you sleep on it tonight. Stay here. You can look over the plans, look over the valley. Its . . . logic will come to you. I'll have Maria make up a room for you. I have to leave now, unfortunately. Got a breakfast thing in New York. But you just stay on and think about it. Call me next week and give me your decision. All right?'

'All right,' Walter said.

'Just tell Maria or Lewis if you need something. I'll tell them to look after you.'

Passer held out his hand. Walter took it.

'Thank you,' Walter said.

'I want this built,' Passer said, nodding toward the model. 'It's very important to me.'

'I know what you mean,' Walter said.

Walter spent the rest of the evening on the roof, drinking the cold beers Maria instinctively brought him, watching the falling evening mute the mountain's vibrant colors into pastel shadows. After dark, the simulated gas lamps that lined the pool flared on. Maria brought dinner and Walter ate it on a glass table near the deep end. There were two burritos stuffed with spicy shreds of chicken and vegetables; pasty beans and feather-light rice; cool guacamole and sour cream. Walter ate quickly, greedily, savoring the rich flavors and the alternating sensations of hot and cool.

When he finished Maria reappeared with a tall glass of frosted coffee. He told her how much he enjoyed the food but she said nothing. He realized she didn't speak English. He took a long time to finish the coffee, remembering his father's habit of letting his morning coffee cool, then tossing most of it into the sink. He'd then go down to River Rouge half an hour early and drink leftover swing-shift brew from paper cups. The only times he'd finished his coffee at home was during that long strike, because there had been no swing shift and the canteen was used by the National Guard. Walter remembered how his father would set off after draining the cup, two police motorcycles following the Buick. He remembered the three a.m. phone calls, the razzing from his schoolmates under instruction from their parents, the time someone painted 'scab' in whitewash on the garage door. And when the strike ended his father didn't say a word, just began emptying his mug of untouched coffee into the sink, leaving a little earlier.

When Walter finished he stood and walked around the pool. The dinner and beers had made him sleepy, yet he didn't want to sleep, didn't want to lose this night. Tomorrow he had a mid-morning flight back to Dulles. Tonight, he just wanted to be in this strange air and silence.

He stopped by the edge of the pool. An underwater spot lit the blue bottom. Small insects darted across the shimmering waves on the surface. There was a hiss at the deep end as something that looked like a long-tailed fish surfaced momentarily. Walter watched the mobile filter as it ducked back under, scraping the bottom. It darted randomly throughout the pool, knocking accumulated silt from the walls to be sucked up by the filter.

He stripped off his clothes and tested the water. Warm, like the water that rushed out of his ears when he got into bed on the days he played with the boys in the above-ground pool. He thought for a moment about the games he used to play with them, the lessons he'd tried to teach. He wished he had known about the Passers of the world then. He wished he'd known about channels and Lewis and UPU and fountains in the desert. He stretched his back and rubbed some circulation into his thighs and flanks.

He dove in, gliding as far as possible with his arms outstretched, legs together. He kept his eyes open in the stinging rush, letting the chlorine wash the journey from them. As his momentum ran out he began his slow crawl to the other end. He paused for a moment beneath the diving board, his heart racing with the effort. The mobile filter popped up close to him, spitting a dare in his face before darting off to the shallow end. Walter headed after it with his steady, even stroke.

He swam a dozen laps, faltering somewhat on the fourth before catching his second wind. The filter lapped at his sides a few times, like a puppy or impatient child. Once his legs became involved in its cord, and for a panicked instant he felt himself tugged toward the spotlit bottom. Yet the cord slipped away on its own, leaving him to resume his swim.

As he moved through the water, he was finally able to admit to himself that Passer had nothing for him. None of them did. He knew that he was capable of only the simplest work now. He'd sink beneath the weight of anything else. What he needed was to put his hands to work on something real, something small and sturdy. To build something that they wouldn't tear down. That wouldn't crash. Not Passer's ridiculous fountain or any other project his computer could belch out. No, he needed to build something private. Something that would last. He thought suddenly of the house in Greece his father-in-law had given him a quarter-century earlier. He wondered if it was still there, what condition it was in. What it would be like to move there for a while and make it habitable. He pressed hard through the last two laps.

He climbed slowly from the water, gulping for air, trying to withstand the tremors in his muscles. He stood for a long time, dripping rivulets into the swirled cement deck. This is how a man should be tired, he thought. This is good exhaustion. Not like the other kind. He dropped into a lounge chair and fell immediately into a dreamless sleep.

Small, hard bunkers of flesh covered him when he awoke, defending him against the surprise attack of chill. He looked around, unsure of how long he had slept. The sky was brilliant with stars. He located his rumpled clothes and dressed quickly. He found the severance watch. Nearly midnight.

An animal began to chant in the valley below the house. A coyote, he thought. Like a dog, only more desperate. The last thing you hear. He walked to the edge of the roof and looked in the direction of the sound. He caught sight of a red glow, about a half mile away, right in the valley's center. After several seconds of looking he determined that there were actually several lights, arranged in a crude circle. They flickered intensely, defining the center of a great, vertiginous whirlpool of darkness. Walter watched them for a few minutes more, then walked to the elevator.

*

The first wound came at the end of the driveway – a clean, deep puncture on the front of his thigh. He jumped back and swatted reflexively at the dark space in front of him, believing he'd been stung by a large insect. Yet all he felt was air. He touched his leg and found a needle. He yanked it out, yet that only caused the pain to increase, throbbing into his bone, rippling down to his knee and up to his groin. He rubbed furiously at the wound and felt a small hard lump developing just beneath the puncture. The animal yelping continued ahead of him.

'Jesus.'

He knew he should turn back, yet the intense glow beckoned to him. You've come this far, he thought, the strange sense of dread and expectancy returning. He began to walk again, more slowly this time, probing the darkness with his feet.

It was no use. After only several yards he was pricked again, this time at the side of his ankle. As he angrily plucked it out, the back of his hand hit another plant, collecting two more needles. A wave of cackling drifted to him from up ahead. He realized it wasn't animal after all, but a human voice.

He decided to move quickly, taking whatever blows the darkness had in store for him. The more he was stuck, the faster he walked, until he was running through the scrub at a steady clip. His legs, hands and chest were soon covered with the two-inch needles. About two hundred feet from the red glow he stumbled down a small embankment, shoulder rolling to a seated position. He sat still for a moment, discovering that the fall had shaken loose a few of the pricks. He stood and walked slowly, silently toward the light. It was clear the rest of the way, just jagged rubble and small mounds of powder. The ground was flat. He stopped about twenty yards away from the camp, just beyond the glow.

He could see two men sprawled within the circle of light created by a dozen sizzling traffic flares. Walter recognized Lewis, his driver's cap replaced now by a plastic batter's helmet. He lounged on what looked to be an old car seat, taking a long pull from a labelless bottle. Walter didn't know the other man, who sat on an inverted tar bucket. He was young, perhaps in his teens, dressed in faded jeans, sandals and a woven sweater with a large hood that flopped against his back. He was thin, with wiry muscles and long fingers. His jet black hair was pulled back in a pony tail and his smooth brown skin showed input from several races. He was sitting in front of a flare, holding a stick over its flame, roasting the indeterminate mass the stick impaled. His shadow was cast behind him on to what looked to be a small clay hut. Walter stepped into the light. Lewis saw him approach.

'Yeah,' he said, nodding slow, smiling wide. 'My man. I hoped you'd come. I wanted to talk with you some.'

The other man was momentarily startled by Walter's entrance. He hid the stick behind him.

'I saw your fire from the roof,' Walter said, his eyes tearing from the clouds of sulphur.

'Yeah man,' the young man giggled. 'It's a landing pad for the spirits.'

'They're from the limo,' Lewis explained. 'Rest it here, my man.'

Walter looked at the flat boulder between the two men.

'Don't worry,' Lewis continued. 'Me and Captain America here are just chillin'. We do this every once in a while, when Mr Passer is away.'

'And the spirits are out,' the Captain giggled.

Walter walked to the boulder but didn't sit.

'Well, sitting is a bit problematical,' he said, holding his arms out to his sides. 'Cactus.'

'Oh man, you been stuck,' Lewis said, examining Walter in the light.

Walter smiled self-deprecatingly and shook his head. Suddenly, the young man was kneeling beside him.

'Let me,' he said. 'Jos be still.'

'That's right,' Lewis said. 'The Captain'll do you.'

Walter stood perfectly still as the young man expertly removed the needles, first from his legs, then his stomach and chest, and finally his arms. He coaxed them out in a way that left no pain or swelling. Walter looked at his face as he worked. He wore alligator clips for earrings and had a row of three tears tattooed below his coal-black left eye. Walter noticed that his other eye was pale blue, so light that it was difficult to tell where the iris began.

'There,' he said, removing the last needle with a small flourish. He cackled with delight for a moment, and Walter recognized the voice he had heard from the roof.

'Thank you,' Walter said as he took his seat. Lewis passed him the bottle.

'Tequila. For the pain.'

Walter took a long sip of the strong, salty liquid. It burned for a moment, then sent out numbing pulses to all his small wounds. He drank again.

'This is good,' he said.

'But who will get the worm?' the young man asked in a melodramatic voice as Walter passed him the bottle. Walter looked confused, so he plucked a flare from the ground and held it to the side of the bottle, showing the mummified bug at the bottom. '*Gusano*. The last one to drink must eat him.'

Walter nodded warily and looked around.

'What is this place?' he asked.

'Dry riverbed,' Lewis said. 'They damned it up years ago to make that recreation lake up near Sun City. Sometimes people come down here on bikes or buggies, but mostly it's just the Captain and the coyotes and the scorpions. Yo Captain, ain't that right?'

The young man cackled his strange laugh. They listened to it echo around the canyon. A flare sizzled out. Lewis took another from the duffel bag at his feet, cracked it alight and planted it where the spent one had been.

'Is that your house?' Walter asked the young man, nodding to the hut behind them.

'That? No man, them's my cosmic wheels.'

'I don't understand,' Walter said.

'Well come on then, *muchacho*, and I'll take you for a spin,' he said, prancing toward the hut like a marionette in the hands of a child.

'Damn nut,' Lewis said forlornly.

Walter followed him. It was a car, almost totally buried in windblown sand. Only the right front door, the back bumper and the front grill were exposed. It was a stationwagon of the same model and year as the one he had owned when the boys were younger. He had used it for long trips, to haul the boys to and from sports practice, for the Saturday morning shopping trips to the lumber yard or home improvement center. The young man snatched a flare from the ground and crawled in through the open door. Walter turned to Lewis, who nodded okay and stroked his scraggly goatee. He leaned halfway into the car.

The front seat had been ripped out, the second seat moved all the way to the tailgate. Flare butts, empty bottles, food wrappers and a pile of frayed Polaroid backings littered the floor. On the dashboard was a large tape deck, with speakers situated in each of the car's four corners. Above it an animal's tail dangled from the rear-view mirror. A large red hooka-pipe was jammed into the steering wheel, a Jimi Hendrix poster was taped on the windscreen. The young man flopped on the back seat, leaning on a two-foot-high pile of comic books. A pile of chipped animal skulls and bones was arranged neatly in a corner at the bottom of the seat. The young man held the flare aloft. His eyes sparkled in the flickering light.

'How did this get down here?' Walter asked.

'Flash flood.'

'I used to have a car just like this,' Walter said.

'Really,' the young man said, half standing. 'Will you take me for a ride then? Please?'

Walter smiled, shook his head and pulled out of the car. He took his seat near Lewis, who was smiling his conspiratorial smile. Music began to pulse from the stereo in the car. They could hear him chattering and laughing along with it. Walter took another long drink of the tequila.

'The thing about that dude is that he's harmless, you know?' Lewis stated. 'He may seem like a psycho or Freddie but he's really very soft.'

'Who is he?'

'Man, I wish I knew, I honestly do. I was out washing the limo one day and he just sort of blew in out of the desert and axed if he could have some food. All's I know about him is he got no family or nothin'. Came up in institutions, foster homes, juvey lock up. I'll tell you one thing, he been spoon-fed plenty of them government drugs. Don't even know who his people are or what they are.' Lewis laughed. 'Tell truth, I don't either. Depends on the light. Somedays he looks as white as you, others I could swear he's about half brother. Other times he looks like fucking Crazy Horse, then he looks like goddamn Valenzuela. It's just where the sun is, I guess, that's where he is.'

'Why do you call him Captain America?'

'Fucking comic books of his. You know?'

Walter stared at the flickering light coming from the car door, shaking his head.

'So what did you think of old Passer?' Lewis asked.

'He's all right, I guess. A bit of a different species from me, though.' Walter stared at Lewis. 'Have you seen his model for this place? His plans.'

'Yeah,' Lewis said, holding Walter's gaze.

'What do you think?'

'Like you said, Walter. Different species,' Lewis said slowly, passing on the bottle.

The young man returned to his bucket seat, murmuring a tune. He stared at Walter's wrist.

'Hey, can I have your watch?' he asked suddenly.

'Yo, Captain,' Lewis said. 'Chill. This ain't no dude to be messin' wit.'

'That's all right,' Walter said, twisting off the serpentine gold band from his wrist and tossing it to the young man, who immediately strapped it on his right arm. 'You know, Captain, you sort of remind me of somebody.'

'Is he cool?'

'He's dead, actually.'

'Ow,' Lewis mocked.

The young man stared angrily at Walter, then turned to Lewis.

'Hey Lewis, let's do some of that button.'

Lewis made a brief, nullifying gesture with his hand.

'Come on, Lewis.'

'What button?' Walter asked.

Lewis shook his head. The boy took a small foil package from his pocket and carefully unwrapped it, removing a small, viscid yellow pellet for Walter to see.

'Peyote,' he said, trilling the 'y'.

'What do you do with it?' Walter asked.

'Nothing,' Lewis said quickly.

'You eat it,' the young man said.

'And then?'

'And then you can drive God's Chevy back there,' he said, jerking his head toward the car. He handed it to Walter. 'Go ahead.'

'Man . . .' Lewis said.

Walter looked at it for a moment.

'This reminds me of something,' he said.

'What?'

'Plutonium.'

'Never done that,' the young man said.

'You seen that stuff?' Lewis asked.

'Plenty of times,' Walter said. 'It's the same color, the same wicked yellow.'

'Damn. I wouldn't never get near that shit,' Lewis said.

'I would,' the young man said, puffing himself up. 'I'd do anything once. How 'bout you?'

Walter smiled at him.

'Go ahead,' he said.

'Hey man, that shit's strong,' Lewis said.

'I dare you, suit.'

'Will it kill me?' Walter asked with a smile. They both shook their heads.

'Go on, society man,' the young man said.

Walter declined, tossing the pellet back to the young man, who gave out a cackling laugh. Lewis pulled the tequila bottle from his mouth.

'Why the fuck you laughin'?'

The boy pointed at Walter.

'Bwah,' he laughed.

'Oh man, you didn't?' Lewis said.

'What?' Walter asked.

'Did you?' Lewis persisted. The boy laughed. 'Where? In the bottle?'

The boy nodded his head.

'What?' Walter asked again.

'Man, this crazy motherfucker solved some button in the tequila,' Lewis said. 'You better stick yo' finger down your throat, otherwise you gonna flip, big time.'

Walter stared hard at the boy, who was only smiling now, nodding his head. His one blue eye glowed brilliantly in the red glare. Walter felt a brief, hot wave of fear pass through his lower back. A small, tight tremor of nausea and dizziness.

'No,' Walter said. 'It's all right.'

Lewis shrugged as he screwed the lid back on the bottle.

'Your funeral.'

'Anybody hungry?' the young man asked, reaching to the ground behind his bucket for the stick he had discarded on Walter's approach.

'Not me,' Lewis said.

Walter could see what he had been roasting. The flame-blackened corpse of a small bird. The Captain dipped it into the flame again and the charred flesh glowed orange. Walter found himself thinking how beautiful that burning color was. Suddenly, it seemed that he had been staring at the flame for some great stretch of time. Hours. Everything in him had lightened, as if the atmosphere had changed to helium. He felt both dizzy and lucid.

'*Mania*,' the young man said, passing Walter the stick.

It took Walter a moment to get his hand to connect with it. He noticed that the dark sky surrounding the clearing had begun a slow centrifugal spin. He finally fastened on to the stick and put the meat to his lips. He blew to cool it, then bit in. The first taste was dusty charcoal, then rancid, stringy meat. Walter chewed the rubbery gristle for a while, unable to force it through his dry throat. The labelless bottle floated before him. He snatched it from the air and took a long drink, enabling him to force the mouthful of bird to a perch just behind his solar plexus.

There was a fluttering at the end of his stick. Feathers were slowly sprouting from the hummingbird's belly, back and neck. Its wings broke through the charred crust that surrounded it and began their rapid flutter. Even its eyes managed to flicker open. It flew off the edge of the stick, approaching the floating bottle, trying to get at the worm inside. Walter could hear the futile click of its tiny bill against the glass.

He felt a great hand on his shoulder and went to brush it off. It was the earth.

'Whoa,' he heard someone say. 'Easy.'

'Put him in the car.'

Strong hands clamped the woolly things that were his arms and lifted him back to his feet. He felt wet all over and saw that there were dozens more needles sticking in him, emerging from the back of his hand. They sparkled in the light, as if they were made of gold.

'Watch his head.'

He felt himself dropped on to the seat and closed his eyes. Loud music flared on behind him, a hard ghetto voice backed by insistent drums, a naked guitar.

> *You thought you were hot,*
> *But you really were illin'!*
> *You wanted to be cool,*
> *But now you are chillin'!*

Walter felt himself teetering on the edge of a great basin of unconsciousness, a wide crater of sleep. The night's gyroscopic sway increased. Go ahead, jump, a voice from below called. Drive on in. No, no. Get where you're going. Stay with us.

> *You started on top,*
> *But now you backslide!*
> *You did a hip-hop,*
> *Now you nationwide!*

There was an instant of silence, a blinding light. Then the rushing sound started, the darkness. It grew louder and louder, hurting his ears. He felt the vehicle plummeting down a steep slope. That yelping animal that had beckoned him was chasing after it. The speed increased, the noise continued.

> *You thought you'd stand up,*
> *And mess with the man!*
> *But he's paying you back,*
> *On the installment plan!*

There was a jolt. Everything stopped – the whirling, the din, the blinding red light, the accusing voice. They'd reached the bottom, reached the ground. Walter opened his eyes, feeling lucid, strangely calm. Lewis slept soundly on the floor under the steering wheel, a sweet smile on his face. Captain America was gone. A young boy sat on the floor in front of Walter. He was looking out the window at the towering pylons that lined the highway they smoothly raced down.

'Hello Edward.'

'Hello, dad.'

The boy was a young man now, handsome, with clear, ironic eyes. Walter wanted to touch him but still could not move his woolly arms.

'How are you?' Walter asked. 'How have you been?'

'All right,' he said, averting his eyes. Walter strained to see his face.

'Tell me the truth, Edward.'

The boy searched for words.

'Edward?'

He said something but Walter couldn't hear what it was.

'Eddie?'

SO

When she moved, webs of static passed through the blankets draped over her shoulders. Matthew could see her face in the irregular light – her eyes half closed, unseeing; her mouth open in a soundless call. Hair moved across her face like a wind-jostled curtain. He touched her temple with his finger, collecting a line of dewy sweat and touching it to his tongue.

The blankets crackled violently as she let them fall from her shoulders and dipped closer to him. He arched his neck forward to kiss her breasts, circling his tongue around one nipple, then the other. She drew back her shoulders at this and he could feel her scapula almost touch. Then she sighed plaintively and he felt her flesh rise, her soft muscles shiver. She drew upwards, her body primed like a filament charged by high voltage, rising so high that he left her. He reached out to steady her hips but she had grabbed the base of his penis, lashing her nut-hard clitoris with its head. He could feel the random aftershocks shudder through her musculature, ripple across the flesh.

He sat up, going back into her, leaning her back until her hair swept the sheets. He came a moment later, engulfed by the waves of warmth. His open eyes darkened for an instant under the same warm, lapping tide. His vision quickly returned and everything in the room seemed close, soft. Like her flesh. She had dropped back on to the sheets, shaking her head slowly from side to side. He settled beside her on the bed, feeling her damp cheek on his rising chest. The wind chimes they'd hung on the fire escape began to sound softly.

'Wind,' he said.

'Dirty city wind.'

He awoke later to the sound of Prospero returning from work – the irregular thump of his limp, the rattle of his many keys, his slight wheeze. Pale light came through the bedroom window. A few streets away, garbage men banged cans into an idling truck. Matthew lay still for a while, listening to Prospero make the tea that he would let cool beside his bed as he fell asleep. He was whistling softly now, and Matthew recognized the song Eleni had sung the first time he'd heard her sing.

Her eyelashes fluttered on his chest. He looked at her face, set in hard concentration, almost like fear. Bad dream, he thought. He stroked her hair and kissed her forehead. She stirred, her eyes still closed.

'Okay?' he asked.

She nodded sleepily and began to trace indecipherable hieroglyphics on his chest.

'I was just a girl,' she said, not really awake. 'I had a friend. A boy from England. He had very pale eyes and his father was a diplomat. Sometimes we would go dancing with other friends at a disco, then he would take me for a ride through the city in a big English car with air conditioning and four speakers and diplomatic registration. Some nights we'd stay out past curfew. The army would let us pass because of the license. But one night there was a commotion and they pulled everybody over. A bunch of ruffians sitting in a jeep stopped us. Draftees, from the country. They told us the emperor had been taken away. They shone their lights into the car and wanted to know who I was. They told me to come out.' She was silent for a while and he thought she'd fallen asleep, but then she began to speak again. 'But Ian just drove away. The ruffians piled into their jeep and chased us, but they couldn't keep up with the English car. My heart was racing so. We parked in a grove of eucalyptus trees by the Africa Hall and lay down in the back seat. It was leather, like warm skin. We could hear the jeeps looking for us, but then they left, and all we could hear were locusts, a million locusts in the trees that hid us from the ruffians . . .'

She had spoken herself back to sleep. Matthew lifted the sheet to cover her exposed shoulder against the morning chill.

He stood in the steam of the large sink, watching water and pieces of soggy bread swirl into the drain, using the small nozzled hose to urge vagrant bits into the main flow. Sweat covered his face and chest, and his hands ached from the heat and the corrosive detergents. The sink cleared with a loud, popping suck. Daniel, the Haitian cook, stopped next to Matthew.

'Sounds like a jeu' fille I knew in Port-au-Prince,' he said, nodding to the drain.

Matthew laughed and followed him to the walk-in freezer, helping him stack the food they hadn't used for that night's dinner and remove meat to defrost for tomorrow's. They worked quickly, in silence, wanting to get out of the cold as quickly as possible. Matthew's hands, marble white from the bleach, began to turn red. When they returned to the kitchen, Eleni was waiting.

'All done?' she asked.

'I still have to scrape the burner down,' Matthew said.

'I'll do it,' Daniel said.

'No, Danny, it's my job,' Matthew protested.

'*L'amour, mon,*' Daniel said, winking. 'I can dig it. You go.'

'Thank you,' Eleni said.

Now that it was warmer, the streets of the restaurant district were beginning to become crowded. Taxis unloaded couples or groups of women who lingered on the sidewalk, seeing which place looked likely. Vendors selling roses or jewelry or umbrellas stood in the doorways of closed shops, surveying the diners with bland fatalism. Police helicopters swooped over the nearby ghettos. On some corners groups of off-duty Marines stood in tight clusters, passing a bottle, scowling at everyone.

Matthew and Eleni passed a commotion outside a disco called Poseurs. A muscular young man, his face and polo shirt smeared with whipped cream and pie crust, was struggling against the restraining arms of several other young men, trying to get a thin man who stood laughing in the disco's doorway. A man in a clown suit hovered nearby, looking at his watch. On his back was a sign that read 'Pie-in-the-Face, Inc.'

'I'm gonna kill you, motherfucker,' the victim screamed, trying to break free, pointing at the smirking thin man. 'You can't do this to me. Not in public.'

'Take a joke,' the thin man said laconically.

'Yeah, come on, Flip,' another said.

'No way. Nobody does this to me. Nobody.'

'Hey, am I gonna get paid?' the clown asked.

Matthew and Eleni walked in silence for about a block, smiling to themselves.

'What's it like to be white?' Eleni asked.

'Oh, a thrill a minute,' Matthew said.

'Hey,' she said sternly. 'You know the rules.'

Once, just after Matthew had moved in, they were watching a basketball game on television before going to work. The commentator referred to an ungainly blond center as suffering from 'white man's disease'.

'What's that?' Eleni had asked.

'He can't jump.'

'Oh. I thought that would have been irony.' She had looked at him. '*That's* a disease I can cure you of.' She had pinched him hard, causing him to hop off the couch. 'And maybe one day I'll even teach you how to jump.'

Matthew looked over his shoulder. The young man had broken free of his friends and plunged back into the bar after the thin man. The clown followed at a safe distance.

'I don't know, really,' Matthew said. 'It's like a being involved in this constant struggle to find out what's important.'

'No, Matty, that's part of us all.'

'Then what do you think it is?' Matthew asked.

'Being white? I think it's not being serious. Oh, I know the business-man and the politician are very serious, but they aren't really, are they? It's just a game, just a mask. On the inside everybody's laughing. Or laughed at. We, on the other hand, laugh on the outside, where our mouth is, and are serious on the inside.' She looked at him. 'That's why I love you, you know. Because you don't accept these jokes and this irony you've been taught. You're not a game man. Oh, you're too often silly and too thin, but there's serious in you. You just don't know what to do with it yet.'

Matthew said nothing.

'We're home,' Eleni said, leading him up the dimly-lit steps to their apartment.

It was situated above a video rental store on a side street continu-ally blocked by delivery trucks. Prospero had rented it since leaving his home country ten years earlier. There were two bedrooms, a lounge and a formica kitchen that smelled of palm oil and natural gas. The scuffed wood floor in the lounge was covered by a large oval rug Prospero had brought from home, woven with fabrics of many different textures and colors. They were forever picking up pieces that had come off its frayed edges, yet the rug never decreased in size. Matthew spent many hours on it, reading or listening to music or kissing Eleni. The furniture was sturdy, old, faded. There were dozens of leaf-tumbling plants in handpainted vases hanging in every corner, giving the apartment a dense, humid atmosphere, leaving resinous pollen over the bookshelves, the mirrors, the rec-ords.

The light switch by the door wasn't attached to anything, so they had to cross the lounge to turn on a lamp. Before they made it, however, Matthew gently pulled Eleni on to the carpet.

'I know what to do with it,' he said.

They kissed for a long time. Matthew could smell the sweet mustiness of the carpet's fabric, the spice of her skin. He helped her off with her blouse and jeans, then kissed down her body until his tongue reached in between her legs. It took him a moment to work through the layers of brittle, rice-paper tissue to reach her clitoris. He could feel the carpet rise beneath him as she gathered it into her fists. The ball of her foot stroked his spine, faster and faster, until she let out that songful moan. She sat up to kiss him but he lifted her from the ground, holding the backs of her knees in his cupped hands. She gripped his shoulders, stroking his hair with one hand, then the other. He leaned her back against the drawn curtain and they could hear the picture window rattle with their motion. They soon moved back to the carpet, Eleni straddling him now. From outside came the sound of approaching sirens, several engines turning up their small street. Matthew could hear the cackle of radios and slamming of doors, could see the strobe of red light on the far wall. They continued to make love throughout, finishing just after the first truck drove off. They lay still for several minutes, then Matthew stood and walked to the window, peering out of a crack in the curtains.

'It's the place across the way. A chair on fire. They've dragged it out into the street. It's still smoking.'

He looked over his shoulder. Eleni was sitting next to the phone, checking the answering machine for messages, as was her habit.

In the afternoons, before work, they'd often go for coffee at a nearby café called L'Artiste Assoifé. It was a single, long room, a few steps down from street level, so that when the patrons could look out the windows they saw the legs of pedestrians. There were a dozen tables of a dozen different sizes. The walls were covered with Parisian theatrical posters, vaguely pornographic postcards, signed photo portraits of unknowns, out-of-date calendars. The proprietor was a hatchet-faced Hungarian who wore garish silk shirts and dropped cigarette ash into the espresso he made. He was forever arguing with the overseas graduate students and failed artists who spent their afternoons drinking coffee and filling the low-ceilinged room with acrid cigarette smoke.

Matthew and Eleni would sit at a corner table, talking, holding hands beneath the table, watching the garrulous patrons. They often talked about the sensations and discoveries of their youths. Matthew would tell her about walking up the imaginary staircase in search of new colors, about the giddy elation of being carried by the waves his father made in their small pool, about the time Eddie stole the small wax bottles filled with candy syrup and they'd sickened themselves eating them whole, about watching Nixon resign on television with Walter saying 'don't believe him, don't believe him' to them. In turn, Eleni would talk about the stifling feel of her school uniform in the late spring heat and the way the nuns would yell if she undid her starched collar, how her father would race through the car-glutted streets on his bicycle with her balanced on the handlebars, the day she was supposed to give a bouquet of poppies to the emperor's wife at some ceremony or other but it was cancelled. She talked about her friend Ian, the son of the English cultural attaché, and how funny everyone thought it was that he gave his dog a name. When Bob Marley came to the sports stadium, he took her and some friends and they sat in a glass booth just above the stage, watching the singer's dreadlocks shimmer in the stadium lights.

One afternoon, she asked him about Eddie's death. Matthew looked out the window at the wheels of a passing stroller. At a nearby table, the café owner and a one-armed Vietnamese man were arguing loudly.

'There's not a whole lot to say,' he said softly. 'My father lost control of the glider and they crashed and Eddie died. It was on our birthday.'

'Is that why you hate your father?' Eleni asked.

'No, of course not,' Matthew said quickly.

The nearby argument grew louder.

'Why "of course?" ' Eleni asked after a moment.

'I don't hate my dad,' Matthew insisted. 'Not any more than everybody else hates their dad.'

'Well, there's something, no? Do you hate his profession or his big car American life?'

Matthew twirled his small spoon through the remnants of his coffee.

'No, no. If that were it, it would be easy, right? I just can't understand him, and that pisses me off. I mean, what does he want? If he wants to be happy, then why doesn't he just chill out in front of the TV and enjoy his big house and marvelous wife? And if he wants to be rich, why doesn't he drop all this integrity crap and make a buck? And if he wants to be a fucking martyr, then why doesn't he just go die?'

'Matty . . .'

'Well, I just want to know what he wants.'

'Maybe he wants to get away from what happened. I mean, that's what you're doing, isn't it? Or maybe he just wants to be forgiven.'

Matthew didn't answer.

Eleni was hired to work as an interpreter at an international trade conference at a retreat west of the city. She would be gone for three days, staying at the conference center so she could work breakfast meetings and the parties that would last well into the night. A limo came for her at six in the morning. Matthew watched her go from the lounge window, wiping a circle in the condensation. Then he went back to bed and slept until noon.

He had arranged to work all three nights in the Nile's kitchen. He would arrive in the afternoon to help Daniel heat the ovens and arrange set-ups of bread and vegetables on the large trays. Then he'd prime the tables – putting out the placemats emblazoned with historical or philosophical treatises, making sure there were large candles in the ornate brass holders, filling up the skull-like censers with stalks of incense. He'd eat when he finished, then read in the back of the kitchen until the restaurant was opened and tables needed to be bussed or trays scrubbed. He'd work furiously during the evening rush, cleaning dishes and glasses and silverware in hot bleachy water that would wash the color from his shriveled skin. Then he'd help Daniel and the waitresses close down, scraping solid fat from the grills with the back of a spatula, wiping down tables, stacking food in the walk-in freezer.

On the second night Prospero stopped by the restaurant just before closing time and asked Matthew if he wanted to accompany him to work at the dispatch office. Even though he was exhausted from the work, Matthew readily agreed. He had slept poorly on his own in the large bed the night before.

The dispatch room was on the fifteenth floor of an old art deco building on the fringe of the city's business district. They rode up on a freight elevator with doors at the front and back, entering a room with a small sign on the door reading 'Unity Cab Co'. The walls were lined with maps of the city, calendars from auto parts companies, posters like those at the Nile. At the back of the room was a large desk, containing a phone with about a dozen lines and a small, upright microphone attached to an archaic two-way radio. There were a few other small tables and chairs scattered around the room, littered with magazines and cups stained with old tea. It had the same musk and incense smell as Prospero's room at home.

A young man with a woven cap holding in dreadlocks quickly took his feet from the desk and tossed his creased magazine on a chair. Prospero acknowledged him with a frowning nod and they shook in their characteristic style, first grasping one another's hands, then slowly pulling them apart, each running his thumb along the back of the other's middle finger so that they could snap simultaneously as they parted hands. The man then handed Prospero a clipboard. He looked it over quickly, then told the young dispatcher he could go. He left without a word.

'Sit yourself down, Matty,' Prospero said, rearranging the few things on the desk. 'It's gonna be a long night. Make some tea if you have a thirst.'

Matthew sat in a large green chair that billowed pale stuffing through random cracks. He picked up a magazine but put it down as soon as Prospero began to talk on the two-way. He leaned forward slightly toward the upright microphone, placing his mouth close to the receiver so he could talk in conversational tones. His body remained completely still, except for the index and middle fingers of his right hand, which he used to depress the talk button at the bottom of the mike, angling his fingers slightly upwards because of his long nails.

He was a short man with veined muscles and large fingers. He had medium-dark skin that had gone black beneath his Berber-blue eyes and a thin gray beard tinged yellow from the incessant smoke of his carved ivory pipe. The ends of his moustache were wire thin from years of twisting. His small, bald head was covered by a cap woven with thick strands of yellow, red and green yarn. He wore an aged tweed sportscoat over a white smock, string-drawn khaki pants and light brown sandals. Matthew watched his eyes as he spoke into the mike. They were distant, alive with concentration on his words.

'*Selah*, brothers. Uncle is on the airwaves. It's a little past midnight which means a new day. So let us pray. Oh sweet Christ bring peace to our troubled nation, and may you bless our drivers to steer courses true and swift, and may you bless the soul of our Emperor and let him rain down wisdom upon us as we struggle with Satan, and may you get David Kingston's wife Carmel all right from her leg pains, and may you help Tadesse fix that damn axle once and for all, and may you look over my little niece Bichu and our new friend Matteus. Amen. Okay.'

He crossed himself from right to left, in the orthodox fashion. The phone buzzed. Prospero released his button and picked it up.

'Yes? Okay, okay, I'll take care of it, sir. Okay.'

He hung up the phone and pressed down the talk button.

'Hey David, wayward brother, come back to me.'

There was no response.

'David, come back to me, brother.'

'Maybe he's out of his car, uncle,' came a voice eventually.

'Yeah, well, Sezwe my friend, you get on down to 15th and K and pick up that fare, pick him up cause he's still waiting there.'

'Yeah, okay, uncle,' came back the voice.

Prospero looked over the clipboard, then went through a time check, calling out the names of all twenty drivers, jotting down their location when they responded. He called David's name first and last, but there was still no answer. As he spoke Matthew looked around the room at the posters and photos. He noticed one on the far wall that showed Prospero as a young man, dressed in running shorts and shirt, standing with two other runners. Matthew recognized the barefoot man in the middle from the poster in the Nile's lobby. He wanted to ask Prospero about it, but he had begun speaking into the microphone again.

'Okay,' he said, settling into his swivel chair. 'Everything looks quiet just now. Yeah. We are all in a quiet city . . .'

'The calm before the storm, uncle,' came a voice over the radio.

'Perhaps, Isayas. We be on Patmos now, looking over a wide water with blind eyes. We are in Nod, waiting for that dry wind . . .'

The phone buzzed. Prospero took the call, then depressed the switch on his mike.

'Hey Peter, get on over to Kalorma, my brother. There's a lady there gotta get to the airport, catch that night flight.'

After giving the address, he turned to Matthew and asked for some tea. Matthew boiled water in the electric kettle, then let the fragrant leaves steep as Prospero did another time check. David still did not answer.

'Come on family man,' Prospero said. 'Answer your call.'

There was only static.

'Hey uncle, tell us about the ride again,' a new voice said. 'Tell us about the Emperor's bug ride.'

'It's a sad story, Mesfin,' he said, taking the cup Matthew offered him.

'Tell us about the Emperor's car, uncle,' came another voice.

Prospero twisted the ends of his long moustache for a moment, considering. His eyes were brilliant with memory.

'This is so. You remember the day, my brothers. Bright and hot, the *simoom* coming in steady from the north, giving flight to the locust. There was fighting at night but the guns had fallen silent by morning. We knew the Colonels had won. You remember those hours, eh? The women hiding in doorways as the jeeps drove past, young men trying to make the airport road but getting stopped at checkpoints. The wail of the locust. Well, I was down by the palace, driving my hack, cause you know I always drove my hack. Day or night, feast or famine, I drive. For some reason the ruffian guards let me through. This is so. I saw the jeeps outside the palace gates, the tanks all covered with flowers, the boys spitting and cussing and holding their Russian guns all proud and nasty. The peacocks on the front lawn were nervous, they were fluttering about. And there were the bodies, too. The palace guard, all in a row. This is so. I pulled over my cab and turned up my collar and pretended like I had business there. Well, it was not too long until they brought him out. They couldn't tie him up, didn't point no weapon at him, the cowards. They just led him down the steps real slow. Then the car pulled up. I couldn't believe the car. A VW bug car. All green and rusted and dented and ugly. Made the Emperor stoop down to get in. All those guards laughed and laughed. This is so. I wanted to drive my Mercedes hack up and give the Lord a ride but I know they would have shot me and maybe shot him. So I just sat there, the engine humming, watching them drive away the King of Kings in that green VW bug car.'

Prospero closed his eyes.

'It's an old story. So. There was a wedding that day. The bride was lovely, the . . .'

The phone rang. Prospero took the call.

'Hey Yacoub, hustle on over to 14th and M and get the pretty lady with a job to do, eh? Now, where was I?'

'The bride was lovely,' Matthew said.

'So.' He closed his eyes again. 'The bride was lovely, the groom tall and strong. They stood in the shade of the omo tree and were wed by the old priest with his beard like a nest, and the gazelle and the yellow bird called out their praise and the people came with gifts of dripping honeycomb and bands of gold and baskets of *teff*, and the wind through the hollows of the omo tree sounded its praise and the bride was lovely, the groom tall and strong. But there's a beggar at the wedding and there are fire ants in the omo tree and the soldiers come in their surplussa jeeps and their shining guns and they trample the honeycomb beneath their blackened boots and throw over the baskets of *teff* and steal the bands of gold, and there's a beggar at the wedding and there are fire ants in the omo tree and the soldiers defile the bride and kill the bridegroom, burning his body so smoke rises into wind that no longer praises, and there is a beggar at the wedding and fire ants in the omo tree, and there is a beggar at the wedding and fire ants in the omo tree. This is so, this is so.'

There was a long silence.

'Hey uncle,' the radio crackled. 'This is David.'

'So, David . . .' Prospero said.

Matthew stayed awake for the entire shift, listening to Prospero's dispatches, making tea when it was needed, answering the phone once when Prospero was lost in the rapture of a song. The old man continued to intersperse the fares with stories, news from home, Coptic prayers and hymns, even a series of riddles the drivers baffled over until dawn. He occasionally took books from the shelf beside the desk, reading from the works of St Augustine, Lamumba, Marcus Garvey, The Apostle Paul, Camus, Jefferson, Gadaffi, Malcolm X, Hermes Trismegistus. Matthew noticed that he never neglected his job, directing the drivers from the map in his mind, keeping an ear on the traffic helicopter reports and emergency calls on the police scanner. Near dawn, a driver named Ras called in to say he'd been robbed by a young boy with two guns. Prospero told him to go home and go to bed. He finished at eight with a prayer, replaced by another young man with dreadlocks and eyes averted in respect.

As they made their way home in an off-duty Unity cab, Matthew asked who the bride and groom had been.

'Lots of people, Matteus,' he said, looking out the window, twisting the ends of his moustache. 'Lots of things.'

Eleni wanted to take a vacation with the money she'd earned at the conference. They chose a nearby island, known for its seclusion and wild horse population. Matthew reserved a cottage for a long weekend. They left after work on Thursday night, taking a bus out to the tip of the peninsula, where they would catch the first ferry of the morning. They thought they could sleep on the bus, but there were many stops, and a drunken party of college kids in the back seats. The bus arrived early, so they huddled under a blanket in a small shelter at the entrance to a pier, surrounded by crab cages and cracked buoys. Eleni put her head on Matthew's chest and dozed. A few cars pulled up and idled outside the pier gate, waiting for the ferry. Small fishing boats chugged by, their occupants folding and unfolding stacks of netting.

André Brand walked into the shed. He did not recognize Matthew, taking a seat at the opposite end of the shelter. He was wearing a large hooded parka with dirty fur lining and blue jean coveralls. He carried a box of computer paper and a case of twelve-year-old scotch. He stared at his shoes, a sour expression on his face. He looked thinner to Matthew, but it was hard to tell with the large hood pulled almost to his eyes.

'Hello, Dr Brand,' Matthew said softly.

Brand looked up with slow surprise. His eyes dilated for a moment in recognition.

'Hello, Walter's son,' he said. His eyes took in Eleni indifferently. 'What are you doing out here at the end of the world?'

As Matthew explained where they were going, Eleni awoke. She sat up, looking Brand over.

'Yeah, that's a nice place,' Brand said. 'Horses. No cars. I live on the other side of the bay. Different ferry. I wish I'd chosen that island, though. These goddamned kids with their dune buggies keep me up half the night.'

'So how have you been?'

'Me?' Brand looked out the door, the sour expression returning to his face. 'Jesus, I don't know. I don't think about things like that, really. I just work and drink and try to sleep a lot.'

'What are you working on?'

'A book. The slating on my roof. Crossword puzzles. Whatever.'

There was long silence. They could hear the backwash from the approaching ferry's engine.

'So how's your dad?' Brand asked at last.

'I honestly don't know.'

'No?'

Matthew shook his head. He could feel Eleni looking at him.

'When are you going to?' Brand asked.

The gate's chain rattled and the cars began to inch forward.

'I don't know,' Matthew said softly. He turned to Eleni. 'The boat's here.'

'So,' she said.

They stood and collected their things. Brand remained seated, staring at them. Just before they left he cracked open the cardboard lid to the case of scotch and took out a bottle.

'Here's something for your stay on the island.'

Eleni took it, thanking him with her smile. Matthew stood still for a moment, as if he wanted to ask Brand something, then silently followed Eleni to the ferry.

They had a small, wooden cottage in the morning shadow of a reed-covered dune, a hundred yards from the water. The front porch was covered with screens that were dotted with small gashes. Inside were three continuous rooms – a lounge with faded furniture and shelves full of cheap novels left by previous tenants, a bedroom with a low bed, and a tiled bathroom that smelled of salt and disinfectant. There was another screened-in porch around the back, as well as an open shower.

'Let's go sleep in the sand,' Eleni said after she dropped their things on the bed. 'Then when we wake up we will begin our vacation.'

'Deal,' Matthew said, leading her out the back door and up the path cut into the dune.

A cold wind was blowing off the bay, but when they lay on the thick blankets it was still and warm. Their beach faced southeast, toward the bay's entrance. A few boats could be seen prowling the fishing lanes, surrounded by flocks of birds. The sun had risen above the horizon – large, dull orange, unradiant. They wrapped the blankets into a tight pouch. Eleni fell asleep immediately. Matthew stayed up a while longer, watching the birds suspended in the stiff ocean breezes.

He felt the rhythm of her breathing, the warmth of her skin on his palm, the flutter of her eyelashes on his neck. Dreaming again, he thought. She'd seemed restless recently, her usual tranquillity disturbed by a number of long-distance phone calls and hushed conversations with Prospero as they brewed tea in the kitchen. He'd asked her about it several times, yet all she'd say was that she was worried about the situation in her country.

He fell asleep and dreamed about his father. They were in the belly of a great ship, shovelling coal from a large pile into a series of giant furnaces. No matter how hard they worked, however, the flames were flickering out, furnace by furnace. André Brand soon appeared from above. He was angry.

'Use your hands!' he said.

Matthew obeyed, reaching down to the pile. But he noticed the coals were flaming orange, like those in the old barbecue grill Walter used on the weekends. He looked over at his father, who had already picked some up in either hand.

'Go ahead,' he whispered.

But Matthew was afraid.

'Go ahead.'

'Look,' Eleni was saying.

Matthew awoke. Eleni sat next to him, facing the island. Matthew rolled on to his stomach. A group of three horses looked down at them. All three were chestnut brown, with black manes that fluttered in the stiff breeze. They munched on strands of brittle grass, keeping a watch on Eleni and Matthew.

'I wonder what they think of us,' Matthew said.

'Oh, they told me,' Eleni said. 'You can see the words in the puffs from the mouths. Like cartoons.'

'And?'

She gently knocked him off his elbows, into the sand.

'They approve.'

They walked all over the island through the afternoon. There were no roads, just a myriad of paths connecting the cottages and running to the beaches. Occasionally, groups of horses crossed a path ahead of them. They saw no other people until they came to a cottage where loud, clashing music played from several boom boxes. They could see kids dancing and wrestling within. Beer cans and food wrappers littered the yard. A boy in a baseball cap crashed through the back door, dropping to his knees in the packed sand and vomiting.

They found a small general store at the island's center where they bought some wine and a bucket of fresh clams from a fat woman who looked at them strangely. She told them it was a good thing they didn't want beer because she'd just been bought out. On the way back to their cottage they saw more horses watching them from a small ravine. Matthew tried to approach them, but they maintained a shy distance, never taking their eyes from him.

It was dusk when they got back to their cottage. They were hungry, so Eleni made a salad while Matthew tried to figure out how to cook the clams. He ended up taking a screen off one of the back windows and placing it over a large pot of boiling water. The steam swirled around them for a long time, causing muddy condensation to run into the water. Finally, the clams began to yawn open. Matthew called Eleni in from the porch, where she'd been leafing through a paperback called *Love's Dark Passage*. She looked over his arrangement with approval, taking the proffered meat with a mincing bite. Her eyes widened with the heat and salt.

'So,' she said.

'You don't like it,' Matthew said.

'It will come. All my favorite tastes are required.'

Matthew let the mistake pass uncorrected. He dumped the clams into a shallow bowl and took them to the screened-in porch, where she had arranged a table and candles. They ate in silence. Occasionally, the sounds of human laughter wafted to them from a nearby beach on night breezes. Once they heard the impatient neigh of a horse.

'Enough,' Eleni said, dropping an empty shell into the bucket. Matthew agreed by pushing his chair away from the table and sighing.

'Let's drink that man's liquor,' Eleni said.

Matthew fetched the bottle from their pile of stuff on top of the bed. He poured it into two wildfowl coffee cups he found in the kitchen and returned to the porch. Eleni took the drink and nestled it under her mouth and nose, inhaling the fragrance.

'So who is this generous stranger?' she asked before sipping.

'He used to work with my father.'

'Why couldn't you answer him?'

Matthew looked out at the screen. Giant mosquitoes swarmed against it with regular clicks.

'Sorry,' Eleni said. 'Let's talk about something new.'

'Yeah,' Matthew said.

'Well?'

'I went to work with Prospero the other night. Listened to his dispatches.'

'Ah yes.'

'What is all that?'

'Well, it's hard to explain. At home he was an *azmari*, who is a man that makes rhymes on special days. If you have a wedding or a funeral or a son is born the *azmari* comes to your home and makes a rhyme story of praise or sorrow. He travelled all over, Prospero.'

'Did he run?'

'You know about it, then?'

'I saw a picture of him with some runners.'

Eleni took a long sip, watching the floating insects.

'Yes, he would run all over. He and his friends. They would run in races and run between jobs and then some of them became very good and began to run in big races and even run in Kenya or Tanzania, against those runners. Then the emperor said he wanted runners for Rome, for the Olympic games. It was Prospero and a boy I don't know his name and the great Bakila. Do you know Bakila?'

'Sounds familiar.'

'He was the greatest runner. He wore no shoes, you see. So none of our runners wore shoes. Well, the nation was very proud of these boys going off to run in Italy, in the country who had shamed us in war. The Europeans laughed at our runners because they had no shoes but by the end of the marathon Bakila had won. He had beaten everybody in the world. It was a great victory for our country, which seems silly now but I think at the time people really were joyous about it.'

'And what about Prospero?'

'Well, when he was running through the yard of the church there, the Vatican, he turned his ankle on one of the cobblestones. He tore something and he should have stopped. But he remembered what the Italians had done to our people in the war. They had shamed us and so on. So, he kept running. Ten more miles, fifteen. He was well behind. It was night now. Everyone else had finished. He says the waiters and drunken kids would stop to watch him pass, the taxi drivers would sound the horn and call out "*avanti*". It took him five hours to cross the line, but he made it. Yet he hurt his leg so badly that he never ran again and must walk with the cane. But I don't think he minds. That dirty rug at home was a gift from the emperor for his courage.'

They listened to the laughter from the beach.

'You're such a sad people,' Matthew said.

'It's a sad place.'

'Do you miss it?' Matthew asked. 'Home?'

'Yes.'

'Do you want to go back ever?'

'I can't.'

'Why not?'

But she didn't answer.

They were awoken by the sound of gunfire. It came from the beach, where the voices had been growing louder all night. Matthew raised himself in bed.

'What the hell was that?'

He looked at Eleni, whose eyes were wide.

'It's guns, Matty.'

There were two more rapid reports.

'They're shooting the horses,' Eleni whispered.

'No, no, they can't be,' Matthew said.

There were two more rapid shots and the sounds of cheering voices.

'We have to go to see,' she said.

They dressed quickly and stole out the back door, heading down a dune path toward the sound. There were more shots, more cheers. The near-full moon was reflected in the white sand, making their way clear. They reached the line of dunes that bordered the beach, peering over its ridge like children at their parents' party.

The first thing they saw was the fire, which smouldered in a deep pit in the sand. Large piles of shells and beer cans littered the beach around it. Some people slumbered nearby, though most stood down near the water's edge. There were about a dozen altogether, most of them holding flashlights. Two stood off to one side, crouching over a large aparatus. The others called for them to hurry. A man stepped out from the main crowd, holding a gun up to his shoulder.

'Pull!'

A clay pigeon was released from the apparatus, sailing over the tide. The others on the beach tried to track it with their flashlights, yet most failed to stay on it. The man fired and missed. The people around him let out a groan. He called again, and another target was released. He hit this one before it left the confusion of flashlight beams, scattering small bits into the surf. The people let out a drunken cheer.

'You see,' Matthew said. 'It's just night shooting.'

Eleni turned and hurried down the dune, saying nothing. When they got back to the cottage she sat rigid on the bed for a long time.

'Let's go in the morning,' she said. 'I don't like this place.'

Spray from the waves the ferry broke lashed their faces and necks, yet they stayed on deck, away from the other foot passengers and the cars below. Eleni had been quiet since they'd seen the shooters, her eyes distant, troubled. Matthew had tried to cheer her up yet she'd only been able to manage a weak smile. They saw just one horse when they walked to the pier, a pewter colt that ignored them.

'I'll tell you,' Matthew said above the sound of the ferry's engine. Eleni looked at him. 'Why I couldn't answer Brand.'

She waited as the boat chopped through water.

'It's because I'd just about gotten to the point where I could hate him from a safe distance. Yeah. From a long way off. Long distance.'

'And?' Eleni asked.

209

'And now, I don't know. I mean, here we are, in the middle of fucking nowhere, and I can't get away from him. He's staying with me, running right along side of me. I can't hate him and I can't ignore what he is, because it's not like he's some other thing from me. It's funny – in losing one twin, I've gained another.' He looked over at her. 'Do you understand any of this?'

'Oh, I understand this,' she said, looking into the broken waves.

They were alone in the restaurant, hardly acknowledging each other as they moved slowly through the lingering cloud of smoke from snuffed candles, wiping tables, stacking chairs and vacuuming. It had been a busy and tiring night – slow at first, with a late rush of customers just before closing. As they finished, there was a crashing noise in the kitchen. They stood perfectly still, looking at the closed door. There was a second, muffled noise. Matthew went in to investigate.

He saw nothing at first, but soon became aware of another presence, in the corner by the alley door. Matthew squatted behind a trolley and reached for the overhead light switch. The lights flickered on, showing a man standing in the corner. When he raised an arm to shield his eyes, Matthew saw that he held two large butcher knives in one hand. He was a short, thin man with close-cropped hair and a drooping moustache. He wore a dirty yellow slicker over a host of sweaters and T-shirts. The bottom of his moustache was tinged with white foam, and Matthew noticed he was holding a whipped cream canister in his other hand. He smiled at Matthew, shrugging his shoulders. Matthew kept his distance, wary of the knives. The man took a step forward and looked as though he was going to speak.

'Easy,' Matthew said, standing, holding his palms toward the knives.

The man stopped, confused by Matthew's tone. He remembered the knives.

'What, these?' he asked, dropping them on to the center table and pushing them away. 'No no, Jack. I was just admiring them. It's not what you think.'

'Then what is it?' Matthew asked.

'Uh, I was looking for the manager,' the man said, licking the cream from his moustache.

Matthew looked at the clock. Two-thirty a.m. There was a long silence as Matthew scrutinized the man. He needed a shave, and the nets of purple vein within the folds of his ears betrayed too much exposure to the cold. Yet his eyes showed lively intelligence, and his small thin hands promised ability. Eleni edged into the room.

'Who's the gentleman?' she asked.

'He's looking for the manager.'

'About employment,' the man added.

'How did you get in?' Eleni asked.

'The door was open,' the man said.

All three looked at the two long creases in the door's metal, the broken padlock on the floor.

'What sort of other jobs do you do?' Eleni asked.

'I'm a performer.'

'Oh yes? What sort of acts are yours?'

The man smoothed out the hair around his ears.

'Cabaret. Comedy, stand up or rep. Satirical medleys. Close-up magic. You name it.'

'I'm sorry,' Eleni said. 'We don't do that here. Just traditional music.'

'What, like Irish stuff? I do that. Listen. There once was a lady from Cork, whose. . . '

'No, no,' Eleni said, laughing. 'I'm sorry.'

The man bit his lip in momentary disappointment.

'Can I show you anyway?'

Eleni looked at Matthew, who smiled perversely.

'Yes, yes, all right. In here,' she said, nodding to the dining hall.

'Primo,' the man said.

'Are you hungry?' Eleni asked.

'No, I'm cool,' the man said. All three of them looked at the canister in his hand. 'Well . . . '

'You go set up and I'll make a sandwich,' she said.

'Come on,' Matthew said, pushing open the swinging door.

Matthew got three Crucial Brew beers from the cooler behind the register while the man walked around the restaurant, squinting at the posters. He took the beer Matthew offered him with a nod.

'Nice place,' he said, looking at the small stage. 'The red spot is a bit torchy, but it's okay for some of my stuff.'

Eleni returned with two cold meat sandwiches and an apple. The man tore hungrily into the meal.

'Obviously,' he said between bites, 'you think I'm a street individual and this performer stuff is a ploy for getting out of B & E raps or conning meals out of kindhearted manageresses. Am I right?'

'So,' Eleni said.

'Sew buttons,' the man said brightly. 'Because that's my gimmick. You see, what I do is lower expectations to such a meager level that success is guaranteed.'

'That's good,' Matthew said, laughing.

The man finished his meal.

'You're on,' Eleni said, checking her watch with a yawn.

The man nodded with curt professionalism. He dipped his index and middle fingers into the puddle of paraffin beside the candle and used it to stiffen and twirl the ends of his moustache. He licked his palms to slick back his thinning hair.

'So,' Eleni said.

He bounded on to the stage, loosening his shoulders with slow shrugs, bouncing on his toes as he pinched the bridge of his nose in concentration. Matthew felt Eleni take his hand.

'There's this guy,' the man said, his voice suave, confidential. 'Just your basic guy. Average job, average life. Except one day, he wins tickets to a football game. Playoffs. Bears and Giants. He can hardly believe it. Great seat – fifty yard line, about midway up. Y'know what I'm saying? The guy can hardly wait for Sunday to come around. Well, when he gets there, it's a mob scene. But does he care? No way. He loves it. Only, he's gotta climb over about twenty people to get to his seat, which is only about eight inches wide. Y'know what I'm saying? To his left is this guy who must weigh about six hundred pounds. Must weigh. To his right is this blonde with garbanzas like the Himalayas, okay? Anyway, this guy gets his beer, his popcorn, his smokes, and is all set for kickoff when someone behind him yells, 'Hey, Steve!' So he has to put down his smokes, ask fatso to hold his beer, ask the blonde with the hoo-hahs to hold his popcorn, stand up, turn around, and look. But what does he see but a sea of faces, none of which he knows. Ah well, he thinks. Don't sweat it. So he sits back down, gets into the game. And it's a doozy. Giants, Bears, y'know what I'm saying? Well about midway through the second quarter, the Giants are driving, you see, and all of a sudden he hears it again – 'Hey, Steve!' Up he stands, jostling the fat guy, bumping into the blonde's knockers. He looks, but again, nothing. Nada. Just strange faces. So he sits down. At half-time he squeezes out to take a leak, a stretch, grab a hotdog and another brew. Squeezes back in, the game starts. Great game. *Tie* game. Y'know what I'm saying? But no sooner is the second half under way than he hears it *again* – 'Hey, Steve!' Well, he's getting mad by now, and so are fatso and the broad with the katangas. He stands up and gives a dirty look to about two thousand people. Nope. Nobody. Down he sits, royally pissed. But soon he's back into the game, which is a classic. Payton. Sims. Taylor. The Fridge. Twenty-one all, fourth quarter. Y'know what I'm saying? The Bears intercept, look like they might get in that barefooted kicker's range. When all of a sudden? You guessed it. 'Hey, Steve!' The guy jumps to his feet, slams down his stuff, turns around and screams at the top of his lungs, "Listen, my name's not Steve!"'

Matthew laughed loudly, twisting in his chair. Eleni shook her head and leaned over to Matthew.

'Expectations met.'

The man bowed briefly.

'Thankyouverymuch. Now, may I please have a salt shaker?'

Matthew handed one up.

'A little magic,' he said as he removed the shaker top. 'In this jar is the most simple substance known to man. Salt. Pure salt. Yet when poured into my hand, it will become as elusive as stardust.'

He inched his sleeves up his arm, then made a flat fist, into which he poured a steady stream of salt. A smaller trickle emerged from the bottom of his hand. His confident expression vanished.

'Wait. Damn.'

He put his hands together for a moment, then opened his right hand to show several moist clumps of salt which he shook off as if they were venomous creatures.

'Take it easy,' Matthew said. 'Take your time.'

He rubbed his palm clean with the napkin Eleni offered, paused for a moment, then tried the trick again, this time without narration. The same trickle leaked from the bottom. He opened his hand slowly this time, revealing more sweat-soaked clumps. His hand began to shake and they fell off like cracked plaster.

'Shit,' he said, tossing the fake thumb to the carpet, its joke flesh cracked. 'Damn.'

'Easy,' Matthew said.

'It's all right,' Eleni said, half-standing from her chair. The man continued to stare into the grains on his palm, sobbing gently now.

'Steady,' Matthew said, showing Eleni the prosthetic thumb he'd picked up from the floor. 'Easy . . .'

Matthew awoke alone. His head ached, the sheets around him were damp and twisted. His heart was racing with light, quick beats that seemed to flutter against his ribs. His armpits and groin were soaked with sweat. Pulses of pain emanating from his left side ran from his neck to his thigh. He lay still for a moment, trying to remember if he'd had a bad night, a bad dream.

He heard Eleni speaking on the phone in the other room. Her voice sounded urgent, somewhat frightened. He tried to listen, but she was speaking in dialect. Sometimes she would emphasize what she said by striking the soft fabric of the chair. When she eventually hung up, there was a long silence. Matthew sat up in bed, feeling a little dizzy. She came back into the room, her eyes moving nervously, her bottom lip beneath her top teeth.

'Good morning,' Matthew said.

'Afternoon,' she said grimly. 'Soon to be night.'

'Hey . . .'

He watched her go to the dresser and nervously rearrange brushes, photos, jars.

'Are you okay?' he asked. 'What is it?'

She stood still for a moment, her back stiffening.

'Nothing. Just bad news from home.'

'What is it?'

She turned towards him.

'Nothing, I said.'

'Eleni . . .'

She approached the bed.

'Are you going to get up today?'

He spun his legs over the side and stood uneasily.

'These sheets are a mess,' she said. 'They are all wet and smell dreadfully.'

She ripped them violently from the bed. Matthew stood shivering in the spring drafts. She rolled them into a bundle, then tore the cases from the pillows. She gathered them all together.

'I'm going downstairs to put these in the machine,' she said, leaving him alone in the room.

He dressed slowly, feeling a little better, although his side still ached. He went into the kitchen and made a pot of tea, then sat by the picture window and drank it slowly. He watched the birds on the opposite buildings and in the quiet streets below. After a while, he began to notice their complex organization, the oblique politics of their movements. Although they seemed at first to be oblivious to one another, the slightest movement by each resulted in reactions by several others, which in turn caused a few others to move, until the chain returned to the first bird. There were borders and zones that had to be respected, or else there would be noisy warnings, raucous flights, even an occasional attack. Once, a nearby car backfired, and every bird took off in abbreviated flights, landing moments later to retake the positions they'd had before the disturbance.

Eleni returned, calm now. She sat on the edge of the chair and stroked Matthew's damp hair.

'You were restless last night,' she said.

'Yeah, I got some sort of bug or something,' he said.

She looked out the window.

'What are you doing?'

'Watching the birds.'

She nodded.

'Let's go out,' she said.

The café was empty except for the owner and a young bearded man with green sneakers. They were arguing passionately. Eleni and Matthew ordered coffee and sat as far away from them as possible. They didn't speak for a long while.

'Hey . . .' Matthew said at last.

Eleni looked up at him.

'You've heard me speak about my nephew, Dawit. The wild one.'

'Yes.'

She took a breath.

'He's not my nephew, Matty. He's my son.'

Matthew felt a wave of heat through him; fear and the fever.

'He lives with my mother. But now he's in trouble. He's been arrested by the government. They will either put him in jail or in the army.'

'What did he do?'

'Sloganeering. He and some other boys painted some nasty words about the Colonels on the walls of their school. They were seen. These things often happen.'

'How old is he?' Matthew asked, not knowing what else to say.

'He's sixteen. I had him when I was fourteen.'

Matthew stared at the reflections of the overlapping posters on the café walls in his black coffee.

'You want to know,' she said, 'why I have left him behind, why I am not with him, and you want to know why I never told you I have a son. These are things you want to know, yes?'

Matthew nodded.

'So. I didn't tell you about him at first because back then I didn't know of a way to make you understand I was not a bad woman. And then I never had the courage. The longer you let it go, the harder it gets. You know.'

'Yes.'

She took a breath.

'I had him because on the day the emperor fell some soldiers stopped me and my friend Ian . . .'

Matthew remembered her dream, remembered Prospero's story.

'I know, Eleni.'

She accepted this.

'Every time I looked at Dawit I thought of the smell of those ruffians, their calloused hands and curses, I thought of the burns they made on Ian's back, the way he yelled. Do you know how they did that? They put their guns next to his head, then shot them off, just missing him. Then they would touch the hot barrels to his skin.' She paused for a moment. 'Dawit has a devilish smile that was too much like those soldiers' smiles. Like his fathers' smiles. He was always reminding me, in all the things he did. I tried for a few years to live with him but it was too much. I was too weak. I was young and ashamed. So I ran to the place where I thought they didn't have shame and pain and things like that.'

The owner came over to pour them more coffee, muttering to himself, his face red from the argument.

'What can we do to help him?' Matthew asked.

Eleni looked up and smiled. But her face grew serious again.

'Nothing, I'm afraid.'

'Let's get him to come here, live with us. We can get a bigger place. He could go to school or work at the Nile or drive for Prospero.'

'One needs a visa.'

'We'll get him one.'

'How?' she asked. 'He has no sponsor.'

'Can't you sponsor him? Or Prospero?'

'They're clamping down. We're not sufficiently resident.'

Matthew paused.

'How about me?'

She smiled.

'Who are you?'

'What do you mean?' Matthew asked.

'I mean are you a university? Can you offer him a job? Are you his dad?'

Matthew said nothing.

When they got home Eleni went to the basement for the laundry. Matthew went up to the apartment and drank several glasses of orange juice. He felt drained by the sickness, yet very lucid. He walked over to the picture window and looked out at the darkening street. The birds were gone. Eleni came in, holding the folded sheets against her chest.

'I want to marry you and adopt Dawit,' Matthew said.

She was silent. He couldn't see her face in the dusk of the apartment.

'Eleni?'

'Yes.'

She walked over to him and put her head on his chest, the still-warm sheets radiant between them.

There was a metal detector in the lobby, an electronic archway manned by two uniformed men. Eleni passed through silently, yet the klaxon sounded when Matthew entered it. He removed keys, coins, his watch, and tried again. Still it sounded. He was drawn aside by one of the guards who divined his body with a device that looked like a branding iron. He failed to locate anything.

'Do you have any metal plates in you?' the guard asked.

'No.'

'Artificial limbs?'

Matthew shook his head. The guards looked at each other, puzzled.

'Strange,' one said.

'Must be some kinda malfunction.'

'But it don't sound for them,' said the first, gesturing to two women who passed through without alarm.

'Weird.'

There was a long pause as they looked Matthew up and down.

'Can I go?' Matthew asked with a half smile.

'I guess,' one of the guards said.

'I thought I was the alien,' Eleni said as they stepped on to the elevator.

They had to take a number. Seventy-four. The board above the door read fifty-one. They found the only two plastic-molded chairs not occupied or littered with gum and paper. There were about two dozen other people scattered through the brightly-lit room – two oriental families with several small children, Hispanic men in tatty sportscoats and baseball caps, an elegantly dressed black couple, a red-faced man who paced nervously in and out of the room.

There were three firmly shut windows at the front of the room. They were unmanned. To their left was a door with a tattered 'Do Not Enter' sign on it. At the back of the room was a shelf littered with hundreds of forms beneath a picture of the president. Piped-in music, interrupted by long silences or garbled static, came from two round speakers on the ceiling. Matthew noticed that dozens of coins, pins and paperclips had been shot into the soft plaster around the speakers.

They sat patiently for nearly half an hour, moving only to take small drinks from the water fountain or play peekaboo with the children. One of them began crying when Matthew made a face, yet stopped when Eleni sang him a short lullaby. The number board above the door stayed on fifty-one. The red-faced man, who had begun to swear loudly, finally walked out. A few minutes later, the elegantly dressed black man walked to one of the three windows and drummed the glass with his long, ringed fingers. He continued until a harried-looking woman with a fallen hair-do and glasses hanging limply around her neck came to the window. She tried to gesture him away, yet he held his ground. She slid the window open.

'Please step back,' she said with mechanical bitterness. 'You must wait for your number to be called.'

'No numbers are called,' he said in a deep, gentle voice.

'Just step back and wait,' she said, slamming shut the window.

The man stared at the window for a moment, firmed his tie-knot, cocked an arm for his wife to take, then led her from the room.

'This is absurd,' Matthew said. He stood and walked to the windows, but thought better of it. He looked at Eleni, who nodded toward the door. He stepped up to it and tried the handle. It was unlocked. He stepped through.

He entered a large room of desks and file cabinets. There was no one around. The desks were littered with manila folders, stacks of fingerprint cards, cheaply framed photographs, paper cups half-filled with scummy coffee. The yellowed walls were covered with maps, FBI posters, crayon drawings by children, another picture of the president. A water cooler by the door gurgled.

'Hello?' Matthew asked firmly.

The ring of a distant phone was his only answer. He walked across the room, following the noise. He discovered a long hallway that had been hidden from view by a file cabinet. It was as devoid of life as the main room. The phone sounded several more times, then stopped. Matthew walked down the hall.

He paused at several closed doors, listening. Nothing. He then heard a chair's squeak and the clearing of a throat from an open door near the end of the hall. He walked to it and discovered a large, sunlit office with a crafted oak desk and several large chairs. A man sat at the desk, working on a toothpick and tissue model of a zeppelin. He was tremendously fat, with ginger hair and small ears. His stubby fingers worked on the delicate model with surprising agility. The nameplate at the front of his desk read 'C. M. Bec'. Matthew tapped on the doorframe.

'Moment,' Bec said as he affixed a rectangular section of tissue. When he finished he looked up Matthew.

'Yes?'

'I've come for some information,' Matthew said.

Bec wiped his hands with a paper towel.

'Yes?'

'I'm marrying a foreign national and I want to adopt her son.'

'Is he in this country?'

'No.'

'Take a seat,' Bec said, nodding to one of the large chairs.

Matthew slid into the chair, smelling the fumes of glue from Bec's work. He examined the man's face. He had very large cheeks, chins and neck, yet his other features were absurdly small. His blue-gray eyes were almost lost in the fat, while his red eyebrows were nearly invisible. He had a small nose that barely surpassed his cheeks and bluish lips that looked as if they were being sucked back into his head. He wore a three-piece blue suit whose seams were strained by his mass. A series of large buttons, latches, fobs and chains seemed to be the only thing holding him in. Matthew noticed he wore a signet ring on his right hand that was almost covered with flesh, like a pan that held an over-risen loaf of bread.

'This is not an easy thing you've set out to do,' Bec said.

'I figured,' Matthew said.

'Where's the little lady from?'

Matthew named the country. A sarcastic smile passed over Bec's face like an underdeveloped hologram.

'I see,' he said, shifting his mass enough to open a drawer and pull out a large folder. He ran a large thumb through it, pulling out papers until he had a stack about a half-inch high. He dropped them in front of the model, explaining that these would have to be filled out. He then recited a hyperlitany of additional information that would have to be supplied: marriage license, birth certificates, tax and employment records, blood tests, chest X-rays, fingerprints, education certificates, fees, waivers, affidavits. Matthew rested the tips of his fingers on the stack of papers.

'How long?' he asked.

'Six to eighteen months.'

'That's long,' Matthew said.

Bec said nothing, the sarcastic shadow again passing over his face.

'Perhaps we could get a temporary visa for the boy, while this stuff is being taken care of?' Matthew suggested.

'No way. The visa has to be issued in the country of origin.'

Matthew looked at the model.

'What if he's in danger of political prosecution?'

'What did you say the country was again?'

Matthew told him and Bec reached for another folder. He looked through it, shaking his head in increasing arcs as he read. He slammed it shut.

'No way. They're not on our hit parade just now.'

'What does that mean?'

'It means people in trouble there aren't necessarily our types.'

Matthew sat in silence. Bec sat back in his chair, hoisting up his arms and with great difficulty locking his fingers behind his head.

'Let me ask you something,' he said. 'What are your intentions?'

'What?'

'Are they pure?' Bec asked, the sarcasm no longer a shadow.

'What the hell is that supposed to mean?'

'Oh, come on, kid. Don't be a jerk. What are you trying to pull here, anyway? How much are these jungle-bunnies paying you to run this little scam? We know how it works. You get your bread and she gets her card and her piccaninny in to boot.'

'It's not like that,' Matthew said softly.

Bec looked him over.

'No?'

'No.'

Bec sat forward, his hands hitting his blotter with simultaneous thuds. A bemused smile caused his lips to edge toward the front of his face.

'You know something funny? I believe you. I actually do. Which is all the more pathetic. You've found yourself a snatch of black twat and now you're going to be her hero. She blinks her bugaboo eyes at you and plays some damsel in distress and so you're going to be the hero and save the day. You gonna be big old bwana, as if that's what she didn't peg you for in the first place.'

'You're wrong.'

'Okay, let's say I'm wrong about that, too. Let's say she isn't conning you. Fine. That doesn't change a thing. The winds have shifted, kid. We're letting different garbage blow in this year. You get nothing from us. You're going to have to figure out another way to be a hero.'

Matthew stood up.

'Fuck you,' was all he could say.

'Great. Wonderful,' Bec said, nodding towards the door.

Matthew began to walk out.

'Hey,' Bec called.

Matthew turned around to see Bec spreading his arms, puffing out his massive chest and stomach.

'When you exercise your conscience, it loses weight.'

Eleni sang at the Nile that night. Matthew listened from the sink, stepping to the doorway to watch her when he had a chance. She sat at an oblique angle to the audience, ignoring their applause and requests. Her eyes were closed during most of the songs, and she simply hummed through several sections, as if listening to them in her imagination. Many of the diners returned to their conversations or meals before she'd finished. Others simply left.

Matthew found his work increasingly difficult as the night wore on. The heat from the kitchen compounded his own, and the strong smells made him nauseous. He had trouble lifting boxes of food or wash racks due to the sharp pains in his side. By eight o'clock he'd had enough. He waited for Eleni to take a break, then told her he was going home. Her eyes awakened with concern when she saw his complexion and his sallow eyes. She said she had to stay, but would be home just after closing.

Prospero was in the lounge when Matthew got home, reading on the tattered couch. After performing the snap handshake with him, Matthew slumped in a chair, dripping with sweat. His limbs were heavy, his side throbbing. Prospero looked him over.

'Are you okay, Matty?' he asked, offering one of the sky-blue eucalyptus candies he was forever eating.

221

'I'm feeling feverish.' Matthew said, declining the offer. 'I think I have a bug.'

'I got just the thing.'

Prospero limped into the kitchen and rattled around for a moment. Matthew heard the kettle sing, then the sound of a spoon clicking against the side of a glass. Prospero returned with a steaming cup of tea.

'This may or may not help,' he said. 'But you look like hell and it will make me feel better to have given it to you. So drink, goddamit.'

Matthew sipped at the hot and bitter drink. Bits of soggy leaf clung to his lips and tongue, yet the liquid in his throat was soothing.

'Good.'

They sat in silence for a moment.

'So tell me about Eleni's son,' Matthew said.

Prospero raised an eyebrow as he refilled his silver cup from the wide-bottomed carafe of sweet wine on the coffee table.

'When Dawit was a baby everybody pity him. Poor kid, they say, and they were right. But as he became a boy and then slowly a man people don't pity him so much. They begin to see in that crooked smile something they don't like. It remind them of what he is. So Dawit begins to be a devil, a troublemaker, a rebel, to show everybody that he's not what his fathers are. Same old story, Matty. The bastard son curses the father who won't give him his due. The wronged son will fight the father. Only with Dawit, the father is a whole fucking government, man. He's got a big battle ahead of him.' He laughed softly, twisting the ends of his moustache. 'Funny world, eh? Dawit paints a wall and they clamp him. Nigger spray a wall over here and they give him a grant and a show.'

'What's Eleni going to do?'

Prospero gave his hand a fatalistic twist.

'She's tried living away from it but I don't think she's at peace like that. I don't know, Matty. Maybe she'll go back.'

'That doesn't say much for me, does it?'

'I don't know, my son. Maybe it says a whole fucking hell of a lot for you. Maybe it says everything for you.'

Matthew's eyes closed with sorrow and fatigue.

'Maybe . . .'

He didn't remember going to bed, didn't remember Eleni's return. He slept dreamlessly. In the morning, the damp impression in the sheets showed that he hadn't moved during the night. He noticed a few small clumps of hair on his pillow.

Eleni was sitting on the couch in the lounge, leafing through a cracked leather book of photographs. Matthew slumped next to her.

'You should see a doctor, Matty,' she said, stroking his hair.

'It's just a bug. I used to get them when I was a boy.'

She shut the book and placed it on her lap.

'I'm going to return home, Matthew.'

He closed his eyes and leaned back his head.

'I know.'

'I . . .'

He stood and walked quickly to the bathroom, dry heaving over the toilet. The spasms came violently, uncontrolled, as if he were being beaten. When they abated he slumped on the floor between the toilet and the tub, clutching his aching side. Eleni came and dampened a washcloth in the sink, then sat on the edge of the tub and wiped his face.

'Can I come with you?' he asked.

She smiled and softly lashed the top of his head with the cloth.

'No, don't be silly. You are part of the lightness I must leave behind.'

'I know.' He looked in the space behind the toilet and saw some theater tickets they had lost. They had stayed home that night, making love on Prospero's carpet.

'And besides, you don't even have a passport, do you?'

Matthew smiled weakly and shook his head.

'Now go back to bed,' she said. 'I'll bring you some tea or weak soup or maybe a chili dog.'

'When will you go?'

'When you are well. I'm on stand-by.'

The fever failed to break that night or the next day. Matthew stayed in bed, sleeping in restless intervals. Eleni looked after him, using the moments he slept to pack her things. There were a few more long-distance calls, and her voice sounded more anxious. She could not sleep or sit still for very long until well after midnight of the second day, when she fell into a deep sleep beside Matthew on the bed. He slept too, waking just before dawn. He felt a little better, although he could tell the fever was still on him. As if I'm in the eye of a storm, he thought. Matthew looked over at Eleni. Her eyelashes fluttered rapidly.

He stood, dressed, and packed his few things. Two suitcases, an armful of books, the videocam case. He deposited them in the lounge,

223

then sat in the chair by the picture window and watched light come to the street. Prospero soon returned from work, his keys rattling.

'Lazarus,' he said upon seeing Matthew, his eyes widening in mock awe as they snap-shook hands.

'Would you call me a cab?'

Prospero stood still in the middle of the room, nodding.

He watched her sleep until he heard the taxi brakes squeak in the street below. Her eyelashes weren't fluttering so much now. He leaned over to kiss her. He could feel the warmth of her flesh, smell the spicy fragrance. He stole from the room.

Prospero helped him carry his things to the cab, then told the cabbie to turn the goddamned meter off. He and Matthew stood next to the back door that jutted out like the wing of a coasting bird.

'She'll be all right,' Prospero said, twirling the ends of his moustache.

'I know,' Matthew said. 'Listen, tell her . . .'

Prospero shook his head, then shook Matthew's hand. The snap which concluded their touch was barely audible. Matthew slid into the cab and could see the dreadlocked cabbie's eyebrow rise in the rear-view mirror. Matthew gave him his home address.

'So,' the driver said.

NOSTOPATHIOS

T he map made no sense. Its scale was all out of proportion with the reality that confronted Walter. What were avenues on the map were actually cramped alleys of tourist shops, while the large boulevards of warehouses and apartments he'd passed were depicted as side streets. And the overlapping cartoons of ruins weren't any help. As Walter tried in vain to figure out where he was, he felt the presence of a person behind him. He turned to see a thin man in a black suit with thick glasses looking over his shoulder. The man nodded grimly at Walter, then reached out and flipped the map right-side-up. He left before Walter could thank him.

He had been wandering through the narrow streets and blind alleys of the crowded marketplace for nearly an hour, trying to find the square where he could catch a taxi to George's house in the suburbs. Yet he kept passing the same shops selling postcards or wineskins or crockery or beads, the same stalls with their spools of lamb and charred kebab and pregnant olives and clots of feta cheese. Someone jostled him hard from behind and he realized he was blocking the way, so he stepped into a dead-end alley.

He leaned against a damp wall, jetlag paralysing his muscles for a moment. His back had been throbbing since the final approach. From where he stood he could see the ruins, dull white above the city's collar of smog. The smell of diesel and burnt fat was less powerful here, so he took the deep breaths he'd craved since arriving in the city. He also took a quick inventory of his possessions to be sure one of the dozens of people who'd come up against him since arrival hadn't relieved him of any of them. Passport. Wallet stuffed with traveller's checks and currency. Shoulder bag with a few days' clothing and photos of his family. A pocketful of drachmas, with their strange alloy and heroic busts. The paper with George's address and phone number. The duty-free Japanese mini-recorder with three blank cassettes and a Greek language lesson. No keys, no licenses, no business cards, no appointment or address books. No return ticket. All there, he thought.

The shop across the alley caught his attention. It was a small, bustling building, almost hidden behind the canopy and the clothes racks spilling over from its neighbor. Walter stepped across the alley and peered at the displays in the window. He paused a moment, then stepped inside.

It was dark, and the dank smell indicated that the door was seldom opened. The only other person in the shop was an old man reading a tabloid paper behind a small counter. Walter examined the shop's only merchandise – toy soldiers, arranged in tight, dustless formations along the walls. Fusiliers, archers, doughboys, Swiss guards, Zulu spearmen, desert rats. The best were on the back wall, a squadron of soldiers in the formal dress of the Greek army, with tassled hats, blue tunics, white skirts and pointed boots. Walter picked one from the ranks and examined it in the pale light. Its facial features were exquisite, somehow suggesting a melancholy pride.

'Hyou like?' the old man asked above the paper.

'Yes. Yes, I do.'

He soon found the main square. Although it was mid-afternoon, the square was almost empty. Mostly police, lounging on corners or sitting in the backs of small buses. In the gutter were several large piles of rocks and crumpled paper that seemed to have been only recently collected. A chemical breeze blew by, causing Walter's eyes to water momentarily. The only human noise was a drunk who yelled at pigeons near a closed taverna. Everyone else moved quickly, avoiding looking at the police.

Walter hailed a taxi. He had to repeat the address several times to the driver, then show him Helen's directions. There was a newspaper on the front seat, and Walter noticed the same cover photo as the other papers he'd seen hanging in the marketplace – a young man tossing a petrol bomb, his face shrouded by a handkerchief. His long, curly hair flowed with the violence of his motion.

The suburbs were squat addenda to the city's prosaic mass. The streets repeated themselves. Vine-covered houses with small balconies, shops fronted by fruit baskets and newspaper racks, bus stop huts occupied by chunky women holding plastic bags. Occasionally he saw clusters of police, but nothing like the presence in the square. Once they were stopped by two officers with large white caps who joked for a moment with the driver, then waved them on.

George's stucco house was at the end of a quiet street lined by cypress and fruit trees. It was a two-storey structure with vine-covered walls and shuttered windows. Walter walked through a grassless yard and rang the doorbell, yet there was no sound. A cat stared down at him from the balcony, licking its flanks without taking its eyes from Walter. He rapped on the smoky glass. There was a banging sound and the scuttle of padded feet.

'G'day, Walter,' George said, grinning broadly as he opened the door. He pumped Walter's hand with savage enthusiasm. 'Come in, welcome, take a load off yer feet, mate.'

'Hello,' Walter said, trying to keep up with the smaller man as he raced ahead down the hallway. 'Thank you.'

'Here,' George said, pointing the way into a room like a tour guide. Walter hesitated, uncertain of what was expected of him. 'Hyou go in, an I'll bring you a fix, neh? Okay?'

'Excuse me?' Walter asked.

'Tinnie,' George said, making a guzzling gesture. 'Beer.'

'A beer would work,' Walter said. George looked at him quizzically. 'Yes, thank you.'

George nodded and shuffled into the kitchen. Walter went into the lounge, sitting heavily on a doily-encrusted chair. The room had the waxy smell of rare use. The magazines on the table and candy in the small bowls were strictly for display. Never-lit candles and polished icons lined the shelves and the mantle. The walls were covered with photographs, all portraits.

George was Helen's cousin, older than her by a few years. He had emigrated to Australia as a young man with his wife and baby, working for twenty years in a warehouse. He'd returned to Greece after his wife had died when a bus crashed into their house as she was cooking dinner. Now he worked for the government. His only son had stayed on in Australia, where he did something with a sound system for a rock band. He had once come to stay at Walter's in New Jersey, a slouching, drunken moron who'd thrown up in their garage and fought with Eddie. George returned with a tray of beer, cheese and cold cuts.

'Welcome,' he said formally after handing Walter bottle and glass. Walter nodded. He saw that the beer was named Fixx.

'Sorry he's not too cold, mate,' George said. 'Electricity's off, hyou know. Strikes.'

'So that's what it is,' Walter said after taking a long sip. 'There were no customs people at the airport. And very few buses.'

'Communists,' George said, making a face. 'Students. That lot.'

'Does it affect you, in your work?'

'*Ohi*,' he said. 'No.'

'What is it exactly you do?' Walter asked between sips.

'Me,' George said, a proud grin coming to his face. 'I am boss at food mountain.'

'The food mountain? What's that?'

George searched unsuccessfully for the words, then hurried from the room, returning with a book of photographs. He stood next to Walter, holding it open for him to see. Walter flipped through several pages of George, dressed in a white jumpsuit and hard-hat, standing next to a massive pile of what looked to be dead insects.

'What is this?'

'Figs.'

'Oh, so you distribute them.'

George drew himself up, a look of shocked insult coming to his face.

'No way, mate. Never distribute. We *keep* them. That's the food mountain,' he said, tapping a photograph. 'Europe pays us not to sell them. To keep prices all right. If we distribute them, then prices go down and the Spains and the Italy get all the money. So we make a mountain. We also have lakes of olive oil, but I don't have photographie of them.'

'But don't they rot?' Walter asked, tapping the edge of the photo. 'Don't they go bad?'

George spread his hands and made a clicking sound with his tongue behind lips that pouted fatalistically.

'So then, you just throw them out?'

'No,' George said. 'We keep.'

Walter handed him back the album and George sat on the couch.

'So, how's Helen?' George asked after a while.

'She's well. She sends her love.'

'Yes, she did that in her letter, too. So – when she come?'

Walter spread his hands noncommitally. George frowned but did not pursue the subject.

'When you want to go to *horio*?'

'Excuse me?' Walter asked.

'To the village. To Nostopathios.'

'Oh, yes. As soon as possible.'

George nodded.

'Tomorrow then, if the strike allows.'

They drank from their beers in silence for a while.

'My father is glad you've come for your house,' George said. 'He's tries keep it fix but he's an old bloke.'

Walter nodded.

'But Walter, what hyou do?' George asked, his thick brow furrowing. 'Why are you halone? Man halone, he's not good.'

'George . . .'

'I know, mate,' he insisted. 'No good.'

'Perhaps not,' Walter said, looking away.

George opened his hands and made that fatalistic clicking noise.

They left for the village early the next morning. Walter hoped George wouldn't come further than the Athens station, but he bought two tickets. The train was delayed, so they went into a small café where a group of conductors were having a heated argument. Walter ordered a coffee that turned out to be about one-quarter grounds. George got two fingers of anis liqueur that became murky when he added a few drops of water from the pitcher on the bar.

Walter remained silent as George rambled on about national politics. There had been a small strike up north that had become ugly. The army was called in, shots were fired, an organizer had been killed. The big unions were now planning a national strike unless the government resigned. Walter lost interest when he started to go into details and describe personalities. He watched an old woman with a black scarf and shawl enter the café, carrying a staff of crossed sticks to which dozens of pieces of paper were pinned. She walked directly to Walter's table, muttering inaudibly. He handed her ten drachmas and she gave him a ticket. He stuck it in his pocket as she backed away from him, nodding and giggling to herself.

'Walter . . .' George was saying. 'Walter, we've been called. We have to go, mate. They won't wait.'

As they trotted toward the platform he saw the old woman again. She stood at the edge of the track, a small cloud of smoke swirling about her crumpled hose. She smiled toothlessly and shook the lottery board at him, but he ducked past her.

Their car was crowded with peasants who ate cold meat and black bread from the plastic bags they clutched to their laps. Walter and George sat in silence, facing one another. By the time they reached the port of Pirea, just south of the city, George was sleeping lightly. Walter watched the

231

freighters being loaded and unloaded by slow cranes, the supertankers anchored in the haze further out. Sometimes the sun would be caught by slicks of oil in the still water, casting blinding glazes at Walter.

The train soon began a slow ascent through a range of treeless hills covered by dark green scrub, flat boulders and goats who stood at awkward angles or pranced over ridges. The valleys were dense with small orchards of olive or fig and meadows of poppy. Sometimes he could see flocks of dirty sheep watching the train as frenetic dogs circled them. The train stopped about every fifteen minutes at small stations where old men played dominoes beneath shade trees. The slamming doors awoke George, who would sit up in his seat and look around, then smile at Walter, saying, 'Not yet, mate.' Walter was surprised how different it was here from Athens. The air was empty of fog and noise, the colors were clear and unsmudged. He felt Athens' nervous fatigue begin to abate.

They reached Nostopathios in the late afternoon. It looked like the other villages Walter had seen on the journey – a series of small, irregular houses starting in the valley and following the logic of the hillside to the peak, where it ended at a cross or monument of some sort. The train track provided the village's lower boundary. Further into the valley were orchards, wells, a looming yellow church and adjacent graveyard. The station was in a copse of large trees that tossed shadows around when the wind blew. Next to the waiting room was a small café with about a half dozen tables, occupied by old men who played the inevitable games of dominoes or fiddled with black beads. George led Walter from the train.

Connie's twin brother John greeted them as they stepped from the train, saying something Walter couldn't hear above the noise of the slamming door. He ignored George, grabbing Walter's shoulders and kissing his cheeks. His face's stubble was wiry, his breath sweet and resinous. John then pulled back and looked at Walter with his watery olive eyes. Walter could see Connie there. But the playfulness and energy seemed drained by age or some sad wisdom. He nodded once and led Walter and George to his table at the café, where there were three glasses and a large, labelless bottle. The men at the other tables looked Walter over with frowning nods.

Walter watched John as he poured out the pale yellow wine with a shaky hand. He wore a brown suit with a tan vest and starched white shirt buttoned to the collar. He was heavy around the neck and waist, and the tops of his hands were a leathery fabric of sinew and liver spots. Old age and long work, Walter thought. His pale lips and Adam's apple were busy with concentration as he evenly topped the glasses. A string of worry beads hung loosely from his right wrist, clicking against the bottle as he poured.

'*Endoxi*,' he said, finishing pouring and passing out the glasses. He said something to Walter in formal tones.

'He says he greets you and is happy you've come for your house and wants to tell you the story of the clinking of the glasses,' George translated.

John spoke in long, recitative sentences, his watery eyes fixed on Walter.

'Wine is a gift from the gods, you see,' George translated. 'It was given to, uh, satisfy the senses of man. The gods had first given woman to him for this, but she turned out to be a big mistake. But wine, this is for the senses. *Eef* you drink it right. First,' he said as John held up his glass, 'you look into the wine, look at its beauty, and the eyes are satisfied. Then,' he continued as John held the glass to his nose, 'you smell it, smell its perfume, and so you satisfy the nose. Then,' he said as John wet his pale lips with the wine, 'you touch it to your skin, feel its feel, and so the sense of touch is satisfied. Yet before you drink to satisfy the taste,' George said as John held up a stubby finger, 'you must satisfy the ears, the hearing. You must hear the wine . . .'

John and Walter touched their glasses together. The noise sounded through the quiet copse.

'*Endoxi*,' John said nodding.

'Now you may satisfy the taste,' George said.

Walter sipped at the cool resin wine. This is the stuff, he thought, looking at John's watery eyes. This will do.

They drank several more glasses, then headed up into the village, passing through a series of balcony-shaded alleys lined with hay and dung. A thin fog that smelled of burnt olive and peat swirled about them. They stopped a few times so John could explain about Walter to old people who leaned out of windows. About halfway up the slope was the town square, built on a small plateau. It consisted of several large houses, a café full of more old men and a post office that appeared to be closed. No merchants, no lights, no cars. John stopped them near the upper edge of the square, pointing to a slightly dilapidated house.

'*Plika*,' he said proudly.

Walter looked it over. It was two storeys, made of the same sun-drenched stucco and red slating as every other house in the village. The ground floor seemed to be a storage or barn area – he could see hollow darkness between the slats covering the bottom door. A vine-covered staircase ran up the side of the house. Walter could not see any structural cracks or signs of seepage. In fact, the occupied houses nearby seemed to be in roughly the same state of repair. He wanted to move right in but kept quiet, nodding appreciatively to John.

'He says it will need some work,' George explained.

'Good,' Walter said. '*Endoxi.*'

John's smaller house was near the peak. He lived there with his wife Haliklia, a frail, near-blind woman who clutched Walter every time he passed near her. They sat in the cramped kitchen, George translating John's stories about the relatives whose photos hung about the kitchen. He passed over the picture of Walter and Helen and the boys, taken ten years earlier. Walter found it difficult to listen after a while, the constant flow of retsina and thin air making him light-headed.

Haliklia finally served dinner, going outdoors to fetch the meat from a brick oven built directly into the side of the hill. They started with a first course of salty goat's cheese piled on chunks of black bread, viscid olives and baked pistachios, grapeleaves rolled around rice and hazelnuts. Then the main course of crumbling lamb spiced with garlic and oregano, roasted potatoes with nearly unbreakable skins and insides as soft as cream, mounds of kale seasoned with wine vinegar and brown sugar. They ate in silence, the three Greeks making sure Walter's plate was never less than full. When he'd finally had enough, Haliklia cleared the plates and John rummaged through an icon-littered chest until he found a stainless steel bottle and three aperitif glasses. They drank the ouzo with quick gulps.

John asked Walter a question.

'He wants to know if Connie was rich,' George said. 'He hears Americans are rich.'

Walter shrugged.

'No. Not particularly.'

John nodded at this news and asked Walter another question.

'No, me neither,' Walter said, not needing a translation. John said something, then made that fatalistic clicking noise, deep in his mouth.

'He asks what's the point of being in America then, mate,' George said.

Walter shrugged and held up his glass for another measure of ouzo.

The outhouse was over the hill's peak, about thirty yards from the back door. Walter walked slowly over the narrow path, lighting the way with a large candle. John and Haliklia had gone to bed just after dinner and George had walked down the hill to stay at a cousin's. Walter was given a cot in the kitchen to sleep on. He had stayed up for a long time, staring at the photos on the walls. He did not know who most of the people were, although he could see his wife's eyes and posture and grim smile in many of them. He wondered about the two times she had come to visit here, on her own and with her sisters. She had told him upon returning that there were a thousand small reasons for being glad she didn't have to live here, as well as a few large ones – the poverty, the treatment of women, the hopelessness of the young. Yet counterpoised with that relief had been a regret, a feeling that she had been cut off from something that generations had been preparing her for. A nostalgia for missed experience, she'd called it. When Walter had returned from Phoenix and told her he had to go away for a little while, she had suggested he come here and stay in the house. She had playfully suggested they could retire there when he was done fixing it and himself up. Walter knew there was a real hope there. He wondered when he would be able to send for her.

He reached the outhouse, a lean-to whose sides were draped with tattered cloth. He slid in, placing the candle on the floor. It smelled of smoke, shit and lime. There was no commode, simply two molded footprints in front of a funnel hole in the ground. A cypress branch half-stripped of large leaves hung from the leaning wall, as did George's newspaper. The fire-throwing youth on its cover danced in the flickering candlelight, as if he were preparing to throw his missile right at Walter, who dropped his pants and tried to fill the footprints with his leather shoes.

Walter went to his house the next morning. It wasn't as bad as he thought it would be. Everything that needed doing, he could do. There were four rooms on the second floor, plus a kitchen with a wall oven and a stone sink which drained into a ditch that ran behind the house. The walls were swirled plaster, the ceilings crossed by dark beams, the floors made of slightly warped wood. It was sparsely furnished – a double bed in one of the rooms, a chest of drawers and a tall wardrobe in another, a table and some chairs in the kitchen. There were about a dozen framed photographs of the same stoic, black-dressed people he'd seen at John's house hanging in the rooms. He left them where they were, adding his own pictures of the boys and Helen above the bed. He then inspected the structure. There were a few sections of plaster missing, a few blotches of seepage, but nothing that some rigorous bunging and patching wouldn't fix. He would also have to refinish the floors and replace the rotted planks. And there was no outhouse. He'd leave that for last.

He began by clearing away the rubble, mouse droppings and cobwebs, using a thatched broom and buckets of water he lugged from the well in the nearby square. He cleaned the clouds from the windows and dug decades-old dirt from the dimpled imperfections where the glass blower had pulled free his pipe. He worked until the early afternoon, when George came by and told him lunch was ready. During the meal Haliklia became offended when Walter made it clear he'd be sleeping in the house on the square from now on, but George and John soon calmed her. The men walked down to the station after lunch to wait for the afternoon mail train that George would be taking back to Athens. John introduced Walter to several of the bead-squeezing old men who sat over wine and dominoes. They laughed at the expensive work gloves Walter carried draped over his belt, showing him their leathery, work-worn hands in comparison. Walter laughed along, yet left at the first possible moment to get back to his work. The train soon arrived and George promised to return in the next few days with white paint, putty, shellac, nails and plaster mix. There would be little need for him at work, with the strikes.

Walter decided to tackle the floors first, using the plane John lent him. The rot in some places went down to nearly a quarter-inch, so he decided to take the floors down that much uniformly. It was exhausting work, causing his legs to cramp and his shoulders to throb, filling his nose and throat with sawdust. He loved it, though, stopping only to drink from the yogurt and retsina mix John had taught him how to prepare. The plane, like all John's crude and time-scarred iron tools, was the best he'd ever used. It moved in true lines, gracefully bringing up centripetal whirls of wood shavings. Walter found that after several hours of constant work his back did not hurt at all.

The hypnotic motion brought on memories of other times he'd worked with tools. As a boy in his father's garage, in shop classes in school, while working around his houses. Running the generators, the reactors. It occurred to him that his life could be seen as the employment of ever more complex tools to ever diminishing effect. Except for building the glider with Eddie. But that had been Eddie's work, really. He was a master with tools, a born craftsman. Matthew wasn't bad, but lacked his brother's instincts, so, as usual, gave up handiwork when he reached his teens. Walter remembered the perfect lines of Eddie's cuts, the way he would anticipate instructions, the dripless solders and even punctures of the screws. Like the surgeon he should have been. Walter was always a step behind, making sure the gradient of a fixture or positioning of a part matched the blueprints. They always did.

He worked until dark, lighting the way with the sputtering candles John had lent him. While removing a plank near the wall, he discovered some old wiring, most of its insulation eaten away by vermin and time. He traced it through the house and discovered that someone had begun to electrify the house, but had stopped before finishing. Walter figured that it would not take too much effort to complete the job, but decided not to. He removed the wiring and tossed it into the growing pile of trash beneath the back window.

Just before finishing the first room, he heard a noise outside the window that sounded like a radio. He put down his tools and looked out. Across the divide of the ditch, slightly uphill, was another house. An old woman sat on its balcony, speaking softly. Walter could barely see her for the black shrouds around her head and torso. Yet when he lifted the candle he could see her eyes – brilliant, without pupils.

'Hello,' Walter said. '*Kalinikta.*'

Yet the woman ignored him, continuing to speak in soft tones. Walter noticed that she was holding a headless doll, stroking its petticoats with her long fingers. He blew out the candles and headed up the hill for dinner.

George returned a few days later with Walter's supplies, although he said he couldn't find plaster mix. He told the men assembled at the station café that the government had turned down the union's ultimatum and that a general strike now seemed inevitable. There had been another killing in the north, more student problems in Athens. Walter slipped away as soon as possible, returning to his house with the bags George had brought.

He decided to mix his own plaster. After looking around for a while, he decided to pulverize the dozens of small icons he had found in a rotting trunk downstairs. Most of them were no more than a few inches high, yet they were solid, yielding a good amount of powder. He had to chip garish paint from them, yet this was relatively easy, given their poor workmanship. He ground them down in the brick oven, using a heavy iron joint he discovered by the railroad tracks. He then collected the dust in a large bucket and added water and flour he borrowed from Haliklia. The mix blended smoothly, a bit darker than the walls.

He worked slowly in an effort to mask the repairs. The plaster dried quickly and evenly, although there were a few lumps from the poor quality of the flour. He would sand them later. He then painted the door and window frames white and used the putty to seal the stonework around the oven. Finally, he sanded and varnished the floor. The wood took it well, shining brightly when the morning or afternoon sun angled across it, sharply echoing Walter's footfalls. He worked slowly, savoring it.

As he worked, he thought of all the houses he had lived in. His parents' cramped frame house in Grand Rapids, with its clanking furnace and laundry chute, its narrow back yard with the single elm that survived the freak tornado that came one year. There was a detached garage out back with papered-over windows, too crowded for cars, where he'd spent long Saturdays watching his father rebuild appliances and engines. That's what Walter remembered most about that house – the way he'd had to shoulder his way through police and curious neighbors clutching draped-on coats to their necks to get to that garage, cluttered with engines and tools and sockets and his father's body, slumped sideways against the workbench. It's strange, Walter thought, how so many years and so many events in a place can resolve themselves into a single memory. There was the frat house in Ann Arbor – dancing to Bix Beiderbecke on the beer-sticky concrete floor in the basement. Then the apartment, and hearing the marching band practise in the lot across the street as he and Helen made Saturday morning love while the twins watched cartoons in the next room. In Chicago, it was sitting in the furnished basement with the boys, watching the horses pull JFK's casket through the city, trying to explain why Helen cried but the woman on the TV didn't. In Cincy, there was the weekend smell of burning autumn leaves that got in your hair and clothes and stayed with you until the first snow. In the first New Jersey house, there were the hot evenings spent playing in the pool with the boys, the feel of their slick muscles as he wrestled with them. In the second Jersey house it was the one a.m. arrivals from work to a cold dinner and the previous morning's paper, to the sound of the refrigerator and the central heating. At the Maryland house, there was the way the funeral guests shocked one another with small charges of static electricity gathered from the carpets every time they tried to give comfort and solace. He wondered what his memories of this house would be.

When he finished plastering and painting he began work on the outhouse. After a brief examination of the neighboring houses he decided to build it near the bank of the three-foot-wide sewage ditch that meandered by the back of the house to a stagnant marsh beyond the railroad tracks. He began to dig the hole first thing one morning, using planks from the storage space beneath the house to support the deepening walls. The work was hard, with many rocks and small avalanches. Yet his back continued to hold out well, suffering no more than muscle fatigue. It took him an entire day and part of another to get down to his own height, where the resonant clanks of his shovel indicated bedrock. He then dug a narrow canal, about three feet deep, from the lip of the hole to the ditch, laying a section of clay pipe he'd found in a trough beneath the house in it. This would allow for run-off should the rock prove not to be porous. He then covered the pipe over, patting the dirt down firmly. Sometimes people passing in the square would wander back to watch him work. They seemed impressed by his work, although several laughed at him for using gloves, again displaying their own work-toughened hands in mocking comparison. He gently refused all offers of help.

The hut was easier to build. Using the remainder of the planks and the nails George brought, he built a small, sturdy structure with several ventilating slots, adding a quarter-moon design to the decor. The final step were the footprints. After narrowing the ground hole with planks and smoothed dirt, he measured out a perfect square around it, using a line chalked with quicklime that he plucked against the ground like the string of a musical instrument. He then poured a square yard's worth of concrete in front of the area, demarcated by two-by-fours. He let it dry for a while, then stepped into the half-hard mass, his feet shoulder width, at slightly outward angles. He stepped away to survey his bid for eternity. Not bad, he thought. He heard a voice outside. He stepped out to show off his creation, but only saw the old woman on her balcony, chattering as she shook the headless doll in front of her.

Having finished work on the house, Walter began to spend long afternoons sitting at the station café with the old men. He had picked up some Greek from the villagers and the language tape he'd listened to while working on the house, but found it did not really matter whether he spoke or not. Language here was mostly a ritual, like the work in the hopeless orchards or the fingering of worry beads or the endless games of dominoes. So he sat among them in silence, drinking wine, watching the shadows the wind tossed around the stucco walls. He began to see why so many of the men he'd worked with over the years had practised daytime drinking. It took the time out of a day, turning it into a single, unfocused moment of reverie, nostalgia, heroic plans, short naps. Only the late afternoon arrival of the mail train, which came and went like a fit of drunken temper, marked time at the station café.

Walter eventually tired of this, however. Memory was the thing he had come to avoid, not indulge. He began to wander the countryside around Nostopathios. He would start at dawn, when the suck of the farmer's boots in the damp clay of the square woke him. He'd choose a direction at random and stick with it, marking his way by the glass-enclosed memorials that littered the countryside, commemorating boys killed in the civil wars or shepherds who had dropped dead at work. Walter was fascinated by these icon-littered showcases, by the way the photographs were preserved for decades beneath the airtight glass. He'd either take a lunch of olives and cheese and cold lamb, or stop at a village where the people fed him without question. He'd return by late afternoon, in time to wash in water he pulled from the well and eat dinner with John and Haliklia.

On a journey to the west he found a marble quarry, not far from Nostopathios. It was about a hundred feet long and fifty wide, with a depth of about fifteen feet. It was almost purely marble, shining brilliantly in the morning sun. Weeds seeped through long fissures in the walls. One end of the pit was terraced, allowing Walter to walk to the bottom. He strode its length several times, his footsteps echoing off the smooth walls. Despite the overhead sun, there was a coolness to the stone. A great, unaffected cold, just beneath the surface. He found a loose slab in a corner, a perfect square of one yard. He decided to lug it back to his house for use in the kitchen.

As he climbed the crude terrace, he slipped on some mud that had oozed through one of the pit's cracks. The marble he carried in front of him acted like a fulcrum, causing his feet to swing forward and violently slamming his coccyx into the marble step. There was a tremendous shudder through his whole body, then the familiar throb of his lower back. Walter sat still for a long time, afraid to move. When he finally tried he could not, as if some great hand were holding him around the waist. He looked down at the slab next to him. It was a loss – one end chipped off, a great crack running through it at a diagonal.

He sat in the pit until late afternoon, when the shepherds found him. There were four of them, an old man in a fedora hat and three young men in sheepskin vests. They walked along the ridge above Walter, leading about three dozen sheep and a handful of goats. Two dogs helped, nipping at the heels of wandering animals. The youngest boy saw Walter first, bringing him to the old man's attention. They scurried down the slope, leaving the other two to follow with the herd. The old man looked like most of the other men Walter had seen: his body sinuous from work, his watery eyes the color of the olive trees, his cheeks covered with a yellowish stubble. The older boys were handsome and strong, with curly beards that grew into angles in front of their chins and noses that hooked almost to their full upper lips. The youngest one had not yet reached puberty, and followed the others closely, waiting to be told what to do.

Walter was able to communicate what had happened with gestures and well-timed grimaces. The old man understood immediately and ordered the boys, his sons it turned out, to lift Walter gently to a standing position. He then stood behind Walter and, placing his arms around Walter's chest, slowly walked him to the end of the terrace. He told Walter to loosen his muscles by shaking his limbs one by one, then grabbed Walter firmly beneath the armpits and slid him off the side of the terrace. Walter felt himself fall about eight inches, caught by the old man just before hitting the next terrace. His back wrenched painfully, but that was quickly replaced by a cramping numbness. The old man called for two sons to help him and they lifted Walter back up to their terrace, twisting him slowly, like a puppet. When they let him go he found he could stand and move slightly with only residual pain.

'Okay?' the old man asked.

'Yes,' Walter said in English.

'Hyou Yank?' the old man asked.

'Yes, I am.'

'Me too,' the man said, puffing his small frame up. 'U.S. citizen. Listen, the congress, he's a bicamereal house.'

Walter smiled.

'Where in America did you live?'

'Dakotas. Black Hills. I was shepherd for thirty years.'

'It's beautiful there,' Walter said.

'Ho, yes,' the man said.

'Why did you come back?' Walter asked.

241

He made that clicking noise deep in his mouth. His three sons watched Walter with fascination while their dogs kept the herd close.

'So what hyou do here, Yank?' the man asked.

'I've come for my *plika*. A house in Nostopathios. I'm fixing it up.'

'What house?'

'It's on the square. It belonged to Constantine Nikitopolous.'

The man's eyes widened and he lifted his arms at his sides, like a flightless bird.

'He was hyour wife-father? Constantine? Hi know him. We were boys together. Went to States on sayem boat. Ho ho!'

He grabbed Walter by the hand and pressed his grizzled cheek to Walter's face. His breath was hot and sour.

'He's good man, Connie. Ho ho! We were boys together in these hills. Fought the Turk at Smyrna. He's very smart, very strong. Not like hees peoples, Yian and them.' The man spit, his foamy spittle clinging to the marble wall. 'So, you're Connie's son? He did many things for me on that journey. Safed me from immigration man, from bad foreman in New York who want me to be slafe to dig canal. Ho ho. Constaninopo Nikitopo,' he sang, tilting from side to side, his eyes watering. 'We were boys together, you see. I went to hees funeral in Detroit. All those police. Some man, that Connie.' He clapped his hands together. 'We must celebrate. Will hyou celebrate?'

'Yes,' Walter said uncertainly.

The man spoke sharply to his sons. One of the older ones fetched a bottle of wine from his bag, while the other climbed out of the quarry and moved toward the herd. He was followed by the young boy, who began to collect leaves and sticks from the ground. Walter watched the older boy enter the herd and pick out a lamb.

'Now, wait . . .' Walter said.

But the old man wasn't listening, instead ordering his sons around with shouted commands. The son with the lamb returned to the pit, cradling it in his arms so that its legs came together like a bundle of sticks. The lamb's eyes were open, unblinking. When the boy got to the bottom of the pit, he flipped the lamb like a wrestler and held it to the ground with one strong hand at the neck. The lamb kicked up its legs in unison every once in a while.

The young boy returned to the pit with an armful of sticks, dropping them near the lamb. The old man said something to him and the boy cringed, shaking his head. Walter figured he could not be more than twelve. The old man spoke again, this time producing a slightly-curved knife from his belt and thrusting it handle first toward the boy, who continued to shy away. The second son shouted over the lamb's squeals while the third son walked up behind the boy and cuffed him hard on the back of the head. The boy took the knife, gingerly, as if it were hot. The old man continued to speak sharply to him as the third son grabbed him by the collar and walked him over to the struggling animal.

'This isn't necessary,' Walter said. 'It really isn't.'

'Yes,' the old man said, without looking at Walter. 'He must learn.'

The boy was kneeling in front of the lamb now. It kicked harder, giving out moaning squeals. The third son continued to hold the boy's collar, shaking him occasionally. The boy slowly reached out the knife. The lamb was struggling harder, its tongue protruding from its mouth. The father said something that sounded decisive. Walter tried to step down into the pit but found the muscles in his back were still cramped from his injury. The boy closed his eyes and ran the knife along the lamb's throat with a quick, mincing gesture. A line of blood appeared and the boy jerked away. With a tremendous kick the lamb sprung free and began to dart around the pit, bleeding profusely from its wound. The father and older boys swore violently at the youngest son, who set off after the lamb. Its nails clicked on the smooth surfaces as it bounded away from him. Every time it tried to change direction it slid on the marble, emitting terse, sucking squeals when it banged into the walls. Before long, the walls were covered with short smears of blood that dripped slowly towards the ground. The father and older sons were laughing now at the sobbing boy's efforts to run down the animal. Walter tried again to move into the pit but his still-cramped back would not allow him to step down. Finally, the young boy slipped on a slick of blood and the knife rattled away from him. The two older sons easily corralled the lamb. One flipped him expertly while the other grabbed the knife from the ground. He spoke sarcastically to the young boy, then slit the lamb's throat with a violent flourish. It died in strange silence, its unblinking eyes still open.

The boy with the knife quickly flayed the lamb, delicately rolling up the bloody skin he had removed in one continuous piece. They dragged the lamb over to the steps, where they smeared it with oil taken from their bags and piled sticks and leaves on it. The youngest boy stood at a distance, sobbing. Occasionally his brothers or father shouted a command at him, yet he ignored them. Walter noticed that he rubbed his bloody hands manically on the sides of his pants, never checking them to see if they were clean. One of the older boys lit the wood, and the lamb was soon engulfed in flame. A few remaining hairs glowed like hot wires, then disappeared. Its limbs gradually gathered together as the muscles sizzled. Smoke soon filled the pit, obscuring the smudges of blood on the walls and floor. Walter noticed that the cramp in his back had gone and he could move freely. He looked past the lamb at the youngest boy, whose crying face was distorted by waves of heat from the fire. After a few minutes one of the older boys kicked the charred wood from the lamb and began to cut sheaths of flesh and fat from the surface of the carcass. He skewered one and handed the knife to his father, who in turn offered it to Walter.

'In celebration,' he said with a curt bow.

When he returned home Walter discovered that someone had wholed the moon on his outhouse door, shaping it into a crude circle with a sharp tool or knife. Splinters and small cracks lined its edges and bits of broken wood lay trampled in the wet clay. As Walter dug at them with the toe of his shoe he heard the voice above him again and looked up to see the old woman twisting her headless doll toward the sky. He went inside to sleep, his muscles aching and head throbbing.

The next day was the boys' birthday. George had told him that the nearest post and telegraph station with long distance lines was in Argos, a city near the sea, about forty miles away. Walter woke up early to catch the first train. The bad-toothed stationmaster said it might not come because of a strike to the south, but it arrived about a half hour late, just before dawn, as the farmers trudged down to the orchards in their unlaced boots and small black caps.

The only other passengers in his car were two old women sitting together and a tall blonde girl in cut-off jeans who slumbered against a weathered knapsack. Walter took a seat equidistant between them and looked out the window at the men beginning to work in the small hills. Nobody got on or off at the shadow-crossed stations where they paused briefly.

Outside Argos, they were shunted on to a side track to let a larger train pass. There were about thirty cars on it, mostly open cattle cars full of soldiers. They squatted low against the sides to protect themselves from the chilly morning wind. Walter looked at their faces as the train clicked past. Some seemed scared, others nonchalant, yet most had fierce, predatory expressions that matched the sharp folds of their drab caps and collars.

'They're being transferred to Athens,' an American voice said into

Walter's ear. 'In case of the strike. They're totally for real, aren't they?'

It was the blonde girl. She leaned against the seat next to his, her wide blue eyes moving back and forth, following the train's progress.

'I see,' Walter said as the train's last car passed. 'How'd you know I was American?'

'Your haircut. Your shoes. Your curiosity. Like, everything,' she said, smiling.

Walter smiled back, gesturing to the empty seat with a nod. The girl slid into it with self-conscious grace.

'So where are you going?' she asked, replacing a strand of hair behind a small ear.

'Argos. To make a call.'

'You calling the States?'

'Yes.'

'It's like three in the morning there now.'

'Is it?' Walter asked. 'Of course it is. Damn.'

The train began to move, pulling back on to the main track.

'You should tour around a bit here,' the girl said. 'It would be a good way to kill some time. There's, like, lots to see. Plus there's a good beach not far from here.'

'Is there?'

'Yes. I'll show you if you like.'

'Yes, that would be fine. I don't want to wake anybody up in America, after all. They need their sleep.'

She smiled.

'My name's Felicia.'

'Felicia? Hello. I'm Walter.'

She looked to be around twenty, though she could have been younger. Her skin was bronzed by the sun, yet her features were fair – pale blue eyes, blonde eyebrows, archipelagoes of freckles on her forearms, cheeks and upper chest. Her lean, graceful limbs were covered with sun-bleached white down. In addition to her cut-off shorts, she wore a gauze blouse brocaded with small floral chains and a half-dozen thin turquoise bracelets on either wrist. Walter noticed that she had a strange manner with her eyes, alternating between intense concentration on him and a distant, vanishing gaze out the window.

'So are you visiting?' Walter asked, nodding toward the sack. 'Touring around?'

'Sorta. I was up at the American college in Thessalonike but I bagged that.'

'Sounds like fun,' Walter said.

'I guess. It's pretty tiring, moving around all the time. You gotta make new friends to figure out where you are or get a place to sleep. But I love the sun and the sea and the ruins. There are some awesome ruins around here. Not like home.'

'I don't know,' Walter said, 'There are some pretty awesome ruins in the States.'

She nodded expectantly, waiting for an explanation.

'Are you going back soon?' Walter asked instead.

She twirled the bracelets on her left wrist, staring at them with intense concentration.

'I dunno. It's like, I'm always just about to go back. But I can never bring myself to do it. Take the final step. I have this open ticket, you know? But I never really go ahead and go for it.'

'I think I understand.'

'Really? So why are you here?'

'I'm fixing up a house of mine.'

'Really? Back in one of those villages?'

Walter nodded.

'Gah, that must be great.'

'It's all right.'

She looked out the window at that vanishing point.

'So are *you* going back soon?' she asked.

'I don't think so,' Walter said.

They were quiet for a while, watching the countryside, which had flattened and become denser with trees, houses and powerlines. Twice they passed trucks that had burned while waiting to cross the tracks.

'Hey,' Felicia said, raising her shoulders. 'Have you ever been to Epidauros?'

Walter shook his head.

'Oh, it's great. They have the most totally awesome theater. I mean it's like, well you definitely have to see it. It's just up ahead. We can go there then go for a swim, then it would be time to make your call. Kay?'

'All right.'

It was a half-mile walk from station to theater, through a small village of ice cream and postcard vendors, then a parking lot jammed with cars bearing international decals and long buses with tinted windows.

At the entrance to the park several stout women in blazers stood holding furled umbrellas above their heads as clumps of tourists gathered around them.

'So is that what you are in the States?' Felicia asked as they walked. 'A builder?'

'No, I'm a nuclear engineer. Or I was. I've retired.'

She began twisting a strand of hair.

'So you made, like, nuclear power?'

'Yes, that's right.'

'But that's like a bad thing though, isn't it?'

Walter smiled patiently.

'Oh god,' she said. 'I'm sorry. I always do that.'

'No, no. Don't be sorry. You may just be right.'

'*I'm* in college. But I've totally wrecked my spring semester. I don't care, though. They're jerks.'

There was no one attending the park gate, although admission prices were posted in several languages. Felicia skipped ahead of him down the cinder path lined by pine trees.

'We have to go to the museum first.'

It was little more than a long room lined with hanging and showcased artefacts. Tourists milled about beneath the floodlit signs, some of them stretching out fingers to aid in reading. Felicia led Walter past the smooth pottery and fractured cornices to the end of the corridor.

'You have to see this, Walter.'

It was a display of terracotta masks, arranged in three long rows. Each seemed to capture a particular emotion – the sybaritic leer of the satyr, the concentrated fury of the soldier, the slack-jawed frenzy of the buffoon. One mask in particular, called 'A Youth', caught Walter's attention. Its emotion was terror, expressed simply by a mute cry from an empty mouth.

'You wanna know something weird?' Felicia asked solemnly.

Walter looked at her.

'I was raped last month. On Mykonos. I was at this campsite and these guys broke into my tent. They were wearing these like hoods with holes for their eyes but not for their mouths. Which was funny because they tried to kiss me while they were doing it but all I could feel was this hot fabric, you know, not their mouths. Isn't that weird?'

'Felicia . . .'

'It's all right. I mean it was gross, but no more than guys I knew back in the States.'

247

Walter looked down at her, but her eyes were focussed again on that vanishing point.

The theater was a great crater of marble and moss built into the side of a hill, so that the top row of seats and the stage were both at ground level. It contained about fifty rows, dissected by a dozen aisles. The seats enclosed three quarters of the stage, which was a perfect circle about fifty yards in diameter. At its center was a small marble disk. Beyond the stage were the ruins of what had probably been dressing and props rooms. Further on were tall pine.

On the path from the museum to the theater Felicia picked a bunch of poppies and strung them into a garland, which she playfully hung around Walter's neck. He watched her carefully, yet saw no signs of distress or even that she remembered making her confession.

'They used to start plays at daybreak,' she explained. 'They'd run all day – comedies, tragedies, clown shows. It was like watching TV all day Saturday, from the cartoons through the old movies to the sitcoms.'

When they reached the stage Felicia clapped her hands excitedly.

'Hey,' she said. 'I want to show you something totally amazing. If you go stand up at the top seats and I stand on that little disk there, you can hear me whisper.'

Walter looked up at the distant seats, and the great expanse of open space above them.

'I doubt that.'

'Oh, you do, do you?' Felicia said in a teasing voice. 'Well, you just go on up and I'll show you. It's really unreal.'

Walter smiled reluctantly and headed for the cracked steps.

'I'll tell you a secret,' she called after him.

The steps were littered with bottlecaps, plastic wrappers, film cartons. Tourists milled about the seats, the younger ones jumping and playing. There were many names scrawled into the rock, dates reaching back hundreds of years. About halfway to the top Walter saw an old couple sitting still in aisle seats, staring at the stage in silence, their mouths set in grim concentration. The man held the woman's hand in his lap, stroking it slowly. Walter could hear birds in the trees above him, idling buses from the parking lot. He reached the top and gave Felicia a surveyor's wave. She cupped her hands and lowered her head slightly, so that she was speaking directly into the marble disk.

'Can you hear me?' came the soft voice.

It sounded as if she were standing beside him. Walter nodded broadly and could see her smile. She lowered her head again.

'Be my father,' came the soft voice again.

It was a short train journey to the sea, about fifteen miles of open land. They passed a small encampment of gypsies on the way, an enclave of rusting trailers. Tin cans and hanging clothes warmed over small fires. As the train passed, naked children ran out from the camp and tried to pelt it with chunks of sod.

Walter and Felicia had said little since leaving the theater. He had let her lock her arm in his, and on the train she asked if she could put her head on his shoulder. He thought she was sleeping but when he looked down at her he saw that her eyes were wide open.

The public beach was a thin crescent of sand bounded by limestone walls, not far from the station. It was crowded with tourists: pink and waistless British mothers marshalling children; topless Germans with thick limbs and majestic nipples; Frenchmen whose buttock clefts showed above tiny shorts. Fully dressed Greeks walked above the beach, ignoring the bathers.

'I know a better place than this,' Felicia said, taking Walter by the hand. 'Come on.'

She led him to the end of the beach, to a dirt path that wound upwards through a field of half-buried boulders. It then ran along a small cliff overlooking a beachless shore of stones and clashing waves. A squadron of jet fighters flew in a low, tight formation above them as they walked along the ridge. After a quarter mile they came upon another beach – wider, rockier, less populated. Most of the people here were totally nude. They were strangely motionless, stretched beneath the relentless sun. For an instant Walter tried to remember if he'd heard an explosion as the jets passed overhead, but then he began to notice small movements from the sunbathers.

'Nice,' he said.

'Totally.'

Felicia giggled as she removed her clothes. Her small breasts were tanned, as were her ovular buttocks. She didn't remove her bracelets, beads or the leather strap around her left ankle. She stood in front of Walter for a moment with a child's mischievous smile, then raced down to the water. Walter followed her slowly, shedding his shoes and rolling up his pants to mid-calf. He stopped at the edge of the sea, watching Felicia do slow dolphin dives about fifty yards out. The waves swirled around his ankles, bringing small fish and cracked shells against his skin.

'Come on in,' Felicia called, treading water. 'It's great.'

Walter waved noncommittally and she plunged beneath a small swell, her glistening legs kicking up like a gesture of defiance. A catamaran raced by further out, its orange sail billowing in the afternoon sun. Down the beach two naked boys had begun to throw a frisbee back and forth, their sunburned penises shaking when they ran or leapt. Walter checked his watch. It was time to call home.

The Argos square was nearly empty as he searched for the post office. Just a few taxi drivers reading newspapers in their cabs and a *souvlakia* vendor forlornly turning the sticks of meat on his grill cart. Walter also noticed a stepvan holding about a half-dozen young policemen parked beneath a large tree.

The clerk at the post office took a long time to notice Walter, then curtly nodded him to a door with a small statue of a telephone above it. Walter gave the number to another surly clerk in the room, who motioned for him to take a seat on a bench. He asked how long it would be but the man only made that fatalistic clicking sound. Walter sat across from a young blond man who was biting his nails. The room was lined with tinted booths bearing phones and posters describing rates and dialing codes. Only two of the booths were occupied, one by a woman who was laughing loudly. After about ten minutes the clerk called Walter's name and nodded toward an empty booth. He shut the door and picked up the heavy receiver. There were a series of clicks, then static and a satellite beep. It was ringing.

"Matthew? Oh good, you're home. Matt? I'm . . . Hello? Yes, yes, it's a bad connect . . . Matt?"

The small stations on the line back to Nostopathios were littered with piles of rotting produce, burst crates of grain or cloth, heaped sacks of mail. There was no conductor on the train, just two young soldiers who checked his ticket after every stop. The station café was deserted when Walter arrived home after dark. He trudged up the hill to his house, not bothering to alert anyone to his return. He took a long drink from an open bottle of retsina and ate some faintly rancid yogurt, then went to bed, falling immediately into a dreamless sleep.

The next day the trains stopped coming. The strike was on. It meant little more than gossip to the village, although George found himself stranded. But he didn't seem to mind. There would be no work in Athens. That afternoon, the old men congregated as usual at the station café. There was plenty of wine.

Over the next few days, Walter found it hard to stay still for long. In the mornings he would carry out unnecessary repairs on the house or hike to places he'd already been. In the afternoons he'd wander down to the station café, then leave, then return. He began drinking steadily, consuming two bottles or more of retsina by sunset so that he could sleep long and hard. His dinners with John and Haliklia were silent and quick. The novelty and nostalgia of his presence had long since worn off, leaving him in the role of eccentric distant relative. He began to think about leaving, yet the strike continued.

He awoke to candlelight, a dull dawn of twenty votive candles placed under the old photos around his house. He lay still for a moment, wondering if this might be a dream, an accumulation of resin on his imagination. No, he was awake. He sat up, sickened momentarily by a cloud of incense coming from a censer near the door. He looked at the candles, wondering who put them here and why they hadn't awakened him. In the flickering candlelight it looked as if the people in the photos were moving slightly, trying to say something. He checked his watch. Nearly dawn.

He heard people passing through the square. Not the usual suck of the farmers' boots, but the shuffle of women. Walter dressed quickly and walked to the window. They moved quickly, in twos and threes, clothed entirely in black. Some carried upside-down bunches of flowers, others candles they shielded with leathery hands.

Walter waited until they had passed, then slid quietly down his steps and followed the procession. They passed through the station, taking the path to the church. Is it a holiday? Walter thought. And where are the men? Then he noticed they weren't going to the church after all, but had instead taken the ancillary path to the graveyard. Yet he was certain there had been no deaths in the town recently.

He paused at the fork in the church path to make sure they were well ahead of him, then started down the weed-crossed cemetery path. It was about fifty yards to the first graves. As he made a bend about halfway along he came face to face with George, who was carrying a shovel. He was sweating heavily, his fleshy face red from exertion. His eyes panicked for an instant when he saw Walter.

'Hey mate, what you doing here?'

'Just walking,' Walter said. 'Couldn't sleep.'

'Better not go down there,' George said, gesturing over his shoulder with his chin. 'They aren't too keen on men for this sort of thing.'

'What sort of thing?'

They heard footsteps of latecomers. George took Walter by the arm and led him from the path, into a small copse of vines. The women passed quickly. From here, Walter could clearly see the graveyard, about twenty yards below them. It was a small field bounded by two rows of vine and two large walls of shelf-like sarcophagi. One of the graves in the ground had been dug open. The women had gathered around it, planting their candles in turned earth. Those with flowers still held them upside-down.

'What is this?' Walter asked.

'Re-bury,' George whispered. 'There are only so many graves so we have to take the dead from the ground and put them in the wall. To make way for the new.'

'Why today?' Walter asked. 'Nobody died.'

'No, it's that bloke's name day,' George said, nodding toward the open grave. 'Five years after he died.'

'I see,' Walter said.

Enough daylight had now seeped into the valley to afford him a clear view of what was happening. One of the women, gathering in her many skirts, began to back slowly down a rickety ladder into the grave. Strong hands steadied her. She disappeared for a few seconds and one of the women at the grave's lip passed down a small spade. About a minute later, the woman handed something up that reminded Walter of the cardboard advertisements of movie stars. He realized it was the corpse, made light as balsa by the dessicating volcanic soil of the valley. One woman held it in her arms like a baby while the others began to examine it, some dusting it gently with small brushes. The woman from the grave emerged and Walter saw her secretly toss something that looked like a piece of crumpled paper into the nearby floor of vine.

'What is this, George?' he asked.

'Well, before they put him in the wall they check him over. If there's still flesh on his bones, then they know he was a man of this world. A man of sin, a bad man. But if all the flesh has rotted away, then they know he was a man of the spirit. A man of God. A good man.'

'Who was he?' Walter asked.

'Just a man.'

'Who was the woman who went into the grave?'

'His wife.'

Walter looked at the corpse. It did not look like a skeleton, but rather a wax figure of a man that had begun to melt. The only part that was recognizable was the mouth, grinning broadly in the early sun. The wife was holding a photograph next to the skull, comparing, sobbing gently. As the women worked the section of leg below the left knee fell off. One of them picked it up and nonchalantly laid it across the corpse's pelvis.

'No limping to the Lord,' George said.

Finally, the woman holding the corpse lifted it up slightly and the others stood away.

'It is clean,' said one of them in Greek.

The other nodded and murmured, those with flowers arighting them at last. Most began to walk from the graveyards while the few left behind prepared the corpse for its crypt. They scrubbed it with alcohol, then heaped on generous amounts of quicklime. Finally, they wrapped it in several layers of gauze, then put it gently into the open shelf.

'I better get down there and close it up,' George said to Walter, who was staring at the spot where only he had seen the woman toss the flesh.

Some of the candles had burned down by the time he got back to his house, which stank of stale incense and paraffin. Walter noticed something he hadn't seen that morning – a small candle placed beneath his picture of the boys above his bed. He wondered again who had put it there, and why it hadn't awakened him. He got down on his hands and knees and pulled his bag from beneath the bed. It took him a moment to find the blank tapes and spare batteries. He then took the duty-free cassette recorder from the nightstand and inserted the first tape.

'Testing, testing . . .'

He played it back. It worked. Walter took a long drink from the half-empty bottle beside the bed, then began to speak.

THE TIME ORCHARD

M atthew watched the landscape of his kidney on the flickering screen as the doctor slowly thrust the catheter deeper into him. It reminded him of the films made by robot submarines at the deepest parts of the ocean. The veins looked like seaweed, the mounds of tissue empty shell. Sometimes he would see gulleys of ancient rivers, populated by single cell creatures that floated in and out of the camera's scope. Suddenly, a glowing eye appeared among the folds, some strange electric fish disturbed by the intrusion. The doctor stopped moving the catheter and Matthew relaxed his tortured grip in the bed rails.

'There,' the doctor said, touching the glowing image on the screen with a stainless steel pointer.

'What is that?' an intern asked.

'It looks like a tracer,' said another.

'We haven't planted anything like that, have we?'

'No, no.'

'Then what is that?'

Everyone looked at Matthew.

The operation was simple, without complications. They had to remove a small pocket of tissue around the pellet, but there was no real damage to the kidney. Antibiotics and bedrest cleared up the fever in a few days, yet Matthew remained weak for almost a week more, plagued by nightmares, dizziness and nausea. He slept often, never for more than a few hours, awakened each time by a recurring dream. He would be standing on a great globe of hard plastic, like the kind they had studied in school. Only larger, much larger. Above him was a net in which hundreds of people were firmly involved. Some struggled momentarily, yet most remained perfectly still, staring forlornly at him. Beyond the net was a flickering neon sky. Then there would be a brief rotation of the globe, causing Matthew to fall to his face and slide down the smooth surface. He could see the globe's topography as he fell, could read the strange place names. He then reached the bottom and fell freely, through a liquid-thick atmosphere, landing in a pit whose walls consisted of hundreds of television screens. His father was speaking on all of them, yet Matthew could not hear what he said because the sound was off. He'd awaken then, his heart racing, his sheets soaked with rancid sweat. The old man with emphysema who shared his room would be watching him from the chair by the window, his head shrouded in smoke from a forbidden cigarette.

Each morning a herd of interns would stop in his room on their teaching rounds. They would stand around his bed as a doctor ran through the details and statistics of his case. None of them ever looked at Matthew's face, except a tall, awkward redhead whose nametag read 'Plumb'. Matthew would often catch him staring down at him, averting his eyes just before they'd make contact.

One night, after visiting hours, Plumb came to his room alone. He was dressed in jeans and a football sweatshirt and smelled of beer. He made a brief pretense of looking at Matthew's data, then pulled up a chair next to the bed. Matthew remained quiet, a bit hazy from the evening's mild sedatives.

'I knew your brother,' Plumb said after a long time.

Matthew nodded, trying to lick the foam from his mouth's walls.

'We did first year together.'

The old man in the other bed had one of his periodic hacking fits, then settled into uneasy sleep. Matthew looked at Plumb. His bright red eyelashes and pale blue eyes made him seem childishly feminine, despite his firm jaw and large, bony hands. He continued to refuse to meet Matthew's gaze.

'Yeah, he was something else . . .' Plumb said.

'I've always thought so,' Matthew said.

'I mean, he was fucking crazy. Did you know that?'

Matthew sat up a little higher on his mound of pillow.

'Is that a term they teach you here?' he asked. 'Fucking crazy?'

'Listen, man, there are some things you get taught here and other things you learn.'

There was a long silence. The man in the next bed stirred for a moment. Someone dropped a tray several halls away.

'So what did you learn about Eddie?' Matthew asked.

'I mean, like, he didn't care,' Plumb said insistently, looking at his track shoe poised on the bed rails. 'I mean, he was a real speed demon, you know? A real Mario Andretti. Crystal meth, amyl, black beauties

– whatever he could organize. We would all of us jam, work late, but Eddie, man, he just wouldn't sleep. Period. That's why his eyes looked like they did. And then he got into these mega-vitamins. B-complex concentration with a dusting of meth. Taken intravenously. I mean, he wasn't the only one who did this sort of thing, but I believe he was the only one who did it all the time.'

The man in the next bed coughed furiously for several seconds, moaned a few times, then fell back to sleep.

'So one night we're all together in a study lounge back at the dorm, getting ready for an anatomy exam or something. There were six in our study group. Eddie comes late as usual, but nobody really cares, since he's the smartest one by a mile. Very generous, too. He'd neglect his own studies to help the rest of us along. I mean, you knew he knew this stuff, yet he'd stay with it, drilling it home by teaching us these wild mnemonics.'

'Such as?' Matthew interrupted.

Plumb stared at his shoe, smiling to himself.

'Shit, there were millions of them. The one that springs to mind is the one for mitosis. You know what that is?'

Matthew shook his head.

'Yeah, well, it's how cells split up. A five-part process. Interphase, prophase, metaphase, anaphase, telophase. Right? What Eddie came up with was to remember it as "I push myself against them". That was how we remembered it.'

They were quiet for a moment.

'Anyway, that night he comes into the study room with this Nike box full of syringes, which he plops down on the glass table between us. I remember the sound of them rattling. We just stared at him. He was on some sort of amazing trip that night. You should of seen his eyes. Anyway, he tried to get us to shoot up with him, but nobody was into it. Come on, he says, it'll be good practice. One of the girls on our group was from India and she had big problems with the idea. So Eddie just says okay and sits down, putting his Nike box on his lap.'

Plumb paused, looking at his hands.

'I mean, what you gotta understand is that in med school people do all kinds of fucked up shit and it doesn't matter, it's like normal. People drink thirty cups of coffee or wreck their rooms or call home with suicide threats but it's basically S.O.P. So with Eddie, well, we figure he's maybe gotta problem of degrees, but not of kind. Or so we thought. Anyway, he starts taking the loaded syringes out of his box and lining them up on the glass table. Side by side, six of them. Then he primes five of them, but leaves one so that it's still got some air in it. I mean, you could see those bubbles on that clear table, like pearls or something. We're all silent now, watching him. He puts the syringes back in the box and shakes it up a little. You can hear the needles tinkle. He ties off his arm and isolates a fat old vein. Some of us laugh a little, like it's a joke. Then he shuts his eyes and reaches into the box, pulling one out with his fist over the clear part. Still, without looking. Then, real slow, he sticks the needle in his arm and injects himself. Like that. Nabjit gets up and splits, but the rest of us just stare. After a few seconds he opens his eyes and begins to laugh. Not mocking or crazy, just gently, like you would if you saw somebody do an incredible move in gymnastics. He rummages through the box and finds the bad needle, squirts it out into the air. It was like rain. And he was just, laughing . . .'

'He knew which needle,' Matthew said softly. 'He had it marked.'

'I don't think so, man. I mean, you know your brother, but I was there. No, I don't think so.'

The old man began to cough.

'I don't either,' Matthew said.

Matthew strengthened quickly after going home. He would rise early and eat breakfast with his mother, then spend the day reading or watching television. Sometimes he'd take afternoon walks through the neighborhood, passing young children on their way home from school. In the evenings he'd eat large dinners and watch TV movies with his mother. They went out to a movie once, but it was too soon, and Matthew had to leave, feeling nauseous in the crush of people.

On Matthew's second weekend home, Helen decided to clean the house. Matthew helped her move furniture, then went up to do his room. He started by going through his books, rearranging some on two cluttered bookcases, packing others away. What pretentious crap, he thought, as he went through them. All the latest glossy daring do from small presses, all the hyped translations, all the remarkable achievements by first-time novelists whose pictures covered the bookbacks like entries in a college yearbook or modeling agency prospectus. What could I have been thinking of when I bought this shit, Matthew wondered? At the back of one shelf he found the two books his father had given him on his fourteenth birthday – *1984* and *The Grapes of Wrath*. He also found the gifts from Mexico, the skin scroll and the grotesque statue, stuffed behind a stack of magazines. He looked at them for a while, then replaced them.

He went into the closet, where he kept the books from his boyhood. The children's books of friendly crocodiles and faithful puppies, the sports biographies, the teen novels of inter-racial pop bands or a shy boy's idolatry of his wayward older brother. He picked out one – *Great Moments in Sports History*. Another gift from his father. Each chapter described some late inning home run, impossible kick-off return, record run on a soggy cinder oval. Matthew sat on his bed and slowly thumbed through it, looking at the black and white photos that accompanied each chapter. He studied the faces – Thorpe, Bannister, Louis, Cousy. Impassive, assured, sculpted by strong thumbs. The strain moving through the face's contours as fluently as blood or sweat, as if they had been engineered specifically for that stress.

He closed the book and thought of his father in Greece. They still had not heard from him. When Helen had told Matthew that he'd quit UPU and gone to work on the house, Matthew had thought it to be a natural and obvious move. He could picture him working with that slow deliberation, muttering to himself sometimes in concentration. Taking his time. Getting it right. Yet he sometimes found himself wishing Walter were around so he could tell him about what had happened, ask him about the things he wanted to know.

Helen came into the room, her hair bound by a bandana, her hands covered by yellow rubber gloves.

'Oh. You were very quiet,' she said. 'I wondered what you were doing.'

'Just looking through this book dad gave me.'

They stared at it for a moment.

'Do you have any idea when he might be coming back?' Matthew asked.

'No, Matthew. I don't even know that he's coming back.'

A few days before Matthew's birthday, they went to an orchard outside of town to pick apples so Helen could make him his favorite pie. She explained that they did things a little differently here – instead of paying for whatever you picked, you were allowed, for a set price, to pick as much as you could over a half-hour period. She had been here a few times before with friends, gathering so much fruit that she'd had to make preserves, which she'd then given away in the shop.

They waited outside a chainlink gate with about thirty other people, mostly fat young couples. The men had double chins and baseball caps with ammunition company logos. The women wore tight designer jeans and pastel windbreakers. Matthew and Helen stood near the back. There was no need to rush. They only wanted a dozen good apples.

An old man finally drove up in a golf cart and opened the gate. Most of the couples rushed to distant points in the orchard, stuffing wicker baskets and plastic bags as they went. Matthew and Helen strolled down the central row, stopping occasionally to examine obscure branches. After about fifteen minutes they had five good apples. Then Matthew saw a thick branch near the top of a deformed tree. He pointed out the ten or so shining apples to his mother.

'How do we get them down?' she asked.

Matthew tried throwing rotten apples or stones at it, but his aim was poor, and when he did connect he only dislodged leaves.

'Oh, what the hell,' he said finally, leaping to grab the lowest branches and hoisting himself into the tree.

'Matthew,' Helen said, alarmed.

'It's cool, mom. There're plenty of branches.'

'Are you sure? Be careful.'

He maneuvered slowly through the branches, stopping after every step to plot his course. Once a branch snapped, but he was able to step off it to another. Helen said nothing as she watched him, her mouth set in worry. Matthew soon reached the top, plucking the apples and stuffing them into the bag he'd looped through his belt. Someone had carved some words into one of the branches – 'John. Tusday. I can see for miles and miles.' He paused when he was done and looked around. He saw the other harvesters rushing around, the fat men stopping to shake trees as their wives scurried to pick up the fruit that fell. Further on Matthew could see more orchards and houses. In the haze to the east he could just make out the remaining cooling tower of Olympic.

'Matthew, why don't you come down now? I don't think you should be climbing around like this.'

He waved to her and began his slow descent. When he reached the last branch he lost his footing and fell eight feet, twisting his ankle and causing the apples to spill from the bag. Helen let out a gasp and rushed over to him as he clutched his ankle.

'Goodness, are you all right?'

'Yeah. Shit. I just sprained my ankle. Sorry.'

'You're as bad as your brother, sometimes,' Helen said angrily. 'You know that?'

She turned violently away from him and began to pick up the apples, examining each one before putting it back in the bag. Matthew watched her for a moment.

'Are they bruised?' he asked.

'Just a little. Don't worry. They're still all right for cooking.'

She finished and he struggled to his feet.

'Can you walk?' she asked.

'Oh yeah. Don't worry.'

'Don't worry,' she said, turning away.

They began to make their way slowly out of the orchard.

'Mom, I want to ask you something.'

'What's that?' asked Helen, still a little angry.

'What was it with Eddie?'

Helen looked quickly at Matthew, then stared down the path.

'I don't know,' she said, her voice gentle now. 'I don't think there's a word for what he was, Matthew. I mean, I wondered. I thought about it all the time. Believe me. There were days when I would look at him and tell myself I was a fool, that he was just high-spirited or whatever. But then . . .'

They passed a couple who were beating a tree with long sticks they had found.

'You know,' Helen said, 'he teethed very early. Well before you did. You were still breast-feeding, both of you. They tell you to stop if they teethe but I couldn't, because when I'd try to you'd throw fits. And I couldn't just feed one of you. So I kept on, you on the right, Edward on the left. And it hurt so much, sometimes. Like when you get scratched by a cat. I'd go to bed with cotton around my ni . . . my breast, because it was so tender. He'd cut me sometimes, yet keep on feeding, drinking the blood that mixed with the milk. I'd be horrified, yet if I stopped you'd cry so hard I feared for your health. And Eddie would join in. So I kept on . . .'

On his birthday she planned to make his favorite dinner – chicken roasted with lemon, oregano and slivers of garlic. Wild rice, broccoli, apple pie. She began preparing it in the morning, since she had to go to work in the afternoon. Matthew sat in the kitchen, telling her about producing the play, about Ben's mural and the way Max had changed his play, about his time with Eleni. Helen listened without comment, smiling when he told her about confronting Sandy Mock at the FIT opening and Prospero's taxi dispatches.

The phone rang just after she began folding the crust's dough. Matthew was able to answer it without leaving his stool, plucking it from the kitchen wall. He could hear a sound like ocean waves, followed by a high-pitched electronic tone.

'Dad?' he asked.

'Dad?' came his voice in echo.

Helen watched him from the counter, nervously rubbing the flour off her hands. Matthew heard what seemed to be Walter's voice, but it was covered by another breaker of static, another series of beeps. Different voices came on the line momentarily, laughing or arguing or explaining.

'Dad, it's a bad connection,' he said.

'Sa bad connection,' he heard himself saying.

'I wanted to call on your birthday,' came Walter's voice in an instant of clarity. Matthew listened closely, yet Walter's voice again broke up into cubist fragments of language – some words clear, others hopelessly distorted, truncated. He heard 'Eddie' several times, as well as 'son,' 'doubt,' 'final'. Matthew tried to interrupt, but his father's garbled speech was relentless. Finally, there was a series of shrill beeps, followed by a calm sea of static.

'Dad? Are you there?'

But the only response was the satellite's mocking echo.

'What did he say?' Helen asked.

'I don't know. Nothing.'

Matthew waited around the house all afternoon for the return call, but the phone only rang twice, with a recorded sales pitch and Helen checking in. She returned from work around seven-thirty. They ate in silence. When they finished she cleared the plates and brought out the freshly-baked pie. Matthew lowered the lights by the dimmer switch on the wall and Helen tried to put candles on it, but the soft crust wouldn't hold them – they either fell over or slid into the pie. She finally gave up, lighting one and holding it in front of him.

'Make a wish,' she said.

Matthew nodded, then blew it out. A bit of soft wax flew on to her wrist. Helen plucked it off and rolled it into a ball, then placed it back on the candle. She then gave him his gift – a handwoven white sweater, with thin horizontal stripes of purple and black.

264

'Thanks,' he said as he tried it on. 'It fits well. I like it. Really.'

'I knitted it while you were in the hospital,' Helen said, plucking at a loose strand on his shoulder. 'Something to do.'

Beth came by later with a bottle of champagne. It was the first time Matthew had seen her since his return from the city. She was still very thin, but not as washed-out looking as the last time he had seen her. The bags beneath her eyes were gone, and her clavicles no longer protruded beneath her gold chain necklace. She had cut her hair short and was wearing a gray suit with a designer scarf and black pumps. She chatted with Helen for a while, then took Matthew for a ride in her new car. Matthew opened the champagne as she raced around a corner, causing the cork to ricochet around the interior.

'Hey,' Beth called out, laughing.

They took turns drinking, recoiling as the carbonation invaded their sinuses.

'So dad tells me you were sick?' Beth asked.

'Yeah, but I got better,' Matthew said.

'What ailed you?'

'What ails us all, Beth?'

'Really.' She pulled on to the main strip. 'Anyway, you look well.'

'Thanks. You too.'

'I am, I guess. I'm working as a para-legal for a firm in the city. They're good. Communications law. I'm going to start law school in September.'

'Sanctuary,' Matthew said in a Charles Laughton slur.

'Hey, Matthew, fuck you,' Beth said sharply, turning her head towards him but keeping her eyes on the road. 'To hell with your sarcasm, you know.'

'Sorry,' Matthew said. 'Really. That was stupid.'

They said nothing for several blocks.

'Let me tell you something about sanctuary,' she said in a firm monotone. 'I was crazy all winter. I did things that like I can't even believe I did. Physical things, Matt. Things to myself. Against myself. I'd wake up shaking and it was all downhill from there. I couldn't eat anything that didn't have sugar and E-additives in it. I'd sit in front of my mirror and smear mascara and lipstick on myself until I looked like Bozo. I'd put my TV on the bed and watch my soaps from my dressing table, in the mirror, over my shoulder. Then I began to hang out with these gay guys I'd met in school. We used to go to those bars in the city.

I'd put on really garish clothes and too much make-up and pretend to be a man in drag. Sometimes . . .'

Her voice caught in her throat.

'Beth . . .'

'No, let me tell it, Matt. A couple times I got really wasted and sucked guys off. Right there at the bar. You can do it in those places, you know. Nobody found me out until one day. I . . . did this one guy and spat out his come into a glass with one of those little umbrellas in it. Another guy came up and drank it down, then said only fag hags don't swallow. They pulled open my blouse and threw me out in the street. I scraped my elbows really bad, Matt. After that I stayed at home. Stayed in bed. I'd eat diet pills and vodka and go swimming. I almost drowned twice. Dad finally drained the pool. So please, for god's sake, don't talk to me about sanctuary . . .'

'Listen, Beth,' Matthew said gently. 'I know. I'm sorry. It's my birthday.' He smiled. 'We're allowed to do one stupid thing on our birthday, right?'

'That seems to be your family tradition, anyway,' she said, still angry.

They entered the vacant parking lot of the mall. A dumpster burned violently near the middle. Some kids ran across their path – jumping, yelling, spinning crude pirouettes. Beth parked under a sodium light and turned off the engine. She gestured for the bottle and drank as they watched the dumpster flare.

'What do you mean?' Matthew asked finally.

'Nothing,' Beth said softly. 'I was just thinking how nuts you and Eddie used to be on your birthday.'

Matthew wanted to challenge her, but decided to tread gently.

'I've been thinking about him a lot these days,' Matthew said.

'That's natural.'

'Yeah, but it's strange. I mean, I have all the same memories of him, but it's like watching a foreign film for the second time with different subtitles.'

'What do you mean?'

'Well, come on, you know Eddie. I think all we ever saw there was that blinding energy and all I could ever feel about him was love and admiration. He just moved too fast and too well to think about.'

'Yeah . . .'

'But now, I don't know. I mean a lot has happened to me in the last year, too, Beth. And seen from this distance, I think there was a lot of pain and confusion and madness in Eddie. I wasn't able to see that burning in anyone but myself before he died, but now I can see it in a lot of people. And I think he was worse off than any of us.'

Beth looked at him.

'Even your dad?'

'I don't know,' Matthew said. 'Him I don't understand.'

'You should talk to Dean, Matty.'

'Why?'

'You just should . . .'

Matthew quietly walked to the edge of the waterless pool. Dean stood in the deep end, peering into his telescope. The pool's bottom was strewn with spine-cracked reference books, empty bottles and crumpled white delicatessen bags. Matthew thought of the summer hours he had spent here with Eddie and Beth. Diving contests, underwater boxing, the ever-increasing record for breathless laps. He had been in the pool the first time Eddie and Beth had made love, up in Beth's room. He had floated on a raft in the shallow end, looking up into the trees as their laughter and sighing came through the open window. Eventually, Eddie appeared naked in the window. He climbed on to the ledge, squatting perilously as Beth's worried voice filtered out from behind him. He smiled down at Matthew, who petulantly tried to ignore him, yet finally had to look at this handsome gargoyle. After their eyes met Eddie leapt, his arms and legs spread wide, his half-flaccid penis shuddering. He seemed to hover for an instant, then dropped quickly, turning into a perfect dive just before hitting the water. His velocity drove him to the bottom, causing both wrists to sprain, a finger to dislocate. He surfaced next to Matthew's raft, his eyes ablaze with excitement and pain. It's great, Matty, he said. It's great. Matthew wasn't sure if he were referring to the sex or the plunge.

'Well, look at this,' Dean said, catching sight of Matthew. 'Come on down. Dive in.'

Matthew backed down the ladder. They shook hands firmly, grabbing each other's right shoulders with their free hands in a military hug.

'So how the hell you been, you pencil-neck such and such?' Dean asked.

'Sick,' Matthew said.

'So I heard, so I heard. But you're looking good.' He smiled. 'For a pussy.'

'Uh, thanks,' Matthew said.

'You seen my Beth?'

'Yeah, she came by for some cake earlier. She's looking good.'

'Yeah, well we had a few problematical months there, but . . .' Dean suddenly tapped his forehead with the heel of his hand. 'Hot damn, it's your birthday, isn't it?'

Matthew nodded.

'Howsabout if I do your stars? Custom job.'

'Dean, I'm an educated young middle-class white American boy. You know I don't go for that stuff.'

'That's a roger?'

Matthew smiled and nodded. Dean went over to his telescope and began to search the sky.

'So what've you been up to?' Matthew asked his muscular neck.

'S.O.S,' he said, still peering into the viewfinder. 'Same old shit. International nightflights over Dulles are now routed over us, so I can scope those out. Fucking Concorde. I wish they'd let the Brits kick that sombitch up to full throttle over land. Just once. To hell with the windows is my theory.'

'Definitely.'

'Being down in this pit is a real bonus, groundfuzz wise. Basic rule of the game – the deeper you go, the further you can see.'

'Uh, let me write that down,' Matthew said.

Dean found what he was looking for.

'Okay, here we go. Ho boy. Yep. You're rising, sailor. Utterly ascendant. Big adventures on the horizon. Discoveries, wealth, travel, all that shit.' He put the telescope upright and looked at Matthew. 'Yessir, you're set.'

They smiled, their eyes averted.

'Now tell me about the past,' Matthew said. 'Tell me what happened a year ago today, Dean.'

Dean ran his hand through his bristle hair.

'You turned twenty-two and Eddie didn't.'

'What happened at the airport, Dean?' Matthew persisted.

'You tell me,' Dean said.

Matthew kicked gently at a white bag.

'Dad took Eddie up. It was too windy and he couldn't handle it. He fucked up and they crashed. The surprise party that everybody knew about got cancelled, but we got to use the coke and chips for the funeral reception.'

Dean looked at Matthew.

'All right, Matthew. All right.' He took a bottle of schnapps from the ground and drank, then offered it to Matthew, who refused. 'Listen, for starters, I didn't want to take them up. As far as I was concerned, everybody was grounded. It was a weird fucking day, you see. Hot sun but very cool ground temperature. Thunderstorms on the southern horizon. Somebody even said something about hail. Lots of vertical action, lots of chop. But the thing was, it was Eddie's birthday present. He wanted to go up. Have you ever tried denying your brother something that he really wants? I mean, successfully?'

Matthew shook his head.

'That's right, amigo. Everything we said was contra-indicated. Walter gave up before me. Finally I said okay, on one condition – dad flies. None of Eddie's bullshit, not in those conditions. You know, you and Walter never understood something about that boy. You always thought he was a daredevil hotshot golden-boy, right?'

He paused.

'Yeah, well, those are civvy terms, my friend. In the service, we got a different appelation for that situation. Death lover. There are lots of 'em, Matt. I seen them by the dozen in Korea and Nam and Houston. They like to look the beast in the eye. Tell him to eat shit and die. You have to use them very carefully, Matt. Else they get people killed, get things broke.'

'But – ' Matthew said.

'Hold on,' Dean said sharply. 'Let me finish. Now you don't know squat about it, so just zip it up and learn something.' He took another drink. 'So up we go. I take them up to about three thousand. It's actually better than I thought. There's some chop, but it's basically clear, except for one nasty bit of business in the southeast corridor. I radio this intelligence to Walter, then release them, clean. Man, I love the sound of that snapping rope when there's a good release. Anyway, I circle around for a while, checking it out, but it looks good. I touch base with them one last time; everything's fine. I head back to earth cause I gotta take a royal pee.'

He stopped, stroking his crewcut with an open palm. Remembering.

'So I'm in the shed, on the horn with Beth about the surprise party for ya'll, when all of a sudden I see that there's a bird down in the approach pond. Well, Walt and Eddie were the only ones up, so I knew it was them right away. I bolt outta the shed like a shot off a shovel, pushing that old jeep of mine for all she's worth. I can see it from a good ways off. She's flipped in about three feet of drink. A power line's down, dancing above the water, raining down sparks like the Fourth of July. I can see Walt sitting on the shore, dazed, just staring at the wire with this curious expression. Just before I get there he comes around, stands up quickly and wades into the water, toward the plane. I can tell he's hurt by the screwed up way he walks. I'm right behind him, hoping like hell that wire doesn't hit the water. Well, we reach the plane about the same time and both go under. And it was bad, Matty. That cockpit was wedged into the bottom mud something ferocious. I could see Eddie inside, his face pinned up against the glass, his eyes open. God, you should have seen his eyes.'

Dean took a drink.

'I try to pry the glass bubble, but it's no good. So then I try kicking it, but you can't get any momentum under water. It's like a slow motion nightmare. Finally your dad just squats underneath the fuselage like a weightlifter and raises up the whole fucking plane. The bubble just pops open. I wrench away the stick and pull Eddie out, but you can feel it. The body just flops. I drag him to shore and try the kiss, but he's gone. The ambulance guys just shut his eyes.'

'Dean, you said you had to wrench . . .'

'The stick. That's right, Matty. Your brother was flying the plane.'

'But maybe in the crash he shifted.'

'Matt, I had to pry his dead damned hands from the controls.'

Matthew listened to Dean's words echo around the empty pool.

'Why didn't you tell me this before?' Matthew asked.

'What would you have done with this six months ago, eh?' Dean asked. 'I thought Walter was going to tell you, anyway.'

Matthew looked around the pool.

'Where's three feet?' he asked.

'There,' Dean said, pointing to a spot about five yards from the far end. Matthew walked there, scrambling up the concrete slope. He stood next to the pool's wall, measuring the depth with his eyes.

'So what happened?' he asked.

'I don't know,' Dean said, his voice echoing. 'I don't know.'

He found Brand a hundred yards into the bay, pulling a rake through shin-deep water. An anchored rowboat bobbed several yards away from him in the small waves. He worked methodically, passing the rake through the bottom's sand several times before twisting it out of the bay, letting the water and silt drain, then dumping its contents into the boat. Matthew removed his shoes and walked slowly through the undeepening water. Brand looked different. Less substantial. What was left of his hair hung from his head in long, straw-like strands. His cheeks were more collapsed, his rubbery ears seemed even larger. His tanned limbs were all bone and sinew.

He jumped backwards when he noticed Matthew, raising the rake in self-defense.

'Whoa,' he said sharply. 'Far enough, punk.'

Matthew stopped and made a calming gesture, his palms down.

'It's Matthew Merriweather,' he said.

Brand let the rake's head splash into the water.

'Walter's boy,' he said, unsurprised.

'Can I talk to you?' Matthew asked.

'Sure,' Brand said. 'Sorry about the greeting. You get used to chasing people off out here.'

He nodded toward the boat.

'Grab a rake.'

Matthew waded to the boat and took a wooden-handled rake from the bed of grit and shellfish. Its head was combination hoe and shovel, with dozens of small perforations in the shovel half. Brand showed Matthew how to work it.

'You pull it through the sand like a garden hoe. When you feel a shell, you dig in, then flip it and pick it up, so that the sand and crap filter out. Then you dump the shell in the boat. We'll sort out the quick and the dead later.'

'How do you know it's a shell and not a rock or bottle?' Matthew asked.

'A certain vibration.'

Matthew began stroking the sand. Several times he struck something solid, yet only once was it a clam. He soon saw what Brand meant – the fractured conches, rocks and rusting cans gave a dull vibration, while the living clam's report was resonant.

'Getting the hang of it?' Brand asked.

'Sort of.'

'It's like everything. You're bad, then you're good, then you're bored. But if you hang in there, do it and do it, you eventually find its poetry.' He looked into the water. 'It's like everything.'

Matthew looked at the rake's artificial curve below the surface. Brand stepped up and took the rake from him.

'But you haven't come here for a fishing lesson. Nor for sunstroke.'

He loaded the rakes, then pulled the cannonball anchor from the bay's bed and piled it on to the bow. He handed Matthew the frayed tow rope.

'Pull this back to shore for me, will you? We'll talk.'

Brand's cottage was a blistered lime-green shack with a large, multifaceted antenna appended to the tar-paper roof. The yard was weed and sand and rusting metal that had spilled over from the lot of rusting auto bodies next door. Brand led Matthew through a small screened porch jammed with buckets of shellfish and chunks of driftwood to a large room filled with garage-sale furniture, waist-high stacks of books and antique fishing gear hung on the walls. In one corner, under a window facing the lot of rusting cars, a hard disk computer and sophisticated graph printer rested on a card table. Beside the table was a thirty-gallon garbage can, overflowing with fingernail-sized bits of torn paper.

Brand disappeared into the bedroom for a moment. Matthew could see through the open door that it contained only a small bed, ceiling-high cinderblock bookshelves, and a console television resting at the foot of the bed. Two VCRs were stacked beneath the television. Brand soon returned, his thin body wrapped in a linen robe.

'Beer?' he asked. 'Iced tea?'

'A beer would work,' Matthew said.

Brand poured out a can into a glass decorated by a reproduction of a newspaper's front page.

'Now,' he said, handing Matthew the glass. 'What is it you want to talk about?'

Matthew read the glass's illustration. Mets win the series.

'Something you said when I saw you last year. At the plant. Something about my dad.'

'Go ahead . . .'

'You said something about self-possession. About holding on.'

'That's right.'

Matthew wiped the foam from the glass's lip, unable to find the words to finish the question.

'All right,' Brand said finally. 'I think I know what you're driving at. You want to find out what makes Walter click, right? You want to know why he's disappeared to Turkey or Morocco or wherever. You want to hear that, after all the crap, he's still a great guy. Well?'

'Something like that.'

'Such as – he's the last of a dying breed? A worker in an age of

272

non-jobs? A master builder in an era of compromised design and structural confusion?'

Matthew said nothing.

'Okay.' Brand said, running a finger through the rubbery gulleys of his ear. 'Sure. He's all those things. Big deal. Look where it got him and you, and especially look where it got your brother.'

Matthew looked up sharply.

'Sorry,' Brand said, shaking his head. 'I told you I spend a lot of my time chasing people off.'

He took a sip from his beer.

'Listen Matthew, and I say this in all seriousness, your dad has a lot of integrity. A lot of character. Walt could send me a telegram tomorrow telling me he's starting a latrine digging service in Biafra and I'd be tempted to give it a go with him.'

He took another sip, smiling to himself.

'I remember once, these dago contractors came out from Baltimore to lay some wiring for us. Alarm and warning systems. Your dad told them to put in treble back-ups, but they only put in doubles, which is perfectly acceptable, but it wasn't what Walter asked for. I guess they'd figured he wouldn't check and they could pocket the margin. That was their first mistake. Well, when they finished, and I mean they put down *thousands* of feet of sensory wiring, Walter went through it with them. Foot by foot. Wearing that stupid windbreaker, holding that big ugly flashlight of his. You should've seen the looks on those wops' faces. Anyway, Walter soon sees what's going on. He confronts them with it. Their leader shoots back that all their work meets government specs. Second mistake. Walter leaps up on to a big switch box – imagine your dad leaping – and rips out a whole section of wiring. Just rips it out. He turns around, holding it up in front of those guineas like it's a scalp or the guts of a soothsayer's beast, and says, "Now it doesn't. Do it again." Then he tosses it at their feet and walks away.'

'I know, I know,' Matthew said, smiling now, too.

'But you wanna know why I'd say no to that telegram? Why I'd turn him down? Because it doesn't make one iota of difference. Character. Integrity.'

'Crap,' Matthew said.

'I'm serious, young man. I'm not being cynical or antimodern or any of that. I'm just telling you that life isn't about character or integrity or truth or any of that garbage. It's about developing strategies against despair. It's about performing the necessary steps, be they real estate or lobotomies or jazz or Scientology, to insure that you don't end up fifty-five and lost. And this is where your dad was wrong. And me. From your age on, we made tactical errors every step of the way. We believed in the wrong gods, built the wrong models, read the wrong myths. We weren't cunning enough. And now we're trying to deal with the regret and torture that all true believing brings. And believe me, Matthew, *that* takes every bit of cunning you got.'

'So what should you have done?' Matthew asked.

'If I knew that . . .'

Matthew put his glass on the ring-stained coffee table.

'Well,' Brand said quietly, running his finger through the gulleys of his ear. 'At least you seem to care. That's something, I guess.'

The power plant was almost completely gone now. Just foundations, raw materials, sagging fences. Only the one cooling tower remained intact. Matthew slowly drove his father's car past the unattended guard's shed and through the empty lot, crunching bits of garbage with the radial tires. He parked near a rusting shed emblazoned with cracked danger signs. When he turned off the ignition there seemed to be a noise coming from the tower. Music. But all he could hear when he listened was the cooling of the eight-cylinder engine, the steady rustle of nearby waves.

He angled back the seat and looked beyond the tower. A squall had developed down-bay, dropping slivers of lightning into the water. Matthew figured the storm was about three miles off by counting the intervals between the flash and the report of thunder. It was a method of reckoning his father had taught him. He remembered some other things Walter had taught him. To shoot a foul shot, you pretend there's a brick on the front of the rim and try to knock it off. To drive a car, you align the hood ornament with the road's edge. To break into the open field, you offer the tackler a limp leg, keeping your weight on the other.

He heard the music again. It came from inside the tower, in pulses carried by breezes from the gathering squall. Something very hard, very fast. Matthew slid out of the car and walked toward the tower, careful not to step in one of the many foundation holes that lined the lot. Instead of entering the garage-sized door at ground level, he mounted the metal stairs that spiralled the building. He could hear the music more clearly as he walked – angry, panicked snatches of mad guitars, spit words.

He reached the upper entrance, a doorless passage just below roof level that led to a platform overlooking the inside of the tower. He could see the dancers from here. There were about ten of them. All boys in their mid-teens, dressed in tattered jeans and T-shirts and heavy black boots. Their hair was closely cropped, a few had shaved heads. They danced within a circle of light cast by four hurricane lamps, whirling manically around the massive boom box that played the music. They danced without rhythm, without plan, jerking across the floor so violently that they seemed to be drawn by ropes. Sometimes two would slam together ferociously, spinning away after contact. But that was the only communication among them. They would stop as suddenly as the music, their eyes downcast, their chests heaving, saying nothing as they waited for the next song to begin. Then they would start again with the same oblivious passion.

It was nearly dawn when Matthew arrived home. He parked the car in the driveway, not wanting to shake the house with the automatic garage opener. Something had been at the garbage, scattering it over the blacktop and part of the lawn. Matthew collected it as quietly as possible then entered the house through the back door. He decided to get something to eat before going to bed.

His mother sat at the kitchen table, a cup of instant coffee cooling before her. The refrigerator door was slightly open, emitting a wedge of coolness and light that crossed her face. Matthew could see that her eyes were ringed with lines of mascara. She held a twisted napkin in her hand. A bottle of aspirin lay overturned before her, its wad of cotton resting on the table like a snowball in the last stages of melting.

'Mom?'

'There's something you have to do, Matthew.'

THE LUCKIEST MAN

M atthew watched the immigration officer shuffle through Eddie's passport. He stared at the photograph for a moment, then at Matthew's face. He carefully examined Matthew's eyes before he continued shuffling the stiff pages. Matthew relaxed slightly. He had taken Eddie's passport rather than wait for one of his own. This had also allowed him to take Walter's credit cards and frequent flyer points for the ticket, since both his father and brother were named Walter Edward. The officer found a blank page and picked up a stamp.

'How long you rest in Italia?'

'As long as it take me to get to the border,' Matthew said.

'*Dove vai?* Where you go?'

'To Greece.'

The man raised his eyebrows as he stamped the passport.

'*Buona fortuna,*' he said, handing it back.

The plane had been late, so he decided to take a cab into the central train station to ensure he made the noon train to Trieste. There, he would rent a car and drive down the Yugoslavian coast, into Greece. He knew that there were no trains or buses in Greece because of the general strike, but not much else about the situation there. Everybody he had talked to about it told him he shouldn't go.

Matthew looked at the Milanese suburbs as his cab raced down the four-lane highway. The morning air was thick, smudged with foggy grays and chemical blues. Billboards loomed every quarter mile, knee-deep in stagnant pools. Beneath the overpasses were fenced lots full of rusting equipment or kids playing dusty soccer. Occasionally, there were clusters of high-rise apartments, isolated in fields of still weed. A jack-knifed truck surrounded by spluttering flares stopped traffic for a few minutes, provoking an alarm of horns from impatient drivers. As they waited Matthew remembered he had forgot to set his watch and turned it ahead seven hours.

The driver ignored Matthew, speaking continually into his microphone, adding his voice to the chaotic babble that came across the receiver. He was a tall, heavy man with connecting eyebrows and a hairy neck. He wore a sweatshirt with the number '32' emblazoned on front and back. He had a filterless cigarette which he never quite lit, removing it from his mouth every time he raised a flame to it to say something into the radio. Several times he burned his fingers with the forgotten match. Matthew noticed that his left eyelid drooped lazily, leaving that eye almost closed.

Once in central Milan they moved quickly through the late-morning city traffic, pulling up to the looming, exhaust-stained station with plenty of time for Matthew to make his train. As he pulled into the line of taxis beneath the giant stone awning at the front of the station, the cabbie popped the glove compartment to reveal a meter. It read 92,000 lire. Outside the airport, the driver had twice quoted Matthew a fare of about 30,000 in broken English. He'd even nodded after Matthew wrote it down on the back of his ticket. Matthew looked at the driver's scrutinous face in the rear-view mirror, his lazy lid dilating. He nodded and got out of the cab, taking his single shoulder bag with him. He took three 10,000 lire notes from his wallet and handed them through the passenger window. The driver shook out his match and removed his unlit cigarette to receive them. He waved the bills at the idling meter, his heavy left lid shuddering now.

'*Scusate, signore, ma . . .* '

'Bullshit,' Matthew said slowly, staring at the drooping lid. 'You said thirty, you get thirty. You want more, come get it.'

The driver was momentarily taken aback. Smoke from the extinguished match swirled through the cab.

'*Io non ha detto tre . . .*'

'Oh, fuck you. I don't have time for this,' Matthew said, turning and mounting the steps to the station. He heard the taxi door behind him slam.

'Oh,' the driver wailed. '*Scusate . . .*'

Matthew kept on walking, kicking his way through resentful pigeons. He heard the driver take a few steps after him, then stop. There was a slight impact on his back, and Matthew heard the hollow rattle of coins around him. He continued up the steps into the looming station, pigeons cooing critically behind him.

He made his train with a half-hour to spare. He found an empty compartment, but was joined at the next stop by an old priest who began to read a paperback copy of *Pane e vino* after settling in. Matthew was soon lulled asleep by jetlag and the train's rhythmic progress. He only slept sporadically, though, awakened at each stop by the sound of slamming doors. At Verona he leaned out the window and bought a can of orange soda and a ham sandwich from a man with an apron and beige fedora. The priest was asleep now, his book resting open on his several chins like a lowered veil.

Matthew stayed awake after Verona, eating slowly as he looked out the window. The landscape had evolved from the flat wastelands around Milan into fields of gnarled olive trees and disinterested livestock. The cities and towns grew less modern, built of stucco and red slate. Matthew thought about how badly he'd wanted to visit here, ever since his early teens. And now that he was here, he wanted only to get through it as quickly as possible.

There was a long wait at Mestre. The priest was awake now, writing something on a large notepad. Matthew watched the activity in the station, as men wearing orange jumpsuits and carrying small lanterns walked back and forth. There were several profound jolts in the train, from either direction. Finally, around dusk, there was a shrill whistle and the train jolted back toward Milan. Matthew was confused for a moment, then realized they were probably going to loop around Venice. Yet they continued west for almost fifteen minutes, then only gradually turned to the north. After a half-hour of travel Matthew's view from the window was still the darkening east, the way he wanted to go. He checked his watch, then looked at the priest, who was staring at him with a faint smile.

'Trieste?' Matthew asked.

The priest shook his head.

'Vienna,' he said hoarsely, phlegm almost drowning his voice.

'Vienna?' Matthew asked.

The priest nodded. He put his index fingers together, then spread them with benedictory precision.

'*Il treno . . .*'

Matthew realized what had happened. The train had separated in Mestre and he was on the wrong half. He walked into the hall and found a map bolted on a wall next to the WC. The next stop was Udine, up near the Austrian border. A very fat man carrying a shaving kit squeezed out of the bathroom. Matthew suddenly felt a wave of exhaustion. He opened a window with a sign that told him in four languages it was dangerous to lean out. He let the cold night air rush past his face, awakening him slightly.

'Damn . . .'

The station was a large, domed room with marble floors and dark wood walls. The doors to the street were chained, except for the center one. The five ticket windows at one end of the room were shuttered. Above them was a large Roman numeral clock and a blackboard that displayed arrival and departure times. Matthew saw that the next train to Trieste wouldn't leave until five-two a.m. He checked his watch. Just before midnight.

He found a seat on a long bench at the end of the hall opposite the shuttered windows, near a row of ticket and concession machines. The wood was hard but he was eventually able to stretch into a comfortable position. He looked around the station. The only other people in it were a short man in a Turkish skull cap who swept cigarette butts into a long-handled dustpan, and two young men who sat near the street doors. Both had long hair and scant beards. One wore a jean jacket decorated with badges, the other a black vest over a tattered white dress shirt. They stared blandly at Matthew. The board above the ticket windows began to rattle. One of the blank columns ran quickly through a series of indistinguishable numbers, then settled back into blankness.

Matthew slept for a few minutes, awakened by the sound of slamming doors, the high-pressure release of steam. A train had arrived. He stood up quickly, but saw it was not even twelve-thirty yet. A group of men with unlaced boots, orange jumpsuits and dim lanterns strolled silently through the station. Mail train, Matthew thought. He looked up at the board. There was no change in the five-two.

He settled back on to the hard wood, wide awake now. Something about the sound of the slamming doors made him think of a summer night when he and Eddie were ten. Walter had sent them to baseball camp for two weeks at a run-down boarding school on the outskirts of Trenton. It was their first time away from home. Walter and Helen had driven them there on Saturday morning, registering them in a large gymnasium where men in baseball caps manned folding tables. Another set of twins were there – two blond boys whose bull-necked father told Walter and Helen he edited a body-building magazine. He produced a recent issue with a photo of the boys, standing in tandem in small briefs. Their effeminate, greased bodies were spring-tight with tension, yet there was not a visible muscle on either of them. Matthew remembered the look his parents exchanged as the man proudly held the magazine in front of them – bewildered, amused, but also a little frightened.

Matthew had been desperately homesick for the first few hours after his parents left, yet soon grew interested in the camp. He was part of a team of twelve boys who did everything together: ate, practised, slept in one large room with six bunk beds. At Walter's request, Eddie had been assigned to another team. The blond twins had also been split up on to Matthew's and Eddie's teams.

The boys would rise early, gathering for breakfast in the cafeteria, then fidgeting through a talk from the retired Triple A league coach who ran the school. They'd jog out to the dusty diamond and practise skills all morning – shagging flies, hitting curves in the batting cage, learning how to run the bases or hit the cut-off man. After lunch, there would be the games among the teams, a round-robin tournament that would end in a championship on parents' day. Then, the day's final run, followed by the *en masse* shower in a tiled room that echoed their screams as they wrestled and danced through the steaming water. At night they would watch films or television, or line up at the phone booth near the cafeteria to call home.

One morning Bob Feller came to give a seminar on pitching. He showed the boys various techniques and tricks, but basically concentrated on how to throw the fastball. How to use the leg muscles for push, how to swing the shoulders before delivery. He lectured for nearly an hour, yet the only player who picked it up was the blond twin on Matthew's team. By the end of the lesson he was throwing ferocious fastballs that popped in Matthew's glove like an ax striking an old oak. The other boys complimented him on it but he ignored the praise, strangely grim with his new knowledge.

The next day Matthew's and Eddie's teams played for the first time. The blond twin on Matthew's team pitched, using his new-found fastball to strike out the first four batters, including Eddie. The fifth batter was the other blond twin. Matthew called for a pitch low and away, yet the pitcher threw a fastball directly at his brother's head. It grazed the brim of his helmet and slammed into the backstop. The batter smiled sheepishly and jogged to first. His brother didn't acknowledge him.

The game proceeded quickly. Eddie managed to keep the other team from scoring with his wild array of pitches – change-ups, knuckleballs, slow curves. The blond pitcher continued to strike out batters with fastballs at the knees, barely more than few inches from the center of the plate. He rarely missed the strike zone and was never wild. The second time his brother came up, he paused for a moment, staring at

Matthew's low-positioned glove. He then threw a tremendous fastball that hit his brother squarely on the temple guard. There was a hollow cracking sound, and Matthew remembered watching the ball shoot up in the air like a weak pop-up. After catching it, he noticed the batting twin crumpled over the plate. His helmet was scarred with a long crack and he looked like he was taking a nap. His brother stood on the mound, silently beckoning to Matthew for the ball so he could face the next batter.

It took about twenty minutes for the ambulance to arrive. The boy revived a little, although his ears rang and he couldn't fully steady himself. There was a large purple welt below his ear, but the coach told everyone that was a good thing, since it meant the pressure was outside the skull. They took him to the hospital anyway.

That night, Matthew awoke around four a.m. to the echoed sound of slamming doors. He climbed down from his bunk, noticing the blond twin had gone from the bottom shelf. He went into the marble hallway, looking out the window next to the iron fire door. There was a parking lot below, lit by a single pale streetlamp swarming with busy moths. A car idled beneath it. Matthew watched as the body-building father loaded his sons' gear into the trunk, then slid into the car. The blond pitcher was in the passenger seat, his face pressed against the glass, watching the moths singe themselves on the light. He looked up and saw Matthew, and seemed to smile slightly. They drove off slowly, crunching gravel and bits of broken glass.

Matthew went back into his room and took the small change wallet from beneath his pillow. As he walked quietly through the large halls, he was beset by various fears. That the sun would never rise again. That the blacks who lived in nearby slums would attack their camp. That Eddie would run away and leave him here. That he would fall into a well. He thought about his own funeral, what it would be like, who would be there, what would happen if he woke up in the coffin after being buried.

A ten-watt light came on when he entered the phone booth. It smelled of urine and wet tobacco. He put all his money in the slot and called his home number. Walter picked it up before the first ring had ended. His voice was clear, although Matthew could tell he'd been sleeping.

'Dad?'

'Matthew, what is it?'

'Can I come home now?'

'Why? What's happened?'

Matthew couldn't think of what to say.

'Matthew, tell me if something's happened.'

'It hasn't. It's just time to come home now, isn't it?'

There was a pause. Matthew could hear Walter's muffled voice as he spoke to Helen.

'Listen, Matty. It'll be time to come home next week. We'll be there with the stationwagon. Just hang in till then, will you? You'll be all right.'

'It can be time to come home now, dad,' Matthew had persisted.

'Come on, Matt. It's not so bad. Just tough it out. It'll be good for you.'

There was another pause. A recording came on to tell Matthew to put more money in the machine.

'Matt?'

'Yeah?'

'Go back to bed now. All right?'

The phone clicked dead before Matthew could answer that it wasn't. He listened to the dial tone for a while, then hung up. He waited for Walter to call back for several minutes, until he heard the sounds of the kitchen staff arriving. He snuck back to his bed.

Matthew walked over to the vending machines. Cigarettes, juice, razors, wrapped sandwiches. He fished sufficient coinage from his pocket and bought a pimento and cheese sandwich in a small roll. He returned to his seat and tried to get comfortable, then ripped the cellophane skin from the sandwich and broke the roll in half. He noticed the insect just before biting into it. Moist, many legged, pigment washed. It coiled in astonishment, shadow boxing with a dozen limbs before retreating into the folds of the cheese. Matthew dropped the sandwich and kicked both halves beneath the bench. He looked around the station. The long-haired men were asleep, the janitor had left. The schedule board began to work, turning the same column through a series of numbers and letters before settling into a blank position.

He was out of Trieste by mid-morning in a rented Fiat 500. It was a tiny, yellow, pill-shaped car that snowed rust from the undercarriage every time Matthew slammed the door. The engine coughed on exactly like the lawnmower he'd used to make spending money in his teens. It was the smallest car he had ever seen, much less driven. From the driver's seat he could touch every window without moving his torso more than a few inches. There was no back trunk, and the front hood was no larger than a section of sidewalk. The only thing that gave it any sense of room was the small sun roof directly above Matthew's head. Once he opened it, however, he couldn't get it closed. As he drove, he could feel his hair flutter through the gap.

He took the coastal road down the Yugoslavian coast. It was a treacherous course – narrow, sharply inclined, jointed by blind curves that often bore flower-strewn memorials to past accidents. Opposing buses and trucks often straddled the center line, causing Matthew to slow regularly and even stop a few times. He soon crawled along the shoulder, passed several times a minute by speeding Volvos and Mercedes that caused his Fiat to shudder in their turbulence. He worked the gears so hard that the head of the gear stick soon came off, leaving a sharp screw that he had to wrap with a T-shirt from his bag.

When he allowed himself glances at the landscape and sea, Matthew was taken with its clarity and beauty. The water was opaque blue, revealing spines of reef that ran from the shore to the church-and-tree-covered islands that guarded every bay and inlet. Still birds hovered above the water and the beaches, suspended by the steady sea breezes. Knots of semi-nude tourists populated the sand, yet most of the people he saw were black-dressed peasants hunched over wooden tools or tight-jeaned youths watching him pass their cafés with hard, uncurious stares.

He stopped in the early afternoon at a small village to fill up with gas and quell his rumbling stomach. He found a small taverna where he bought a ham and cheese omelette, a large roll and several cups of thick coffee. He ate quickly, so as not to lose any time. He wanted to make Athens by the following morning at the latest.

By early evening, when he was almost to the end of the coastal road, he discovered that his headlights didn't work. He pulled over to the side of the road and checked the connections, but couldn't see anything. A truck passed very close, its horn sounding a Dopplered complaint. He would have to find a place to stay overnight, then head out in the morning.

Not far ahead was a turn-off to a city called Split. He made the town just as it was becoming too dark to travel. The city's suburbs were nondescript, slightly run-down – small houses, bus stops, cars under repair, a few billboards. He followed the signs for the town center, discovering it to be an old harbor town of alleys, cobbled streets and stone buildings built around a large palace. The tree-lined hills surrounding the city were dotted with villas and a few churches.

Matthew found a bed and breakfast near the harbor that would take his father's credit cards. He locked himself in his room, wanting to go to sleep immediately so that he'd be ready to leave by first light. Yet the mattress was creased by lingering impressions from past occupants, and the garish wallpaper reflected streetlight at him. He almost dozed off once, but just then a loudspeaker van passed by his window, then passed again. After that, he lay wide awake, listening to a rhythmic scraping sound in the alley below his window. He finally scissored out of bed and looked through the lumpy curtains. An old woman sat in lantern light, cleaning a large basket of thin silver fish. Matthew looked down the alley, to the main street. Groups of people were making their way toward the palace, the youths doubled up on Vespas, the older people strolling in pairs or fours. The loudspeaker van passed again. Matthew dressed quickly and left the hotel, following the crowds to the inner harbor.

The palace had originally bordered the harbor directly, yet ruin and silt now left about a hundred yards of flatland between it and the water, land covered by a wide promenade. The palace's seawall had crumbled, leaving only the two loggias at either end. A series of terraces, like tall, wide steps, now provided frontal entry to the palace. Each was about ten feet high and a hundred wide, covered by the umbrella tables of cafés and the awnings of souvenir shops.

After wandering around for several minutes, Matthew climbed up into the palace's southern loggia to get a better view of the city, dropping a paper-light coin into an unattended donation box at the bottom of a tightly spiraled staircase. The top of the tower was a single room with open windows. To the north and south he could see the slopes that ran up the enclosing shores of the harbor, dotted with lights from the villas. The eastern view showed the remainder of the palace, with its maze of streets and alleys. There was a large square at the center, with more shops and what appeared to be apartments. Beyond the palace was the less concentrated topography of the city's outskirts.

The western window overlooked the bay. There were only a few boats in the water – small, lantern-lit pleasure craft and what appeared to be a tourist ferry, returning from the islands beyond the bay's mouth. A well-lit barge, busy with workmen, was anchored several hundred yards offshore, near the center of the bay. Matthew watched it for a while, trying unsuccessfully to figure out what they were doing. He then looked down at the promenade below, where hundreds of people strolled slowly back and forth, stopping occasionally to speak with acquaintances moving in the opposite direction. At the northern end of the promenade a group of workmen were setting up the last of several hundred folding chairs, arranged in rippling semicircles that afforded a view of the palace. The chairs were bordered by a string of colored light bulbs that ran between wooden poles. At the opposite end of the promenade, more workmen scrambled around several flatbed trucks that held banks of searchlights.

As Matthew spent several minutes watching the moonlit ribbons of spume on the bay's breakers or following the regular procession of people below, he felt himself relax for the first time since leaving America. There was something calming in the small waves, in the walkers' pointless procession. He knew that tomorrow, the next few days, would be difficult. Tonight he would breathe the salt air and rest.

After a large dinner of schnitzel, boiled potatoes and steamed vegetables at a terrace café, Matthew wandered on to the promenade, losing himself in the meandering crowd. The people were dark, with light eyes and heavy brows. Most of the men wore tight, beltless pants and silk shirts. The women wore boldly printed knee-length dresses and sandals that laced up their thick ankles. Matthew walked only a few lengths, then stopped at the assembly of chairs. They were cordoned off by a thin chain. Women with sashes stood at the entrance. He felt himself led gently toward the entrance by the crowd. As he inched forward he noticed that the women's sashes bore the names of languages. 'English' was a tall woman with bowed legs. Matthew paid her ten dinars.

'Are you an English speaker?'

Matthew nodded. She handed him a box-like cassette player and a set of bulky headphones from a nearby table.

'This is your translation of tonight's performance,' she said mechanically. 'When the loudspeakers instruct you, just depress the red button and affix the headphones over your eyes.'

Matthew laughed and she returned an oblivious smile. He wandered into the rippling chairs, finding a seat in the last row. Most of the people around him seemed to be tourists. He heard snatches of German.

The string of surrounding bulbs was dimmed when the chairs were nearly full. The flatbed searchlights at the far end of the promenade flared on, sending crossing beams over the city and the harbor. The loudspeakers on top of the nearby wooden poles crackled momentarily, then repeated a message in several languages. English was last.

'When you hear the tone, please start your recorder.'

There was an interval of silence, then a prolonged, shrill tone. Matthew put on his headphones and started his recorder. There was a fanfare of tinny music as the spots were lowered on to the palace. They played haphazardly over the stone for a moment, then focussed on to the southern loggia. There was an ominous basso flourish and an authoritative English voice began to speak.

'It is four hundred AD. Twilight has descended on the once brilliant daytime of the Roman Empire. Internal strife, outbreaks of plague and barbarian attack all threaten to bring down the once great state. Only one thing holds it together still – Diocletian, the last great Roman Emperor. For two decades he has presided over the last flowering of Rome, using his tremendous political skill to hold his vast empire together. He has pacified rebellious provinces, centralized the diverse economy, reinstituted the old religion of Jupiter and Mars, even reined in those powerful kingmakers, the Roman Legion. Yet now he is a tired old man, exhausted by his struggles, desirous only to live out his last days in peace. So, after handpicking a successor, he relinquishes power and retires here, to the harbor of Spoleto, now Split. He builds a palace . . .'

Light flooded the entire structure.

'A building that merges the desire for opulence and beauty with the need for safety and refuge in an increasingly complex and dangerous world.'

There were more shrill trumpets. Matthew removed the headphones, although he let the tape continue to run. The lights began to penetrate the palace, casting full frontal views on Corinthian columns, bottom-lighting arches, shrouding the loggias or terraces with gauzes of red or blue. Matthew could hear the narration continuing on his loudspeakers, interspersed by fanfares and trained voices performing skits. When the lights concentrated on a small domed roof tucked in a corner of the palace, Matthew put his headphones back on.

'It was here that the Emperor had artisans from all over the Mediterranean create his most elaborate and yet most personal room – the celestial vault. Painters, sculptors and architects conspired to re-create the heavens on the ceiling of the room, so that the aging and infirm Emperor could look at the skies where he would soon go as a god . . .'

289

Matthew again removed the headphones. The performance ended not long after, with the narrator's voice raised above a symphonic swell as the light fully illuminated the palace. Then everything went dark. There was a hissing sound in the bay, followed by a willow of light reaching down from the sky above the palace. The boom followed closely. Matthew watched the sky for a moment, then turned his attention to the launching barge. There were four men working there, moving agilely through the thick smoke and flares of ignition. Sparks from ascending engines showered them occasionally, yet they seemed oblivious. Once, a small rocket misfired, lurching horizontally just after launch. It shot through a low arc, hitting the water about fifty yards from the barge. There was a momentary phosphorescent glow, a puff of sea steam, then darkness.

Just before reaching the Greek border, Matthew was forced off the road by a jolt of wind from a passing truck. He skidded across the gravel shoulder, then came to an abrupt stop against a small turf hedge. He sat still for a minute after impact, then got out to examine the car. The front right fender was dented a little and had collected a wedge of turf beneath it. He walked around to the driver's side, yet before he could get back in he heard an insinuating hissing coming from the rear of the car. He knelt next to the back left tire and saw the gash. He smeared spittle across it, then watched the small bubbles. The tire was soon flat.

He found a spare beneath the back seat, but no jack. He looked at his watch. Nearly noon. If he didn't get going soon, he would have to stop again for the night before reaching Athens. To hell with that, he thought. He sat on his haunches, looking at the four large lug nuts holding on the tire. He tried one with his hands, but knew that wouldn't work. After staring at it for several minutes, he stood and went back into the car, searching beneath the passenger seat for the knob to the gear stick. He took it to the side of the car and fitted its bottom over the lug nuts. It was a bit too small, so he found a sharp rock and whittled it until the knob's square hole resembled the nut. He tried it again. It fitted the lugs tightly.

The next thing to do was get the car off the ground. He looked around for some sort of lever, but the landscape around was desolate – rocks, turf and small branches. There were no houses or buildings within sight, just pastures bounded by crumbling rock walls. He walked to the side of the road and tried flagging down the occasional cars and trucks, but their drivers passed obliviously, intent on maintaining great speeds. Matthew walked back to the side of the car, rocking it slowly.

'Fuck it,' he said.

He walked over the turf hedge into pasture and began to gather rocks from the top of its crumbling wall. He took about two dozen in all, most of them roughly the size of dinner plates, piling them beneath the car's back left corner. He layered them in rows of three, until the pile was snug against the chassis's bottom. He placed one last rock on the ground next to the tire, then squatted beside the tire and tried to get a good grip on the chassis. He could feel the rust flaking off in his hands. Great heat still came from the muffler, just inches from his fingers. He counted to three, then jerked the car off the ground. It took about ten seconds to get it up the necessary few inches above the rock pile. He could feel the muscles strain in his back, could feel small cuts open on his palms. He slowly maneuvered his right forearm and knee so that they were under the car, pressed up beneath the chassis. Then, moving as quickly as possible, he took away his left hand and snatched the rock from the ground. He could feel the car sag and shoved his right arm further in. It touched the muffler. He could smell the burning hair immediately, but he managed to slip the rock on the pile before instinct took over and he jerked away. The pile settled a little, but held. Matthew fell back into a sitting position and watched the wheel turn slowly, an inch free from the ground.

He looked at his arm. It wasn't too bad. A burn about two inches long and a quarter inch wide, just above his wrist. There was a cut within the burn's valley, lined by a row of red spheres. He peeled back its edges – it wasn't very deep. He took the T-shirt from the naked gear stick and wrapped it around the wound, then used the gear knob to remove the lug nuts.

The border was marked by a long, low building that looked like a toll booth and was manned by soldiers. Only a few of the slots were occupied by cars. Matthew pulled into an empty bay and was slowly surrounded by three young soldiers carrying large carbines. One stood with a probationary foot on the front fender, the rifle strap wound around his forearm like a bandage. Another examined beneath the car with a mirror on the end of a pole. The third leaned toward Matthew's window.

'Passaporta.'

Matthew showed him his passport. The soldier glanced at the cover, then handed it back to him without opening it.

'Hyou money?' he asked.

'Uh . . .' Matthew produced the clump of dollars, dinars, lire and drachmas from his breast pocket. The soldier looked at the thin fold of crumpled bills, then made a clicking noise in the back of his mouth. Matthew took the wallet from the dashboard and displayed his dad's credit cards. The soldier nodded and backed away from the car.

'Excuse me,' Matthew said, getting out of the car. 'I wonder if you could help me.'

The other two soldiers joined the first. Matthew removed the reddened T-shirt and showed them the burn on his arm. The spheres of blood still came up every time he wiped it. It was beginning to throb.

'I've done myself here. I wonder if you can give me a bandage of some sort.'

'*Ti léi?*'

'A bandage,' Matthew said, displaying his wound for each of them. 'For the cut.'

The first soldier looked closely at the wound, then frowned slightly and shrugged. He pulled his shirt from his pants, showing a short, waxy scar on his abdomen. He pointed to Matthew's wound and clicked critically. The second soldier said something, then pulled down his collar to show a thin, purplish wound running along his shoulder. They began to argue until they were interrupted by the third guard, the one who had looked beneath the car. He had removed his shirt entirely and was displaying a long surgical scar that ran near to his spine. There was a moment of silence, then the first soldier said something. The third soldier shouted back at him, and immediately all three were talking quickly, gesturing to their scars and shaking open hands in each others' faces. Matthew walked slowly back to his car and drove into Greece.

The highway was busy with northbound traffic, yet the southern lanes were almost empty. Matthew noticed that the Esso and BP stations were almost all closed and hoped he'd have enough gas to get him to Athens. Everything else appeared to be closed, too, except for occasional tavernas or shops hidden behind mounds of uncollected garbage. Matthew drove quickly, ignoring the terrain, keeping his eyes on the road.

On the outskirts of Athens there was a roadblock manned by several more soldiers. Matthew was stopped by a middle-aged Captain who asked him a series of sharp questions in Greek. Matthew held up his passport. The man shook a splayed hand at it and complained bitterly, as if it were some great irrelevancy.

'I don't understand you,' Matthew said.

The Captain continued to ask questions. Matthew sat still, looking at the shadow of beard on the man's face, at the stains on his powder-blue cravat. Then he slowly let out the clutch. The car inched forward. The man drew back from the window, his eyes surprised. The soldier who had been standing in front of his car moved slowly out of the way. The Captain asked him another series of questions, yet Matthew continued to move forward, gradually gaining speed. The Captain had grown silent. Matthew looked in the rear-view mirror at his astonished face. None of the soldiers moved. Finally, when Matthew was about twenty yards away, the Captain gestured toward him with his splayed hand and said something to his men. They laughed. He then turned around and waved down an approaching truck. Matthew drove on.

He arrived at the embassy at four o'clock. Although it was located near the town's center, there was little traffic. Just occasional cars, a few vans carrying soldiers. He parked a hundred yards past the entrance, bumping the Fiat on to the sidewalk. The pavement was strewn with rotten figs from the trees that overtopped the high, barbed wall. There were also broadsheets and newspapers, and several mountains of odorous garbage. As Matthew walked toward the gate a dirty sheet of paper blew against his leg. He peeled it off and looked at it. It was the front page of a tabloid newspaper, its banner photo depicting a young man in the middle of a rubble-strewn avenue hurling a firebomb at an unseen adversary. Matthew crumpled the page and tossed it on to one of the piles.

The embassy gate was manned by a Marine inside a small shack with a thick, slightly tinted window. He stared down as Matthew waited, checking off some sort of list.

'I would like to see the Vice Consul,' Matthew said finally into a small speaker on the glass.

The guard looked up slowly. He appeared to be Matthew's age.

'Name?'

'Matthew Merriweather.'

The guard looked back down at his list.

'I have no clearance for that name,' he said after a moment.

'Yes, but I have to see the Vice Consul. I was told to get in touch with him when I got to Athens. He has some information for me.'

'You still have to be cleared.'

'Maybe you could call him and he could say it's all right.'

'Maybe,' the guard said slowly. 'Maybe not.'

'Um, why not?' Matthew asked, trying to stay calm.

'He has to call me. It's procedure.'

'But then how could I get this information from him?'

'You would have to call.'

'Are the phones working?'

'Some of them.'

Matthew looked into the embassy grounds. There was a courtyard with a fountain. A limousine was parked near the main entrance, its hood up. Two men in shirtsleeves sat on either side of the main door. One was rubbing the face of his watch with a salivated finger. The other sat with his chair tipped against the wall, reading a paper.

'What if I said something like I'm not going to leave here until I get to talk to the Vice Consul?' Matthew asked.

'Don't do that,' the guard said.

Matthew looked up at the sky.

'Damn it,' he said softly.

'Listen,' the guard said after a moment. 'Normally I'd cut you a break, dude. I mean, you're all right. I know that. But this fucking strike, man. You just don't know. It's by the book, else it's my ass in a sling. You know what I'm saying? So what you gotta do is you grab yourself a crib, call the number on this card and ask to speak with your man. They'll sort you out. They really will, man. It might take a little while but it'll happen. Awright?'

Matthew took the card from the dish beneath the window.

'All right.'

'What you after, anyway?'

'My father's body.'

He found an open hotel on the city's central square, opposite the Parliament building. He parked the Fiat in a forbidden zone on a narrow sidestreet, doubting anyone would challenge it. The square was quiet. Although dusk was setting in, there were no commuters at the bus stop, no drinkers or diners at the several large cafés on the tree-lined traffic island. Only police, driving slowly in small cars or lounging in stepvans.

The hotel was a thin brick building wedged between two solid-glass office blocks. The lobby was small and dark, filled with old furniture and framed tourist posters. It was empty except for a short man in a baggy suit behind the desk who was speaking rapidly into a phone. He held up his index finger to Matthew as he concluded his conversation.

'*Kalinikta*' he said warily after hanging up.

'Hello. I need a room. Maybe for a couple days.'

'Yeah, sure. Passaporta and . . .'

Matthew dropped his brother's passport and father's credit card on the desk. The man smiled grimly and produced documents of registration.

'We have little staff, I'm afraid,' he said as Matthew filled in the forms.

'That's not a problem. Do the phones work?'

'Yeah, sure. But everything else . . .' He shrugged.

The room had a low ceiling and a crater-like double bed. Several long fissures ran through the walls, beneath the brittle wallpaper. Matthew looked out the window, on to the wide square. More police had gathered in front of the Parliament building. The phone buzzed and it was the manager with an outside line. Matthew called the embassy and left his name and number with a harried-sounding woman.

There were some candies and a bottle of mineral water on the nightstand next to the bed. Matthew unwrapped one of the candies and put it into his mouth, only to spit it out immediately into his palm and examine it. A watermelon rind, drenched in sugary syrup. He tossed it into the tin garbage pail and took a long drink of water. He then took off all his clothes and stretched out on the bed, but couldn't relax, his muscles still tensed and cramping from the long drive.

He walked into the bathroom, a small room whose plaster walls had buckled with humidity. Colonies of yellow mold grew in the corners, behind the elevated tub and toilet. Matthew wiped some paint chips from the bath, then put the rubber stopper into the drain and turned on the hot water faucet. There were several subterranean rattles, followed by a vomit of rusty water. Matthew filled the tub almost to the rim. He was surprised at how hot the water was – it took him over a minute to lower himself in. He submerged himself to the chin, letting the heat loosen his muscles. After he'd settled, he thoroughly scrubbed the crusted wound on his arm with the lye soap on the edge of the tub, cleaning away the incipient infection that tinged its edges. He then lay perfectly still, watching the cataracts of steam swirl through the room's drafts.

He thought of Eleni, the times they had bathed together. He wondered about her, how she was. He had spoken to Prospero before leaving, but all he had heard was that she was still working on Dawit's case. He had seen a flight for her city listed at Milan airport. Perhaps later, he thought. After all this.

The water eventually cooled. He slowly dried himself and lay, still naked, on the tatty brocaded bedspread. He fell asleep immediately.

*

He awoke to the sound of echoed footfalls, excited shouts, blasts of horns and sirens. Flickers of flamelight played over the ceiling above him. Matthew sprang to his feet and ran to the window, thinking fire. Yet it was only a procession of young people entering the square, many of them holding torches. He watched the procession. There were long-haired boys with banner-carrying girls riding on their shoulders; groups of students walking with linked arms, singing anthems and laughingly crossing steps; solitary marchers wearing large, papier-mâché heads, some of Uncle Sam. Occasionally, packs of young men in balaclavas stole past, staying in the shadows, lumpy sacks slung over their shoulders.

The students began to fill the large square, moving slowly toward the Parliament, which was now guarded by several hundred police. They were massed in three lines – two on the street, a third at the top of the high steps. The officers in the street wore their regular duty uniforms: black waistcoats, white peaked caps, small truncheons hanging from their belts. Those on the front row wore gas masks. They watched the students impassively, pointing out the more outrageous banners and papier-mâché heads to one another. The third row, those on the steps, were dressed in riot gear: black jumpsuits and lace-up boots, plated vests, shields and long staffs, helmets with tinted visors.

The students had gathered on the traffic island and were being harangued by a long-bearded man who stood on a café table, holding its umbrella stem with one hand and a megaphone with the other. The crowd quieted eventually and began to form a long, arm-linked line under his direction. The police responded by tightening their own two lines. The men on the steps remained perfectly still. Matthew noticed that the balaclava-clad men remained at the back of the square, out of sight behind a copse of cypress trees.

The students began to advance slowly on the police lines, singing and laughing. They met the police in the street and there was a moment of sustained shoving, the two lines writhing like mating serpents. Other students rushed up to thicken the original line, and the police began to give ground. There was a whistle and the second police line rushed up, putting their shoulders to their colleagues' backs. Again, there was wavering stalemate. This continued for about a minute, when clouds of smoke began to emerge from the crowd of students. Tear gas, rolled in by the police. The students retreated quickly across the street, clutching handkerchiefs or cloth banners to their noses and mouths. The police withdrew to the foot of the steps, leaving a half dozen canisters smoldering in the street.

To the cheers of the students, a nimble young man raced into the street and expertly kicked one of the canisters with his instep. It bounced twice before hitting a policeman on the thigh. The policeman steadied it with his foot and corner-kicked it back with similar skill. Other students rushed forward, and soon all half dozen canisters were being booted back and forth, leaving trails of smoke hovering above the street. Matthew could hear shouts of encouragement and laughter echoing through the square.

Suddenly, there was a shatter of glass, and one of the policemen stumbled back from the line, alight. Other police tackled him on the steps, patting out his flames with their jackets and caps. There was another explosion just in front of the police, a small lake of flaming liquid in the street. Matthew saw that the balaclava-clad men had crept through the lines and were now dancing through the street, hurling Molotov cocktails and large stones at the police, who retreated hastily up the steps.

There was a shrill whistle that echoed through the square. The third line of police raced down the steps, brandishing their staffs like lances. Stones and bombs landed ineffectually around them as they moved forward. They raced across the street, catching some of the hooded men in the square and beating them savagely. They beat other students too – whoever they could catch. Most of the students were able to stay ahead of them, fleeing down side streets. The square was soon empty except for a few dozen wounded students and police. Heavy smoke lingered in pockets near the ground, illuminated by dropped torches and blue siren lights.

Matthew's phone rang. Two quick pulses, then silence. He stared at it for a moment, then picked it up.

'This is Armand Debakke from the embassy. I have the information you need . . .'

Matthew hesitated at the hotel lobby door, making sure none of the riot police were around. The square was almost completely empty now. He slipped out and moved quickly along the sidewalk, hugging the walls to stay out of the light. The street where he'd parked the Fiat was littered with banners, stones and shoes. They had sprayed an encircled 'A' on the driver's door and another on the back window. There were several dents in the hood, as if it had been danced on, and the side-view mirror had been bent down, like a wilted plant. But the tires were unharmed and the lawnmower engine revved with the first turn of the key.

His directions were straightforward. Through the square, up the northern artery on which he'd come into Athens. The hospital was a half-mile past the embassy. A large white building across from a memorial park. You can't miss it, Debakke had said. He had notified them that Matthew was coming but warned him things would be in a chaotic state. He told Matthew to call him once he'd secured a release and they'd make further plans.

He drove slowly through the square. The streetlights showed the way, yet in a few places his lack of headlights blinded him. Once, he drove through a cloud of tear gas that lingered in a depression in the road. A small amount wafted through the sun roof, causing his eyes to water momentarily. As he emerged he thought of a movie he'd seen as a boy, in which a man on a yacht had passed through a mysterious glowing cloud that caused his skin to sparkle with radiant drops of condensation. Weeks later, the man began to feel strange. His shoes no longer fit him, his clothes were baggy. His wife didn't have to stand on tiptoe to kiss him anymore. He was shrinking . . .

Matthew shook off the memory and paid attention to the road, which was deserted except for racing police vans and small cars that travelled slowly along the curb. Some of the piles of garbage that lined the road were alight. Groups of police stood on corners, watching him pass without interest. He thought again of what Debakke had told him, Walter had been to the embassy a few days earlier, trying to organize the sending of a small parcel back to the States. He had walked and hitched to Athens from somewhere in the south. Debakke had finally arranged a spot in a diplomatic pouch, but Walter had never been back. Then the police had called.

Matthew soon reached the hospital. It was a large building, set off from the road by a hedge of denuded lemon trees. In contrast to the nearby shops and offices, it was busy with light and activity. Two ambulances were parked in the crescent drive at the front, their rotating blue lights playing over twenty or thirty soldiers who sprawled beneath the trees. Matthew could see human forms moving busily through the hospital windows.

He parked in the street, walking around the crescent drive and through the glass front doors. There were about a hundred people crowded into the large lobby. Most appeared to be waiting for relatives or friends, although there were several with minor wounds – soldiers with bandaged heads, young men clutching their ribs, women dabbing tearing eyes with lace handkerchiefs. A group of soldiers sat on the floor in the far corner, playing some sort of card game with muffled excitement.

Opposite Matthew was an unoccupied desk with a ringing phone. Behind that was a door. He felt someone touch his arm. A short, black-shrouded woman with several large moles on her face was speaking to him, trying to explain something. She pointed to a bulletin board covered with lists. Another old woman nearby joined the conversation. Matthew walked away from them, around the desk and through the door to a dimly lit hallway lined with scales. There were several doors, most of them closed. Only two of the rooms showed light. Matthew walked toward the first one, nudging the door open enough to look in. A young boy dressed in a paper gown sat on the edge of an examining table, singing to himself. Matthew walked to the second light, which was some sort of office. Two nurses were inside – one writing furiously at a desk, the other watering potted plants.

'Excuse me,' Matthew said.

They both looked at him.

'*Ne?*' the one at the desk asked.

'I'm looking for my father.'

'*Ti léi?*' asked the other.

'My father. He's an American. The embassy called about him, I think.'

They spoke to each other, saying 'Americanou' several times. The one watering the plant finally nodded at him and pointed toward the floor with the spout of her can. A few drops fell out. Matthew nodded and walked to the stairwell across the hall.

He paused at the top of the concrete steps, suppressing a sudden swell of nausea. A hedge of sweat appeared on his hairline and his rapid gasps of breath seemed to fall a few inches short of his lungs. The way he felt when Eddie would frighten him in the back of the stationwagon. Look at them, Matty. The exhaustion he'd felt as he walked down that imaginary spiral staircase in the woods behind the house, after searching in vain for the new colors.

There were footsteps below, then a half step and a crash – the sound of flesh on concrete, of breaking glass. Curses. He walked quickly down the steps. An orderly had fallen, dropping a box of thermometers on the tile floor. He was standing by the time Matthew reached him, angrily brushing the slivers of glass from his white trousers. He was young, younger than Matthew, with incongruous blond hair. When he saw Matthew he shook his head and shrugged, then squatted to pick up the thermometers. Matthew knelt next to him to help. They worked quickly, silently. About a dozen of the thermometers had cracked, yet only one had shattered altogether, allowing its drop of mercury to escape. Matthew stopped working to watch the orderly try to pick it up with his fingers. The residueless liquid squirted from his grasp each time he pressed it. He tried mashing it down, scooping it with a large sliver of broken glass. Nothing worked. Matthew left him there, still trying.

The hallway was dark; most of the bulbs did not burn. The walls were covered with water stains, the floors littered with white pans full of crusty cotton balls. Matthew heard a calm voice coming from a nearby room. He listened for a moment. It was his father.

'And you just took off and ran, all the way to the outfield?'

He walked quickly to the door. It was a small lounge with a tattered sofa, several wooden chairs, pale lamps and dozens of styrofoam cups. A young man in a white uniform sat on the sofa, operating a mini-recorder.

'And hyou took joos off hran, aloway out feelt?' he said, then turned the recorder back on.

'Like if you ran fast enough you could outdistance that awful sting-ing . . .'

'Lie heef hyou run fast enough you can outdiss that stinking . . .'

'. . . numbness, keep it from overtaking you.'

'. . . none of thees, keep hit from hover you.'

'What are you doing?' Matthew asked hoarsely.

The young man turned around, startled.

'Practise English.'

Matthew stared at him. He had a heavy brow and dull, dark eyes. His mouth worked rapidly, as if he wanted to smile but wasn't sure if he should.

'I go one day to America,' he continued.

'Where did you get that?' Matthew asked, nodding to the recorder.

'From the American.' The orderly stood up suddenly. 'Are you for him?'

'Yes.'

'Okay. Come with. Everything ready.'

The orderly dipped past Matthew, leading him to a door across the hall. He turned on the light in the room, then stepped back to let Matthew past.

'Wait out here,' Matthew said. 'Don't go.'

'Okay.'

Matthew stared at his palm for a moment, rubbing several areas of it with the index finger of his other hand. Then he stepped into the room. It was empty except for a stainless steel gurney that his eyes avoided.

The walls were tile to about chest level, then plaster, covered with more water stains. At one end was a deep concrete sink with two tall hooked faucets. Above that was a clock. The room was lit by fluorescent lights that hummed slightly and flickered through various degrees of brilliance. There were no windows.

The clock double clicked away a minute. Matthew checked his watch against it, adjusting it slightly. He suddenly felt a great thirst and walked quickly to the sink, opening one of the hooked faucets. There was a momentary rumble, then an underpressured stream of water dropped out. He drank long from it, water running down his cheek and tilted neck. He could see some hair caught in the drain, like seaweed.

When he finished drinking he turned quickly and approached the table. He was surprised to see him almost naked – just a hand towel over his groin. Matthew's first thought was that he must be cold. His chest had been shaved, and there was foot-long scar running down the middle of the ribcage. It looked like the laces on a football. The skin there and around his neck, armpits and stomach was covered with some dull yellow paste. Matthew looked at his father's hands. The fingernails and large callouses were drained of color and shone brilliantly in the overhead light. There were purplish intubation punctures further up the arm.

Matthew looked at his face. The chin and cheeks were covered with several days' growth of beard. Matthew remembered how that stubble would scratch him when he wrestled with Walter in the pool as a boy. He reached out and stroked it with the palm of his hand, careful not to touch the skin. It was soft now, not rough at all. He looked at the eyes, not quite completely shut. Small crescents of white showed, covered by a patina of caked rheum. He reached down and touched his neck. It was cold from the refrigerator. He pressed hard then drew away his hand, noticing that his fingers left no impression.

He turned away. The orderly stood watching in the doorway.

'How did he die?'

'Okay,' the orderly said, nodding. 'I look.'

He walked past Matthew and squatted near the table, taking a clipboard from a shelf beneath the gurney. As he read Matthew squatted next to him. In a silver tray there were other things – passport, wedding ring, change, a ticket of some sort. There was also a miniature model of a soldier, dressed in the Greek uniform. Matthew picked it up and examined it for a moment, then placed it in his pants pocket.

The orderly pointed to the clipboard.

'It says here his heart was attacked by a rock of bone that came loosed.'

Matthew nodded slowly.

'What is this?' he asked, holding up the ticket.

'Lotto.' The orderly's dull eyes brightened. 'Hey, maybe he's winner . . .'

They stood up.

'Take it,' Matthew said, handing it to him. 'You can use the money for America if it is. You'll need it.'

They looked down at the body.

'And what's this yellow stuff?'

'To kill the dirt.'

Matthew nodded.

'All right. Thanks. Can I have that recorder now?'

The orderly handed it to him and nodded for a moment, then left the room. Matthew walked over to the sink, took another long drink, then sat on the cold floor and rewound the tape. He stared at the machine a moment, then depressed the 'Play' button.

'Matthew, this is your father. I tried to call you on your birthday, but there was a bad connection. I don't think you could hear me. Then the lines went down. I tried to call back but everything was dead. And now I'm stuck here with some sort of big strike. They say it might be weeks till things get back to normal. So I'm going to say what I have to say into this thing. Get it off my chest while the time's right. It's better than the phone, anyway. It gives you time to collect your thoughts . . . I suppose the first order of business is to explain what on earth I'm doing over here. Well, that's not too easy to say. I suppose after things at UPU reached their logical conclusion, well, the idea of looking for another job was just too much. There was really nothing much for a washed-out old engineer like me anyway. Not even in the damned Middle East. But then it wasn't just work, Matt. It was something deeper. The fact of the matter is I couldn't bear to look at the mess I'd made of my life. All those familiar things were, well, painful. The house, the photos on the wall, the little league trophies. It was as if they had all turned against me. I just had to go, to be someplace where I wasn't being, what, hunted by my own life. Accused by it. It was like . . . well, remember how you felt that game when Ricky Smith hit you on the funnybone with a fastball? And you just took off and ran, all the way to the outfield? Like if you ran fast enough you could outdistance that awful stinging numbness, keep it from overtaking you. Even though it's not the ball, it's your arm. Well, there's a large element of that in what I've done. Trying to keep from being overtaken . . .

Coming to this village was your mother's idea, and it was a good one. It's so very different here. I've managed to rebuild Connie's house, or fix it up anyway. My house, I guess I should say, although that's a strange notion. It's good working with the hands again. But still, it's not the work . . . it wasn't until I'd been here a while that I could see why it was I'd left, what it was I was looking for. Perspective is the best word for it. Wisdom, maybe. Remember what Dave Dixon used to say about that? Wisdom is knowledge you can't use any more. Like most things Dave says, it turns out to be true. Which is ironic, since my whole life I've equated knowledge with utility. Construction, design, results. Yet now I'm saddled with the most, what, important knowledge of my life, and it's of no use to me whatsoever. Would you believe it? And so in the time-honored tradition of aging windbags, I'm going to try to pass it along to you. So here we go . . .

I think you know what I'm going to tell you about. But before I do there are a few other things I want to explain. Now don't fast forward me, Matty! The thought of spilling my guts into this Japanese recorder only to have it come out like the high-pitched garble from Mission Impossible is, well, just please be patient with me, all right? Because there are a few things I've got to say . . . The first thing is about your hardness on me. Your contempt. At first I thought it was just your blaming me for what happened, though now I realize it's much less simple than that. I think you have contempt for a lot of the choices I've made, a lot of the work I've done, the things I've believed. I don't think you know how much it hurts, Matt, that contempt. Because it's not as if it's something other than you that's hating you. How do I explain this? All right, I know . . . You never knew your grandfather. No big loss, really. He was a very somber man. Very close mouthed. What your mother would call an old grump. From a very early age, I had the same, well, contempt for him and his life that you've had for me and mine. For those long silences in that easy chair, broken only by the sound of the Detroit Tigers can opener biting into another Stroh's. Contempt for the lodge meetings with other grumpy men. What did they do there? Have stare-down contests? And his job. Years and years of pouring his guts into that line at River Rouge for an hourly wage. I don't think I ever told you what he did. Installed ashtrays. Ashtrays. At River Rouge. You know how it got that name? There was a massacre there in the French and Indian War and the river ran red with the blood of the dead and wounded . . . He just slaved away there. Never doing anything to move up, get on. His only gutsy action there in thirty-nine years was to break a strike. And it was a decent strike. Jesus. So, my contempt. And now I can see how important that contempt has been to me. How it's been what the people at seminars call a motivating factor. How I've tried to flee that, that dark, crippling thing in him. That thing that landed him in the

garage that night. I became competent. I became social. I joined. I contributed.
I got things done. I filled up every moment of my waking life with energy and
effort. To avoid him. To spite him. Stupidly, stupidly believing that if I could
act, if I could live differently than him, I could be different from him. Achieve
a different, what, fate. Carve or sweat or will that dark silence out of me . . .
You know, after he died, all I got was those cardigan sweaters you took from
my closet when they became fashionable and this big B & O conductor's watch
from his days on the railroad, before he got railroaded into marrying mom. I
always thought those things were my inheritance, my paltry inheritance. But
there's something else, Matt. And it isn't paltry at all.

I guess my point is that you can't choose your inheritance. And I know old
Dale Carnegie will go wild when he hears this, but you can't do much about your
character either. Because that's your inheritance, Matt. Character. Or rather,
this dark and restless thing that feeds on character, nibbles at its edges, devours
it maybe. And in your case, well, in both your cases I've seen things you've got
from me that aren't all that good. And my mistake as a father was not to teach
you this. Not to let you know that you've gotten a bit of a rotten deal in being
my sons. To deny it in you, to brick it over. To wean you away from the, the
dissatisfaction . . . ah, words are no good for me . . . the dark . . . remember
the praying mantis, Matt? You probably don't. It's a little thing, really. Small
memory, yet it sticks with me. You two were young. It was Father's Day, I
remember, and you had given me this quart bottle of atrocious aftershave you'd
picked out on your own from the five and dime. So of course I had to go into
the bathroom to shave so I could try it on. You sat on the edge of the tub and
watched with that look of fascination of yours. Then Eddie comes in, all dirty,
his hands cupped. I hadn't finished yet — there was still cream all over my face.
What you got, Edward? Present, dad. Let's see. It's a sammy bug, dad. Oh.
That's called a praying mantis, Eddie, because of the way it holds its hands.
See? Only you've killed it, Eddie. You were too rough with it. It doesn't matter,
dad. It's all right. Here. And I took it, Matt. Without another word. Just, took
it. Placed it next to my shaving kit and kept right on scraping my face so I could
slap on that cologne you'd bought. Boy, did it stink . . .

That it was it, though. That was my greatest mistake. That was my fatal
mistake. Not confronting that thing in you. Hoping against hope it hadn't been
passed on. Trying to shelter you, to force-feed you character and strength and
mindless self-confidence when really I should have . . .

Because it hit me like a truck on a foggy night, Matt. Suddenly it was all
wrong. All those years of building this bulwark in myself, well, it just crumbled.
Under its own weight, perhaps. It began, I guess, with the end of my craft,
the redundancy of my skills. I suppose if I'd been cunning I could have seen

the writing on the wall, but cunning comes from practised cynicism, which is exactly what I didn't have, what I wouldn't allow in myself. I just ground along, ground on. And yet the rules changed. They changed the definition of work on me, Matt, of hard work. Nowadays, you can apply your cunning for one hour and it'll get you farther than applying your back or brains for ten. Lesson one . . . But listen to me. Blaming the world again. Jesus. If I keep this up I might get fasted forward. No, no, the problem isn't the world, Matt. Not really. The problem is that I'm a driven man, as they say. Driven by . . . That's why we moved so much, you know. Every job I've had was perfectly good. Every place we've been we could have stayed. Especially the first, at U of M. Could you imagine how good it would have been if I'd stayed on that course, become a professor there? There was this big old frame house your mother and I used to pass on our walks, pushing that dual-buggy. Painted shutters, a crow's nest on the roof, twin willows in the front yard, detached garage with a loft bedroom. The sort of place you'd always be working on: painting, cutting the lawn. We dreamed of getting it once I got tenure. What a good life that would have been. Grad students would have always been hanging around, eating Helen's pastries and playing catch with you boys and cramming for exams. I would have worn bad tweed coats and written books that sold eighteen copies. Your mother would have kept on with her studies and become smarter than us all. Eddie would have become an intern at the hospital. You would have been the best, though, Matty, hanging around in the student union with angry Detroit blacks and Utica hippies, talking about socialism and art and whatever it is those kids in the student union talk about. But something drove me on. I couldn't settle for that house, that life. I drove myself on and on, until I ended up with that monster by the bay. That's what's been puzzling me recently. Why did I choose such a powerful and dangerous thing to toil with? Yes, at the time I saw it as a challenge and an essential technology and all that rah-rah stuff and, to be honest, it was a very exciting field to be in. For years and years. Unlimited possibilities. But was there something else there? Something else about splitting the atom that drew me on? Some dark fascination with it, because it is such a violent and dangerous thing? As if I were drawn to the negative side of that energy just as strongly, more strongly, than the positive side. I've been wondering about that recently. A lot. And I think it might be true.

Remember that photograph Eddie had above his bed? Of Einstein? The hair all frizzy, the droopy eyes, the sweatshirt with the pen clipped on at the neck? For a long time people thought that's the face of the atom. Gentle, saintly, avuncular. Harmless. But that's not true, Matt. There's another face that's the true face. A man I saw speak once. A man called Oppenheimer. A very different face. Thin, hard, ringed with dark and unforgiving lines. The eyes cold and deep, frightened and arrogant with what they've seen. 'I am become death, shatterer of worlds.' I wish I'd put that photo on Eddie's wall. Another lesson I forgot to teach . . .

Well, anyway, in your case it didn't matter so much. The teaching, I mean. My attempts to mold you into something you aren't. Because you don't take teaching well. You teach yourself, I think. You're very sly and watchful and you always have been. You have the sort of ruthless honesty that breaks fathers' hearts but also lets them grow old without worries. You're the wanderer, really. Driven on and on by this internal combustion engine. Always will be, I'm afraid. That's the cardigan you get from me. But Eddie. Well, your brother was different. He bought the teaching. Hook, line and sinker. He grew not to give a damn for that, that thing. Jesus, I wish I could find a word for it. It fed him, thrilled him, gave him all that energy. And it . . .

So that's where I failed you as a father. Using my skills as a builder to make a house with thick walls and barred windows and a hundred bolts on the doors, to keep the wolves out. Only when it was all over I knew I'd only succeeded in locking them in that much more tightly . . . I'm going for a walk.'

'This stuff is always cool, this marble. Oh, I'm in an old marble quality, uh, quarry, not far from the village. I come here sometimes. It's a remarkable place. Always cool, even after the sun has a day long burn directly on it. The surface of course gets hot but somehow the coolness comes through. Like the pool in the spring. Remember the whirlpools we made? Can you hear the echo in here? Just one. Echo . . . cho . . . I fell down in here once. A couple weeks ago. I jarred my back quite badly, but then some shepherds came along who had known Connie. They did some folk orthopedic maneuvers on me and cured it. Completely. Like before the accident. No stiffness, good mobility. As if the pain has been removed or dislodged altogether. This stuff, this marble, I wish I could have worked with it. It's an ideal bedrock, really. Non-porous, stable. Breaks elegantly. That's its most remarkable quality, really. How it ruins. The things we use, concrete and plaster and drywall and thin ore, just fall apart as they will. But this stuff absorbs stress and fatigue along very subtle and beautiful lines. That's the key, really. Not how something goes up or looks in its heyday. But how it ruins. You should see it here. Or in the monuments. Come visit and I'll show you.

I wonder if you understand now why I started soaring so late in life. Your mother always thought it was some macho, mid-life thing. I wish. I think you thought it was just another contemptuous absurdity of this person who . . . But there are very specific things about it, Matt, that drew me toward it. Dean'll tell you. Very gratifying things at work there, all stemming from the fact that there is no engine, no manpower. Because although that means you can run out of steam immediately, it also means that your potential energy is unlimited. Did you know for example that a thunderstorm contains more energy than the Hiroshima bomb? One of André Brand's favorite clichés. But it's true. It's there – you just have to find it. You're like a sky prospector. Only there's a limited amount of time to do your probing and sifting. Because for every wrong step you take, you take one back. Or down, I should say.

Have you ever heard the saying that as you rise above the earth the last thing you hear is the barking of a dog? It's true. Travels further than sirens, even. But we heard nothing that day. Not even the bark. Just a strange silence. Which should have told me something. Lesson two, Matt. Always pay attention to silence . . .

When we popped the rope it slid away like a snake. Dean gave us a little draft-lift as he always did and away we go. Contrary to the latest isobar charts, things were actually very smooth. Minimal chop, a steady but light sou'wester. Maybe ten knots, gusts up to fifteen. I can sense Eddie's disappointment. Down west of D.C. I can see a squall that's slowly approaching, but it looks to pass below us, then out to sea. I figure one loop to the northern bay and we'll be safe. Dean radios in about the squall and says he thinks my idea about the bay is a good one. Eddie takes the mike and clucks like a mother hen. Dean comes back with some nervous laughter. Away we go . . . As usual I'm trying to stay within the wiggle of the least threatening isobar. Eddie's making impatient mutters of the faster faster variety. We pass over Advance. Cul-de-sacs, loop roads, parking lots. It looks like some great old primitive sundial or clock. Then we pass over the orchards, the rolling hills. We catch some small thermals there, but nothing to write home about. Eddie begins to fidget and to be honest I must agree that it was a pretty tame ride. Lousy lift-drag ratio. Every yard we lose causes a little of my caution to dissipate. Thrown to the winds, so to speak. The bay shows up on the horizon, to the north is Olympic. We hear something on the radio about small craft warnings. I check behind us – that squall is still moving at an angle that'll take it south of us, but just. And it looks a little bigger than I remembered. To hell with it, I decide. Helen and Beth have had plenty of time to set up their streamers. I begin to slow loop home. Eddie asks if he can take it in. Some other day, I say in a pre-emptive voice. He does a little aw-dad sulking, but keeps quiet. We're going into the wind now, so it's a little more choppy. You can hear the air through the gaps. We lose speed, altitude. But Advance is back in sight and it'll be no problem to make the gliderport. Suddenly Eddie gets all tense. I can feel him behind me. Look, he says. To the southwest. Next to the squall. I don't see anything, I say, thinking in terms of light planes or flocks of birds. 'It's a thermal, dad. Can't you see?' A monster, he calls it . . .

Now let me tell you something about Eddie. He had a nose for thermals, an instinct for uplift. He could find one in the angle of a flock's wedge, in the refraction of a lowering sun, in the swirl of a cumulus or bend of a vapor trail. If there was one in range, he'd spot it. So even though I saw nothing, I knew something was there . . . I'll be honest with you, Matt. My initial reaction was to turn into it, to let it carry us for ride. But with the storm that close, well, it was no good. But Eddie wanted it. Please dad, he says in a very serious voice. Just one spiral. One pass through that beast. It's my birthday, he says, as if that's got anything to do with anything. Everything in me says no. No, no, no. There's a long pause. All you can hear is the wind. Insinuating. And then, then it's as if everything in me scatters away except for this, that, thing. Racing out from a place way deep in me, that I didn't know was there. And the idea of being pulled up by some great thermal on my sons' birthday in that total, total silence is the only idea I'm capable of holding . . .

I nod. I don't even say yes. We roll over each other awkwardly and Eddie's at the stick. He peels off gently to the south. After about a mile he half turns to me and says, Okay. That's all. Okay. There's a bit of a jolt, then the press of air, the whoosh of entry. It's like a great gentle hand just pulls us up. The variometer indicates an incredible angle of climb, but you can see that for yourself. There's just blue sky ahead. Eddie is on top of it, though, taking us through a tight, through a controlled spiral on the northern edge of the thermal . . . That feeling, Matt. It's like nothing. Nothing else. To be in an unpowered craft and still to be surging with all that energy. Eddie makes three, perhaps four circles, slowly drawing us toward the center. The silence grows a little louder. Finally, he announces he's going to the south side, the storm side, because he's running out of lift up here. No, I think. Yes, I think. I say nothing. Off we go . . .

What happened next, Jesus, it took me months to put it into some sort of order. We crossed the thermal and started to spiral even faster, even higher. But he must have lost track of the edge, because after just a minute or less there's this thumping sound and the variometer blinks its big eye. We're out, back in still air. Level. A ways ahead of us is the storm — very small, very black. I remembered that scene from the Wizard of Oz when Dorothy looks out the window of her spinning house and sees the people floating by. Eddie banks to the right, heading home. I pat his shoulder. Well done . . . All of a sudden that same big invisible hand pushes our nose down. Hard. I'm pitched forward into Eddie's back. He bounces into the glass, which is starting to rattle. We'd hit a wind sheer, wedged between that thick storm and Eddie's thermal. The variometer's eye shows we're almost vertical. The compass oscillates like one of those tops you used to spin across the kitchen floor. Shit, I remember hearing Eddie say. Get the nose up, I said, as if that needed saying. And all the while we're picking up speed, shaking and rattling. This, this loud whistle starts to come through. Eddie's fighting like mad but the nose wants that ground. There's no way to stop the speed we've got, the energy we've tapped. We have parachutes of course but there's no way, just no time. Eddie manages to point us toward the airfield, but we have too much speed, too much angle to stabilize. We're very low now and I can see that approach pond, the pylons on either side of it like sentries. Then your brother turns around and looks at me. He's very calm. It's all right, he says. It's all right. His eyes are peaceful and so very light . . .

I saw the wires just before we hit them, or rather, I saw those orange balls stuck on them. Like a string of setting suns. Then the whip hits us. Hard. We flip and hit the water. Upside down, as luck would have it. My head slams into something and the bottom of my back, just, shifts . . . The next thing I know is I'm sitting in mud, watching sparks. Beautiful. Then I come to my senses and rush toward the plane. Somebody's with me. Dean. We can't get through the glass, so I decide to lift the plane . . .

I don't know. I don't know. I must have got out before the plane sank. Probably my efforts to flee are what caused it to settle so firmly in the bottom mud. I don't know. I have this memory of looking at Eddie's eyes in that murky water, through the glass, and it seems to me that that was before I went to the shore. Not after coming back. Before he drowned. But how could that be? How could I have done that?

And so what you want to know is why did I lie to everyone about what happened? I felt, I felt as if I had no choice but to say I was flying. Not because I wanted to take the blame off Eddie. Not because I wanted to be a martyr. No, it was just the opposite. I wanted to take the blame off myself. Because the guilt is in admitting that it was Eddie who flew. The guilt is in confessing that my son died because I wanted to ride his madness . . .'

'When I was a boy you could only see great athletes on the newsreels that preceded the Saturday matinees. For some reason they were always sped up, moving in fast motion. And we, being young and unschooled, had no way of knowing that this superhuman speed was just a technical trick. Red Grange's churning legs, Dempsey's hands. All so fast. Later, of course, you learn the truth. And nowadays when I see athletes they're always moving in slow motion. In replays. A lifetime without the proper pace.

No, that's not true. There was one. I'm reminded of him by the echo in this pit. I only saw him once. Just before the war, at Briggs Stadium. My dad took me. Afternoon game – the Yankees were in town. We sat in the upper decks, first base side. My dad was very animated, which was unusual for him. He pointed out the players, spoke of their strengths and weaknesses. Then he showed me the Yankee's first baseman. He looked older than the rest. A different breed, as they say. He moved slowly, with dignity. I couldn't take my eyes off him. The way he warmed up the infielders. The way he cleaned his spikes with a tongue depressor he kept in his back pocket. The way he pressed that pine-tar rag against his bat handle. How he tucked his hair under his cap. How he tapped the near and far extremities of the plate with his bat before receiving a pitch. I studied him for three hours, Matt. It's all so clear. As clear as a dream . . . He was out his first two at-bats. Infield fly, grounder to short. He also missed a throw at first because he couldn't stretch far enough. He's getting old, my dad explained. But he's still the man. His third time up he hit a foul ball that sailed over our heads. I remember following it, tilting my neck back. It rattled around in the empty seats above us. Go, my father said. Go Walt, he said in a tone of voice I'd never heard before or since. I bolted from my seat and ran like mad, banging my shins into folded chairs, his voice ringing in my ears. Go, I thought. There were two skinny kids on my tail. But there was no way those Hamtramack bleacher rats were going to beat me out. Go, I thought. And I got there first. Found the ball on the edge of a step, a little scuffed but white as a cloud. I held it up above my head, above those green-with-envy runts, for my dad to see. He smiled big and gave these jerking nods of his head. Raised his fists up next to his ears. Like it was the best thing that ever happened.

A couple months later he called me into his study, where he's pulled his chair up really close to the radio. It was a sunny day but all the curtains were drawn. Gehrig Day at Yankee Stadium. Retiring his number. Live broadcast. We stared at the radio and listened to that echoing voice together as he thanked the crowd. Today, today. I consider myself, myself. The luckiest man, man. On the face, face. Of the earth, earth.'

When the tape was finished Matthew stood slowly and turned on the hot water tap, letting it run until it was tepid. He took a sponge from the shelf above the sink and soaked it in the water until it was soggy and warm. The clock double-clicked. He carried the sponge to the gurney and began slowly to wash the stains from his father's skin. It was such a strange color in the fluorescent light, brilliant yellow on the pale flesh. He thought again of that imaginary spiral he used to walk. The paste resisted removal at first, sticking resiliently to the skin. Matthew scrubbed harder and it began to come off, running from Walter on to the gurney, drops of gold on stainless steel.

A NOTE ON THE AUTHOR

Stephen Amidon was born in Chicago. He writes for the *Literary Review* and the *Financial Times*, and had a short story in *Soho Square II*, a literary anthology published by Bloomsbury in 1989. *Splitting The Atom* is Stephen Amidon's first novel. He lives in London with his wife Caryl and his daughter Clementine.